RITES OF CATACLYSM

LITURGY OF WORLDS BOOK 4

NATHAN HARTLE

To friends gone too soon

PART 1

— · —

PROLOGUE

HUIRE WATCHED FROM HER cage as the Guardian came to her. "You have returned." Not much surprised her, but that did.

The Guardian was a small thing. Though older than she was, he had always given her the impression of brittle youth. But he had changed more in the short time since he left her presence than he had in all the time she had known him before.

"How did you survive?" she asked. "This place was built by greater minds than yours."

His spectacles rested unbalanced on his nose. "Or yours."

"Greater, perhaps, or simply different."

"Make no mistake," the Guardian said. "I died. What remains is someone else."

"If there is something left, then you haven't really died. Not totally, yet."

He shook his head, a gesture so human that it struck at her heart. "You still do not understand us. I've learned about you, though, and the things you've done. Your people are still coming, but I'm going to stop them."

"You can't," she shot back. "You're too small."

"I may be small, but this place is not."

"You wouldn't dare to use its full force. You lack the will."

"You're right. It can stop them on its own."

1

ARUMIN

ARUMIN HID BEHIND A tree and struggled to breathe. Something must have been blocking his throat. He wanted to tear away whatever it was, but his hands were clamped to the folds of the tree bark, refusing his commands to move.

He heard voices. Their jolly amusement set his heart pounding. He heard his name—"Weylan!"—and sank farther into the tree's knee-high roots.

He realized a few things at once: where he was, how he had gotten there, and whom he was hiding from. He was barely a teenager, and his scrawny arms and legs made a surprisingly small bundle when he gathered them together.

This is a dream. He seized that thought. Others in the Ronian company were having similar experiences, dreams of powerful memories that gripped them night and day, but the condition lasted only a few days. His turn had come—that was all.

But his senses argued otherwise with amazing persuasiveness. The voices had come closer. He leaned around the tree trunk to peer out.

His brothers pushed through the undergrowth nearby. He leaned back to hide, but he had already seen what his eldest brother, Rhys, held. The sight tied his stomach in knots.

Rhys plucked the strings of Weylan's lute, and a grotesque twanging and plinking followed. The instrument was crying out as if in torture, and Rhys knew it. "Come on out, then!" he called, singing the words in no particular tune.

Weylan doubted they would beat him. When they had hurt him before, it was usually an accident. But the thought of stepping out—of exposing himself to their mostly good-humored verbal assault—was almost worse.

So he waited until they passed. He did not even move when a forearm-length spider emerged from somewhere to climb fearlessly over him.

Even when his brothers and the spider had all left, he saw no reason to return to his family's hut. His mother would be there. He felt no desire to go anywhere, really.

An hour passed in patched-together fragments. Then he heard footsteps in a little clearing nearby.

Angry voices arose. He left his tree and risked creeping closer.

A man and a boy were arguing. They looked so alike that they must have been father and son. The man was youthful and handsome. Weylan knew of him, and his eyes narrowed with dislike.

"No more of that," the man was saying. "If I see anything or hear anything—"

"All right," said the boy. His eyes were keen and his face narrow and beautiful. He was perhaps a year older than Weylan.

The man sighed. "I mean it." He sounded a little calmer.

"All right, I said. What are you going to do?"

That made everything worse. The man gritted his teeth and leaned close to the boy. "That depends. Why don't you hit me?"

The boy wilted.

"It's time to be a man."

"I don't want to."

The man hissed and shook his head. "Of course you bloody don't."

"Why do you want that?" The boy's lip trembled. "Do you want to hit *me*? I'll bet you do. Are you scared to?"

The man thought about it then spat on him. "I won't do you no more honor than that." After a quiet moment, he told the boy, "Don't come back."

Weylan did not think of intervening. He could not conceive of exposing himself to danger. It was a wonder how little he had changed in the years since that moment.

When the man left, the boy looked around as though wondering what his life would hold from that moment on. Weylan had come to think of himself as a ghost, and he jumped when the boy saw him and their eyes met.

Weylan hid, but he was far too late. He heard the boy approaching and stepped out from behind the tree.

"Hello!" the boy said. His ingratiating smile did not hide that he had been crying.

Weylan did not answer.

"You're a quiet one. What's your name?"

Weylan told him, though he felt like he was giving something precious away.

"I'm Dram," the boy said. Except for his reddened eyes, he seemed to have forgotten his abandonment.

"I know your father," Weylan said.

"Is that so? Most people do, sadly."

Weylan could stand Dram's smile no longer. "He's cruel to my father. My father says he wants to work them all to death."

The boy's smile fell. "He might, at that."

Anger boiled up inside Weylan. "It's all his fault. All of it!"

"I know."

"No, you don't. I hope you starve out here." Weylan marched away. He suddenly wanted his mother.

2

—·—

ARUMIN

ARUMIN'S EYES HUNG OPEN, but he didn't really wake up until he slipped on the ice midstep and nearly fell. The latest snow squall had smothered the land, leaving exposed only the sharpest, cruelest angles of the rocky crags that were all the company knew of this planet. The men walking at the front of the column trampled the snow into a path, but their newly packed boot prints were slick and untrustworthy.

None of them had ever seen a place like that, and no one was dressed for the cold.

The bishop had never slept easily, and the thousand aches of old age made it worse. His chest still hurt where a vine had gashed it on Caidfell. Now, he had stumbled on the ability to sleep standing up—while marching through a snowstorm.

They had come to this planet from another, and to that one from another. They caught only glimpses of each one, of nights alive with mystery or days that revealed them to every wonder and terror. They saw only what lay between one gateway and another, a journey of sometimes minutes, sometimes days.

The gateways to each new world tended to cluster around the point where the gods had first arrived on the planet. Wherever a deity's journey through the Outer Dark ended, it had constructed passages by which humanity could follow. Since the gods' disappearance, many worlds were now environmental and geological ruins. On others, the lifeforms that the gods had forged and the atmospheres they had breathed into being had, inexplicably, paraded along apparently undisturbed.

Though he was awake, his dream had not ended. While part of him was occupied with ice and wind, another part was reliving his childhood. His turn for the dream sickness had come, and he would endure it as he endured all else.

During their hours of walking, the snow had become deep enough to conceal whole chasms beneath its gray blanket. More than ever, the company must depend on the Lady for guidance. But perhaps even she could not remember the terrain of every step of the journey.

No one in the company spoke much anymore, but the silence from Shada was the most harrowing. The girl was the Lady's vessel, the voice through which she spoke, and the company took her words as if they came from Huire herself.

But Shada was constantly on edge, staying quiet whenever she could and saying little about the Lady's thoughts and words. As the snow fell thicker and the path grew more doubtful, Arumin became certain that something was wrong in this arrangement of girl, spirit, and deity. One of the links was faulty, and it could hardly be either of the latter two.

He picked up his pace, taking bigger steps until he reached the captain's side. He had avoided dealing with the man since the company left Om—he didn't know how many gateways they had passed through since then. Arumin had encouraged an attempted mutiny that would have put him in charge of the company. The attempt had failed, but to the bishop's surprise, the captain had yet to seek vengeance. Arumin had no wish to anger him further, but certain issues could not wait any longer, not for the captain's temper or even the end of this snowstorm.

"Emberly," the bishop said.

The words passed over and around the captain like one more sigh of the wind.

"You heard me," Arumin continued, though he wasn't sure that was true.

In this place, with their pitifully unsuitable clothing, one's face stung and one's feet tingled and grew numb. Ignoring everything but the fear that drove one to keep moving was easy.

Arumin raised his voice to penetrate Emberly's reverie. "What will you do with Nor?"

Emberly turned his head the bishop's way for just long enough to make it clear that he had heard but was choosing not to answer.

"You can't keep him chained forever."

The captain replied in a throaty rumble, "I'll do what I want with Brother Nor. You'll find out what that is when the others do."

Arumin huffed, adding a new layer of frozen breath to his mustache and beard. "This is extraordinary, the way you're acting. However angry you are with me, you've got to put it aside. You're lucky to be alive right now."

Though he did not break stride, Emberly turned his head again, eyes aflame. He spat snow as he answered. "You are the lucky one."

Staring straight ahead, the bishop spoke conversationally. "If you dared to punish me for the mutiny, you would have done it by now. The truth is, you can't lose me—any more than you can lose a third of your men by punishing those who mutinied. You should do now what you did then: pick one man and let him suffer for all."

Beneath the wetness of Emberly's face and its sliding crystals of ice, his face darkened a little more. The memory of executing Iwan, his own lieutenant, must have been near to his mind, but still, he would not enjoy the reminder.

Soon after, the captain said, "Roark is dying."

Somewhere behind them, a pair of men were helping the wounded officer along. Roark needed a chance to rest but would probably not get it.

Anger rose inside Arumin. "Am I your confessor after all?" he growled. "Find your comfort elsewhere. Lieutenant Roark did as he was ordered. What else is a soldier for?"

"If I were you, I wouldn't speak to me any more than I had to."

But Arumin could not leave it at that. "Putting Nor in chains is not enough. He must be punished. I suspect it is the entire reason that he is on this journey—perhaps the reason he was born."

"Now you approve of killing holy men?"

"Goddess, no. We're not there yet. There are other forms of punishment."

"Most of my men wouldn't touch him."

"Captain, several of your men put Nor in chains of their own volition. You may be underestimating the rest."

Emberly wiped an arm across his mouth. He hadn't shaved in some time, and ice was forming in his new mustache. "The Lady disappeared for days. She left us in deadly danger. Have you thought about that?"

"It is not my place to think of it."

"Does it truly not worry you?"

The sheer incredulity in Emberly's voice brought the bishop up short, silencing him.

The captain finished, "Because it worries me."

The bishop answered haltingly. "Everything happens for a reason. We are a body, and one of our hands—Norhim—has betrayed us. We cannot complain when we have not purified ourselves."

"Only one hand?" Emberly's mouth cracked into a smile. "And what of you and the men you convinced to betray me?"

"We are the loyal ones. You considered joining the Shining Realm."

"That's a lie."

"In Om, you were gone for a long time. I couldn't risk your handing us over to the enemy. Are you sure that you weren't a little tempted?"

Emberly turned shadowed eyes on him. "You don't know yet how much I am willing to risk."

The two walked silently for a time, side by side.

"Let's hope the snow is covering our tracks," Arumin said.

They both knew the Shining Realm was coming.

3

SHADA

THE LADY'S MOST RECENT words to Shada had included the whispered command that she must walk at the very front of the column. For hours, Shada's had been the first pair of boots tramping through each new snowdrift. Shorter than most of the men in the company, she pushed ahead more slowly than they might have, and she constantly felt them pausing to wait for her. At first, she had pushed herself to exhaustion to keep up a speedy pace, but she soon realized she would help no one if she collapsed. She had slowed down and accepted their eyes upon her and their breath on her neck.

As the company moved, everyone had donned every article of clothing they still possessed. A few soldiers had given Shada jackets or scarves, and since she was meeting each cutting gust of wind before anyone else, she had accepted them all, turning herself into a rack of disused clothing. Still, the snow found its way into her boots, and though she kept moving vigorously, an eerie tingle was creeping into her toes.

She heard no talk from anyone beyond the occasional muffled voice. The wind had picked up, and she thought she could talk to the Lady without being overheard.

"So this is it, is it?" she asked aloud. "You've decided to kill me."

To her relief, a humming arose in her ear, and a voice came. "Is that not what you want?"

"I don't know," Shada said. "It has one benefit—I would be out of your service. Regardless, if we go on like this, I'll either freeze to death or take a bad step and fall into some ravine."

The Lady replied, "If you still think I enjoy hurting you, then you understand nothing. You have chosen to be my enemy."

"I wish I'd made the choice sooner. I should never have been your friend."

"I think you have spoken enough for now."

Shada felt a little warning flash of pain in her throat, a throb that was there and instantly gone. The Lady stored much of her shapeless mass there, letting her torment Shada at will. She now dwelt permanently in Shada's body, having abandoned the box where she used to dwell. Shada, despite her horror at the development, had been happy to leave the box behind when the company left Om.

"You've at least got to tell me where to go next. I can hardly tell where the path is. If you don't help, you will soon be alone out here."

"I will tell you when you need to know," the Lady said.

"What about the others? They will start asking questions soon, and if I have nothing to say, they will doubt both of us."

The Lady answered in a much louder voice that resounded painfully in Shada's ears. "Must you depend on me for everything? Once, you said you would resist me however you could. Tell me: where is that spirit now? Now that you are cold and hungry and lost?"

"Have you gotten us lost on purpose?"

"You will know when I tell you. Or perhaps you will never know."

"You want to scare me?" Shada asked. "Well, you have. But I think you're scared too."

"I have much to be scared of. I have exposed myself to extraordinary danger for the party—danger that you cannot understand—and still you scorn me. You claim I abandoned you."

"Has Huire spoken to you?"

The hum of the Lady's voice rose in pitch and intensity. "Not since I first left her presence. That was long ago."

"Why not?"

The hum rose then petered out to its usual level. "I don't know."

Shada looked at the sky, which seemed to be an opaque ceiling hanging a few meters over their heads. "Will she really welcome us when we find her?"

Either the Lady had tired of the conversation, or else she had no answer.

4

—·—

EMBERLY

THE FIRST NOTICEABLE CHANGE in the company's surroundings came when the cliffs on either side of the path drew close. The sky became a narrow road visible only because it was a little darker than the snow. Emberly's chest felt lighter. To him, any change seemed good. Then the path turned downhill.

His strong misgivings about Shada leading the company grew. Nobody could tell what lay even a little way down the slope, and if she fell, nothing but the snow could stop her from sliding out of sight and into oblivion. The Lady might rescue her, he hoped. *Surely.*

As the company stepped one by one onto the treacherous decline, he realized that each of them was a danger to everyone in front of him. Anyone who fell and slid could bowl over others on his way down. If he wasn't stopped, he could take as many with him as his flailing limbs could reach.

His wife, Charlotte, came to his mind. She often did at such moments, when he was wondering how he had come to be where he was. He would have given a lot to know what she was thinking right then. He wondered where she imagined he was, if she was thinking of him.

As the company advanced down the slope, the journey slowed like creeping tar. Shada was feeling sensibly for each new foothold with no previous prints as a guide. Roark and the other wounded could move no faster. Emberly considered removing Nor's shackles for the monk's own safety. He rejected the idea because the monk had reverted into a quietly feral state that Emberly did not trust.

Beneath the snow, he periodically felt flat surfaces. Someone had cut steep, irregular stairs into the rock. Still, ice covered everything.

As the captain gained a sense of the true pitch and scale of the descent, he called, "Halt!" Catching up to Shada, he told her, "I'm going to send some men forward to dig out the way ahead."

"No," Shada said. The refusal held such calm authority that he immediately understood she was speaking for the Lady.

In that case, he could do little but obey, so he sighed and nodded, and the march continued as before. He could not imagine what the Lady must be commanding Shada to do and why.

The way down ended suddenly. Shada had stopped, but Emberly could not tell why. The way ahead remained gray and indefinite. He got very close to her before he realized she was standing on the very brink of a precipice.

He crowded in with several of the others in the narrow space between the cliff walls. She was heart-stoppingly close to the edge, her feet on a sharp incline and the toes of her boots over thin air. He gasped, afraid to speak and startle her into a fall. From the gulf below, wind assaulted them—the only thing in this madness that had any direction. It blew so hard that it bent him back.

Shada was leaning slightly forward, out over the abyss, letting the wind bear her up. Emberly's innards clenched at the sight.

"Caretaker, please," he said, just loud enough to be heard over the wind.

"The sea is down there," she answered.

He would have to take her word for it.

Until then, he had managed to ignore their obvious plight. The path ended there, at the bottom of this slender chute in the rock, a road into nothing. In moments like that, one embraced faith most eagerly or cast it away—sometimes both and sometimes more than once.

Something awful whipped about in the air, in the space between snowflakes. "Where next?" he asked Shada.

Shada turned. Her face was not the inscrutable mask of divinity that he was hoping for. It was a young woman's face and very much mortal. "I don't know."

Everyone waited for someone else to react—all but Arumin, who had squeezed through the crowd to join them at the edge.

He spoke kindly to Shada as he nearly always did. "Just ask the Lady, dear."

"I can't. It doesn't work that way."

He left no space between her words and his. "But that's exactly how it works. You are the Caretaker."

Shada turned her face away.

"What does that mean? Why are you shaking your head, girl?" Arumin would not let it rest, and as happened occasionally, Emberly agreed with him.

She craned her neck to see behind Emberly and Arumin. Everyone else was lined up on the path and straining to hear, even Nor, whom someone had forced to his knees. She called out to all of them.

"The Lady will not answer me."

People leaned closer, cupping their ears more tightly. Few wanted to accept such news when there was a chance they hadn't heard properly.

Then Shada bent over as if in sudden pain. Her hand clutched her throat, but she quickly withdrew it.

His voice now pitiless, Arumin asked, "What have you done?"

She said nothing. Her eyes watered.

A rumble spread through the crowd. Nor sprang up, pushing others aside. "Why don't you leave her alone, you old bastard?"

With a stifled thump, he went silent. Someone had hit him, perhaps in the stomach. Emberly did not protest the abuse. "Shada," he said, his tone barely controlled, "I'm sure this is all terribly difficult, but we need an answer. Not later—now."

Something swelled inside Shada. Her shoulders shot back, and her spine straightened. Her voice boomed above the wind, above their muttering. "You'll get it when we are ready to provide it. Not sooner or later. Until then, you will damned well wait."

Had there been room, everyone would have stepped back a pace. No one said anything or even looked at each other.

Emberly sank from surprise to weariness. He exhaled, and his shoulders slumped.

Arumin swelled with fury but released it with a sigh of odd satisfaction and a knowing smile. "Very well," he said. "We must wait."

The others coughed and murmured. Few had faith like the bishop's.

Emberly spoke for them. "But the Shining Realm could be here at any time. Would the Lady have us wait until—"

"Watch yourself, Captain," Arumin said. "Affairs like these are not yours to manage."

"I am making them mine."

"That is blasphemy."

"If that is blasphemy, how can I not blaspheme?" Emberly shouted. He knew he should not be speaking thus in front of the men. "How can we obey the Lady when she won't even bloody speak to us?"

"Excuse me?" A voice came from the crowd. In the nonplussed silence, its owner emerged. It was Private Robir. He had been quiet since his attempted mutiny in Om, his voice heard mostly in whispers. Now, it rang proudly: "We are here at the Lady's convenience, in case you've forgotten."

Emberly's face grew numb as he regarded the private. "I was hoping you had the sense never to speak again in my presence. But since you haven't—"

"*Since I haven't...* what?" Robir exclaimed with mockery and chilling vehemence. "What do you think you're going to do? If she wants us to wait, we will wait."

Everyone froze. Emberly stared at Robir then at Arumin, who waited with mouth open in anticipation. The captain pondered the reality of trying to enforce his will here, amid numerous increasingly hostile and rebellious men, on the edge of a cliff. He felt his bitterness petrify on his face, becoming permanent. His wounds, the cuts on his arms, all he'd suffered for this company and its mission, ached anew.

Finally he said, deathly quiet amidst the storm, "Very well."

Shada's eyes lit up as if she'd been waiting for an opportune moment. "There is a path," she said. "We have to find it."

Emberly forced her to repeat herself. Then he hushed the men's impending celebration and sent groups to look for the path.

Shada said, "There's a ledge along the cliff to one side. It's hidden by the snow, but it's there. That will lead us down to the sea."

The men heard their orders. Then most of them did something strange: they looked at the bishop, who pondered the matter briefly and nodded his permission.

As the company shuffled into motion, Emberly thought of Charlotte one more time, of her smile. He wondered, if she could see him at that moment, whether she would be proud.

5

NOR

MEN SPREAD OUT ALONG the newfound ledge. As they went, the bottom of the path grew a little less crowded. Nor, on his knees, sensed the space around him and allowed himself to sag.

He hadn't seen who hit him, and he didn't care. He felt beyond personal grudges. The soldiers were mostly a mob, faceless and without individuals who could be fought or reckoned with.

The punch he'd just received was the latest of many. The blows came now and again, whenever no one of authority was looking. A few of the men committed most of the abuse, with others participating once or twice, seeing how it felt. Nor hadn't told anyone about it, not even Shada.

Private Tabard was foremost among his tormentors. The private had lost a thumb on Caidfell, and with it, he had lost his future in the Ronian army. Nor had spoken a little to him while visiting the company's sick and wounded. But then Nor had left, and in his absence, a sick man named Carrowy had disappeared.

Nor wouldn't have guessed that Tabard and Carrowy were friends, but sometime between then and now, Tabard had decided that Carrowy's loss was Nor's fault. The company's last, nauseating glimpse of Carrowy had surely not helped.

Nor didn't know whether Carrowy's fate was really his fault. He had come to realize how little such questions meant. He knew he resented that bastard Emberly for choosing to save him over Carrowy.

They kept him in chains at all times. Tabard and a few others had volunteered to look after him, giving them ample opportunity to torture him. They often denied him food or spat in it before handing it over. Nor did not hate them for it. More and more, he saw them as meat and bones, eyes and tongues, mindless assemblages that were moved by forces they did not understand and that, themselves, understood nothing. And Nor was no better.

To the monk's surprise, Sergeant Orund had played no part in the others' games. The sergeant made no secret of despising Nor thanks to the monk's terrible wounding of a Ronian soldier—*How long ago? Great Mother, has it been only half a year?* But since he had a chance for revenge, he hung back, not stopping the abuse but taking no part in it.

He watched Nor often, though. Nor had repeatedly caught the sergeant gazing unabashedly at him, measuring him like a cat would a mouse. He was planning something, and it could come at any time.

Nor's clothing hid his bruises. If Shada knew what was happening, she hadn't said anything. In fact, she had barely spoken to him since they left Om. She sat with him sometimes during moments of rest, but she was as blank and closed to him as he felt to everyone else. An old silence gripped him, a silence as worn and familiar as his skin, and he had no notion of how to begin speaking to Shada again. Perhaps the company's journey was meant to end this way, with all of them engaged in their own battles, in separate worlds, each forgetting the others existed.

Emberly had been gone for a few minutes, helping to clear the narrow ledges of snow, when a shape moved in front of Nor. It was Tabard.

"Taking a rest, are you?"

Nor decided that he wouldn't answer, not in words, at least. To reply would be to classify Tabard as a man.

"Think you deserve it?"

Nor felt the corners of his mouth turn upward. He might have stopped the smile from coming had he wanted to.

His face stung as Tabard slapped him.

The private yanked upward on Nor's chain, forcing the monk to his feet. "Get up, you lazy—"

Without planning it, Nor drove his forehead into Tabard's face. Other men rushed on them. Nor kicked out, aiming for someone's groin with his knee. His shin made contact instead. The man grunted in pain as they piled on him. They grew heavier and heavier, driving the air from his lungs, and his mind reeled with panic as he realized that, even then, he didn't want to die.

The weight left him little by little, and all at once, he was free. Arumin had saved him. The bishop twisted about, swearing, screaming at everyone, his face bright red and his eyes aglow.

He ended with Nor. "And you. An utter disgrace. What would Huire think?"

Nor smirked, and the smirk became a grin. He laughed, and it felt good, so he cackled.

He saw the others through the snow and the haze that filled his eyes. They were watching him, their rage extinguished. They were seeing a power greater and more evil than theirs.

"You're an animal," the bishop told him.

"I must tell you a secret, Arumin," Nor replied.

The bishop glared and leaned close. For his life, Nor could not understand why the bishop trusted him enough to come that close.

When he had the old man's ear, he gleefully confessed, "There is no Huire."

The bishop stood up straight. "Take that back."

Having said it once privately, Nor felt free to say it aloud. "Huire does not exist," he told them all.

"Repent, fiend!" Arumin grabbed Nor, one hand around his throat and the other on his jaw. He squeezed Nor's cheeks and mouth, trying to pry the words out.

Striking like a snake, the monk bit the bishop's fingers and tore at them like a dog.

The others attacked him again, punching and kicking. Arumin was among them that time, kicking Nor while clenching his own hand, face dark with pain and wet from tears.

The sound of the melee must have reached those on the ledges. Through a gap in the kicking legs, Nor saw Emberly arrive, his face contorted with fury. But one large soldier stood in his way and would not let him pass.

Some of Nor's attackers drew blades. But angry though he was, Arumin stopped them before they went any farther.

After they all stepped back, the bishop said, "We must pray that Brother Nor finds his humanity."

As the captain raged, the big man blocking his way claimed that he could not hear him over the wind, that he did not understand what Emberly was asking, that the captain must repeat himself.

Emberly finally shoved past the big man, but the fight was over. A couple of soldiers were kneeling on top of Nor as he bled. The bishop watched over them all like a stone idol.

Emberly seemed to realize everyone was looking at him. Breathing hard, he glanced around. His eyes settled on Nor, and he said, "I will deal with you later." Then he returned to the ledge.

6

ARUMIN

THE TRAIL DOWN THE cliffside was almost invisible until one stood on it. Starting with a thin ledge, it dove immediately into the rock face, which created a partial ceiling over the path. However, any hope for shelter from the storm was quickly dashed as the snow, borne horizontally on the wind, plastered everyone's skin. Squinting, they trod carefully and close to the wall.

As the way switched back, turning one direction then the other, Arumin kept his eyes on the man in front of him. If that man passed safely, without plunging off the cliff, then Arumin, who followed precisely in his footsteps, would also. The circumstances were harrowing but monotonous, and the bishop allowed himself to think about what he should do with Emberly.

With Lieutenant Roark a walking corpse and Sergeant Orund already turned against the captain, few obstacles remained. If Emberly was killed, Arumin could concoct a story that would satisfy his enthusiastic supporters and let many others tell themselves that, sad though it was, it could not have been avoided.

He did not know why he was hesitating. He had felt no such doubt when, in Om, he had arranged a mutiny against Emberly. The company's situation now was just as desperate, and they still could not rely on Emberly to put the will of the Goddess above his own.

But even during the mutiny, he hadn't ordered Robir to execute the captain. *Why not?* That seemed an obvious move in retrospect. He regretted needing to work with Robir at all, after he had cut Brin's face in Om, but he told himself it couldn't be helped.

The bottom of the cliff came slowly into view. A rocky crescent of beach bound an inlet, all of it snowy and colorless. Night had not yet fallen, though Arumin was not sure he would know when it did. The beach was lumpy, scattered with gray mounds that he identified in the thin light as buildings. They were huts, a small village's worth, gathered mostly near the cliff and close to where the company's path emerged.

Arumin watched the beach as the company descended. Nothing moved but the snow and the rippling water. The thought of sentient life existing there was startling enough to give the whole scene a supernatural aura. His skin crawled at the sight of many oblong lumps near the water's edge. He soon realized they were numerous small boats. Later, he could not remember what he had imagined them to be.

No one felt like talking, but as the company set foot on the beach and walked among the buildings, their silence seemed enforced from the outside. Nature might have preserved the place as a monument to her fallen enemies.

A figure appeared by the buildings closest to the water. Everyone jumped and hissed, and Arumin was surprised that no one shot the stranger by reflex.

The figure was short and stooped. Its outline was hazy, and as it stepped closer, the bishop realized it was wearing fur. Under its thick hat was a face, but it was barely recognizable as such. Its eyes were round and black and set strangely out from the rest of its head. Where it should have had a mouth, it had only a set of vertical lines, the outlines of ridges that stretched down and out of sight under the stranger's coat.

Few but the very rich in the city of Ronia could pass a day without seeing one of the Changed. Huire had preserved humanity in its natural form, but many other gods, in their corruption, had felt no such qualms. At one time, the holy men of Huire's temple had seen the other gods' playthings as incurably cursed and damaged. In this more enlightened age, Arumin and his fellows saw them for who they were: unlucky wretches still beloved of the Goddess. They might never have been permitted to hold high office in Ronia or its temples, but they were part of Huire's family—or could be if they wished.

The thing walked with a wobbling, troubled gait and passed into the company's midst, apparently unafraid.

"Let it come," Emberly told the others.

It turned toward the captain and stopped in front of him.

Emberly raised a hand, palm facing the stranger. "Hello."

The figure shed its cloak and hat. The light revealed what lay beneath, and Arumin's chest filled with the cold air. The stranger's arms were spindly, its hands segmented, fingerless extensions. Rows of similar appendages extended down its torso, and it used some of these to prop itself upright haphazardly. Those limbs sprouted forward from its body, which was bent like a crooked finger. Arumin's back hurt just looking at it. It had a set of legs like a man's, but they looked out of place and did not seem to work as they should. Its face was no better. Its eyes were black bulbs on stalks, and the lines by its mouth were a bouquet of whipping, clenching proboscises.

Emberly grabbed for his pistol. Cries and pleas to Huire went up from the men. Everyone spoke at once.

"What does it want?"

"We ought to kill it."

"It would be a mercy."

"Not yet," the captain snapped.

"Not until it tries to eat us, you mean?"

"Wait!" the bishop thundered.

That silenced them for the moment.

"No," someone said.

A finger pointed, then several pointed in different directions. More figures had appeared. They were lumps large and small, covered with fur. Some seemed to arise out of the storm. Most stepped out of the huts, where they had waited so still and quietly that the village had felt long dead.

As the company watched, more of the strangers removed their coats and hats. By that point, Arumin had no idea what to expect.

He recognized only parts of them. An appendage, a sound, or a smell recalled things within his experience. But the whole of the scene overpowered the mind, leaving him grasping at details. Their skins were mottled and stained, slick and glinting, or plated and rocky. Their hands—for those who had them—were fanned and jointed, wandering or purposeful. Their bodies were twisted and wrong or shapely and wrong. Their eyes were wildest of all, none the same. Looking into them, he contained a scream.

They outnumbered the company. They did not seem armed, but he had no idea what their bodies could do, with all those spines and folded angles.

Emberly bowed, still facing their first many-legged host.

After a moment of stillness, unreasonably long, some of the things bowed in return. Not all looked able.

The many-legged fellow walked to Emberly, pressing himself against the captain with a closeness found in nature between such different creatures only when one was about to devour the other. Arumin, who had pondered killing the captain moments before, cringed in sympathy for him. For a few seconds, Emberly was within that forest, his arms and face caressed by whipping feelers, and he held impeccably still. A few of the things' right arms rose, and the captain turned his head to follow where they pointed. All Arumin saw there was a darkened, snowy beach.

The thing took a few wobbling steps in that direction. Then it stopped.

"It wants us to follow," Emberly said.

If anyone questioned the wisdom of following such an unknown, animalistic being, they did not ask aloud. Few of the strangers had eyes that could be properly looked into or reasoned with. They followed their leader, forming a shambling crowd that herded the Ronians in the desired direction.

The combined army approached the cliff face. There, a recess in the rock came into view. Arumin heard a rumble as of water passing through tunnels and lapping at air. In the floor of the alcove gaped a hole as wide as two men's height.

In it, water rose and fell. He could not see far below the surface, but at the water's lowest ebb, he saw the tops of what seemed to be tunnels. From the hole and echoing off the walls of the little cave came every sort of noise water could make. Arumin didn't want to get any closer to the edge, and he could tell the others didn't, either, but the strangers crowded in behind them. The Ronians, in thrall to the creatures' primal authority, let themselves be nudged to the very brink.

One of the strangers tossed a heavy rock into the hole. It smashed the water's surface with a deep *plunk*.

Seconds later, a shape broke the water. It was a low island of glossy darkness, and its shape hinted that much more of it lay under the surface.

Arumin realized that the creatures might be about to feed them to this beast, whatever it was. He nearly screamed a warning to the others, but he did not want to be the one who panicked.

The many-legged leader of the strangers shuffled to the front of the group and bowed. His antennae dipped to brush the glistening skin of the underwater beast, tracing a pattern on it. The beast was still, lapped by little waves. When the leader finished its task, it stood upright.

The shape in the water grew larger, and a hole appeared by its edge nearest the company. The hole puckered and huffed, then with an explosion like a sneeze, wet, warm air engulfed everyone. Near the front, Arumin was splattered with tepid water.

Then came one splash then another. The strangers hurried forward, hopping and trundling, to leap into the water with the beast. They encircled it, and a couple of them climbed onto its bulk. Its hole bubbled in a lively way.

"Looks like they're not going to eat us," someone said.

7

—·—

STAUBEL

MANY OF THE VILLAGE'S huts were empty, and when the Ronians entered them at the villagers' urging, they found ample warm clothing and blankets waiting. Doctor Staubel paused in suspicion when he entered, having expected nothing but a rocky floor and damp walls. Surely, the piles of fur coats and blankets contained some living creature or would themselves lurch to terrible life when disturbed. But that was not so.

Staubel did not know what he feared more, the village and its strange people or his own chief patient, Lieutenant Roark.

Even before the mutiny in Om—a mutiny the young doctor had joined—Roark had rarely spoken with Staubel. Since the mutiny, the lieutenant had maintained an icy, foreboding silence. He had hardly cried out despite what must have been constant pain from his wounds. His love for Emberly was well known, and Staubel had found himself in the unfortunate situation of trying to save a man who probably wanted him dead.

Staubel could not blame him. When the doctor joined the mutiny, he had been simultaneously terrified and angry. He'd been terrified of the Shining Realm's intrigue and trickery and of Emberly's apparent indifference to it. He'd been angry at the Realm for healing all his patients with apparent ease and removing the only purpose that consistently kept the black waves of depression from closing over Staubel's head. He had betrayed Emberly out of principle and self-preservation.

Once he had tasted betrayal, however, he learned he never wanted to taste it again. He wished he had followed Emberly to whatever dismal end instead of turning a weapon on him.

But in that wishing, he had found a strange freedom, even peace. He had done the worst and could sink no lower, and he had simply to wait for whatever vengeance Emberly or Roark wreaked on him. The struggle to be a good man was over, he had failed, and he could be just a man. He no longer felt depressed.

Thanks to the Shining Realm, Roark was not just Staubel's chief patient, he was currently his only patient. Staubel had given up on closely monitoring the soldiers who came down with the dream sickness, that strange ailment that had visited each member of the company in turn. It came and went on its own in a few days, paying no mind to Staubel's efforts to help it along. Even the healers of the Realm had seemed nonplussed by it. Those who came down with it suffered from intense, vivid dreams of past experiences. At present, it had passed through almost everyone but Staubel himself, and none of the sufferers was affected enough to require close watching. That meant Staubel was alone with Roark, waiting for the man to put a knife in his back—or in his front.

Once the men helped Roark into the hut and left, he laid the lieutenant down and briskly removed his shirt. He hoped to change the man's dressings quickly and leave the hut, as they both doubtless preferred. But before he could finish, Emberly entered.

The captain's eyes passed over Staubel with only a hint of icy rage, then they warmed when they fell on Roark.

Roark's face grew bright. "Still here, sir," he said.

The captain smiled. "I expect you'll be here a while yet."

The sentiment felt false, and the conversation faltered. After a moment, Roark shrugged, disrupting Staubel's work. "Not much left to teach you."

"You're wrong there." Hoping to stay invisible, Staubel nonetheless risked a glance at Emberly. The captain clearly had something he wanted to say but couldn't quite manage it.

Staubel knew his presence was impeding their talk. In his newfound freedom, he dared to speak aloud. "Should I go, sir?"

Emberly regarded him as he might have a crustacean crawling across the floor. "Stay."

Staubel went back to work.

A few seconds passed before Roark told Emberly, "You'll win."

Emberly dug up a rock with his toe. "It's not looking that way."

"They'll see."

One corner of the captain's mouth turned upward. "Where will I be by then?"

Roark's eyebrows creased. "The worst that can happen is you'll be with me."

"Goddess." Emberly chuckled as though to say, *Anything but that.*

They passed a few moments quietly. Then Emberly patted Roark on the chest, careful to avoid his wounds, and left.

Staubel watched him go. He felt without knowing why that any danger to him had passed for the moment. As he finished Roark's dressings, he said, "I'm sure the last thing you want is my advice."

"You're right," the lieutenant muttered, staring at the door.

The doctor nodded, understanding. Doomed and free, he spoke without fear. "I've been thinking about what I did, and—"

"I don't care why you did it. Makes no difference."

"I disagree. Still, I'm sorry." Staubel licked his lips and stepped back from his completed work. "Should I expect you to kill me?"

Roark's eye shone with such unutterable sadness that Staubel wanted to embrace him. "Truth is," the lieutenant said, "I don't think I could anymore. Not even you. I can hardly walk."

"You've made it this far. Anyway, I hope you're feeling better before you try."

Staubel left the hut, feeling strangely elated. "You're going to need me for that much, at least."

8

BRIN

NIGHT WAS TRULY FALLING. The villagers had passed around bits of driftwood they had gathered and kept dry. Bishop Arumin claimed a hut for himself, and Brin was waiting for him there. This would be their first time sleeping indoors in several nights, and Brin hoped to find himself welcome.

After Arumin abandoned him during the battle on Caidfell, Brin had closed himself to the bishop, acting cold and polite at best. His anger had waned over the following days, but not before he had an affair with a woman of the Shining Realm. The bishop had been hurt and was clearly hurting still. The two men had spent their nights apart. Brin didn't know if Arumin would keep him out on a night like this, but as the sky darkened and the air grew chillier, he had decided to chance it.

Arumin still cared for him. He knew it. The constant burning in his cheeks, where that damnable Private Robir had cut him during the mutiny, reminded him of the bishop's face when he'd seen the cuts. A ghastly pallor had come over the old man.

Brin clung to that image whenever a more poisonous knowledge crept up on him—the knowledge that Robir's knife had disfigured him. He had depended on his looks so deeply and for so long that losing them, even in part, felt like losing a limb. He hadn't seen his own reflection since it happened, but he had felt the new ridges, which were on their way to becoming scars. He wondered if his face was no longer to Arumin's liking.

The thought wouldn't leave Brin alone. The more it advanced, the more he needed the bishop to want him again.

That need wrestled with a bone-deep weariness. He was tired of the back-and-forth with Arumin—tired of this journey, tired of struggle. He just wanted to be safe.

He was sitting on a fur-lined blanket inside the hut when Arumin appeared in the doorway, speaking to someone in a hushed voice. In the patch of firelight that escaped the hut's doorway, he glimpsed Sergeant Orund's face. Not so long ago, Arumin had been angry with Orund for publicly disrespecting Brin. Apparently, the needs of the bishop's holy mission superseded such concerns.

The same had happened with Private Robir for the same reasons. And the hurt in that case had been much worse. Brin struggled not to resent Arumin's extreme pragmatism—Brin respected the necessities of survival—but he felt himself failing.

Arumin did not seem surprised to see Brin. In fact, the bishop did not acknowledge him at all. He sat on a blanket close to the fire, not close to the young priest but not deliberately far away.

Brin asked the bishop, "Has the doctor seen to your hand?"

"Mmm," Arumin grunted in the affirmative. He did not ask about Brin's face, but the grunt was better than total silence.

Brin turned from the fire toward the old man. "Can I look at it?"

"Why?" The bishop's tone ridiculed the idea.

Brin didn't pursue the matter further. "The things in this village live like animals. But you still found us a place of our own. You always care for us."

The fire popped. Its smoke escaped through a little hole over their heads. The bishop did not look at him.

Brin continued, "You won't believe this. I saw them chaining Brother Nor to some rock outside."

"I believe it. And?"

"And... are you sure that's the way to help him?"

"Help him?" Arumin growled.

Brin struggled to recover. "I only mean—"

"The villagers wanted him kept so." Arumin said it as if that answered all conceivable arguments.

Looking at the bishop's profile, Brin tried to hunt down his eyes. "You're killing him, then. Leaving him out there."

"You don't know what will become of him. Don't concern yourself with these things." The bishop's tone was openly condescending.

Brin snorted but restrained his anger. "Well, did you leave him a blanket?"

He heard Arumin's teeth grind. "So, I am to obey your commands," the old man said. "Let us suppose I did. What would you do with Nor?"

Brin shrugged. "What would the Lady do? That's what I would have done." It sounded like the answer the bishop would expect of him, and for once, he agreed with it.

Arumin scoffed. "Have you become interested in what she wants? What a sudden and profound change you've undergone."

"It's not that easy!" Brin hissed. He would have shouted were not others around to hear. "I am who I am. But I want to try. I've seen her power now. She saved us all."

"You'd seen her act before. But this time, you benefited. That is what made the difference. A fine thing, that."

The confines of the hut suddenly felt intolerably close to Brin. The middling fire felt like a furnace. He was trapped between its hellish aura and the bitter dark and cold outside.

"Or was it something else?" Arumin asked. "What could have changed your mind when I couldn't? Was it *her*?"

He didn't mean the Lady.

Brin wanted to remove the coat but was ashamed to expose any more of himself. "What I did with that woman was for us." That was a lie, but he wanted it to be true. "I do what I must, just like you."

"You don't do what you must. You do what you want. That is all you know how to do."

Arumin still had not met his gaze. Wishing he could leave, wishing the night wasn't so cold, Brin lay down and failed to sleep.

9

EMBERLY

THE HUT THAT HOUSED the officers seemed so large that Emberly felt guilty. That was nonsense—it was a pile of sticks and hide—but then, he was bunking with far fewer people nowadays, when he bunked at all. Iwan was dead, and Roark was passing. Orund was off somewhere, no doubt as listless and dispirited as he had been since Om.

That left Sergeant Feng, who was no particular threat or ally and would get along with whoever was around.

Emberly had felt peaceful enough when he left Roark. But as he thought about their conversation, irritation ate at him.

"You'll win," Roark had said. "They'll see."

Emberly didn't know what had given the lieutenant the wisdom—the right—to say anything of the kind. Words of comfort only comforted if one had any reason at all to think them true. Charlotte had never recognized that, and his annoyance at her kindly intentioned words had started any number of quarrels. Roark had unwittingly taken up Charlotte's cause, and as the captain reviewed their conversation, the old, ritual anger flowed through his chest and jaw.

Roark simply had to see what was happening. His pain hadn't rendered him blind. When the words "They'll see," had come out of his mouth, Emberly thought of that moment on the cliff when Robir had challenged him. The captain had looked at the faces of his company and known he lacked the heft to go against their collective will. He had lost too much credibility in their eyes. Even the men who didn't hate him outright had lost trust in him during their endless march to seemingly nowhere.

Killing Iwan had made everything worse. That had been a desperate gesture, a grasp at control over a situation slipping between his fingers. He had done it to remind them all who was in charge. His brother, Rayan, had convinced him it would work. *And where is that bastard now?* Emberly hadn't seen him since that moment.

Most telling, during the confrontation on the cliff, had been the bishop's expression—that look of open-mouthed anticipation, like a dog waiting for a piece of meat. He had sensed the change in the soldiers as well as Emberly had, and he knew the company would soon be his. His expression had said, *"Your road has ended. If you care to*

*contest my authority over the men, do it now. We'll see which
of us is heaved over the ledge."*

Emberly had not realized how much he, himself, had
changed until he found himself backing down. Giving in
to the bishop would keep the captain alive, if only for
the moment. He had thought about falling from the cliff,
tallied what he had left, and couldn't bear to give up even
the little that remained.

Sergeant Orund belonged to the bishop now. That had
been a blow. But Roark's slow march toward death was
what had tipped the balance.

For the moment, Emberly would keep giving commands to the company. It was a habit, and he knew no
other way to talk to them. But the soul had been ripped out
of the thing, and it was only a matter of time until everyone
realized it.

Then he had heard Roark say, "You'll win."

The simple fact that the man remained loyal, all the way
to this bitter end, made Emberly clench his fists and dig his
fingernails into his palms. He wondered how Roark could
not see how much sense it made to give up on the captain.

Thankfully, Emberly had contained his annoyance during his conversation with Roark. But his restraint didn't
erase the desire he had felt—to hurt the feelings of a dying
man.

As Emberly lay on the fur blankets, wishing someone would come in and ask him for something, feet pounded the rocks outside. Staubel entered at a run.

He was out of breath after what must have been a sprint. "Roark," he gasped.

As Feng awakened, Emberly jumped up. "Is he gone yet?"

Even as he stood, he knew the rush was unnecessary. Roark would want to be alone at the end. The most Emberly might do would be to stand outside the hut and silently wish him well. He could offer a prayer for the lieutenant's soul, though he'd begun to suspect the Goddess turned his prayers to curses. In any case, Roark hardly needed prayers. His participation in the crusade had earned him the forgiveness of his sins.

"Come on!" Staubel cried and ran off.

Emberly's mind caught up to his senses. The look on the doctor's face had been stranger and graver than a simple death would warrant. Emberly followed.

They didn't run straight to Roark's hut. Staubel stopped between it and the water nearby. He turned toward the captain, looking even more like a boy than usual.

"Where is he?" Emberly looked at the hut, but he couldn't see inside from there.

Staubel's eyes caught the scarce light. "He died suddenly."

"Well, take me to him."

"I can't. He died—"

"Where is his body?" Emberly snapped. "We need to bury it."

"Then something came for him."

The world spun.

"I could barely see it."

Emberly's mouth hung open, desperately gulping air. He sank into a defensive crouch, hands raised, looking for someone to fight. He whipped his arm around, pointing at every hut in the village. "Was it one of them?"

"I don't know." The doctor's voice broke and squeaked. "But it came for Roark first, out of everyone. It was like... it smelled death."

"Where did it go?" Emberly shouted, demanding an answer from all the world.

"I saw it go toward the water." Staubel's voice heaved as he began to cry. "I couldn't stop it. I couldn't look at it. It was so terrible."

Emberly left him and reached the water, running too fast to stop. He splashed in with great arcing strides, up to his knees then to his waist, shouts echoing behind him.

The fires of the village got small, and he was alone with the calm sea.

The water was as warm as a bath. He spared no thought to understand that fact. His only real thought was of his own folly. The surf was wide and indifferent. The black sea and the night sky met in a barbarous sludge not far away. No one was there to find, and Emberly would have found nothing anyway.

Perhaps the right thing to do was to dive in and search until he grew exhausted and sank. He fell far short of that, splashing around and shouting the lieutenant's name.

When he came back to the beach, several people were waiting for him. He dismissed them with a muttered word. He gave no reply to Staubel's pleas for forgiveness.

He walked away down the beach until he felt alone, where no one would hear him no matter what he said.

Rayan was nowhere to be found.

10

— · —

NOR

NOR'S ARMS HAD BEEN pulled behind him, stretched around a rock, and chained together. It was a standing stone shaped like a dull knife and looked like it had sprouted from the underlying rock in the early ages of that world. Though close to the village, it had been invisible in that weather until the villagers dragged him to it.

Rattling the chains, he managed to slide to a sitting position. He was on an outcropping of rock that sprouted from the base of the cliff enclosing one end of that forsaken beach. The water lapped the rocks close beneath him.

Shortly after they chained him there, soldiers had begun to visit him one at a time, offering bits of food or spare blankets from the village. Perhaps they were genuinely sympathetic to his plight, but he told himself that was unlikely. They were probably superstitious about leaving a holy man to die. One of them, glowering, had announced that he had brought a coat for Nor only because the captain ordered it.

The covering quickly put to rest his immediate concern of freezing to death in the night. The blankets, hat, and coat were piled on him awkwardly. He could not adjust them to cover exposed areas, but they kept him warm enough.

Shada arrived with an armful of blankets. Seeing his coverings, she stopped and said, "Ah."

After a moment, she shrugged and said, "Oh well, then." She put a couple of blankets on the ground next to Nor and sat on them, covering herself with the rest.

Nor tried to speak but coughed. "You're…"

She returned his gaze. "Yes?"

"You're not planning on staying here."

"Of course I am. Honestly."

Nor shook his head. "No. It's too cold." He wanted her gone, though he couldn't have said why.

"We've got blankets."

"It's dangerous out here."

"It's dangerous everywhere," she said impatiently.

His need for her to leave grew with each refusal. Something about her being there scared him, scared him so much that he didn't want to know the reason why.

"I don't need company," he said harshly.

"Well, I do," she replied.

Then it came to him. Tabard and Orund would come for him that night, soon. They might never find him so defenseless again. The thought of facing them with his hands chained petrified him but not as much as the thought of Shada defending him.

"Well, I don't," he snapped. "Or doesn't that matter to you?"

That got her attention. She looked at him and said nothing.

"Try listening for once," he added. He was almost there—a bit more, and he would drive her away.

The task wasn't hard. Under his feigned anger was a spark that was real. "Go back to your Lady. And your Goddess."

That did it. "*My* Lady?" Shada shot back, her voice threatening. "Do you really think I chose her?"

"You choose her every day!" Nor said. "You think I don't see it? How you whisper to her?"

She no longer seemed surprised or confused by his outburst. Probably, she no longer cared why he was saying these things, only that he was saying them. "How dare you blame me for that! You, of all people—a monk!"

He laid his head back on the stone, and his voice emerged as a low rumble. "I've made my bed. I'll lie in it. But I'll do it with integrity. I won't lick her feet like you."

She stood, letting the blankets lay where they fell. She looked at him, and her gaze was painful. "I don't understand," she said. Then she walked away, out of his view behind the rock.

As seconds turned to minutes, he became sure she was gone, and he breathed a little more easily.

Until night fell in earnest, he had thought of this world as one of perpetual twilight. The "day" was hardly worthy of the name. Still, as the hour grew late, a deeper gloom descended.

His eyes were keen, but he no longer trusted them. When he saw faces in the water beyond the edge of the jutting rock, he stared critically, waiting for them to change into something else. They did not, instead drifting steadily toward the rock and him. More followed them. Their movements were strange and inhuman, each different, but all gave the impression of stealth. With the scraping of feet and claws, they began to climb the rock.

He had thought Tabard and Orund scared him.

As the creatures came closer, he raged against his chains. He would almost have left his arms behind if that meant he could run. His heart pounded until his chest hurt, and his breath rushed in loud little gasps. He felt like he was watching it all from a distance.

He heard the smack of fins and saw the glint of shells, the whip of antennae. His knees leapt to his chest, his body twisting as it willed itself elsewhere. Someone or something gave him a choice: he could lose his senses, enter a fantasy, perhaps even faint. He shook his head.

The shapes were climbing up all around him, segmented legs unfolding and scratching. He had to see them—he had to look away. He turned his eyes to the sky and saw something less strange than what was happening down here: clouds were gathering swiftly overhead. These clouds were different from the blanket that girded the whole sky—they circled each other, so low and thick that he could see them against the murky ceiling.

The creatures from the water reached the edge of the jutting rock. They waited, peering at him.

Voices from the beach were coming toward him. As they approached, the creatures around the edges of the rock sank out of sight.

Perhaps four men were there, Orund and Tabard among them. They gathered before Nor, who realized how he looked: shrunken, pressed against the rock as if to burrow into it. He straightened.

"Look at you." That was Orund.

"Warm as if he was in his own bed," someone else said.

"Who brought you all this?" Orund asked. He laughed, a sound empty of joy or even satisfaction. "I supposed some won't ever see what you are."

Nor looked up. Past the sergeant's head, the clouds were descending. The sky must have been sinking to crush them all.

"Nothing to say?" Orund asked him.

Nor swallowed, wetting his mouth. "Nothing worth wasting on you." He hacked.

"I'll do it." That was Tabard.

Orund's eyes were desolate. He gave Tabard a nod and said, "Do it, for Carrowy."

Tabard drew a knife. Every muscle in Nor's body convulsed, a futile bid for escape.

The sky fell. A cloud swooped down with unholy speed and swallowed them all. Nor's skin prickled and stung; all around him, the cloud buzzed like a million hungry insects. He gasped and got a lungful of raging sand.

The air cleared as he sank against the rock and coughed. Someone screamed in a voice that grew fainter and fainter. Nor opened his eyes, and through a veil of wetness, he saw the others huddled on the ground, covering their heads. Tabard was gone.

The screaming was more distant but no less desperate. Nor turned his head slowly skyward. The cloud was returning to the heavens, an arm that had briefly extended before rejoining the whole. Carried in the cloud was its prize, of whom Nor glimpsed only arms and legs.

Tabard kept screaming until the cloud lifted him out of hearing, out into the sky over the water.

The men on the rock hardly moved. They looked around for things that they recognized: each other, the rock under their hands and feet. The creatures had crawled back into the water, but their heads remained above the gentle waves. They sent up a great, cacophonous symphony of croaks and whines. Orund and his men groaned, covering their ears and shutting their eyes. Nor buried his head against his chest and shoulder, blocking one ear and then the other, never free of the sound.

Emberly arrived, skidding to a halt after what must have been a sprint. "What in Huire's name!" he shouted at them over the roar of the creatures. "That cloud!" He looked around, knees bent, ready for action. "What's happening?"

Nor waited while each of the others spoke in turn. Their minds were scattered, and their thoughts came in pieces. The captain often shouted at them to speak up over the creatures' noise.

Finally, Nor added his part. "They came to kill me. The cloud came down, and it took Tabard away."

"Took him?"

"Yes. I saw it."

Emberly sneered, maybe more in denial than disbelief. "I don't understand."

"It grabbed him," Orund whimpered. "Like a toy."

Others had gathered. The captain looked at the men on the rock, disgust on his face.

"No. I cannot…" He stopped and listened to the things in the water.

The sky was too dark to see them clearly. They were not only screeching but pounding the water with legs, fins, and hands.

Emberly bent and put his hands on his knees. "Oh, Huire. Oh, Goddess." He dug at the corners of his eyes with his fingers. "What is happening to us?"

Shada pushed past the others and crouched next to Nor. "What happened?" she cried. She held his face in her hands. "Are you hurt? Tell me!" She seemed to have forgotten their argument, and Nor was happy to do the same. He looked at her and smiled. Though he knew her well, he felt the joy of recognition.

"What is this?" the bishop's voice thundered over all others.

Emberly did not answer. He glanced at the company then at Nor. His movements were controlled, but his eyes were wild.

He turned slowly toward Orund and his remaining friends. "Who's got the key?" he asked them.

No one answered. Maybe no one understood him at first.

"To the shackles. One of you must have it." He pointed at Nor. "You were going to dispose of his body when you were done."

Sergeant Orund seemed to awaken. He looked upon Emberly with wonder. "You're going to release him?"

"Give it to me!" the captain cried. It was not his deep, commanding roar but a high and ragged shriek.

Nor's stomach turned.

The creatures' awful sounds had faded, their shapes dispersed into the night. The new quiet resounded.

Orund fumbled in a pocket and offered the key. Emberly took it and removed Nor's chains. Nor sagged and felt Shada's arms around him. She tugged at him, trying to remove him from harm's way. He put a hand on her, asking her to stay, and she did.

Emberly studied the chains in his hands. He turned toward Orund. "Get up."

"Why?" the man asked.

"Get up."

No one moved but Orund. The sergeant stood slowly, wobbling and looking his age.

"Against the stone."

"What?" the bishop asked.

"No," someone else said—Robir.

Emberly ignored them. Looming over Orund, he said, "Stand against the rock."

Shada pulled at Nor again, and with her help, he moved away from the stone—just far enough to make room for Orund. The sergeant shuffled into place.

Emberly leaned close to his ear, hissing one command after another. "Turn around. Arms back."

"If you do this..." Robir stopped as though his sentence was complete.

Emberly hardly spared him a glance. He shackled Orund to the standing stone, facing the sea.

"Emberly," the bishop began through gritted teeth.

The captain turned on him. His voice was calm, and his eyes were empty. "Yes?"

The bishop's mouth moved. The silence of the night was unbroken.

"Do what you want," Emberly said lazily. Then he attacked Orund with his fists.

Nor was so close that he heard it all—thumps and cracks. The captain grunted with effort. Orund groaned and shouted, each sound cut short by the next blow. Gasping for breath, he began to cry for help then fell silent.

Emberly stopped soon after. Nor opened his eyes to see blood on the captain's knuckles. He did not look at Orund.

Everyone watched as Emberly caught his breath. "Where's the doctor?" he asked at last. "Find the doctor. Help him."

His eyes fell on Shada. His hand leapt out like a snake, grabbed her arm, and yanked her close to him. Nor cried out in protest and tried to rise, but his legs gave way.

Emberly pushed his face against Shada's and said, "Take me to the Lady."

11

EMBERLY

EMBERLY MARCHED TOWARD THE hut where Shada stayed alone with the Lady. His hand was fixed around Shada's arm, and though he had commanded her to take him to the Lady, he knew the way and was pulling her along.

"Is she in the box?" the captain muttered, watching the door to the hut as they came nearer.

"I suppose," the young woman said.

That halted him. "You suppose?"

Shada's eyes were cool. "She is not in my charge, Captain. Or yours."

"What does 'caretaker' mean, then? Friend? Servant?" Not waiting for an answer, he dragged her on again toward the hut.

Some distance behind them, Arumin was calling the captain's name. Emberly disregarded him as he would a gnat.

As they entered the hut, he felt the muscles in Shada's arm tighten. She said, "This isn't going to get you any answers."

The fire was dying but provided enough light to reveal the Lady's box, which was sitting on the floor in one corner. An ornate and alien metal thing, it glinted red in the firelight.

Emberly strode toward it, each foot falling deliberately, crunching in the little rocks around his boots.

He leaned his head forward and watched the box. "Are you in there?"

The thing remained decidedly inanimate. If any life was inside—or whatever nonlife the Lady consisted of—it did not deign to reply.

"Can you hear me?" he growled, louder.

He might as well have been demanding conversation from a stone. He looked around, wondering if the Lady might be hiding elsewhere in the room and what it would take to bring her out.

Shada watched him. "It's no use, Emberly. Not until she is ready."

"Wrong!" His shout filled the little room. "That's not good enough anymore!" Emberly said to the box, "You're in there, all right," as Arumin entered, puffing.

"Get a hold of yourself," the old man wheezed.

"No," the captain said. He crouched, feeling somehow closer to the Lady's eye level. "Not until she speaks to me."

To Emberly, Shada never seemed quite like the domestic servant she had supposedly been. That was never truer than when she said, "Believe me—you don't want that to happen."

"Not to you!" he told her defiantly. "She must speak to me!"

Her eyes were pitying. "Do you know what she could do, Emberly?"

"I don't care!"

Arumin coughed. "Well, you should! We all should!"

The captain glared at him and spoke derisively. "She doesn't care!" He turned again toward the box. "Do you? And yet... that cloud was like you, wasn't it? It was a being like you."

The bishop shuddered. "Stop this. While she has any mercy left."

"And all along, she knew it was here!" Emberly continued. "Didn't you? Where is Tabard, you monster? Where is he?"

Arumin dared to approach Emberly. "What is one man compared to eternity, Captain?"

"I know nothing of eternity." Emberly picked up the box. The metal was smooth and cold. He stood. "You are going to answer me. What if I break you out of there?"

Shada looked from Emberly to the box. "Captain, do you care for my life?"

He looked at her. "You." He laughed. "You always know what to say, don't you? Do you know where she is?"

"No."

"Let's find out!" He hurled the box to the ground.

It bounced, sang, and rattled but did not break. Landing upright, it tipped slowly and fell on its side. Its door opened. Nothing was inside.

Emberly drew a miserable, empty breath. He dropped his hands to his sides. "Where did she go?" He sniffed. "Has she left us?"

Shada said, "She is watching."

Perhaps she meant that to be comforting, but Emberly snapped his head toward her, startled.

He stepped closer to her. "Is she with you?" He enunciated each word carefully. "Inside you?" Another step.

Shada met his eyes.

"Emberly," Arumin said, "for the love of everything..."

As Emberly slowly advanced, Shada asked, "Are you going to hurt me? You might as well. If you won't stop, I'll soon be dead anyway, and so will you."

"No!" someone cried from far off, outside. The voice had a frantic pitch.

Emberly recognized it as Nor's. He stopped and listened to the voice of the man he had saved. Nor must have been some distance away, but his sharp senses had not failed him, and he could apparently hear enough to guess what was happening. He staggered in seconds later and stood by the door, wobbling.

"Don't hurt anyone," he said.

Emberly felt Shada's eyes still on him. Her gaze was suddenly painful.

Nor went on. "I know how you feel. And you're right." He looked at the bishop. "It's all been a lie."

Emberly remembered something. "You said there is no Huire." He wondered if the monk had been serious.

"I don't know if that's true," Nor admitted. "But I know we can't trust what the Lady says."

The monk's arrival pulled Emberly entirely out of his rage. Some of the things he had just done were beginning to seem strange, even to himself. "What choice do we have?" he asked. "We can't go back. The Shining Realm is behind us."

"None," Nor answered. "The Lady's trapped us into taking her to Huire. She needs us for something. But if I'm right, the Lady may not really be Huire's servant. If so, we don't have to do as she says."

Bishop Arumin said, "Curse that Cadmon. Curse the day he took you under his wing."

Emberly was transfixed. "And if you're wrong? If the Lady is doing Huire's will?"

The monk smiled, an event so rare that it was eerie. He said sadly, "Then we'll do her bidding until the end."

12

— · —

SHADA

A THOUGHT STRUCK SHADA after everyone else left. As she was sitting in silence by the dying fire, hoping the Lady would not threaten or even speak to her again that night, she realized Nor might have no place to sleep.

She dressed again and stepped out into the cold. The latest snow flurry had come and gone, and she was stunned beyond reason to see a clean sky heavy with stars.

She found Nor sitting against the standing stone, right where he had been, and anger flared in her as she wondered if someone had chained him there again.

"What in the world?" she asked, standing over him.

He smiled, apparently enjoying her shock. She believed she could read his blank eyes better than most, though, and suspected he was embarrassed.

"Where else am I to go?" he asked.

"You will stay with me, of course."

He was momentarily speechless, and she was a little charmed to realize that the idea had not occurred to him.

"Come on!" she insisted. She had managed to forget until then how viciously cold the air was.

"Would that be...?" He appeared to correct himself. "Yes, thank you. But not yet. I will come in a little while."

His tone did not invite her to ask why he was waiting there. She looked toward the village and sighed before sitting down next to him.

He blinked. "You're staying?"

"Obviously."

He turned his face back toward the sea. "Good."

She looked hard at his profile. "I should have known to keep an eye on you. I won't leave you again. I'm sorry for Tabard, but I am grateful for whatever took him."

"It was a thing like the Lady," Nor said, "wasn't it?"

"Emberly wondered that too." She cursed herself for bringing it up.

Since the company had come to the village, the Lady had fallen into blessed but mysterious silence, and Shada suspected that the cloud that had seized Tabard was at the heart of it. Throughout the argument in Shada's hut, even as the captain had threatened them, the Lady had not whispered even a word to her. As Shada had struggled to prevent Emberly from getting himself killed, she had darkly wondered if, by refusing to listen, the man was simply asking for what he got.

Fearing that speaking of that thing in the sky might provoke the Lady into action, Shada said, "But I don't know."

"She doesn't tell you these things?"

"No," Shada replied, more harshly than she meant to. To go along with the Lady was to keep everyone alive, and again, she found herself thinking: *Why can't they just damned well wait? What does knowing bring them?*

Eager to make Nor forget the anger in her voice, she asked, "Do you ever regret joining your order?"

"Yes."

"Oh. Why?"

"No women."

Laughter blurted from her throat and echoed across the rocks. She replied, "You should feel right at home with soldiers, then. You share their struggle."

"Soldiers take leave. Monks take a vow. But that's not really why I regret joining. The real reason is what I said before: it's all been a lie."

She winced aloud at a sudden swelling in her throat. The Lady was not pleased and wanted her to know it.

"We don't know that," she said quickly. It was the truth. "We don't know anything."

"I've seen enough to feel sure of this."

"What did they do to you? The Shining Realm?" She needed badly to change the subject, and she had wanted to ask him this since they left Om. Only now did it occur to her what an invasive question it was. This man had nearly been murdered that very evening.

He was frighteningly quiet for a while. When she opened her mouth to say something, anything, he replied, "They only continued what I'd already begun. I asked for this. I've been asking for it my whole life."

She was about to ask what he meant, but he continued without prompting.

"I never listened to anyone. At least, I heard what I wanted to hear. My abbot, Cadmon, tried to instruct me in the Temple's ways, to set me straight. But it didn't work—I wouldn't let it. I could never just... obey." He sighed, and the weariness of the sound pricked Shada's heart, mixing with her own soul-deep exhaustion. "I wouldn't take the Temple for what it was. I used it. Serves me right that it was using me all along."

Coming from Nor, that was an abundance of words such as Shada might never get again, and she absorbed them with guilty happiness. "But here you are," she said.

"What does that mean?" he asked with more than a hint of impatience. Then he shook his head. "Sorry. I just... really want to understand."

Shada shrugged. "What I meant to say is that you're still trying. Still fighting."

He grimaced. "That's not much."

"It's all you have. And you're good at it."

His barely perceptible smile warmed her body. Neither of them spoke for a while, but the silence no longer bothered her.

Finally, he said, "I don't know whether to be grateful for that letter or to curse the day I laid eyes on it."

"What letter?"

He looked at her. "Hell, you don't know, do you? And you've been tolerating my nonsense." He gulped as though steeling himself. "Cadmon gave me a note when we left Ronia. I wasn't to read it... well, I didn't read it until I was captured by the Shining Realm." He took a deep breath. "Shada, are we alone?"

They weren't, of course. But she could not say that. She could only hope whatever he said would not displease the Lady. "Yes. We are."

"This will hurt, and I'm sorry. Here goes: the letter said that the gods were false. They were machines created by man in the ancient world to serve him but who became his masters."

He stopped there for a moment. Many things collided inside of Shada, but they left a great stillness at her center. She could not tell what the Lady knew, whether she believed it or not, or if she was even listening.

Nor continued, "When I read that, I remembered that moment on Caidfell and all the other things I've done. I knew that what Cadmon said was true and that I deserved it to be true."

Shada huffed. "You've made mistakes, of course. But you meant well. You have to move on."

"Whether I meant well isn't the point, though. It doesn't matter. There is nothing to mean, and—here is the worst part—there is no one to mean it."

Shada sat up straight. "I can't accept that. You're not throwing yourself in the sea, after all. You must have hope that there's something. Why go on otherwise?"

He looked out to sea, and for a moment, Shada feared she was giving him ideas. But then he touched her hand. "You're right. I should expect that by now."

She beamed in the darkness. But her warm feelings curdled when she noticed a soft churning in the water. Something large was swimming down there.

"What is that?" she whispered.

He squeezed her hand. "Wait."

In the starlight, dim shapes broke the surface. Splashes came from all around them, and something—more than one something—climbed onto the rock. She would have run except that Nor didn't.

Shadows rose here and there around the rock's edge. Glints of wetness hinted at breathtaking shapes. They came no closer.

"They are not our enemies," Nor said.

"Who are they?"

"I think they lived in the village once. All those empty huts."

"And then they decided to live in the sea?"

"Or something changed them—so much that they had to live in the water."

Shada and Nor sat in the presence of that strange company for some time. The shadowy figures watched them, and she discerned what she could of their shapes. As she became accustomed to them, they ceased to be a parade of night terrors.

The cold had reached deep inside her. She asked Nor, "Would you be breaking your vow if I put my head on your shoulder?"

He laughed. "I'm not a monk anymore. Haven't I told you?"

13

— · —

EMBERLY

THE NEXT MORNING, WORD came to Emberly that the Lady had finally spoken. She had given the company a new direction: out to sea. The men, newly clothed for the cold by their hosts and fed on raw seafood, inspected the boats on the shore. They were narrow, ice-crusted things that might hold four occupants each. To Emberly, who was no seaman whatsoever, they looked long abandoned.

Hoping to use the boats, Emberly led some villagers over to them using gestures and an encouraging tone. But he could hardly get them to look directly at the craft, and when they did, their gazes slid away to the sea.

"They don't seem to care about the boats in the slightest," he said to Arumin.

"What use would they have for boats?" the bishop replied. "They swim like fish. These must have belonged to someone else."

"I'll bet we can take them," Emberly said.

Arumin agreed. They had not spoken of the events in Shada's hut.

A few of the men knew something of boats. They went among the fleet, inspecting vessels, looking for any that might still hold up against the sea. Not many qualified, but they would be enough. Oars were scattered among and under the boats, and the men collected several of the more intact ones.

Things proceeded efficiently, but when the company gathered its few possessions and began carrying them to the boats, a number of the villagers stood in their way. Foremost was their many-legged friend from the previous evening.

Emberly cursed silently. Their hosts must have felt attached to the vessels after all. If they did, he didn't know what the Ronians could do. They had no way to purchase the boats. Arumin would not let such a thing stand in their way, but the thought of attacking those unassuming creatures was as unpalatable as anything Emberly had been forced to contemplate.

He was both relieved and alarmed when, after a lot of muddled communication, he realized the villagers were not concerned about the boats but about the company itself. They did not want the Ronians to leave.

"At least, not in that direction," he said to Arumin, pointing toward the ocean.

The old man replied, "You know we have no choice."

Emberly hesitated but could only nod in agreement.

He ordered the company forward. They walked into the midst of the villagers, who parted to let them through. The creatures made no further protest as the company gathered the usable boats then loaded and boarded them. Assigning occupants to each, Emberly watched them all board. Staubel had to guide Orund, whose eyes had swelled nearly shut. Before Emberly stepped into his own craft, he turned back toward the villagers and raised a hand.

They did not respond. Perhaps the Ronians had offended them by ignoring their warning, or perhaps waving was an unfamiliar gesture to them. *Or perhaps*, Emberly thought, *they've given us up for dead.*

The half dozen little boats paddled directly away from the shore, following the instructions passed from the Lady to Shada. The sky was overcast and threatened snow, but the air before them was clear for the moment. Many imposing shapes, spired and knobby rock formations, lay ahead in the water.

The captain breathed a little more easily as the beach and its cliffs grew smaller. The Shining Realm might still find a couple of usable boats among the hulks left behind but not enough to follow the company in significant numbers. He could not imagine their pursuit was over, but he did not see how it could continue.

He had chosen to sit behind Robir. As everyone was busy heaving and rowing, Emberly leaned forward and spoke softly to the private. "I have not forgotten anything."

Robir didn't answer.

Emberly went on: "When we step off this boat, we will go somewhere alone. Then one of us will kill the other." He paused for a couple of passes of the oar then continued, "There is one other choice. We can leave this vendetta behind, forever. I want your answer when we land."

That said, he leaned back and rowed. A whiteness was encroaching in the water on either side of the boats. They were being forced into a channel between two ice floes. The landforms ahead were approaching quickly. He hoped the channel did not close ahead.

The splashing of the oars sprinkled him with sea water that was shockingly warm. He wondered if whatever was heating the water was also keeping that narrow stretch of ocean from freezing over.

From a distance, he had taken the formations to be a mere clump of rocks. Now, he saw they were much more: a fantastic landscape of which only hints broke the water's surface. The shapes were rocky and crystalline. Among them lay jagged obsidian edges of shining masses and the crumbling remains of towering flutes and pinnacles. The floes had mostly stayed away except for a few brave ice sheets that had broken off to melt in that zone where the surface steamed and air bubbled from beneath the water.

Emberly's boat led the fleet. They had two options: to venture among the formations or to land on the ice and proceed on foot.

Someone shouted. Emberly whipped his head around just as a monstrous underwater shape flashed out of sight under the ice. He looked around, but nothing else moved.

His heart thumped. He told the men in his boat to stop, and they waited until the other boats pulled alongside them.

"You and you, off," he said.

Two men left his boat, stepping carefully onto one of the others. Only Emberly and Robir remained.

"Where's Shada?" he called.

"Here," she replied from somewhere.

"Pass the box to me," he said.

She obeyed after a long moment. The box passed from one set of hands to the next until it reached the captain. "Stay alert," he told them all.

They set out again. Emberly and Robir rowed well in front of the other boats, which followed in a cluster. Emberly was seated foremost, with the box braced between his feet.

The channel through the ice narrowed but did not close. They reached the rock formations and paddled among them.

Emberly asked Robir, "Are you happy now?"

"Happy?" the other man grunted.

The captain's eyes darted about. Every second, thousands of bubbles broke the water's surface, obscuring what lay beneath. He felt like he was floating in a stewpot. "I know why you turned on me," he said. "You didn't always hate me."

"No, I didn't," Robir admitted. "I learned to."

"It's about that scar you got on Gallobraith. You rode with me that night, and you were shot. We had to try it, man. We were trapped."

The private snickered. "Is that what you think? Has it occurred to you that, perhaps, I hate you because I've come to know you?"

"I thought of it," the captain replied, "but I don't believe it."

"Think whatever you want. Or face the truth: you are a bad man, and good men should oppose you."

That quieted Emberly for some time. He let the boat drift uncomfortably close to a multicolumned rock formation, then he pushed it away with his oar. At last, he said, "You will be rid of me soon, one way or another."

Snow began falling again. They rowed deeper among the rocks. Emberly tried to keep watch, but his thoughts kept moving back to their conversation.

Watching more carefully would have made little difference to what happened next. The beasts moved incredibly quickly. A vast furry arm darted from the water and effortlessly crushed their boat.

14

NOR

NOR DID NOT SEE Emberly disappear. Water exploded where the captain's boat had been, and bodies fell in the spray.

Before he could think, monsters were everywhere. Rifle shots rang out. Shapes in the water appeared and vanished. Another boat tipped, casting people overboard.

Nor stood reflexively. His boat rocked and almost overturned. Someone pushed him—it must have been Swinburn, the young soldier behind him—and he plunged into the warm water.

His head broke the surface into light and air. Then everything was torn away. Arms like trees pressed him against a gigantic body with horrible force.

Light faded, and his eyes burned. The beast dragged him down. Struggling was worse than useless—when he thrashed, air leaked from his mouth. One of his arms was free, but as he flailed it, it touched nothing but bubbles and the whipping current. He dug his fingernails into the beast's skin to no effect.

He debated the worth of maintaining his senses. The evidence favored panic and despair.

Perhaps only sheer bitterness convinced him otherwise. He had always lashed out at whatever the world decided for him, and he would keep doing so. He would not die. Yet he was dying.

The sea was shallow there, and they were near the bottom. The odd rock formations on the surface showed their full glory, a dream landscape. The beast turned Nor's body and shoved him into a dark hole in one of the towering rocks. The only light came from an ugly pink glow. Relieved at being released, Nor kicked his legs. Searing pain shot through them, and he nearly spewed the air from his lungs. Something sharp lined the narrow hole, and it had cut his skin.

He had no sense of up or down, in or out, only of being enclosed somewhere deep in a rocky tomb at the bottom of the sea. He wished the beast had killed him quickly.

Then something marvelous happened. He embraced his death. It was a fact, and he knew he could endure it, as had everyone who ever lived. In return for his acceptance, death took away his fear.

He was a new man. He collected himself enough to look around. *Why not play the game a little longer?* He raised his head to look past his feet. The pink glow lay that way. Maybe it was a vestige of light from the surface.

He grasped at the walls and found them covered by bony spikes, all tilted sharply toward the glow. Grabbing those, he pulled himself that direction. Pain washed his hands—the spikes seemed to have small barbs of their own.

The pink glow brightened. Through the burning salt, he saw parts of it stretch, groping along the tunnel toward him—tentacles. If it was blocking his escape, he would have to go through it or give up.

As he hesitated, a glowing tentacle wrapped softly, like seaweed, around his calf.

Its touch was fiery agony. It felt like a bolt of lightning come alive. He screamed into the mute water, losing air. It tugged gently at him, fixing against his skin like jelly. He quickly lost feeling in his foot and ankle, and the numbness spread up his leg.

His feeling of peace vanished. He was a miserable coward, terrified of dying in the clutches of that thing. To feel that fire all over himself was beyond imagining.

Using the spikes, he thrust himself along the tunnel in the other direction. The glowing tentacle stretched like mucus then fell away. Ahead of him was only darkness. He couldn't tell if he was moving deeper into the creature's lair.

His lungs screamed for air. Soon, he would inhale against his will and fill them with water.

His cloak caught on the spikes. Wrestling frantically, he freed himself one arm at a time. The pink glow increased, and he looked backward.

The creature had followed him. Its tentacles reached to caress his skin.

Remembering that everything was a game, he used both hands to grab the spikes lining the tunnel. If he gathered all his strength, he might fling himself face-first toward its end. The spikes were pointed toward him, waiting to cut or stab him.

A tentacle licked one of his legs. Convulsing with pain, he launched himself down the tunnel. He flattened his body and pressed his arms to his sides.

He was beyond joy or surprise. When his momentum flagged, he saw the tunnel's exit ahead. It was a forbidding circle against the darkness, barely wide enough for him to pass. The beast that had put him here must have assumed he would drown.

Seizing another pair of spikes, he gave himself a last push, knowing his aim must be perfect lest a spike lodge itself in his eye or mouth.

He missed them all and found himself in open water.

His lungs gave in. His chest heaved as he inhaled a burning chestful of briny water. He shuddered as the sea began to take him. The light of the surface was far away.

Still, he kicked. And he bent his legs and kicked again. Each great effort brought him closer. His fate was a question that he seemed to study from a distance as his body worked its last.

Freezing wind stung his face. His flailing hands found ice. A final spasm of muscle and bone thrust him out of the water and onto an ice sheet.

There, he lay like one already dead, only slightly aware of the air playing over him, filling his nostrils, tantalizingly close but useless because his lungs were full of water—water that was killing him.

15

ARUMIN

THE SHOCK OF EMBERLY'S almost certain death set in slowly. As the boats crept along through the deepening snowfall, Arumin forgot and recalled it over and over. The captain was dead. He must have been. The bishop couldn't keep the statement in his mind. It was a step along Arumin's way, and though he had expected the captain to die one way or another, such luck was not to be celebrated. It must be offered up to Huire.

The long channel in the ice was bordered by ever larger spires of rock that seemed to lean in over the boats. The water could not be very deep there, and no one who went overboard could disappear so quickly unless the beasts had taken him.

The other men in the tipped boat had been rescued, and the other boats had not reported anyone missing. And the beasts, whatever they were, had ceased attacking and vanished almost immediately.

That was certainly not proof that the creatures had come specifically for Emberly. The bishop could hear Abbot Cadmon, that old bastard, chuckling at the suggestion. *Faith in reason. What would a pack of undersea monstrosities on an alien world want with Emberly in particular?*

Along with the captain, the company had lost the box in which the Lady dwelt.

Arumin should have stopped him. The bishop had power to thwart the captain now. He should have used it the previous night when Emberly beat Sergeant Orund. That had been the perfect moment, when the captain's impulsive and bloodthirsty tendencies were at their highest. Now, with Emberly dead, he would never be publicly overthrown, which left Arumin with a pent-up feeling of business left unfinished.

He had seen the same in Robir's face. When they pulled the private from the water, shaking but unhurt, he had instantly demanded to know where Emberly was. On hearing that the captain was gone, he looked at Arumin with questions in his eyes and then fell into silence.

The Lady had remained with Shada, thank the Goddess. Arumin didn't think the entity capable of drowning but had no wish to find out. As the company had collected itself after the attack, she commanded them, through Shada, to move on at once. No one had argued, though the bish-op heard one soldier crying softly in one of the boats. Arumin halfheartedly wished the beasts would come back for that man.

The air became thick with snow and ice. Ahead, on what passed for the horizon, a looming shadow appeared and grew.

It was an island, Shada informed them, and on the Lady's orders, they made to land on it. A steep rocky beach sloped up to a sheer cliff that darkened the sky. As they approached, Arumin realized the company was not alone.

More of the beasts were waiting for them. They stood in a line, their hulking shapes larger than any man's. The bishop had seen them only in flashes under the water, but he had no doubt that they were the same creatures.

Others saw them, too, and as each successive boat be-came aware, murmurs rose to shouts. Arumin stuttered, not knowing what command would keep everyone calm. Behind him came the rattle of weapons and calls to sur-render. "Not yet!" the bishop yelled, and he hunched down in case someone decided to open fire.

Then the creatures bowed. It was not a reverent mo-tion. They flopped over, landing on their hands and knees. They were near enough that Arumin could see their faces.

His mouth hung open. They were shaped like men but giant and covered with fur. Their limbs and chests were of terrifying girth, and their hands ended in claws like scimitars. Their ears were high and pointed, and sharp teeth protruded from their canine jaws.

He had met their kind before—one of their kind, in Ronia.

"It's the caretaker," he breathed.

Awestruck as he was, he realized the statement contained a number of stupidities, and he was glad it had been quiet. A caretaker was with them already, and she was sitting in a boat behind him. The previous caretaker had indeed been one of those—men?—but he had died on Ronia, killed by the Lady herself.

The company's boats plowed through fragments of ice congregating by the shore. As the hulls scratched shallow rocks near the beach, Arumin could hear the creatures breathing.

By the time the beasts rose to their full height and trotted into the water, the bishop was no longer afraid. His boat ran aground before they reached it, but one of them still laid hands on the prow and pulled it to a secure spot. Arumin could feel the strength in those hands through the wood on which he sat.

Other beasts waded out and roughly hauled the rest of the boats to shore. The men inside bounced and clung to the sides until they were dropped with a jolt on the rocky beach. The shore stretched away in both directions to disappear in snow. The upper reaches of the cliff in front of them were lost in the gray, and near the ground, boulders had piled against it. Amid these, and hidden in crannies farther up, were the shadowed openings of caves.

The soldier sitting foremost in Arumin's boat yelped as one of the creatures grabbed him with two great hands. Holding him around the rib cage, it hoisted him out of the boat and set him upright on the beach like a piece of baggage. Other beasts began doing the same with everyone in the boats.

A few men took offense at this treatment, and one offered to fight the nearest beast rather than let it lay hands on him. Arumin tried irritably to convince him otherwise, but the situation only escalated. Eventually, Sergeant Orund, lying in the back with a blackened, welt-covered face, reassured the man of their safety and convinced him to let himself be taken. The creature handled the man more gingerly than it had the others.

When Arumin was lifted ashore himself, he gave the nearest of the creatures a small bow. "Thank you," he said.

It was a reflexive response. There, beyond the edge of the known universe, no one they met could possibly speak the Ronian language.

He eyed the caves cautiously and the cliff doubtfully. He could see no means of ascending the rock face. Perhaps the beasts lived in the caves and would expect the company to enter with them. Arumin had had his fill of confined spaces during the company's journey, and he had no desire to enter another.

After all, he didn't know what else might dwell there. The being that had taken Tabard, whether it was one of the Lady's kind or not, might make its home nearby. Nobody knew the intentions of these creatures, who had attacked them moments before but were now greeting them so amicably.

Those thoughts came at once in a swirl, and Arumin regretted not opening fire on the beasts at once. But the thoughts were chased away just as abruptly. One of the beasts handed him something small with one of its great clawed hands. It was the box in which the Lady dwelt. The creature handed it to him without ceremony, not as a gift but as a lost possession being restored to its owner.

"It was them," Doctor Staubel said.

Those who had not realized the beasts were their attackers from earlier knew it then. Arumin feared that might cause a fight, but none of the men reacted, at least outwardly.

Staubel pointed at the box and asked the creatures, "What happened to the man who held this?"

The wolves, of course, made no reply. Their faces, like those of wild dogs, seemed to show little but raw emotion.

"We must go on, Doctor," Arumin said.

A small hand fell on his arm. It was Shada. The sensation was odd, and he realized she had never touched him that way.

Her eyes were large. "Bishop, where is Nor?"

Everyone looked around. Nor was not among them.

She raised her voice. "Where is he?"

The wolves were as unavailing on that question as on the last.

"Whose boat was he in?" she cried.

A long silence passed. Clearly, someone had an answer and was struggling over whether to share it.

"Mine," said a young private named Swinburn.

Arumin knew him only as one of those who had joined the mutiny on Om.

"He fell overboard," Swinburn added with a shrug.

Shada's hand touched her cheek. She trembled. "How?"

"I don't know," the man answered. "I assume that's what happened. I didn't realize he was gone until it was over."

"Why, why didn't you say anything?"

Swinburn looked around, eyes wide. He had not seemed to expect a reaction of that magnitude. "Things were so confused. He was a traitor. Wasn't he to die anyway, Bishop?"

A sick feeling bloomed in Arumin's stomach, but he angrily willed it to be gone. No one had openly spoken yet of his part in plotting to kill Nor. But he was in command and felt he ought to make such decisions fearlessly.

His lips betrayed his newfound boldness. "It's no matter now."

Shada put a hand over her mouth. Bending over, she reached out for balance and took the hand of one of the beasts. Her hand barely wrapped around one of its fingers. She sank to her knees.

Minutes passed as she knelt there. Everyone, even the beasts, waited.

Finally, Shada said, "Let's continue."

The men relaxed a little. The beasts, perhaps sensing that an important matter had been settled, went back to work. Each leaned over and took the hand or arm of the nearest Ronian. Then they led their visitors like children, one after another, toward the cliff.

The rock face and its piled boulders became even more forbidding as they came nearer. As Arumin was resigning himself to entering the caves, one of the beasts stopped and squatted. Looking at its accompanying soldier, it clapped its hands on his shoulders. The man got the idea and climbed onto the creature's back, asking the other Ronians with his expression if he was mad to do this. He got no answer as the beast scampered up the cliff face, climbing effortlessly.

The other beasts and their Ronian companions followed.

Just before Shada's turn, she looked at Arumin and said, "I can't come with you. I have to go there instead." She pointed at a nearby cave.

The men rumbled in apprehension.

"Why?" Arumin asked, though he could guess well enough. "Think of the last time you parted with us."

"This time, it's intentional. The Lady commands me to go alone."

Private Merin spoke up, expressing a rare opinion. "It looks dangerous. Are you sure, Caretaker?"

Shada said, "She protected me then, and she will now."

Arumin looked around. "Let me send a few men with you."

"Absolutely not. What did I just tell you?" Her stare was cold.

That got everyone's attention. Arumin was forced to realize that she could speak to him that way, in front of everyone, and he could do nothing.

"Farewell," he said and turned away.

16

SHADA

SHADA FELT LIKE SHE'D been there before—an odd feeling, as these tunnels were different from the ones underneath the city of Ronia. These were moist, with the constant drip and trickle of water and the distant roar of waves. Also, this cave was unexpectedly bright.

When she entered the tunnel, she had quickly realized both that she had no light source and that she didn't need one: every surface there was aglow with a soft golden light. Perhaps foolishly, she touched one of the walls. A greasy film transferred itself to her fingers, and her prints remained as a dark patch on the rock.

Nor's death had left her dazed. She had known as soon as she heard it that she could not deal with it right then. She would absorb and accept it sometime later, whenever later was. In the meantime, she moved mechanically, following the Lady's commands. As she walked, the tunnel branched.

"Which way should I go?" Her whisper seemed to fill the place.

"Forward," the Lady hissed in her ear. "Quietly."

Nearby, rocks crunched and clattered. Shada held her breath and tried to feel as small as she could. Above the dying echoes of the sound and the movement of water, she heard something even deeper: a rising and falling, like breathing but too slow, unless it was the planet itself that breathed.

She took a step and realized she was a little closer to whatever that was. Her instincts screamed at her to stop, and she obeyed.

The Lady said, "Trust me."

"I'm trying," Shada replied. Every sound from her lips seemed to announce her presence to that whole underground world. "But, as a favor, tell me: why are we here? Why did I just leave everyone—"

"Be silent and listen," the Lady said. "When will you simply obey me? Would it please you to know that we may be in the worst danger we have yet seen? Not if we stood in the very fires of Huire's wrath would our peril be greater. If we are to survive, you cannot break your silence to bleat at me. Haven't you learned yet to listen, if nothing else? Can't you abide by the same commands that you gave the others?"

Shada swallowed. The Lady was right. Shada had just admonished the company to be silent. Whichever way she turned, she was wrong.

Teetering near panic, she squealed, "But why do you need me? If your own kind are here, what use am I?"

For an instant, she was sure her throat would burst. She leaned over, and her hands clutched at her neck, where the Lady was blocking her air passage. Her eyes watered with the pain. Struggle was useless. She prayed the agony would be gone soon, and it was.

"I didn't want to do that," the Lady said. "Now, child, you must be silent until spoken to. You and I must be one: you are the vessel, and I am the mind."

Shada nodded without hesitation. She was unsure if the Lady wanted her to keep walking, and she was afraid to ask. So she waited for instructions.

The wait felt long, though she couldn't measure time there. She jumped when the Lady spoke again.

"Since you cannot do without comfort, I will tell you something. I have my reasons for bringing you here, and one of them is that I dislike being apart from you."

Shada listened, as was her part.

The Lady continued, "I've become used to having you near. You help me to think. I am afraid—I admit—of what I may do when you are gone. And I will admit something else. Do you remember when, on the beach, I told you that I had seen Nor drown?"

Shada cast about for how to respond.

The Lady said, "You may nod."

She did.

"It was not completely true. I saw a man push him, and I saw him fall. I do not know what happened after that. He is almost certainly dead."

Air rushed into Shada's lungs. Her chest burned. She looked straight ahead, down the tunnel.

"I thought you might go back for him," the Lady said, "and I could not allow it. I did not wish to hurt you—as I've always said—if you tried. Whatever his fate, it is sealed now. Do you understand?"

Breathing deliberately, Shada coaxed herself to nod. The gesture would have been nearly invisible to anyone watching. She understood, and she hated it, but she could do nothing about it.

The Lady continued, "You are my partner. More than that, we are one and the same. I will learn to keep fewer secrets from you. Nod if you agree with all that I've said."

Shada nodded again. That time, it was easier.

Rocks clattered again, farther away. Shada looked back but saw nothing. She faced forward and gazed into the face of a ghost.

The wave of fear that should have swept her seemed to miss her by an inch. Rather than jumping or shrieking, she stepped back to a proper conversational distance.

"Greet him," the Lady said.

He was a slight form with the thin face of a boy in early adolescence. Beneath his puerile features were a splendid robe and trousers, too layered and voluminous to feel modern. His whole presence hummed audibly. "Who are you? I demand to know." Like the Lady, his voice was a chorus of numberless smaller voices, but his was higher and thinner than hers.

"Say you are a visitor," the Lady whispered. "Nothing more."

"I... am a visitor here."

"A visitor?" the apparition said.

Shada could not help but think of him as a child. Though his body was nearly transparent, she saw him put a hand to his belt, where the hilt of a blade protruded.

"You weren't invited. Whom do you serve?"

"You serve the Goddess Huire," the Lady said.

"I serve Huire."

His eyes swelled like balloons. Shada realized for the first time that he was speaking the same language she did. The accent was strange but contained an uneasy thread of familiarity.

He asked, "Can we risk it?" She could not see whom he was talking to.

Then he looked hard at her. He grew taller, thinner, and even a little fainter. "Yes, I understand." He drew his blade, a narrow dagger, which was faint but still looked far too real.

The Lady told Shada, "You must make peace."

"What?" Shada asked her, surprised.

"You heard me," the boy said. "Didn't she hear me?"

The Lady: "If you don't, we are doomed."

Shada held out her palms to the boy. "Please, no."

"Shall I do it here?" the now grotesquely tall boy asked eagerly. "Perhaps we should take her home and make a toy of her."

"No!" Shada shouted in naked fright.

He seemed to notice her in a new way. "Why shouldn't I?" he asked her.

It seemed like a genuine question. Shada saw apprehension in his face and took a gamble. "Because we serve the same master!" she cried, raising her shoulders to seem larger.

He seemed to believe her and shrank a little. "You serve Huire? But you may be lying."

"I may. But if you hurt me, and you're wrong, Huire won't be happy."

"But she's not here," he said. Then, not speaking to Shada: "Is she here?"

"Enough of that! You speak only to me now," Shada commanded. "Huire's not here yet, but she's coming back. Soon! And when she does, you'll have to answer for what you've done."

A shimmering appeared around his eyes that, she decided, must have been a facsimile of tears.

"Is she really coming?" he asked.

"She is. She's watching you right now, in fact."

"Very well," he said. He looked at his toes. "Shall I take you to my family?"

Shada waited a moment for the Lady to direct her, but no whisper came to her ear. Afraid she would lose her tenuous authority over this being if she delayed, she ordered the boy to lead on.

17

—·—

EMBERLY

EMBERLY WOKE UP BURIED under weight and heat. A great mass had just shifted, squeezing his chest, and the lack of air jolted him awake.

His eyes popped, and his limbs thrashed, meeting darkness, soft fur, and tremendous mass.

The dog men were everywhere. He was piled among them where they lay asleep, and one of their arms had fallen across him with crushing weight. With a tremendous effort, he shifted it to lie across his stomach, and air returned to his lungs.

Since he could not move, he craned his neck and turned his head. They were in a rocky grotto. He was naked, but the heat of the cave was still overpowering.

A small fire lit the place, its smoke draining through fissures in the rock overhead. The entry was blocked by a pile of roughly made blocks of ice that glowed blue in the light from outside. Tiny gaps around the edges of the blocks admitted unfiltered daylight.

He saw his clothes drying on rocks by the fire. When he saw them, he remembered.

He was lucky to be alive. Those creatures had wanted him otherwise. They took him there half drowned, having carried him under ice floes with only occasional stops at the surface to let him breathe.

The one that snatched him when he fell from the boat threw him into a corner of the grotto. They hemmed him in on all sides and tossed him his knife, taken from his belt. The one that had captured him hunched down and bared its claws and teeth while the others sent up a storm of growls and yelps.

As he was reaching woozily for the knife, ready to take a swing or two before they killed him, another dog man arrived, slipping out of a hole filled with water that must have led to the sea under the ice.

The others spoke to the newcomer in whines, grunts, and howls. After he delivered his message, they turned and bowed deeply to Emberly, some even falling to their hands and knees.

He was loath to give up the knife but convinced himself that if they still meant to kill him, the weapon would not save him. At their urging gestures, he let it fall.

They took him by the shoulders and manhandled him to a spot before the fire. There, heat and freezing cold met inside him, and he shivered until he thought he would fall to pieces. Warm but still soaked, he must have fallen asleep sitting up.

Since they placed him among them while he slept, they likely no longer meant to harm him. But they had meant him harm at first, and they might change their minds again. They had walled off the grotto's entry, so they did not want him leaving just yet.

He had to return to the company. He didn't know his odds of finding them on this desolate, frozen sea, but he was obligated to try. Obligations, as they often did, relieved him of the burden of choice.

He decided to escape, and he thought he saw how to do it. At one edge of the blocked-up entrance was a streak of daylight wider and longer than the others, which might be large enough to slip through.

Pushing at the treelike arm that lay across him, he found he could hardly budge it at that angle. His shoves grew increasingly violent until the creature rolled away, removing the arm. Liberated, Emberly sprang up, only to fall to his knees with the place wheeling around him. Unwilling to take time to recover, he crawled through the musty air and across the hard ground to where his clothes lay. Those, he could not do without.

None of the creatures had stirred since he rose. He pulled on his clothes, shuddering at their dampness. Once he was outside in the cold, he would not be able to stop moving.

Then he moved to the entry, nearly twice his height. He whispered a curse: the gap through which he planned to escape was smaller than he'd hoped. He tried to squeeze through anyway, but in vain.

He had seen another way that he had dismissed at first, but now, it was his only chance. Another, larger gap existed at the very top of the ice wall. To get out, he would have to climb.

Testing a few handholds, he found the ice rough enough to grip, along with places to step or wedge his feet. He caught himself hesitating, thinking about falling from that height, then threw himself into the climb.

He was still dizzy, and he weighed more than he remembered. The grit that covered the ice hid slickness underneath.

When he was halfway up, one hand slipped. The other gave way before he could recover. He landed on his feet and fell onto his back, nearly cracking his head. The impact pressed a groan out of him that sounded like a monster's roar in that small room, and he lay still, expecting the creatures to leap on him.

Hearing no movement, he rose. One of the dog men had sat up. It locked eyes with him.

Panic consumed him. He leapt up and climbed the wall in a mad rush. A fall might hobble him, but the thought of remaining at the mercy of those beasts made any risk worthwhile.

Through luck or desperation, he reached the top. As he hooked his fingers over the far edge of the top block, he felt the cold outdoor wind brush his hand. Still in full flight, he pulled himself atop the wall and risked a glance back.

The creature stood directly below him, watching. The others were still asleep. If the one below him stretched, it might have reached him.

Flailing his arms and legs, he crossed the top of the ice wall and faced a blizzard. The block under him moved, sliding back into the cave in the grip of massive hands.

He scrambled toward the light and jumped. The snow softened the impact a little, though he knew he would be sore later. Behind the ice wall, the grotto had come alive with barks and whimpers, and the beasts were quickly dismantling the wall. Cursing at the realization that he had forgotten his knife, Emberly turned to get his bearings.

Not much was there to see. The rock that held the grotto stood nearly alone in a frozen waste. Here and there, breaks in the ice told of the sea beneath, and in the distance, many more rocks protruded from the ice. The rocks seemed to form a belt that stretched out to sea from the shore, where their friends the villagers lived.

One rock much larger than the rest caught his eye. Though it was farther away than most and nearly hidden by falling snow, he judged it to be an island.

His people could not have gone anywhere else in their tiny boats—nowhere else the being that had taken Tabard might hide.

18

—·—

EMBERLY

EMBERLY RAN TOWARD THE island.

Within seconds, a crack in the ice loomed before him. A wobbly leap saved him from a probably fatal plunge into icy water. He landed on ice that cracked and tilted beneath him, and he scrambled blindly until he found a stable surface. After that, he forced himself to slow down.

His progress lagged as the snowfall grew heavier. Soon, he was kicking his way through piles of it and could no longer see the island or anything past his immediate surroundings. He continued in what seemed the right direction but grew increasingly unsure. If he encountered the rock formations, he could follow them to the island, but in those conditions, he might pass right through them and never see even the nearest one. Beyond the rocks would be no landmarks at all.

He stopped. His chest rose and fell faster and faster, and he wondered if he was about to cry. "Come out," he said aloud.

When no one appeared, he spun, searching the invisible horizon. The loneliness was so terrible that he was almost ready to return to the creatures in the grotto.

Then his brother appeared, walking easily out of the snow. He was still ruddy and filthy from the jungle of Caidfell, and the hole in his face still bled. In his shattered visage curled the smile that Emberly knew so well.

"Where have you been?" Emberly roared.

Rayan's smile was unperturbed. "I'm always here."

Emberly gnashed his teeth. "And what have you got to say?"

"What do you want to hear?"

"I..." Clenching his fists, the captain trembled. "I did just what you said. I trusted you."

"And?"

"And you don't know anything!" Emberly cried. "You told me to kill, and I killed. I killed Iwan. I nearly killed Orund. But you were wrong about all of it! If I'd kept it up, I would've had no one left."

Rayan's eyes shot from side to side, indicating the empty horizon. "Brother, you're alone right now."

"And it's your fault! You needled and taunted, and I gave in, like I always do." Emberly stopped, his chest heaving. "But you're nothing. A fool."

Rayan's face fell. "I did my best, Cyril. But there were never any guarantees."

"No guarantees." The captain dropped his hands to his sides and giggled. "No..." He wrapped his arms tightly around himself. "All the things I've done to please you. I killed Iwan. I opened..." He paused then forced the words out. "I opened your cell on Caidfell and got so many Ronian soldiers killed." He stopped again then said, "I want you to leave me, forever."

Though falling snow hid them from the rest of that oceanic plane, none fell between the two of them. Rayan gave Emberly a lopsided grin. "How many times will you say that before you realize that you don't mean it?"

Once, Emberly might have tried to strangle his brother for that. But that urge was gone. The cold was cutting him to the bone. "I'm serious," he said. His teeth were chattering, and the words came out with a childish stutter, but he spoke with such calm that Rayan found nothing to laugh at.

Instead, Rayan's smile slowly crumbled. Feeling no thrill of triumph, Emberly pushed on. "I don't want you. I don't love you. I can't stand the sight of you."

Rayan crossed his arms, perhaps finally feeling the cold. "I'm not the reason you're tramping through the snow. You left that cave on your own. Perhaps if you'd asked for my—"

"It's not about the cave. Or the snow." Emberly dropped his arms, letting the cold fill him. "It's all I've done to make you happy. All the things you were too scared to do."

All mirth was gone from his brother. A stone wall had been erected in its place. "I tried to make you a man," Rayan said. "No one else was going to do it."

The captain spread his hands. "Here I am. Here's what you made. Are you proud?"

Rayan said nothing, but his eyes burned.

"Do me one courtesy," Emberly said. "Don't make me die next to you. Leave me... forever."

Snow fell like a curtain between them. When the flurry cleared, Rayan was gone.

Emberly turned slowly in all that emptiness, feeling no better, wondering what to do. The blizzard lightened momentarily, and his eye caught something moving a long way off. Though size and distance were mysterious there, he guessed it was large. It moved frenetically but remained still. It was growing.

He could not believe he had dared to stop, even for a moment. The creatures from the grotto were coming.

19

— · —

ARUMIN

WHEN ARUMIN, CLINGING TO the back of one of the creatures, reached the top of the cliff that rose from the beach, he saw the island was shaped like a bowl. They stood on a craggy ridge that stretched off to both sides and curved ahead, forming a rim the far side of which must have lain in the invisible distance. While the island's interior was partly shrouded in fog and snow, what he could see took his breath away.

What had at first looked like a forest was nothing of the kind. It was a graveyard. The trees were bones, ribs, and portions of skeletons, all tremendous in size. Under them lay globular shapes that must have been skulls or maybe the shells of ancient creatures, undersea titans.

The place seemed to be the home of the beasts. As the creature that carried Arumin walked down the gentler interior slope, he saw their canine faces peering from openings in the hillside. Paths and steps had been beaten into the slopes, and the Ronians could have made the descent themselves. The bishop wondered if the beasts continued to carry them as a courtesy.

As they climbed down the slope, more of the beasts emerged, and soon the company was the center of a parade. They swept into the mountainous collection of living remains, where Arumin became grateful again for the beasts' transportation. Walls of soft gray and blue bulged, and bones lay like ancient fallen trees. Their hosts slipped around, over, and under the barriers with feral grace.

They soon neared the center. There, they saw a thing out of the Dark itself: a rounded, pallid shape as tall as any five of the beasts and with sets of gaping holes in its gray mass. More of the beasts watched from those. It was a skull, and the thought that such a large object had once been part of something alive gripped the bishop with fear and wonder.

It had no lower jaw, and its upper teeth hung close to the ground. The teeth were set in rows, with molars half as tall as Arumin and a pair of fangs even taller. Behind the skull, at what seemed the very middle of the island, a hill rose into the fog.

As the bishop watched, the beasts carried the foremost Ronians under the gate formed by the teeth. Arumin was close behind. Fighting the feeling of being swallowed, he closed his eyes until it was over.

The space inside was not as dark as he'd expected. In notches and crannies of the skull's interior, small open shells had been filled with fatty, translucent liquid that burned steadily, illuminating the corners. A large hole in the skull's pate, which arced overhead, admitted a flood of pale light that pushed back the shadows.

The floor was mostly rock except for the chamber's rear, where the curve of the skull swept down to form a shelf of tarnished ivory. The beasts led the company to that shelf.

A group of the creatures was already present. Those were smaller than most others and were proudly decorated with jewelry and headdresses made of shells and bone. They moved with restless energy, wrestling on the floor or hopping on their toes as they observed the newcomers.

In the center of the room, just under the hole in the ceiling, a round pit pierced the rocky floor. As they passed it, Arumin glanced down into it and saw nothing but inky black. A chill passed through him that went deeper than the cold, and he shivered as the beasts placed the members of the company on the bony shelf one by one.

With the visitors in place, a few of the beasts entered with a heavier burden: baskets full of wet, moving shapes. They overturned the baskets in the middle of the room, covering the floor with mounds of twisting sea life. The mounds expanded as some of the things flopped or crawled away.

Arumin's stomach tightened, and he pushed himself farther up the sloping shelf, away from the piles and the overpowering stench of the sea. The soldiers turned and shifted uncomfortably.

The beasts who had brought the baskets were larger and looked older than the others. They embraced each of the youngsters, licking their heads and ears, then left, dropping to all fours to pass under the gate of incisors.

No sooner had they left than the youngsters tore into the writhing piles, breaking and devouring. The sounds and smells that accompanied their meal would not be easily forgotten, and Arumin pulled his knees up and placed his forehead on them, giving himself a little space to feel alone.

The respite was short lived. "Bishop?" Sergeant Feng said.

Arumin raised his head. Feng was standing on the floor downhill from Arumin. Next to him was the much larger form of Private Hulgar. Feng wavered for a moment, and Arumin snapped at him to get on with it.

Feng said, "Some of the men have come to me."

"Some," Arumin repeated.

Several were sitting or standing within earshot.

"And I agree with what they've said. Now that we're here, it's time we went hunting for Tabard."

Arumin gaped. "What?"

"He may be on this island, sir. Or in it." Feng glanced nervously at the pit in the floor. "Whatever took him was big, and we've seen no other place where it could land."

That last point had occurred to Arumin, though he hoped his icy face would conceal it. The idea of rescuing Tabard had not entered his dreams.

Hulgar spoke up. "We figure it may live down in those tunnels."

"Why else would the Lady go there?" Feng added. "She's looking for her kind."

Their hosts' feast was ending. Most were sitting among the torn and chewed remains. As Arumin watched, one of them stood. It was a little smaller than the rest—though still larger than Hulgar—and it wore a necklace made of fangs from a menagerie of predators. From its clawed hand dangled a long, scaly fish.

It brought the fish to the nearest Ronians and held it up in obvious offering. No one accepted, but the beast persisted, moving from man to man.

Arumin told Feng and Hulgar, "We can't leave yet. We don't know these creatures' intentions. If we search their island, we may antagonize them. I've seen what one of their kind did to a whole room full of men—I will not risk it."

Hulgar rumbled. "Maybe a few of us could slip away, Arumin."

The bishop decided not to reprimand the use of his name. "No such group would go undetected, especially if you are in it, Private. These beast-men seem to be everywhere. You don't even know how to access the tunnels or where to go once you're inside them."

Coughing, Feng replied, "If you'll pardon me, we should try anyway—I mean, with or without these animals' permission. Sooner or later, we'll have to find out if we are prisoners here."

Arumin leaned forward to look hard at them both. "The Lady did not ask us to follow her underground. She was content to leave us where we are, and her reasons for doing so are clear. If we leave, we will risk catastrophe."

Hulgar's face was stark. "Last anyone heard, Tabard was still alive. We are in the lands of strange gods, Bishop. They'll take who they want, no matter who deserves it."

"Your curiosity about this being is unnatural, Private."

"If he's alive," Feng pleaded, "he may need help. When it took him away, they heard him screaming..."

Cruelty swelled within the bishop, and he snarled. "And why do you think he was taken? What do you think was done to him? He's dead, if there is any mercy. Whatever that thing was, we have no way to fight it. That will be done by the Lady or not at all. And that's the last I'll hear of it."

Feng looked crestfallen but not terribly surprised. Hulgar was silent and ominous.

The beast had given up on its offering and returned to its fellows. Hulgar walked across to stand over them. Then he bent and took something from what remained of the banquet. It was a round-shelled, many-legged creature. He broke its shell with his hands and reached inside. His fingers produced meat and pushed it into his mouth. He smiled. "Good."

The young beast had watched him. Hulgar leaned over and clapped it on the back. The creature reacted like a compressed spring, leaping up and tackling him to the ground.

The Ronians jumped up, reaching for weapons. Hulgar and the beast rolled and grappled.

Arumin scrambled within himself, deciding what to do, what chance they had. Then he saw that the other beasts were all still sitting and chewing or sagging lazily. Finally, he heard Hulgar laughing and realized the thing was licking his face.

20

SHADA

SHADA PASSED THE OPENINGS of many tunnels on her way down. The clattering noises she'd been hearing became more frequent, and she knew they were coming from those holes. Things were growling and skittering, whining. Some, perhaps, were trying to speak. The smells were bitter and sweaty.

Though she feared drawing attention to herself, eventually, she had to know: "What are they?"

"Bad things, bad indeed," said the tall boy in the comical robes. He seemed to take joy in telling her.

The noises grew more frequent. In the faint luminescence of the main tunnel, she could see the way forward, but the glow only hinted at what was moving down the side tunnels. Something nearby screeched with a mouth not so different from hers. Its cries became so loud that in the enclosed space, it sounded like it was right next to her.

Many of the other noises seemed intended to frighten her, and they were quite effective. But that one was worse—in the vocal slashes that came so close to being words, she heard desperation.

Soon, her feet might try to turn and carry her out of that place no matter what the rest of her wanted. When she was just about to speak to the boy again, he stopped and hissed. The noise fell perfectly within a break in the clamor, and the sounds in the tunnels fell silent.

Then he told her, "Some of the things we make don't turn out well. Some cannot move or even think. But these are the best."

Shada's voice wavered as her chest rose and fell. "I want to... I can't..."

"You will do no such thing," the Lady whispered.

The boy kept moving, and Shada followed, and after what seemed a long time, the noise faded into the distance. Once in a while, a burst and flurry of sound close by announced that they had awakened or startled something, but aside from such heart-freezing moments, they passed unhindered. The last of the half-animal noises came from behind when all the others had faded. It was a high, lonely wail that reached into her chest and took hold of her lungs.

Finally, the descent ended, and the tunnel opened. They entered a wide chamber with a blotch of piercing light in the center of its floor. Shielding her eyes, Shada looked up to see a corresponding opening to pale daylight far above their heads. On a floor as shiny and hard as a diamond, outside the painful brightness of the light spot, bones and shells were scattered. In addition to the beam of light from overhead, she thought she detected a faint glow, red and angry, that shone through the crystalline floor from far, far beneath.

The sudden light was astonishing, and for a few seconds, she overlooked the room's most remarkable feature: a set of towering metal doors. Built into a round frame, they met in interlocking sets of teeth.

She knew what it was. She had seen one in the caverns under Ronia after the Lady's first appearance. Aside from Shada, only a few holy men had ever been permitted to stand before those doors. Now, as she realized what she was looking at, a great many fears and wonders awakened in her. The Ronians were not her people—she had no true people—but one did not spend her life on Ronia without absorbing a vulnerability to the weight of certain powers. Her scalp prickled.

"Is that...?" she began.

She expected the Lady to silence her, but the Lady said nothing, leaving Shada in the middle of a question the answer to which she already knew.

The boy turned this way and that. He did not move his feet, and the dramatic twisting of his body made her wince. "I want to go."

Shada looked at him. "But you've just come home."

"Now I want to leave."

"I forbid it," Shada said, taking on her new threatening tone.

"I hate you!" he cried.

The Lady whispered, "Do not let him leave!"

The doors rumbled.

The boy fled without listening to another word. His shape stretched into a stream of smoke as he shot away into the tunnel from which they had come.

The doors ground open, and a thunderstorm poured out. Shada had not seen that thing when it attacked the men on the beach, but it was even bigger than she had imagined. Filling the room almost to its distant ceiling, it displayed its size and yet made the room seem bigger, as though the two complemented each other. Even when it filled the chamber, its mass stretched back through the open doors and showed no sign of ending. Shada wondered how much of it remained hidden.

It swirled around them. Nearly as overwhelming as its size were the voices that came from it. They were too many and different to reckon with. She heard curiosity, rage, sympathy, and sadism. Underneath it all was a humming loud and deep enough to rattle her teeth.

If the Lady was speaking, Shada could no longer hear it. She shouted, though her voice seemed lost in the tumult, "You must speak with one voice! I cannot understand so many!"

The voices, each comprised of a thousand voices of its own, went to war with each other, simultaneously and universally. They assaulted, cajoled, wheedled. The cacophony spun with her at its center, filling her eyes and ears. She held her breath and waited.

In a few seconds, wars were fought, kingdoms crumbled, and a world turned around her. Finally, one voice reached out. It was a miscellany of tones and pitches, and smaller voices dripped from it like melted wax, their words only partly spoken and melting to nothing.

It asked, "Who?"

Despite all the noise, Shada found the silence in her own ears intolerable. The Lady apparently chose that moment, of all moments, to stop commanding Shada what to say.

Her own voice emerged in a squeak. "A servant of Huire."

Even the ambient hum of the being was enough to wash the sound of the words away. Still, the thing heard her.

Its unified voice was lost to chaos for a moment. When it returned, it was deeper and angrier. "A servant? What use could she have for one like you?"

"It is not my place to ask."

It said, "You look like the ones in the boats once looked."

It was not a question, and Shada thought better than to answer.

The voice moved, coming from one place and then another. It spoke in a wild arrhythmia, as if the speaker was being pulled this way and that by the arms. Each sentence came as a declaration.

—"They have learned fear."

—"Have you?"

Shada said honestly, "I have."

—"I don't believe you."

—"How shall we make you look?"

A chill ran down Shada's spine. She replied, "Do as you will, but if you change me, I'll be unable to deliver my message."

—"Message."

—"Liar."

—"What message?"

Shada had no message. She was struggling to invent one when she fell to her hands and knees. Gagging and coughing, she vomited the Lady into the room.

21

SHADA

When the Lady appeared, the storm returned. The cloud filled with voices of spite and hatred, fear, and here and there, relief. Shada even heard a single expression of joy.

The Lady took on a form both familiar and not. As usual, she appeared as an elderly woman whose skin and clothing were colored soft gold, but now, she was far grander, standing taller and wearing a costume from a fairy-tale court. Her voice boomed. "I will talk only to one of you. He knows of whom I speak."

The voice of the cloud responded instantly, sounding quite different. "Is it really you?"

She said, "Come out and speak to me."

A man emerged from the cloud. His form was an elderly gentleman in robes that rivaled the Lady's in splendor. On his head was a weighty, ungainly hat with dangling tassels. The edges of his form were a blur lacking detail. His face, like hers, was a painting that showed emotion without feeling, and always too emphatically. His smile pushed the limits of the possible. "You have returned."

The Lady replied, "And I find you still here."

His smile dropped like a curtain. "Things haven't been easy."

"For any of us," she said. "But look at the state you are in."

"I am not proud," he admitted.

"You are worse than before."

He swept his arm across the room. "Please be careful. You are not entirely welcome here."

The Lady turned from him and spoke to the cloud. "I had hoped at least some of you would remember our purpose."

The Gentleman's eyebrows became a series of deep, wide creases. "What were we to do? You weren't here."

"Why does that matter?" the Lady asked. "You were to maintain order, at least. But never mind. I have returned, having found what we sought."

He stared at the Lady with glassy eyes. "Are you to help us, girl? What has she told you?"

Shada realized belatedly that he was speaking to her. But the Lady answered him before she could. "Look at her when you speak to her. Else why take human form at all? Have you remembered none of Huire's words?"

"Huire's words," the Gentleman repeated. "She allowed us nothing aside from her words." He turned his head toward Shada. It was an instantaneous movement like the snapping of a neck, making Shada cringe. "Are you the only human here, girl?"

Again, the Lady answered for Shada. "Of course not, you fool. Don't you remember the man you took from the boat people?"

The Gentleman's eyes popped. "We knew that one was different. But—"

"It's not important," the Lady replied. "The others were essential, as Huire said, but when the time comes, one human is all we will need."

"I see." His smile was metallic. "You have a lot of work ahead if you hope to convince everyone here to follow you back to Huire."

"Why? They can't really want to stay here forever."

He said, "They do, and I think you know why."

"And what of you?"

He shrank back a little. "They are my family, more even than Huire was."

"So none of you have changed a bit."

"There's been no reason to," he answered. "What Huire did to us cannot be undone." His arm swept again. "This is all she has left us."

"What foolishness," the Lady said.

He breathed deeply, his chest inflating in a shape too perfectly round to be believed. "You still trust her and believe in her. As much joy as seeing you gives me, I find that shocking."

The Lady made a sound not unlike a sigh. "Huire told me this might happen."

"Told you, did she?" He emphasized the second word.

"She told us all, though it has done little good. She warned that, over time, we might waver. She said when that happened that we must think of her there, waiting for us."

His eyebrows tilted inward like the hands of two clocks. "Our circumstances are of her creation. We have done what we can. The fur-covered men serve us so that we leave them unharmed. The boat men—"

"We've already seen what becomes of them," the Lady said.

His eyes themselves tipped toward his nose, making him look like an angry character in a children's book. "Meanwhile, you, her favorite servant, are off on a fanciful quest of your own devising."

"Of my devising?" The Lady's eyes grew round as she fell momentarily silent.

The Gentleman turned toward Shada. "And what of you, girl? Do you also trust Huire to help when the time comes? What faith you must have."

Shada had followed only pieces of their conversation. What she heard made her think of trust, of friendship, of Nor. She sensed that the Gentleman didn't really want an answer, so she gave none.

The Lady looked around again at the churning mass. Her wide eyes vibrated. If Shada hadn't known better, she would have thought the Lady was about to cry. "You must come with me. You must believe there is better in store for us than this!"

"None of our family believe that," he said. "And neither do I anymore."

The Lady was quiet for a time. Then, she said, "I knew that I would come back here someday. Knowing that, I let myself hope for you. But I should not have sought you out again. I should have left you to the little mockery of a world you have created."

Another voice emerged from the cloud. It boiled with rancor. "We have all been fools. You for trusting Huire beyond all reason and we for hoping you might return to us."

The Gentleman's face was a parody of sadness.

The Lady said, "If that is all, then…"

She stopped speaking as the cloud began to withdraw through the metal doors, funneling into the pitch-black space beyond. The Gentleman turned slowly to follow.

"Will you wait a moment?" the Lady asked.

He stopped.

She continued, "We have not properly said our good-byes."

His form inverted so that he faced her. His expression had softened. The cloud had disappeared, but the doors were open and waiting.

The Lady faced the Gentleman for several moments. As they hovered, seemingly absorbed in each other, Shada began to hope they had forgotten her.

She had realized something as they spoke. As the Lady had left her family, as Huire had apparently left them all, Shada had left Nor. She should have gone back and looked.

Once she realized that, she quickly decided to try. She quietly crept toward the entrance to the tunnel from which they had come. Despite her hope, she half ex-pected the Lady to shout at her or seize her, but that did not happen. Maybe she had forgotten Shada. Maybe she wasn't looking. Maybe she thought—probably rightly—that Shada could never hide from her in any place. If that was true, Shada would learn it for herself.

She slipped into the tunnel. She could still hear the giant beings' conversation.

"Won't you stay?" the Gentleman asked the Lady. "We are right about Huire, and I believe you know it."

The Lady said nothing.

He continued, sounding a little uncomfortable. "You have always been here. Since the beginning. May I profess how much I have missed you?"

Their mutual hum increased in volume, rising and falling along with great rushes of air. Shada did not know what they were doing, and she didn't care.

22

SHADA

As she climbed along the glowing tunnel, Shada expected she would not be alone much longer. She stopped and listened several times for the bestial noises that had accompanied them on the way down. She did hear noises, hisses and rumbles as if the land itself was awake, but nothing she could identify as definitely alive.

Afraid of the Lady's keen hearing, she waited longer than she would have liked to begin calling out. She spoke softly at first: "Hello? Are you still there?" As she came nearer to passing the creatures that lived in the side tunnels, each step became a fight against terror.

"Can't you hear me?" Then, a few moments later, "I know you can. Come out this instant."

She took a few more steps, thought about what lay ahead, and stopped. As the echoes of her footsteps dissipated, she finally heard grunts and shifting somewhere in front of her.

She swayed. Looking at the ceiling, she spoke more loudly than she had yet dared. "If you don't come out, I will punish you personally when Huire comes."

At that, the grunting became more aware. It swelled to a wet rumbling and sputtering that nothing possessing lips and a throat could have produced. Then it grew clearer. The thing making the noises had come out of its hole and entered the tunnel, the same one in which she stood.

She would have preferred to never speak again than to draw those sounds closer. But unless she was to leave Nor—or Nor's corpse—alone and locked in ice, she had to say something. She heard either a buzzing sound or the rush of blood in her ears.

"Speak to me, please," she said.

Her voice seemed to shake the walls. The creature ahead came for her as she had known it would, its multitude of feet thumping merrily in her direction. But the buzzing also became louder. The wall's faint glow dimmed as something hazy circled her. The skin of her hands and face tickled. Amidst the matter drifting lazily around her was a bright, fist-sized mass that emitted a muffled light like a sun behind clouds.

"I'm sorry," she said, crying to be heard over the creature's approaching gallop. She backed down the tunnel the way she had come. "I want to be friends. But you must help me!"

The creature was in sight, waist high and wide enough to fill the tunnel. She turned to run with the sickening knowledge that she would not be fast enough when the haze condensed into a human form between her and the creature. The mass of light exploded, filling the tunnel with an immensely concentrated burst of the same glow that shone from its walls.

In that flash, all was revealed: the boy they had met in the tunnel, who had kept the light and flung it to the ceiling; the tunnel itself, bare and ugly; and the oncoming monster.

The creature was low and broad, its underside covered by a shell that curved like a shield. It had a tail that arced up to hang near the intruders' faces like a whip in midstroke. At the burst of light, it reared, revealing legs thick like stumps and an underbelly full of working, twitching parts. Its eyes and mouth, if it had them, were hidden in those innards.

It landed with a thud and, though it shifted and feigned lunges, came no closer. The sparks of light settled to the floor like a snowfall. When the boy moved closer to the thing, it stumbled back.

"He and others guard this place. Stay close to me," the boy told Shada.

Then began a series of advancements and withdrawals that took them slowly up the tunnel. In moments of boldness, the creature lurched this way and that, trying to get around the boy to reach Shada, but the boy shifted back and forth to block it, and the creature would not confront him directly. After an unguessable time, it turned away, and its bulk disappeared down a side tunnel.

"He was quite worked up, you know," the boy said.

"Is that his home?" Shada asked.

"Yes. I think you'd better walk in front for a little while, in case he comes back."

She did, though she felt no safer walking ahead of him. Soon, she heard other noises from the dark to either side, but the boy quieted those with a simple shush. He said, "We should talk. It will let them know we are coming."

"I'd like that. To start, who are you?"

He paused. "I'm a boy."

"Yes, but what's your name?"

"We don't have those."

"Oh." Glancing into the shadows, Shada kept talking to calm herself. "What should I call you, then?"

"Call me a boy. That's what I am."

"Okay, I will." When something chittered in the dark, she gasped, doing all she could to stay composed. "How long have you lived here?"

The Boy sounded entirely casual. "Always."

"Did you come here with the Lady?"

"No. One of the old ones made me."

"Oh." Shada didn't know how to answer that.

"They're not always together, like you saw. Sometimes, they go off alone, but they don't want to be by themselves for long."

The Boy's calm openness encouraged Shada, as did their shared language. Unlike the Lady, the Boy did not hesitate to answer questions, though Shada might not understand the answers. She probed deeper. "Where did the old ones come from, before this?"

"From her."

"Huire?"

He said nothing. Perhaps he did not understand that she was asking a question. She tried again. "Do you mean Huire?"

"Yes."

The bleak white of true daylight appeared in the distance sooner than she expected. They approached the tunnel entrance.

She could breathe again. "You rescued me. Thank you."

"You're very welcome."

She turned to him. "I'm leaving to find my friend. Would you like to come along?" She felt a kinship with the Boy, and she could not deny that she wanted the company. If he could command other life-forms like he had the creatures in the tunnel, finding Nor would seem far likelier.

He stopped. "Out there?"

"Of course."

He turned his head to look back down the tunnel. It was one of the more anatomically believable motions she had seen his kind perform. "Can I?" he asked someone invisible.

He seemed to listen for a moment, then he looked at her with a mournful expression. "I can't."

She looked into the tunnel. "Are you speaking to someone besides me?"

"Yes. To Huire."

Shada noticed an extra chill on the breeze. "Are you sure? I don't hear anyone."

He shrugged. "I miss my friends."

"You mean... the ones you ran from when the doors opened?"

He shook his head. "No. I mean the young ones like me. We live here." He pointed to a few of the tunnels that branched from where they stood.

"But why don't you live with the others? The old ones?"

"We don't like it."

She sympathized. "Well, you'd better get back to them, then. I—"

"Goodbye!" he called as he vanished.

Shada closed her mouth. She turned toward the beach and the ice floes offshore. She had made a decision and would have to go through with it. She made her way down the beach to where the boats waited.

23

ARUMIN

THE COMPANY WAS RECOVERING from the shock of its new surroundings. Upon finding themselves in the temple-sized skull of some ancient leviathan, they had at first huddled together in a clump. Since then, they had come unknotted and were sitting or lying scattered across the shelf of bone at the back of the skull.

Still, only Hulgar had yet dared to really interact with the beasts. He was whooping and cheering two of them, who were engaged in a wrestling match that verged on bloodletting. Though telling the beasts apart was hard, Arumin thought the smaller combatant was the youngster who had offered the Ronians food when they arrived. Hulgar seemed to have developed a particular attachment to him.

Having space to think let Arumin breathe more easily, although so far, thinking was doing him no favors. Since the moment he forbade the others to look for Tabard, a tangible coldness had separated him from the company. Not even Brin, who had remained at his side, seemed quite the same. Arumin had always been aloof from the men, but this felt different. He wondered if he should try to correct anything, not knowing if he was just imagining things. Emberly had given many unpopular orders.

Robir approached. "Bishop," he said.

Arumin was watching the wrestling match without interest. He grunted.

The private continued, "I'd like to see you alone when I can. I need to repent."

The bishop sighed. "For what?"

"Well... You don't know? But you were there."

Arumin looked at him and waited.

They were far enough from the others to remain unheard if they kept their voices down. Still, Robir looked around, frowning. "Emberly beat the sergeant. He could have killed him. I just stood and watched it happen, and I don't know why."

The bishop saw Orund lying face up on a flat edge of the shelf. The man could walk, but he lay down every chance he got. The bruises on his face formed almost a single large welt. Arumin said, "In coming on this crusade, your sins have been forgiven."

Not watching Robir's reaction, he only heard the private ask, "Just like that?"

"Yes. Nothing more is needed."

"I'm sorry, your Eminence, but that's hard to accept. If that's true, it means we can all do whatever we want."

The bishop felt his ability to care about the man and his spiritual crisis dwindling to nothing. "That's what the Temple has promised."

"But... it doesn't feel true, your Eminence. My guilt won't go away. I let you down and Huire too. Emberly's tyranny was allowed to stand."

Arumin tried to smile, but his muscles resisted. He wound up grimacing. "Emberly is not a problem anymore."

Robir waited. When he realized the bishop was truly finished, he said, "Don't you have something to admit as well?"

The bishop knew he should respond with outrage. Instead, he thought hard about how to end the conversation. "What should I say?"

The soldier glared. "It wasn't just me who let it happen. You were also there."

"I didn't intervene because I used my head. What would you have done? Would you have killed Emberly right there?"

"It's what we planned to do before. But when another chance came around..." Robir's inner struggle showed on his face. "I know why I failed: I was afraid. If we'd tried to kill him when he beat Orund, would we have succeeded? I didn't know what would happen. Bishop, if you watched Orund get beaten because you were smart, that's one thing. If you didn't act because you were afraid, I think you ought to repent."

Arumin felt the corners of his mouth draw back like a lizard's. "Repent, should I? It seems that you've got plenty to repent for without worrying about me, Emberly, or anyone else."

"Of course I do. But surely my advice isn't off the mark."

"It was unasked for and insolent. If I need your help again, I will ask for it. Don't come to me."

Robir's arms and legs grew tight like wires. "I wonder, Bishop, if you are really the man Huire expects. Everyone knows you were a coward in the past, but not everyone thinks you've truly changed. I hope you have."

"From this moment, you are to be seen and not heard. Begone."

Robir passed a quiet moment of decision then walked outside, ducking under the row of incisors in the front of the skull. No one else seemed to notice him leaving, and the beasts did not try to stop him.

All was quiet for a while in Arumin's little corner of the room. But he felt something building, a static charge between Brin and him.

Finally, the boy said, "I could have prayed with him."

Arumin snorted. "That's not the point."

Brin persisted. "Perhaps we should go down into the tunnels after all. Shada's been gone for too long."

"A dangerous prospect. I wouldn't have expected a suggestion like that from you."

In one corner of Arumin's eye, Brin leaned back, away from him. "You still don't understand. I'm trying to change."

"If that's true, then the next step is to trust the Lady."

"I do. She isn't the problem."

The bishop furrowed his brow in feigned disbelief. "Are you really worried about Shada?"

"Aren't you? You've seen how she's been acting. She can't be relied upon."

Arumin turned fully to him. "What's brought this on?" He faced forward again without waiting for an answer.

Brin muttered with restrained contempt, "This is why you're having such trouble. You can't see when you're wrong."

"You've followed me this far. Where would you be if it weren't for me?"

"Dead." Brin spat the word.

"Instead of thinking about Shada, think about that."

24

— · —

STAUBEL

To Staubel's relief, Sergeant Orund had chosen to rest on the side of the room farthest from the bishop. This allowed the doctor, in remaining dutifully by his patient's side, to stay away from Arumin.

The sergeant barely seemed to hear Staubel's questions and attempts at conversation. The black-and-purple swelling of his face hid his feelings as surely as a mask. He was relieved when Private Hulgar, wounded in a playful tussle with one of his new friends, came to Staubel and submitted himself for treatment.

With Hulgar sitting on the floor in front of him, the doctor sat on the shelf of bone and cleaned the wound as best he could. It was a gash on Hulgar's shoulder, and as the man watched the play and antics of the beasts, he kept leaning forward to shout or rocking backward with laughter, making stitching difficult. A few times, Staubel snapped at Hulgar—he was one of the few who dared to—but finally sought to keep him still by engaging him with chatter.

"It's ugly," he said, his mouth close to the soldier's ear, "but not like the last time I treated you." He wondered if Hulgar even remembered losing his mind one night in Caidfell's jungle. For anyone else, that would be impossible to forget, but Hulgar had a way of setting reality as he would have it and convincing others to go along. To avoid any tension, Staubel made a joke. "At least you're not getting by on your looks, like Orund here."

Orund didn't laugh. Hulgar laughed, but at something else. Staubel had given up and consigned them all to dismal silence when Hulgar startled him by speaking up. "They're nothing to mess with, this lot."

Staubel cocked an eye from his work. "Eh?"

"That monster in the sky takes away the wretches in that village whenever it wants. But it leaves our friends here alone. It knows not to try." He snickered.

That theory about the politics of the island was as likely as any other Staubel had heard. He could think of no plausible explanation for their mystifying circumstances.

Once Hulgar began to talk, he was off and running. "Think the Realm will be along soon, Sergeant?"

Staubel looked at Sergeant Orund, who shrugged. Hulgar couldn't see the gesture from where he sat, so Staubel relayed to him: "The sergeant doesn't know."

"They will," Hulgar said. "Of course they will. And that'll be the end for this lot."

Orund did not respond, so Staubel took it upon himself. "We don't know that. They seem able to care for themselves."

Hulgar said, "But no one can fight the Realm. We can't. When they come, we'll run off."

"We'll do what we must."

"Can't they just leave people be?"

Staubel suppressed a laugh at the private's newfound concern for others. "Well, I'm glad this place has been good for one of us."

"We'll run off," Hulgar repeated. Then he finished the thought. "If the bishop is in charge, that is."

Staubel stopped. "We had thoughts like that in Om about the captain. Both of us. Didn't we learn where that goes?"

Hulgar huffed, a huge motion. "No," he said, unabashed.

Staubel thought better than to press for a wiser answer. "The sergeant here was the smart one," he said. "He knows, once you start, it's hard to stop."

Orund rolled onto his side, away from Staubel and the rest of the room.

25

—·—

MERIN

AFTER MERIN FELL AT last into a doze of sheer exhaustion, a clamor of Ronian voices rose above the constant din of their hosts. He raised his head to see the men crowding near the pit at the center of the room. They gathered around one of the beasts.

Merin's heart jumped at the thought that a fight had begun. The beasts would finish them off before they could find their weapons. That was the kind of fear always leaping about inside him, bouncing against his throat and rib cage. When he saw it was false, he slumped against the bone shelf and looked around, hoping no one had witnessed his mouselike temperament in action.

The Ronians' voices were high and excited though not celebratory. Even Orund had sat up to peer at them. Merin did not approach the crowd, knowing he was too short to see past the others. Instead, he took a few steps up the curved incline of the shelf. From there, he saw the beast and the soldiers around it were looking down at something.

Perhaps Bishop Arumin had been sleeping, too, for he was one of the last to converge on the group. "Make way!" he barked, and they did.

As the crowd parted, Merin saw the beast holding a knife. Fragments of overheard speech told him what those with a better view already knew: the weapon was Emberly's.

Arumin snatched it from the beast, impressively heedless of any danger of doing so. He looked at it and then up at the creature. Though speaking to their hosts was impossible, the bishop looked like he wanted to pry answers from its jaws.

The beast turned and walked out of the room without a sound.

The men's shouts had turned to murmurs. Someone said, loud enough for all to hear, "Well, if they found this, that means—"

"It means nothing," the bishop cut in. His voice was not as loud as the others', but the final word was hard enough to be heard nonetheless. His tone held an urgency that somehow ran counter to the urgency in the air.

The same person answered—Sergeant Feng. "But we thought he was lost in the sea. And here's his knife." His voice sounded strange, as if carried by some higher energy.

The bishop, perhaps conscious of his grating tone, softened it. "They found it on the sea bottom, Sergeant."

"Maybe," Feng said. "But why would they bring it to us? They might be trying to tell us something—that they have him somewhere."

"If they had him, they would have brought him to us, not just his knife. If they haven't found him, we have no chance of finding him. And let's not forget that they are likely his killers."

"Sir," Merin said. He spoke before realizing he had decided to speak. His voice echoed from the walls of the skull.

Everyone looked at him. He had often seen hate in their eyes when they did so—hatred of him for betraying them on Caidfell. That he had been out of his mind at the time was little help; they hated his weakness in allowing it to happen. Their faces now were an opaque wall, and he wondered how much of their hatred was—and had been—a product of his own mind. His imagination, like his fear, couldn't hold still for an instant. He was weak, after all.

"Your Eminence," he corrected himself, "shouldn't we look anyway?"

The bishop's eyes were narrow but shone like lanterns. "It's hopeless," the old man said.

Merin's thoughts were oddly clear. "If you think so, then let a few of us go. Those who volunteer."

"Why should we waste more lives?"

"Because we need him."

The bishop's mouth froze, and Merin heard a scoff or two from the crowd.

"I will go," he said, "along with whoever else wants to come."

Arumin's voice glistened with condescension. "Not so long ago, you helped try to kill this man. Now, you say that we need him?"

"I was wrong," Merin said weakly. "I don't know what I was thinking."

"That's exactly right. You never know, do you, Private? We couldn't rely on you on Caidfell. Who would ever rely on you now?"

Merin had expected such a question. He felt the blow fall and accepted it. "Don't send me, then. But someone should go."

Arumin's eyes were glassy and nearly rabid. "He is gone. And no one else will follow. I forbid it."

"You can forbid it," Merin reasoned aloud, "but you cannot stop us if we decide to leave." He had no idea if anyone else even wanted to leave.

The bishop raised his voice to the ceiling. "Anyone who leaves will be cast from the Temple at once. When the Goddess returns, she will turn her back as you drift away into the Outer Dark."

Merin had heard it all but did not believe. "I have a feeling."

"A feeling?" Arumin seemed to vomit the word.

"Yes. About the Goddess. I think this is what she wants."

"So. You know nothing else—not even whether you want to kill a man or save him—but you know the will of Huire."

Merin felt like the bishop had pulled a string and finished untying a knot, and a smile took hold of his face. "Yes, I think so."

"Go. And anyone who believes you should follow. Let us see, for good and all, who the unfaithful are."

Merin went. The room was so quiet that he could hear the distant murmur of the sea. Even the beasts were quiet, perhaps realizing something was afoot that they did not understand.

He dared to glance back as he neared the hanging set of teeth and the pearly fang-pillars. No one had followed him. They all stood watching him still. Mostly untroubled, he passed under the teeth and out of their sight.

He emerged in the forest of bone. The space was little brighter than inside the skull. *Will this day never end?* Someone called his name.

It was Robir. For some reason, the sound of the man's voice was no longer recognizable. Robir was sitting against the jaw of the skull, near its teeth. He told Merin, "Could it be true, do you think?"

"About Emberly? It might be. I have a feeling."

Robir stared at the ground as if contemplating its murder. "How could you possibly want him back?"

"He has a part to play. I still don't like him."

Robir squinted at Merin. Then he laughed and leaned back, relaxed. "I'll join you, if you don't mind."

Merin could not help but frown. "I thought if anyone hated me for this, it would be you."

"I do not hate anyone. The Goddess does not permit it."

26

The Lady

The Lady walked among many wonders.

She had known, in the vaguest sense, what lay behind the metal doors, though she had never entered them and had forbidden her siblings from doing so. In her absence, they had given in, as she had suspected they would. That left her no choice but to follow. She wondered if Huire could feel her excitement at the prospect of seeing beyond those doors, as well as how Huire would feel about it.

That vault, like thousands of its kind on other worlds, was more than the vacated lair of this planet's god. It had been a home, and now, it was a kind of tomb. This god and a few others had done something forbidden. It had preserved bits of the technology of the old world—the utmost expressions of the power achieved by humans before the gods superseded them all. She wondered if they were mementos or perhaps tokens of rebellion.

The faithful gods, Huire foremost among them, knew and abided the need to destroy all such things so that man and god could proceed uninterrupted into the blessed future. But some gods had failed to perfect themselves, allowing sentimentality to escape its proper place and infect their minds.

When each of the gods created a home from which to transform a raw world into a life-filled one, they had known just how it ought to look and work. But few felt compelled by that knowledge. Each vault was a kingdom of its own. But this one, like all the others, was finite, and the Lady knew she would find her family if she plumbed its depths sufficiently.

She came to a great spherical chamber. It was so large that if its surface were stretched flat like a sheet, it could have housed nations of men. Its sustained existence had sent eddies of disarray through the surrounding rock—disarray that could only be kept in check by a great and commanding will such as the chamber's current occupants distinctly lacked. She found them clinging to its insides, roosting.

When the Lady and Shada confronted the family in the cave outside the vault, they had witnessed only the uttermost extremity of its combined greatness. Though they were not large enough to fill the vast space, they nearly rivaled Huire herself in might. They were large enough to reshape a planet, given time. Clumped all together, they were awake but inert—until the Lady entered.

She bore the appearance of the Gentleman, and what remained of him trembled within her. The family left their perches and rose as one to meet her, a miasma that groped and stretched, gained and lost wings, crawled like something wet and newly born. The noise was maddening.

As they approached, the Gentleman spoke from within her. She could mimic his favored form but not his exact voice, so when she devoured him in the chamber outside the vault, sweeping away pieces of him and making them hers, she had preserved a piece of him within herself. That piece knew what had befallen it and how much greater it had recently been. Now, it feared savagely for its very existence and did her bidding eagerly. Whether it still loved her in its way, she could not know.

He spoke to the family convincingly. He said that the Lady spoke truly and that they must return to Huire.

Though few in the cloud protested, one voice presumed to speak for the rest. "We do not wish to return."

"Yet we must," the Gentleman said again as the Lady wondered if what remained of him was too stupid to be useful. "Since you do not trust her, trust me."

They replied, "You are under her sway, as always."

"Is that what you all think?" he asked. "It would be the first time all of you have agreed on anything."

"It is what we think."

"None disagree? I do not believe it. Some among you must dissent. May I hear from one of you? Are there none who want more than this?"

Voices had begun to chatter, to others and themselves. The Lady knew them all. They grew in number and intensity until the cloud bubbled with them.

The Gentleman's voice boomed. "If any would be free of this place, now or ever, let them stand apart."

The cloud began to disintegrate. The first were those who agreed with the Gentleman but had been too timid to say so. As they departed, the fighting among those who remained grew more intense, and more individuals broke away to seek a semblance of isolation. None of those who dwelt in the cloud were larger than a speck in comparison to the whole, but as many more followed those breaking away, the writhing mass at the center shrank. The chamber was soon filled with individuals, some dressed in finery like the Gentleman, some in forms meant to be fearsome, some in simple shapes or amorphous masses. None could warp itself beyond the boundaries of what it knew.

Some began to leave the chamber, swooping out in a rush or in a sad procession. As she watched them leave, the Gentleman's voice spoke. "Friends, remember that this is what I want." The Lady wondered if that was true but contented herself with never knowing.

Then she annihilated him finally, wiping away all trace of his identity. The others saw his exterior eaten away, to be replaced by her gleaming visage and golden robes. He managed a scream in a voice that became hers and ended in a laugh.

The free-floating fragments nearby had an instant to become alarmed before she surrounded them. They, too, became parts of her whole. She had fully doubled her mass since coming to the island.

Those who remained certainly knew what she had done, though they had probably never before seen it happen. Their family's one unbroken pact had been that they did not forcibly devour each other.

The family panicked, as well it might have. Some individuals flew around the chamber, while others fled into the tunnel. None dared challenge the Lady alone. Most of them snapped together, joining in a single colossal form that writhed and raged.

She was an insect in comparison. She spoke to all those she had not yet devoured, using her own voice at last. "See what we've done? We are one now."

No single response came from the cloud of others. Shapes like arms and legs and knives reached for her, but those who comprised them disagreed about speed and strategy. She shifted about, and none could touch her.

She said, "Think of it! All our thought, knowledge, and power!"

"What have you done?" one of them asked belatedly.

"He will live in me. He won't know it, but I will, and that is enough."

"We must remain ourselves. Huire told us what would happen."

"She lied!" The Lady let emotion overcome her for a moment. "To keep us apart, she forced us to speak in words like humans. She feared what we could become. If we want to rescue her, we must do it in our own way."

The other wailed, "How can you expect us to surrender our very selves? You would never make such a sacrifice."

She said, "But I have a choice."

She advanced on them. Those who wished to fight could not agree on how, and those who wished to run could not agree on what direction. As one of the cloud's arms extended, she swept through it, cutting it off from the rest. It drew together in infantile confusion before she swallowed it.

The rest of the cloud pulled away, thrashing, fleeing from one wall to the next. She reached the opening to the tunnel before it could. Trapped in the chamber, it reared and spun. Through it all, her brothers and sisters clung to each other.

27

— · —

ARUMIN

THE BEASTS SENSED IT first. They shuffled around anxiously for several minutes, mostly on all fours, sniffing, barking, and snapping at each other. Finally, they gathered around the pit in the skull's floor. Then the Ronians heard the noises emanating from its depths.

This was not the first such disturbance. Shortly after Merin left, a rumbling had sounded from the pit, accompanied by distant voices. The sounds had shaken the Ronians, who had been looking anxiously at the pit since they arrived. But the beasts were undisturbed.

This time was different. The beasts huddled together, whining nervously. Arumin's own men joined the beasts on the precipice, peering down and chattering. His ears were not as sharp as they had once been, but even he soon felt the ground moving under him.

"What is it?" Brin asked.

The bishop shook his head.

Brin slid from the shelf and stood in front of him. "We've got no choice now. We've got to look for the Lady."

Arumin sneered. "You would go down there now?"

"She could be in danger." The young priest ran a hand over his face. "Look, we know that she doesn't know everything. Who knows where that scamp, Shada, has led her?"

"Danger." The bishop scoffed.

"Do you still think our faith is being tested? Well, what if this is a test? A test of whether we can think for ourselves?"

"Many a damned fool has told himself the same."

"The ground is shaking, you old bastard! This is not a part of anyone's plan!"

A sharp rumble came from under the island. The vibration passed through each of Arumin's bones to the next. He took a breath and was able to speak calmly. "What is meant to be, in times and places like these? I don't know, and neither do you."

Brin reached up as if to pull out a fistful of his own hair but stopped short. The newly forming scars on his cheeks shone red. In a carefully contained tone, he said, "I wonder if you really desire to serve Huire. Maybe you're simply worn out."

The bishop's heart was ice. He wished that all of him could be so. "If you want to live to be my age, you will learn when to be silent."

The way Brin straightened himself was so childish that at another time, it would have been endearing. "Maybe it's time for someone else to be her voice."

When Arumin stood up like a shot, Brin stepped back, raising his hands, and almost tripped.

Arumin hollered, "Attention!"

In the fearful muttering that had descended on the room, his voice sounded like a cannon shot. Heads turned.

"It seems I may have outlived my usefulness. Father Brin wishes to supersede me."

The faces of the Ronians were a study in reckless contradictions. They looked dumbfounded, amused, even suspicious of a prank. The faces of the beasts were blank as always.

"Since it seems the mob is destined to rule us all," Arumin said, "I will put it to a vote. But first, you all ought to know who it is who will lead you."

He strode to the edge of the pit. "Though the rest of you may lose faith, I will still be confident that Huire watches over us." He turned and looked Brin in the eye across what seemed a vast distance. Everything else faded to smears on the edge of his sight. "And I am confident that if I do what I must to show you the way, she will protect me."

Brin's face was dark. Arumin took a final step so that his toes hung over the brink. "If I throw myself down there, she will lift me up and place me before you."

A particularly sharp tremor from the ground shook his knees. He relaxed, letting himself wobble. Brin stood sharply. The bishop sighed, assured that he knew how the boy really felt.

The pit erupted. An explosion of gray smoke struck Arumin, rumbling like the purring of a cat in a mouse's ear. It burned him, filled him, and sanded him away to nothing. The last particle of him that was still aware of itself sighed knowingly before submitting to sleep.

28

ARUMIN

ARUMIN—KNOWN MOSTLY AS WEYLAN then—stood on the bar, lute in hand. He remembered this night with a special clarity.

The crowd clapped as he picked. The hairs on his neck rose, and his cheeks and forehead felt chilled. His song, a jig, had drawn the patrons from their circles and pairings and captured their eyes and ears. His brothers dominated the nearest table, and behind them were most of the men he knew. In the back, most numerous of all, were the new strangers who had moved in from the hills to work in the mines. All were dusty, sweaty, and riled.

Arumin had never felt more popular than he did that evening. He shivered each time a splash of ale struck him. Near the end of the tune, a new face appeared at the door, unseen by any but him. It was an oval of savage pallor.

Dram had become famous in recent months: the boy who lived in the woods, who haunted the village by night.

Weylan was the only one outside Dram's family who knew his name and where he came from or who had met him face to face.

As soon as Dram realized he had been seen, his face vanished from the shadowy doorway.

Weylan finished the song and jumped straight into the next. He had learned that if he stopped, the ruder men would spit or throw food.

The face in the door appeared again shortly thereafter, joined by a hand. A finger crooked, beckoning the boy on the bar and his lute. Weylan looked away before anyone else noticed the face. He wanted it to go away, but he also didn't. Most of all, he wanted to keep the face in the doorway to himself.

It vanished again, and fear pierced him. It was warmer and sharper than his cold dread of being at the mercy of so many drunken men. When they met, he had told Dram that he hoped he would die. Weylan didn't understand why he felt tempted to run off with the boy now.

When the face appeared for a third time, he saw it only from the corner of his eye and, after that, ignored it completely.

One song blurred into the next. All were standards, things he could play even if he'd forgotten his head at home.

When each tune ended, he barely left them a second to cheer. He placed his fingers on the strings but jerked them away as the door shot open to rattle against the wall. Dram sprang in at him.

It was revenge. Weylan wondered only that the boy had waited so long, planned so meticulously. Weylan was not a difficult boy to kill.

He watched in frozen wonder as Dram hopped up on the bar like a sprite and grabbed Weylan's wrist with calloused fingers. The boy wore a grin like darkness triumphant. Weylan flailed, and the grip tightened.

Weylan would have jumped from the bar to take refuge among those whom he hated—he would have leapt straight into Rhys's arms—had he not dared to look into Dram's face one more time.

The grin that had seemed demonic now looked glee-ful. The eyes that had shone with sadism now seemed joyous.

In the furor that arose in the pub, Weylan could make out no single voice, but he saw the words on Dram's lips: "Come *on*."

People were rising to their feet. Dram pulled him toward the door, and he followed, dropping from the bar to the floor. When he landed, the lute fell from his hand.

Dram had turned to race for the door, but when he heard the tuneful *thunk* of the instrument, he stopped and looked back. "Grab it!"

Weylan picked up the lute just before several sets of advancing boots reached them. The instrument's body was chipped. Rhys's eyes were locked on Dram, who everyone knew would bring in a bounty if captured.

The boys fled. Several men moved to block their exit. Only one was fast enough, stepping before the door as they reached it. But Dram's unabashed charge knocked him onto his backside. From the ground, the man fumbled for Dram's leg then Weylan's. He missed both.

Trees muffled the cool night breeze as they raced into the woods. Dram moved without hesitation, seeming to know where each branch hung and fallen tree lay. Weylan did nothing for a long time but hold on and follow.

When they entered a clearing, a flood of moonlight seemed to reveal every blade of grass and flower petal. The walls of surrounding trees were unnaturally straight.

"Where are we?" he asked.

Dram's teeth were bright under the moon. "Don't you know?"

Then, suddenly, Weylan did know. A hillock rose near the clearing's center, and the bright streak of a road led away into the forest. Beyond it, machines lurked, bent and crooked like broken trees. At the base of the hillock, the darkness hid the entrance to one of the mines.

Dram saw Weylan looking toward it. "We can go down there if you want."

Weylan's spine tingled. "Do you... live down there?"

"No. I could if I wanted, though. I'm not afraid of it anymore."

"My mother says never to go down there."

"Your brothers go down there every day."

Weylan conceded that with a nod. The thought of entering the mine by oneself transformed his feelings for this boy from fear and attraction to awe. Surely, Dram was not solely of this world.

"Well," Dram said, "we can't just stand here all night. I've got an idea!" His eyebrows jumped. "Will you come with me?"

Weylan offered his hand but soon regretted it when he saw where they were heading. "But I can't!"

"Don't worry so much. We won't." Dram's neck and hands shone with a light like the otherworld as he guided Weylan across a bridge of darkness. Low grass tickled Weylan's ankles as they approached the hillock. They rounded the hillock and sat on a crate by the entrance to the mine.

The mine's opening gaped immediately to Weylan's side, and he pushed himself closer to the other boy, who smiled and said, "You're safe with me."

That bright face, undimmed so close to the jaws of hell, enthralled Weylan.

"Can I play for you?" he asked. He could think of nothing else to offer, and a tribute of some kind was assuredly needed.

"I hoped you would," Dram said. "Do you like it?" He patted the instrument.

"Yes. I think so. I'm good at it." Weylan laid it across his legs.

"You're getting by. Can't fault you for that." Dram touched Weylan's hand, and the boy felt stirrings throughout himself. "But you'll have to go down there with me someday." He cocked his head toward the mine.

Weylan shut his eyes. Even the scarce light of the clearing was too revealing. "Please, let me play."

"Fine. But I want something different. None of those things you play for the others."

"Those are all I know."

"Well, give them some new words, at least."

Weylan coughed. He felt like he was failing at something terribly important. "It's not that easy. Some singers can make up words on the spot, but not me." Then he slapped his knee. "I know what to do."

Dram laughed and moved away. He was only giving Weylan room to play, but the distance still hurt. Weylan wanted to bring him closer again but didn't want to ask.

He played a slow song. He had never played that one in the pub, for it wouldn't have pleased him or anyone else, but it pleased him right then. The chords progressed oddly for such a popular tune, dipping sadly but, at the moment of crescendo, darting in a new direction. They asked a question that they never exactly answered, though they promised that an answer existed somewhere and that the answer was a fine one.

He sang—not the common lyrics but wordless syllables. His voice followed the tune closely at first before venturing out on its own. He found he could put meaning into the sounds, though they lacked denotation. Soon, his lips and tongue intervened, adding words in a language that was birthed as he spoke it.

He sang to the mine, which had broken the limbs and backs of so many strong men, begging it to forgive human effrontery, then to the trees, then to the night itself. In doing the Ronians' bidding, his people had struck great wounds in their planet, of which that mine was only one. Now, their world had turned against them, embracing them with newly toxic arms, holding them close to the labyrinthine hole in its heart, which was the mine. Shoved inside, forced to commit their deepest violation yet, his people would face the great lie that they had told themselves, sworn by, and lived by. There, it had been left to fester and swell.

He thought that the same repeated chords would grow quickly tiresome, but when he looked at Dram, he saw the boy had been deflated. His elbows perched on his knees like the last standing poles of a collapsing tent, barely propping him up as he swayed in a storm.

Weylan let the last notes fade as his voice dwindled to a scratch.

The other boy looked at him with great need. He looked at Weylan's hands and seemed to notice they had stopped. "Oh," he said with trembling lips.

Weylan knew what would make the night complete. "Would you like to sing?"

Then he saw the thing he would remember most vividly about that night. For an instant, Dram's eyes blazed with fear. The boy's face transformed into something gaunt and hunted, barely human.

"I'm sorry," Weylan said quickly.

Dram smiled so brightly that Weylan could almost have forgotten what had come before. "Think nothing of it," he said. "I just can't do it now." He tossed off the statement with casual amusement. Then he leaned toward Weylan, who was amazed to find their foreheads touching. "Thank you. I will sing for you someday. But now, I'd better take you home."

He stood and extended a hand, leaving Weylan still sitting on the crate. Weylan took the boy's fingers, held them against his cheek, and said, "Someday."

29

SHADA

BY THE TIME SHADA'S arms became exhausted, she had paddled well into the forest of rocks protruding from the sea. She stopped rowing, let the boat drift, and began to freeze.

When she abandoned the Lady to search for Nor, whom she somehow could not accept as fully dead, she had been quite aware of her foolishness in doing so. But not until she came outside and saw the blinding snow, which parted occasionally to unveil the great frozen ocean, did she realize it in her gut.

The hopelessness of her search lightened her. She would not find Nor. He was and would always be dead, regardless of the romantic notions she dreamed up, and if she braved the elements to find him, she would soon follow. Still, she did not doubt that she would go.

Now that she had slipped from the Lady's watching eye and was free to fail and die alone, she could not imagine how she had borne that eye's weight for so long. The Lady had gathered her so close lately that she had thought little about herself.

Shada wondered how far she might have gone if she hadn't slipped away from the Lady. Perhaps she would soon have been persuaded to forget herself for all time. She wondered how long the Lady would take to find her again. Whatever grotesque kraken that sea might dredge up, Shada felt she would leap into its jaws before going back. As dearly as she wanted to see Nor again, the line between wishing to find him and wishing to end her own life was as murky as the water bubbling under the boat.

Those thoughts and all else fled her mind when she looked ahead. Nor had just stepped out of the storm on a nearby ice floe.

She stood with a gasp. For a moment, she just stared, afraid to believe it, as the boat rocked beneath her. Then too many feelings to express crowded in—she wanted to cry, laugh, cheer, and rush to him all at once. None of them would have equaled that instant, the seeming impossibility of him standing there.

He was hunched like a beggar and wreathed in fur. She knew him only by his eyes, the whiteness of which glinted in reflection of their surroundings. Behind him, partly hidden by a curtain of snow, two figures towered. They were the same type of fur-covered men who had greeted the company on the island—the kin of a man who had frightened her once in a temple in Ronia.

He shuffled toward her. She sat, found the paddle, and clumsily moved the boat to the edge of the ice, allowing him to board.

She stared, still dumbfounded, as he settled on the next seat. "I can't believe it!" She hoped that her silence had somehow said it all.

He eyed her inscrutably from under the expanse of furred hide. "I can," he wheezed. "Thank you."

The tall figures had already vanished. "Who were those men? Why aren't they with the rest of their kind?" She realized belatedly that he probably knew nothing of the island and its city of beast-men.

Still, he said, "Outcasts."

Then a thought fell upon her like the shadow of death. Against all odds, she had completed her mission. Now that she had Nor, she had to return to the island.

"Shall we go?" she asked. Her voice felt hollow.

His eyes were dull with distance, but his smile lit his face and warmed her inside. He nodded, showing no sign that he sensed her dread. "Did you come just for me?"

"Yes. Why?" She meant the words to be playful, but they sounded sharp, and she grimaced. Yes, she had come just for him. Perhaps he had not expected such courage from her. Or maybe he thought she had been stupid to come.

He placed his frozen hand on hers and shook his head as if to dispel whatever suspicions had come between them. She took pleasure in watching them scatter to the wind.

"What happened to you?" she asked.

Without much change in his expression, he told her a brief, horrific tale that sounded like the fever dream of a dying sailor. He used words as sparingly as ever, and she had trouble discerning one monster from the next, but she did not press him for more. He would have died, he said, had the beast-men not found him and cared for him.

She tried to take it all in. "That's terrible."

"It's over now, anyways. Something is happening to me. It was happening already, but now, it's almost finished. I just don't mind anything anymore."

The passionless emptiness in his voice sent uncomfortable tingles through her. "I don't like the sound of that. You ought to mind some things."

He looked at the bottom of the boat. "You're right. But I think it's too late to stop it. There aren't many things, now, that can move me one way or another. Maybe only one thing."

He gazed into her eyes as frankly as they had ever been gazed into. It was almost too much for her, those eyes like clean dishes, but she wanted it to go on.

"You're sure that you aren't a monk anymore?" she asked.

"I should never have been." His eyes did not leave her, but his face became dark. He received the pain willingly and showed it to her without hesitation. "Huire is a lie."

For a moment, she forgot to row. "But the Lady has seen her. Unless..."

"She may exist, but the Lady is lying about her. This journey is taking us no place that's good. We must convince the company of that."

Shada wrapped her arms around herself as her heart began to pound. "Isn't it still possible that Huire herself is good?"

Nor breathed fog into the air. "I just don't know."

The water rippled faintly as the boat drifted toward the island, and the knowledge of what waited there squeezed her heart, lungs, and stomach all at once. "But... what then? We've come so far."

He paused, and when he spoke, a new determination filled his voice. "We'll go back to Ronia. Or try to. Or maybe we'll find a new place."

She wondered if his newfound openness might instead be the encroachment of madness. "The Lady won't allow it, Nor. She never would have, I think, regardless of what she said at first. And now... she's changed." She continued, "I can't. I'm sorry, Nor, but I don't know whether I'm glad I found you or sorry I won't freeze out here. Here, at least, I would be myself." More imaginings of the Lady's wrath came to mind, and she doubled over in the boat.

His hands touched her, one on her shoulder and one on her head. He said, "I'll take you away."

She spoke to the sloshing water at the bottom of the boat. "Where?"

"Away from the island. Back to the shore."

Sitting up, she cried, "There is no going back! The Shining Realm may be there already."

"Onto the ice, then. We'll walk across the ocean. Whatever comes after life ends, we will go there together."

"You're serious?" She took his hands. "But what about the company?"

That must have struck him deeply. His lips tightened, and he looked down. "I think, for you, I would leave them behind. It's wrong, but I am not a good person."

She thought of spending a little time in his arms, waiting on the ice as the cold made them free. "I don't know."

"Listen." He touched her hand. "You came out here to save me or to die if you couldn't. Do you care about anything else that much? You've got to if you intend to go on. If you don't want to be like me."

A sound cut across the water, through the snow and wind. She twisted to look. There, in the gray where the dim outline of the island loomed, darkness gathered in the sky. It swept up from the island itself. As they watched, it roared so that the air and water vibrated.

That sound stole her breath. Air returned to her lungs with a long gasp like a yawn, though she had never felt farther from sleep.

She covered her eyes. "I think... I think that's the Lady."

"Are you sure?" Nor asked. "What about—"

"It's her." She knew, though she wasn't sure how. "Goddess, it's her."

She wondered many things as, in the distance, the Lady filled more and more of the sky. Maybe Shada had been wrong to search for Nor. Perhaps he, along with anyone else she touched, would suffer for her betrayal of her one true mate.

Surely, Nor deserved better than someone who had to consider such things.

30

Shada

Soon after the Lady appeared in the sky, she moved away. Despite her vastness, she vanished from sight for some time. Shada began to think that she and Nor might reach the island undisturbed.

Her heart sank when the darkness returned to the sky from the direction of the mainland. As she rowed, she heard cries and an immutable humming from above.

The island was almost within oar's reach when the Lady descended on them. She came as a dark column, the tip of a funnel that ended just above the water before the boat. Her face appeared amid the turbulence, twice as tall as Shada and much wider than the boat.

"Come," the Lady said. Her merest whisper was as loud as a roar.

Shada looked at Nor. He did not look afraid, and though she envied him that, it made her feel a little more alone.

The monk sprang to his feet, and Shada turned to see that the Lady's mouth had opened. The maw was cavernous, unnaturally wide, and its bottom was a little higher than their heads. A wide, flat tongue unfurled over its skeletal teeth and reached all the way to her feet—a bridge.

"I have to go," Shada told Nor.

"I know," he said. "It's too late."

As she turned to go, he cried, stumbling, "Let me come with you!"

Shada shook her head. "No. She would kill you."

Since the moment she first saw the great cloud in the sky and knew in her gut that it was the Lady, she had entertained a series of awful suspicions about how the Lady had grown so much. The notions all would have seemed insane if not for the insanity taking place before her eyes.

She looked at Nor one last time and found, to her immense comfort, that she didn't need to say anything at all. They looked into each other's eyes, and it was done.

She placed a foot on the tongue, the tip of which hovered just off the boat. Her foot entered the mass, which hardened to support her weight just as her heart jumped with the fear of falling. She removed her other foot from the boat, feeling its deck sway with her movement, and put herself entirely in the Lady's power. She began to climb the slope toward the mouth, but the tongue retracted on its own, slowly so that she could keep her balance.

Passing through the mouth, she entered a place such as she had never dreamed. Ahead and to either side lay a series of marble halls, fabulously decorated, with vaulted ceilings lit as though from within. The walls were packed with shelves, and despite their thickness and grandeur, those bent and creaked under the weight of all the books they held.

"Is this a library? Where am I?"

The Lady's voice was everywhere. "In a world that I have made for you. Do you like it?"

Shada looked closely at one of the shelves. "It's hard to believe in, you know. Is there writing on any of these pages?"

"On all of them. Any one you choose to try. I have grown, and not just bigger."

Shada gave in to a shudder that began in her belly. "How? Did you convince your family to join you?"

"They *are* me now. When two of my kind meet, the stronger can take the weaker and add it to oneself."

"You... devoured them? Your whole family?"

"Almost entirely. I became so excited that I took off for the skies before I could finish. I was on my way back when I noticed you returning to the island."

Shada touched a shelf. It felt solid under her fingers. "Were you surprised that I returned?"

"I can't say that I gave it much thought. As I watched you leave, I knew that I could hunt you down whenever I wished. Now, I wonder if I should have bothered."

Shada touched the books' spines, felt their realness, and wondered if that last statement was true. "What will you do next?"

"I will leave this world very soon, after I attend to a few small matters. Your company of friends has served its purpose."

"You won't need to hunt me down this time, Lady. I am here."

The Lady's voice boomed from the walls, the floor, the books themselves. "But, child, don't you see? I don't need you anymore. I need no caretaker. What have I to fear?"

The thought of what the Lady might do with someone she no longer needed chilled Shada. She tried to think. "Something destroyed the gods in ancient times. Whatever it was, you've been quite worried about it until now."

"It is a threat no longer. For the final part of the journey, I will simply need someone—any human will do, as long as they obey me when the time comes. Since I cannot count on you, I will pick from among your companions."

Shada fought a sinking feeling—the Lady might dispose of her at any moment. "I don't believe it," Shada said. "You may not need me, but you've gone to a lot of trouble to keep me alive. I think that you want me along."

The Lady's pause was almost undetectable, but it was there. "I will leave the choice to you. There is a hill in the middle of the island. When the sun sets, I will come to the top of it. If you are not there, I will go hunting and take the first human I find."

Around Shada, the world of marble turned back into smoke. She fell, screaming, only to land immediately on rock, even managing to keep her feet. Recovering her senses, she saw she was on a ridge that seemed to form the island's rim.

The Lady's face hung above her for an instant then turned away. The cloud moved off over the island and vanished.

Shada followed. Hurrying down the slopes, she wandered awestruck through a forest of giant bones until, following the growls of the beast-men, she entered the giant skull that served as their camp.

The beast-men saw her first but paid her no mind. The Ronians were gathered around a fallen form that she recognized as the bishop. The old man was clearly hurt, and she tried to feel sorry for him.

Brin noticed her presence first. From close behind her, he said, "You've been with the Lady," making her jump.

"Yes," she answered. She wished to confide very much in someone, but it would not be him. "Is the bishop all right?"

Brin's scarred face was blank, and his eyes were empty. He stared past her at Arumin. "He'll be fine." Even his voice sounded dull.

Shada looked at Arumin again. The bishop was unconscious, his face red.

"Fine?" she asked aloud.

Brin shrugged.

Shada peered at him curiously. Despite how intimate Brin was with Arumin, the sight of the fallen bishop seemed to spark no feeling in him whatsoever.

She cleared her throat. "Soon, I've got to go up the hill over there. Has Nor returned?"

"He just came back. They've put him somewhere." He made a dismissive gesture toward the forest of shell and bone.

Despite Brin's apparent apathy, his eyes never left Arumin. Wondering what kind of man he was, Shada left him there. She caught herself backing away, strangely reluctant to turn her back on him, then walked in the direction he had pointed. The others had yet to notice her, and she did not feel like being the center of attention.

She might not have found Nor in that maze if not for his grunts of pain. She followed the echo through the smooth opening of a shell and into its polished interior. He lay there alone, nursing multiple wounds, but he stood to meet her. He stammered something about how worried he had been, but she did not want to hear it. She placed a hand on him in a way that silenced him instantly.

"Enough of that," she said, and pulled their mouths together.

31

— · —

BRIN

WHEN THE GREAT BLAST of smoke from the pit felled Arumin, no one had dared to approach him at first, least of all Brin. Everyone waited until the smoke passed through the hole at the top of the skull and spent itself into the sky. Once in the clouds, too big to be seen all at once, the smoke departed with the swiftness of a city-sized sparrow.

Then the Ronians rushed to their fallen bishop. The blast had snapped his head back and rubbed his face raw. Only his cry of pain had assured them he still lived.

Under Staubel's direction, the men settled Arumin on the ground near the pit and placed a blanket over him. They crowded tightly around him—all except Brin.

As the others cried out in dismay and touched the bishop's head, trying to soothe him, Brin backed away. The sight of Arumin flimsy and helpless, the memory of what the bishop had almost done, made Brin almost physically ill.

There lay his protector. There lay the man he'd tried so hard, for so many years, to please.

He had tried to kill himself.

Brin imagined Arumin's face in front of him, those big puppy eyes so often filled with pitiful desire and need, and wanted to claw that face to pieces. He'd seen, now, how much the bishop really cared about him, how strong he really was.

Brin pictured that sad old face again and said to it, "You were going to leave me." *Going to leave.* He mouthed the words again and again.

When Shada appeared, Brin said enough words to make her vanish again. But their conversation echoed in his mind. *She was with the Lady.* She had a protector, the ultimate protector, and she was too dense to appreciate it.

Brin knew who he was. He survived. He'd thought he knew who the bishop was too. But in Arumin's nearly deadly fall, he had glimpsed a behavior so alien that he felt the pieces of the world they had built together shatter and rain down around him.

He was not the only one in shambles. Soon, the beasts began to go mad. They leaped and trotted in circles. Their dance had lost all its feral joy as they bumped into each other and exchanged shoves. The Ronians huddled to protect the bishop and themselves. Brin backed a little farther away.

Finally, one of the Ronians stood and shouted over the din, "Stop it, all of you!"

The beasts paid him no mind. He shoved the next one that passed, and the creature slapped him. It was an off-hand blow, not seemingly meant to hurt, but it threw the man backward, and he nearly tumbled into the pit.

Other soldiers rose in fury. They pulled the man to his feet and shouted at the beasts.

One voice pierced the rest. "No!" Hulgar roared, spreading his arms as if to contain his comrades' anger.

He stepped between them and the nearest beasts, but he could only watch one group at once. Behind him, one of the beasts responded to the Ronians' challenge in kind. He backed some distance away and squatted on all fours then leapt at Hulgar. None of the Ronians noticed him in time.

Something struck the beast down in midair. It was an-other beast, the small one that had befriended Hulgar. The two beasts landed on the ground side by side. The attacker, teeth bared, turned his fury on the youngster.

Brin watched it all with contemptuous disinterest. He couldn't believe he had tried to please these people, to please Arumin most of all. None of them were worth a damn.

From the sky came a voice of fury and elation. It was the Lady. Brin looked up, mouth open. The voice roared, consumed by triumph. Brin knew what he had to do.

32

THE LADY

THE CAVES AND TUNNELS of the island were numerous, and strays from the Lady's family were hidden in every part of it. She was large enough to fill the whole warren of tunnels. Each time her ever-swelling mass found another of her siblings while pouring through some crevasse, she smothered it, digested it, and grew a little more. Most did not bother to speak. Lacking her courage, they would not venture into the larger world, even then. Rather than fight or even beg, they waited for the end, sedentary.

In the bowels of the island, in a place deeper than she had known existed, she found a huddling mass of little ones. One of them spoke to her.

"Please don't!" It was the one they called the Boy.

The Lady halted her nearly ceaseless forward momentum to answer. "I want to."

"Huire will be angry with you," the Boy said. He turned and addressed someone who wasn't there. "Won't you?"

The Lady rumbled. "Do you think she speaks to you?"

"She does."

"Then why doesn't she speak to me?" So much rage lay behind the question that the Lady forgot to express it in her tone.

"Because you're wicked!" the boy cried. "She says so."

For an instant, the Lady was poised on a razor's edge of indecision. Could it be true?

Then she laughed, an unnatural gesture that gave her no satisfaction. "Why would she speak to you and not to me?"

She devoured the Boy and his friends without another thought.

When she finished searching the depths, she found a vertical shaft in the rock. It led upward to a fissure that crested the hill at the heart of the island. One person waited for her in that place, hidden from the rest of the island by peaks and ridges of giant bones. It was not whom she was expecting, and a tremor of disappointment ran through her.

"Lady," Father Brin said. He did not fall to his knees or genuflect, but his voice was awed nonetheless.

She wished to leave and saw no reason to bother with little men like him anymore. "What do you want?" she asked, giving her voice the growl of a giant wild dog.

He flinched but stepped closer. "To serve you, Lady."

She wished Shada had come instead. "Return to your master, and do his bidding."

"It's not right that he is my master. The order of things should be changed. He's been broken, I think, by all we have been through. He's of little use to anyone."

"And how do you differ?" she countered. "You exist not to be useful but to prove yourselves worthy. Huire needs none of you, and neither do I."

"Surely not. But might a human servant prove convenient? To work your will in ways that you wish to stay secret."

"Obedience to our will is your duty, not a special dispensation. You might as well say that you are a Ronian."

"Then there are few true Ronians left," Brin said. "I am one of them, and I can be your voice to the rest. If you will let me."

She laughed. "Your fellows think little of you."

The boy's face grew white, and he bared his teeth. "They aren't worth the skin on their bones. To a worthy master, my obedience is absolute. No one has seen yet what I am capable of."

The Lady heard and recognized Shada's footsteps from a good way off. She watched the girl appear through a narrow gap between fragments of bone. The boy did not hear her.

"What can you do for me?" the Lady asked Brin.

"I know that you're leaving—I want to come with you. I want to be by your side when you meet Huire." Then he noticed Shada and turned toward her.

The Lady replied, "I see no benefit to me in this."

"You need someone," Brin said. "You must, if you are taking her along."

Shada stared at him and said nothing.

The Lady was anxious to be gone. "I need one, and one only."

"You cannot trust her." He was looking into Shada's face, though his words were addressed to the Lady, and his accusation did not change the girl's mournful expression. He continued, "She has always doubted you. I know that she has. Am I wrong, girl?"

"You are not wrong," Shada said.

Brin whirled toward the Lady. "There you have it! Accept my service, and your worries are over. How could you refuse that for"—he sneered at Shada—"this two-faced bitch?"

"Father Brin," Shada said, "If you've got any wisdom left in your whole body, you will go back to the bishop."

The young priest's hands turned to fists. "You mean that bedraggled old thing swooning on the rocks back there?" A tear ran down his cheek. "I am fit for better things." He turned to look up at the Lady. "Aren't I?"

The exchange was bringing out a new feeling in the Lady. She recognized it as partly amusement, partly black joy. "If your current master is laid out and half dead, what kind of servant must you be?"

Brin took a shuddering breath as though trying and failing to accept her words.

"Please." He clasped his hands. His body drooped, and he fell onto one knee then, slowly, the other. "Please!" he yelled, a sound that began in his belly.

The Lady decided idly, the outcome making little difference to her. "I will grant you one chance."

The boy laughed and cried at once. "Yes."

Shada turned away from the sight of his face, one hand covering her mouth and cheeks.

The Lady continued, "You will remain here."

His face fell as he grunted in dense confusion.

"You will make yourself master of this company. You will rid it of everyone who lacks the faith or strength to do whatever must be done. Your bishop is one of them, of course."

"Kill them," said the boy dimly.

"I will return here, and when I do, it will be in the wake of the Goddess, basking in her glory. I want to form a company of zealots ready to remake the world. Huire may have room in her service for such as those."

Brin squinted as if looking into a great light. He nodded, though he scarcely seemed to understand.

The Lady went on. "She will know her true servants from the false. If you want a special place at her side with me, you must prove you can manage without your old nursemaid."

"I will." With a series of uncertain movements, Brin stood. He looked at Shada with pale hatred. "Though I cannot understand why you favor this one. I wonder if she'll be reluctant to leave, knowing what I'll be doing to some people she thinks highly of."

Shada looked through him and off somewhere else. "No. There are worse things than you, Father, no matter how much you wish otherwise."

Brin glared. "Something to think about, then. Until I take your place."

"Come, Shada," the Lady said.

The girl looked at Brin with pity that, for some reason, irritated the Lady. Then she cast a glance toward her distant friends. Finally, she walked toward the Lady, who opened herself to receive her. Shada stepped off the edge of the fissure and into a hidden world, the brightness of which shone on Brin's face.

Then the light disappeared. The Lady slithered out of the fissure like a serpent emerging to encompass the world. Her body was still pouring from the opening long after her face entered the clouds.

33

NOR

WHEN NOR WOKE TO find Shada gone, his first assumption should have been that she had simply wandered off somewhere, perhaps to find food.

But he gave little thought to that. The empty spot beside him resounded with finality. Their kisses had felt eternal in the best way. By the time they lay down together, he had wanted more than anything to look at her. She had seemed to want the same, and looking quietly into her eyes, he had lost track of time and finally, in unlikely relaxation, slept.

Now she was gone—not just for the moment but truly gone. The yawning pit that had opened in his belly would accept no other explanation. As he searched the encampment, winding his way through the ins and outs of ancient bones, the notion that she had vanished grew slowly and achingly from fear to knowledge.

The state of affairs on the island had changed since he arrived. At first, he had found chaos. The wolf-men who lived here were the same kind who had rescued him from the ice, but they were in a panic. Their whirlwind of aimless activity had reminded him of the dogs that their god had shaped them to resemble. Presently, they were lumbering around, morose but accepting of whatever had terrified them—perhaps the giant living storm cloud that had burst from their island.

Inside the skull, Arumin had revived and was sitting upright, his face cleaned and bandaged. Nor had felt no satisfaction on seeing the man's fallen form earlier. He would have feared the awakened bishop's wrath had Nor's feelings not been given over entirely to Shada.

Some soldiers had gathered around the bishop, while others stood in clusters. Most talked little while a few spoke unceasingly. A pall of fear hung over everything.

Doctor Staubel was standing alone. Nor pressed him for information and learned that the Lady had left again. Nobody had seen a sign of her for hours.

Shada was with her. That, Nor did not need to be told.

He understood why Shada had gone, but only the smallest, most sensible part of himself could accept it. She had wanted to spare the rest of them the Lady's wrath. But her disappearance had some additional cause—it must—and Nor could not shake the feeling that it involved him.

As Nor stood amid the Ronians, his heart raced, and his blood ran wild. The Goddess had been listening, just as Arumin and the Lady always said. She had heard the things Nor said about her, watched his loss of faith. And she was taking her revenge. He had come to think she was evil, and in an onslaught of foolishness, he had tried to convince Shada of that. Shada had not entirely believed him, but Huire had taken her away nonetheless—thanks to him.

He didn't know all that for certain, but the longer the story wreaked havoc in his mind, the more invincible it became. Then it took on a new shade: Cadmon had been wrong. The Goddess was real, and more dreadful yet, she was good. Not only had Nor wrongly doubted her, but by kissing Shada, he had broken his vow of chastity. Shada's disappearance was not vengeance but punishment, for him and Shada both. *But why, why couldn't I have been the one made to vanish from the world?*

He ran his hands over his chest and face. Noticing the others looking at him, he regained a hint of self-awareness and dropped his hands to his sides. He'd had his reasons for thinking of Huire as he did, and so had Shada. He had seen no way around them, and furthermore, none of them had changed. Huire could not be who the Temple thought she was—she could not be good. And, even more certainly, neither could the Lady.

"Brother Nor," Private Hulgar said, approaching from nearby. "A word?"

Hulgar probably wished to pray with him. Nothing would make Nor more miserable than praying to the Goddess right then. Still, he could hardly refuse the man in his distress, especially there in front of everyone.

Nodding, Nor said, "Over here." He led Hulgar out of the skull's mouth and down the nearest open path through the forest of bone. When they had gone far enough to speak privately, he stopped and turned. He found the massive soldier kneeling.

"Alongside me, please, Brother," Hulgar said.

He meant that they should kneel side by side to pray, touching their heads to the ground as one. Few flat, blank surfaces were available that might represent Huire for the purpose of prayer. Hulgar seemed to have simply chosen a direction to pray and bent his knees. Nor was of no mind to dispute him.

He knelt, but before he could begin, Hulgar bowed and touched the ground with his forehead. Nor followed, not much caring for proper form anymore.

As their foreheads rested close together, Hulgar whispered, "I have a message."

Nor's head swiveled to look at the soldier.

"It's very important," Hulgar said. "You must stop praying to the Goddess at once."

Nor's breath stopped, and he had to force out his next words. "Why is that?"

"Things aren't as you think."

Unwilling to lead another person to face Huire's vengeance, Nor replied, "However things are, we know that she is watching."

"No," Hulgar said with an authority many holy men would have found offensive. "Not Huire. Someone is, but not her. She's imaginary."

Nor would have shaken his head had it not been resting on the ground. Huire's existence, in some form, was a matter of historical record. Not even the leaders of the Shining Realm, who wanted humanity free of gods for all time, believed Huire was entirely dreamed up. "Who is watching, then?"

"The old gods," Hulgar breathed.

"Who?"

"I've known about them since Caidfell. They showed themselves to me, asking for blood."

"You haven't answered my question."

"Because I don't know who they are. But they have us by the throat—I'm sure of that. I've tried to keep them happy, but sacrificing a villain here and there isn't enough. And praying to Huire only makes them angry."

Nor found himself playing along with Hulgar's premise. "What do they want?"

"I told you. Blood."

Nor's heart pounded. A thought had occurred to him, and suddenly, the private's description of his "old gods" sounded terribly familiar. If Huire still existed, that made him wonder about the gods of his own people, the Newat. Nor had left them behind long before, believing himself to be under Huire's protection. But if Hulgar was right, such protection might not exist. And some of the Newat's gods were violent things, adoring warriors over all other people. They might have taken vengeance on him by abducting Shada. It was not beyond them. They might have been the ones whispering to Hulgar.

He suspected the Abbot Cadmon had been right: the gods, Huire included, were not creations of human love but soulless machines. But they were awesomely powerful nonetheless. His thoughts turned to the beast-men, with their fear and dread of the mad god under their island. Perhaps, out of everyone, they had the truest sense of how mortals ought to feel toward the otherworldly. At the bottom of everything, order might not exist at all.

"Hulgar," he asked, "are you planning on killing some-one?"

The soldier said, "The Realm will be along soon. We'll start with them and pray the gods will be satisfied."

"What if the Lady returns? She may wish to lead us somewhere." The notion seemed hopeless, but Nor was frightened by how far and wide Hulgar's mind was drift-ing and taking his own along with it.

"She won't. Look at the beasts if you don't believe me. They're getting ready to leave."

"How do you know that?"

"A few have gone already. As for the rest, it's obvious if you watch them. That god they had was their protector. It's why they stayed here, and without it, they'll move on."

Hulgar lifted his head from the ground and tipped upward to a kneeling position. Nor had forgotten the absurdity of their posture. He lifted himself to his knees with relief and a wave of dizziness.

The soldier frowned. His lower lip protruded, child-like. "There was one I was fond of. A sweet fellow. The runt of the litter, you might say. But he was the first to leave."

Nor tried to imagine the friendship that might have developed, in such a short time, between two men who lacked a single word in common.

Hulgar went on. "After the Lady left, he stopped us all from tearing each other apart. So the other beasts made him leave the island. Forever."

"What makes you think so?"

"He started a fight. He was heading off a bigger fight, but that's no matter. He and his mates, you see—the ones in the skull—are the warriors, chosen specially for it. But it's a hard way to go. They live like kings, get whatever they want—until the first time they draw blood. After that, they're dead or are treated as such. They go out into the cold."

Nor replied, "I met some of them out there, I think."

"That fellow I liked, he wouldn't look at me when he left. Wouldn't look at anyone or even make a sound. He just walked away."

"When I came to the island," the monk said, "there were beast-men in the water all around the beach."

"They're the ones I mean, the outcasts. That's them."

"They were piling things on the beach: shells, fish, creatures from the sea bottom. Then the beast-men on the island gathered those and carried them up onto the island."

Hulgar's eyes were glazed. "Offerings, you might say. This island is a holy place, you see. They can't have violence here or even the smell of it. But those warriors out there, the outcasts—they still defend the tribe. That's their lot. When the tribe leaves, I bet they will follow—from a distance."

34

ARUMIN

ARUMIN WAS ON HIS feet but still aching all over when one of the soldiers entered the skull at a run. It was Sergeant Feng. He burst into the midst of a group of men. After an exchange of frenzied words, the crowd approached the bishop, with Feng in the lead.

"Bishop," he cried, "the captain is still out there!"

Arumin stared until Feng continued, "I've seen something, Bishop. The beasts showed it to me. One made me follow him, and when we got to a ridge over the sea, he pointed. And there was a light out there. A fire!"

Others were gathering around. The group that had followed Feng was abuzz.

Arumin's gaze remained cold. After the noise died down a little, he asked, "And what do you think that means?"

Feng squinted as if questioning Arumin's wits. "It means the captain's alive, Bishop. Who else would be out there starting fires?"

"We know almost nothing about this place. It could be more of the beasts."

"Why would they have shown me that?"

"These are animals!" he snapped. He knew that was not true, but it felt good to say.

Looking thrown off balance, the sergeant replied, "We don't think so, Arumin. And we're going to look."

The bishop's eyes danced from face to face. "Is that so? You might have gone earlier, when Merin set out alone."

"Now, we've got to. This is proof, or as close as we're going to get. Something's got to be done."

"And what if it's the Shining Realm? They are coming for us. What if you find an army waiting for you?"

Feng looked down. "Something has to be done."

"When the Lady—"

"The Lady is acting all wrong," the sergeant interrupted with a hint of irritation. "We figure, maybe, she's turned against the Goddess. Who knows if she'll even come back?"

Arumin looked at him bitterly then at the sky, and he laughed. "Go, then. If you want to cast yourselves into the Dark, I will not stop you."

Sergeant Orund had gathered himself and climbed to his feet. Approaching them, he muttered, "It's not about the Dark, Bishop. It's about seeing sense."

Arumin eyed the bruises that warped Orund's features. "Are you anxious to see Emberly back, Sergeant? I hope he will let you live the next time he loses his mind."

Orund's eyes were desolate. "It's what the men want. The Lady is gone, and now, we need a purpose. That's all I know to do."

One of the beast-men had come to the edge of the crowd, which included most of the company. Someone saw what he was carrying and cried out in dismay. It was Private Merin, unconscious.

35

— · —

EMBERLY

THE SNOW HAD THICKENED, the wind had picked up, and Emberly had, some time before, lost sight of the island and all other landmarks. Marching over cracked ice and leaving deep boot prints, he could not imagine how he had evaded the beasts, but he hadn't caught a glimpse of one in some time. Perhaps they were biding their time. At his rate, he wouldn't last long.

By luck, he stumbled on what seemed to be the only other object in that great gray waste: a tower of rock that protruded from the ice and rose to the height of a large house. He nearly turned back when he saw the opening of a cave in the rock, but after a few moments of listening from outside and hearing nothing, he risked entering.

Someone, perhaps the beast-men, had been there recently. Near one wall was a pile of ashes and embers, and not far off was a small stack of driftwood. In a spasm of inspiration, Emberly plunged his hands into the ashes.

Feeling heat somewhere underneath, he gasped in excitement.

Digging more cautiously, he uncovered glowing coals. Sputtering with delight, he snatched up several pieces of wood.

He had an idea, though it might have been clever or idiotic. Out there, he felt so isolated from human life and reason that he could hardly judge properly.

Minutes later, he emerged from the cave with a smoldering brand in one hand and most of the driftwood under the same arm. That made the climb exceptionally difficult. The rock was steep and tapering, and he reached the top after about ten minutes of scrambling.

He feared he had escaped the beast-men at the cost of becoming permanently lost, himself, to everyone and everything. Soon, he would test that fear.

He had an idea of what direction he had come from—the same direction toward which the cave opened. On that side of the rock, on the highest and flattest surface he could find, he brushed away clinging snow and built his fire. The wind was blessedly low, but still, he used his body to shield his project from the elements.

The wood soon lit. He added most of his brands. The minuteness of the resulting fire, compared to all that nothing, tempted him to despair. He wondered if anyone would be able to see it from far off even if they were looking. He weighed whether to build the fire by adding the rest of the wood or to save the remaining brands to keep the flame alive. He chose to wait. The visibility of this fire versus that of a slightly larger one could not be much, and the longer he kept it going, the greater the odds that someone out there would look in his direction.

The wood was quite dry and burned bright with alarming speed. Helplessly, he surrendered piece after piece of driftwood until his hands were empty.

Far too quickly, the fire dwindled to embers. He sat near it with his hands out, warming them as best he could without blocking the fire from sight.

He watched it die, afraid to turn away because he knew what lay behind him: a gray wall made of millions of drifting snowflakes, opaque as stone. Imagining that anyone had spotted his short-lived spark of light seemed absurd.

He lost track of time, warming himself by the ashes. A gust of wind awoke him from a doze that might have been fatal. He clambered down the rock, slipping several times as his feet shuffled carelessly from hold to hold. Back on the ice, he found the mouth of the cave but did not enter. He turned to look at his surroundings and asked, "Are you still there, Rayan?"

The wind moaned. The drift ice there was cracked all over, leaving shifting chasms of water between broad floes.

"Don't tell me you really left," Emberly called. "I'll never believe that."

He waited a few more seconds as the snow turned his head and shoulders white.

His voice carried a hint of a whimper as he called, "Come out, you sneaky bastard!"

A man's shape moved to one side. Emberly whirled with a delighted gasp to see a bundle of white fur comprising a hat, jacket, and trousers. A pistol hovered under the reddened face of Private Robir.

"This is no surprise," the private said in a voice that quivered with hate.

36

— · —

EMBERLY

"WHAT?" EMBERLY ASKED IN a daze.

"It's no surprise that you're insane," Robir said. His teeth were bared, and his mouth twisted into a species of grin. "You thought you could hide it forever..."

Emberly's hands twitched, but he was unarmed. His limbs felt numb and slow.

Robir completed his thought suddenly. "Or until you were the last one standing."

As Emberly held still, the cold dug into him. His teeth chattered as he said, "Let's get on with your speech, then. You've got one, haven't you? About how I'm reckless, how I'm a glory hound. How I'm out of my mind."

Snow had coated the pistol and the hand that held it. Robir wiped the flakes away. "You wouldn't listen."

Emberly saw Robir very acutely, as if under a magnifying glass. With no other option but to die, he began talking. "You must have asked yourself: why is it that the Goddess chose Emberly instead of a worthier man?"

The private's face was bright with rage.

Emberly said, "You got a bullet in the chest on Gallobraith. Shot from your mount and left in the dust, while I get to tell the story of our ride at every holiday. Did the Goddess make the wrong choice?"

"I've prayed over you for so long," Robir said with a cough.

"And? What did Huire say?"

"That you're a plague on us. I asked her to give me the strength—"

"I am a great man," Emberly said. "I know it, and so do you. I am also terrible. You, meanwhile, are a small man. Most of your kind learn, but you don't. You continue to nip at my heels, a pitiful little thing who's got hold of a gun somehow. Are you going to shoot me?"

Robir drew a knife from his belt and tossed his pistol away into the snow. "I'm not that kind of man."

Emberly did not see where the weapon landed and thought it might have fallen through one of the gaping cracks in the ice.

Robir slipped his knife into a reverse grip. "Your time has finally come."

Emberly shook his head. "Then you know nothing of history."

Robir shed his coat and hat and marched toward Emberly. The man would've killed him straightaway had he not snatched an icicle hanging from the cave's entrance.

The shard of ice was flimsy in Emberly's hand, but Robir would see only its evil sharpness. Emberly met him with a grunt, thrusting the shard forward again and again. Robir stayed away from the gleaming tip, slashing when he got the chance.

The shard was the only thing keeping Emberly alive. When it snapped in his hand, a shroud fell over his mind. He tried to hide that it had broken. Robir, not fooled, began cutting him to ribbons.

Emberly needed all his willpower to not run for his life, which would end quickly if he turned his back then. He was nearly frozen, and his legs were growing stiff and slow. As the knife sliced his clothing and forearms again and again, the pain became general, with no particular location. Paralysis was taking his body and mind, protecting him from the suffering that lay ahead.

Finally, watching himself as if from outside, he ran. A gap in the ice a meter wide lay just ahead. The water in it bubbled from the openings in the sea floor beneath. He thought he could jump the gap, but he slipped just before he reached it. He struck the ground hard, sending a jolt through his bones.

Robir was too close behind him to stop in time. The private fell over the captain and landed on the edge of the gap. A deep, dark crack sounded as the ice they lay on broke away from the floe. The world tilted, and water swept up to meet them.

The sea was warm, and Emberly felt greater heat below. He flailed to stay afloat, trying to remember where he was. Robir came to the surface an arm's length from him, facing away. Emberly plowed toward him, arms spinning like a windmill. The captain thought he might stun the man and let him sink, but Robir leaned back, searching for something. *He's lost his knife!* Emberly collided with him. The captain wrapped his arms around Robir's neck and held on.

Robir's nails dug into his arms. The man's head pitched forward and back, striking Emberly's face. The captain's skull rattled, and his arms slipped. He saved himself again by managing to keep one around Robir's neck. He tried to lock that arm in a choking hold, but he could hardly see through the water burning his eyes.

He wound up punching with his free arm, landing just enough hits that Robir thrashed to be free. Then Emberly clasped his hands and locked his arm on the man's throat.

The thrashing went on and on. Emberly kicked his feet to keep his mouth above the water, but his legs felt stiff and dead. The two men sank together.

Emberly held on to Robir as long as he could, but he soon ran out of breath and pounded to the surface. He grabbed the nearest piece of ice, but it was too small. It sank as soon as he placed weight on it. He paddled to another, and that one held him. He pulled himself up and into the freezing air.

Shivering, he waited for Robir to surface. Seconds passed. Intent on the bubbling water, he jumped when it exploded in a massive splash.

He looked up to see two beast-men standing on the far side of the watery chasm. A third had just leapt into the water.

He ran, fell, and ran again, turning away from the cave. In seconds, he saw Robir's pistol and dived for it.

Rolling onto his back, he pointed the pistol at the beasts. "Stay away!"

They were not far behind but came on slowly, at a walk. Emberly didn't dare waste his bullet on a warning shot, so he screamed his order again.

They stopped. If the weapon caused them any great concern, their lupine faces did not show it. They turned upon hearing another splash. The beast that had jumped into the water had emerged. Robir, limp and apparently lifeless, hung in its arms. A series of yelps passed between that beast and its fellows. They looked at Emberly, who waved the pistol and shouted again, though no one knew what he was saying, not even himself.

Then the beasts left, stepping lightly over the gap in the ice and disappearing into the gray. They took Robir. The captain should have been appalled at the thought of one of his men, even a traitor, being devoured by animals, but he was mostly grateful that the beasts were gone. Robir was dead—he must have been—so he would feel nothing when they cooked him.

37

Emberly

Emberly's fingers and toes burned like fire. He felt rather calm about it, almost sleepy. He remembered walking firmly from the cave in a certain direction, but he couldn't say what direction it was. He could have followed his tracks, of course, but he didn't know what he would find there that he couldn't find here.

He obeyed almost everything inside him and lay down in the deepening snow. The falling flakes quickly formed a tickling layer on his face.

The hole formed by his collapse left walls of snow between which he could see the white sky. Looking toward the far edge of that small horizon, he snorted and said, "Of course."

Rayan did not dispute the inevitability of his arrival. He merely replied, "Well, here we are."

Emberly nodded. He searched for his usual anger and found it was missing. It had been transmuted to something else.

Rayan sat in the snow and leaned over, peering into the hole. The blood from his open facial wound dripped onto Emberly. "And here we'll stay, it seems."

"Where have you been?" Emberly's lip trembled. "Where is it that you go?"

"Nowhere."

"I banished you. You must have gone somewhere."

"I am nowhere if not with you."

Emberly felt a thin blanket of snow forming atop him. "Soon, I won't be here anymore. What then?"

Rayan's eyes were wide and severe. "I will move on. To whatever is next."

"Are you happy about it?"

Rayan shivered and looked about as though expecting an attack. "No."

Emberly's lips hurt. He realized he was smiling. "Is that why you push me to keep going? I am all you have."

Rayan wrapped his arms around himself. Once in a while, the cold seemed to reach him. He spat his words in visceral rejection of his brother's. "You need me."

"Not for long."

Rayan jumped to his feet. "Get up! Move, you bastard!"

Emberly laughed. "No." At the sound of the word, he laughed harder, inhaling the sting of icy air.

Rayan ground what remained of his teeth. "I knew you were a coward, but this is a new low."

"I am not afraid, not much. I took a vow."

"You think your Goddess will forgive your sins if you just lie here and die?"

"I don't know." Emberly felt a genuine warmth, a glow that did not lessen the pain but made it bearable. Soon thereafter, he said, "Those beasts wanted to help me. I should have known—I think I did know it. But I made my choice."

"So now you must freeze? I don't know how you can accept that. I can't."

"You must." Emberly smiled again, the ice on his lips crackling. "I stopped here because I've thought of something, and I need to understand it. You've got to also."

"What?"

"That I don't deserve to live. I am not worthy of it."

Rayan's face twisted as if to spit. "What self-pitying—"

"Stop that! We've only got a little time now. I am not worthy, and neither are you."

"You can't speak for me."

"No, but I'm still right. After all the things we've done, you can't say it?"

"I won't."

"Just once, for me. Please."

"For you, you bootlicker? You mercenary?"

"Please. This means more than…" Emberly couldn't think of a large enough word.

Rayan had ceased to snarl or grimace. His eyes were glassy. "What if it isn't true?"

"Then saying it won't make it true. But you've got to try it." Emberly barely finished his sentence as a coughing fit overtook him. He had no arguments left.

Rayan's mouth shaped unfamiliar words: "I am not worthy of it."

Emberly cleared his throat and echoed the words. Embracing his wretchedness, he felt the cold that filled him beginning to burn like a branding iron.

Rayan's grotesquely misshapen mouth smiled at the ease of it. "I am not worthy," he said again.

Seeing his brother smile turned the heat within Emberly into laughter. "I am not worth a damn!" he shouted.

He lost track of time after that. He found himself and his brother roaring with merriment, rolling and wrestling in the snow, chanting the truth over and over in wet, savage howls that reached the sky.

Eventually, Emberly ran out of breath and energy. He returned to his hole in the snow, and Rayan lay down against him. "Will I see you soon, brother?" Rayan asked.

"Sooner or later," Emberly said, entering what he hoped would be a sleep of eternal winter.

38

BRIN

MOST OF THE MEN left to search for Emberly. Brin's only immediate company inside the skull were Arumin, the unconscious Merin, and a few soldiers suffering from what the company called the "dream sickness." Some who came down with the mysterious ailment could push through the dreams and continue with their duties, while others were nearly comatose for a day or two. Most of the men had been through it already, and it had yet to recur in anyone.

Brin stood some distance apart from Arumin, who looked at him now and again, saying nothing, his eyes as wide as a puppy's. Something had changed in the bishop. He was no longer cold to Brin. That old need was in his eyes again—the need to please, to possess. Soon, Brin could take no more and left through the skull's mouth. He hiked to the island's rim, where he found the beasts in a state of heightened activity.

Sensing his intent, one of them picked him up and set him on the shoulders of another. Brin tried not to cry out as the beast swung out over the edge of the cliff and began to climb down, giving him a view of the narrow beach and the icy sea far below.

Since Brin made his promise to the Lady, all human contact had felt poisonous. What had seemed so attainable, so desirable in her presence took on the weight of impossibility once he reentered the world. He had no idea whether he would follow through with his end of the Lady's deal—whether his promise had even been sincere—or how he would go about it.

The bishop's pleading face pierced his thoughts once again, so he focused on something preferable: the terror of the precipitous descent to the beach. Words meant little. That much was obvious to anyone who walked through the world with their eyes open.

He could go back on his promise if he wished, he assured himself. It had been a precaution, nothing more, a way to stay on the Lady's good side. But he did not know what he would do if he saw her again and had failed to follow through.

That was what the little black vial was for. The Realm had used him as a backup plan, a last card to play if their own people failed to kill the gods. But nobody had said he had to use the vial for their purposes. If the Lady came back and meant him harm, he had a card of his own to play. It was an awesome thought, forcing a god to back down. That would tell him something about himself that none of the voices in his mind could erase.

When the beast dropped him off at the bottom of the cliff, he immediately regretted going there. The rocky beach was piled high with the remains of dead and dying marine life, and as he watched, more beasts arrived from under the ice to deliver new, reeking offerings.

His regret turned to shivering horror when other things came ashore. The sky was growing dark, but it was not yet dark enough to hide their shapes. They were the dragging, scuttling things from the village on-shore. More and more of them emerged from under the ice, shedding the water of their passage indifferently and lining the beach. Brin found himself alone but for them.

Some of them approached him. He backed toward the cliff wall, ready to run into one of the pitch-black tunnels to escape from the creatures.

Then the beast-men of the island descended the cliff like a landslide come to life. They landed all around Brin, facing the villagers with snarls and guarded stances. Torn between relief at their arrival and the dread of a likely battle, Brin edged farther toward one of the tunnels, figuring nothing in there could compare to this.

Then both groups turned, and he followed their gazes to a third party crossing the ice toward the island. He thought he might be dreaming. The newcomers moved in a line, torches fore and aft. As they came closer, he counted a couple dozen of them—a small number compared to the groups that awaited but enough to earn their rapt attention.

The group was the Ronians who had searched for the captain. A few of them were carrying a prone form between them.

They traveled slowly, finding gaps in the ice narrow enough to step or jump over. Somehow, they made their way to the island while getting little but their boots wet. As they carried the captain up the beach, the beasts and creatures parted and stood as though in vigil. When they reached the cliff face, they stumbled to a halt. Brin stepped past the beasts, moving closer to the abominations gathering by the water's edge, and called Emberly's name.

The Ronian soldiers let him pass, some grudgingly, until he faced the captain, who stood supported by two men. The sergeants, Orund and Feng, were both present. Seeing the color of Emberly's face, Brin could scarcely believe he was alive.

"Father," Emberly said, his teeth chattering.

"Captain," Brin replied. Seeing Emberly, one of the men he should be preparing to kill, filled his chest with warm relief. The ice and snow had nearly done the work of killing for him. And what of all the blood on the captain's arms and body?

Emberly turned his head with visible effort to look at the creatures lining the shore.

"They began arriving just before you did," Brin said.

"This must be everyone in their village," Emberly said.

"Why are they here?" Brin wondered aloud. The answer might be simple, but the monsters all around and the captain's return to life were occupying his mind.

The captain said, "I don't know. This island is the home of their tormentor."

"Was," Orund said, his bruised face inscrutable.

Emberly looked for an extra moment at the sergeant. If he had something more to say to the man, he kept it to himself. "Only one thing would drive them here—refuge from something even worse."

Sergeant Feng completed his thought. "The Shining Realm has come."

39

EMBERLY

EMBERLY COULD STAND ON his own, but clinging to one of the beasts while it ascended the cliff was still beyond him. Someone found a rope and made it into a harness, and the captain had the humbling experience of being tied to a beast-man's chest like a babe.

Once he was atop the cliff and free, his exhaustion overcame his pride, and he sat and waited for the others. Orund and one of the privates were the first to follow him, and they supported his shoulders for the long walk down the inner rim of the island to where a sort of megalithic boneyard filled the valley.

Despite the wonder of the scene, his weary attention drifted. Before he could prepare himself, they approached an enormous skull, outside of which Arumin faced him. Unsure what to expect from the meeting, Emberly almost froze when the old man gave him a careworn smile. If he was surprised by Emberly's arrival, he did not show it.

"Captain," he said. "Thanks to the Goddess for your safe return."

"Yes. I'm afraid I owe her a few words."

"There is no need. Your job is complete, Emberly, as is mine. The Lady has left us and gone to complete the final phase of her journey."

"She's gone?" The news moved him shockingly little. He accepted it like he was hearing of the latest misadventure of a troublesome relative.

"She took Shada with her. She needed us, and we fulfilled our vows. Now, she has left us with a final gift: our freedom."

That last part annoyed Emberly. "Freedom to die, perhaps. The Shining Realm will arrive soon."

"And in between, we have a few hours to spend as we will. When death comes, it will be on our terms. Will you die before the guns of the enemy? Or perhaps cast yourself from a cliff?"

Emberly's skin prickled as he wondered, more seriously than ever before, if the bishop was becoming unhinged. Not long before, the captain had been prepared to die, but since then, something in him had shifted. Perhaps his acceptance that he deserved death had, ironically, restored his will to give life one more try. The thought of passively accepting death at the Realm's hands revolted him.

"It need not be so. This island is a natural fortress, and if our hosts and the villagers fight alongside us, we'll be far more powerful than we were the last time we faced the Shining Realm." His mind was off and running, and he spoke quickly. "We need to gather food—I suppose it will have to be that rubbish the beast-men have piled on the beach—and water. They must have a drinking supply. There must be some way to speak to these men, at least a little bit. There may be tunnels that need to be guarded."

The men were crowding around. Hulgar was among them, though he had not been a member of the search party.

He said, "I've got something to show you. A gift."

He turned and walked away, and after a moment, the captain followed on unsteady feet. They passed the bladed towers of a rib cage and the round, high flare of what might have been a scapula. Behind him, Emberly heard footsteps. His men, almost all of them, were trailing behind them in a solemn parade. Those closest to Emberly held out their hands as though to catch Emberly if he fell.

Hulgar approached a rocky slope on the island's inner edge. There, a narrow cave opened. He stepped back to let Emberly enter first, which he did slowly, limbs tense. Once inside, he found the tunnel to be short. On a chipped-away shelf of rock to his right lay a figure, hauntingly white.

Lieutenant Roark had been wrapped with pitiless tightness in pale fabric that covered him head to toe. Only his face had been spared, and it was whiter than Emberly had believed a man's face could be. He looked like a doll, a skillful facsimile of himself.

For an instant, rage surged in the captain as he concluded that the beast-men were playing some trick on him. And if that was Roark's body, then they had abducted him in the first place.

But the lieutenant had been dead when they took him. Emberly could not have done his body any more honor. Perhaps he could have buried Roark under the rocks on the beach or left him to the villagers, but that was as close to burial in Ronia as the lieutenant could have hoped for.

Another notion followed. Roark had simply begun a transformation, one that had been his destiny since birth. Any day now, he would emerge with wings.

"The beasts took him to hide him, I think," Hulgar said from the cave's entrance. "Their gods show no mercy to the living or the dead, and the beasts felt he ought to be saved. Many of their own are bound up like this. They let no one fall into their gods' hands alive if they can help it."

Emberly took a step toward Roark and fell. His head landed on the lieutenant's chest, looking up at the dead man's face. Several people moved to help him, but he waved them off like a testy old man. Gathering himself, he rested there for a moment. He gazed over the landscape of Roark's face, all shrunken and diminished, and felt sleep overtaking him.

Rather than dozing off in that embarrassing position, he tried to stand. That time, he was not fool enough to refuse help. The shoulder that boosted him belonged to Dr. Staubel.

The young man, his beard grown fuller since the mutiny on Om, looked at Emberly without shame. "You're all torn up, sir. You need looking after."

The captain wondered, as he did periodically, how to feel about the men, including the doctor, who had betrayed him. The number had been too large to shoot or flog them, and the company's nonstop movement had given him little opportunity for any lesser discipline. He had taken Iwan then Orund as sacrificial lambs in place of the rest. Still, an imbalance remained, and perhaps it would exist until he meted out vengeance.

But he didn't know if it would end, even there. In the crowd stood Orund, scarcely recognizable yet terribly so, underneath the mass of bruises. Emberly could not tell, in the wreck of his own body, whether his knuckles still felt the pain of those blows.

Fewer Ronians were there than had ever been. Back in Ronia itself, an invasion was likely underway in which his people would fall like cut grass. He wondered if he would eventually be alone with beast-men and sentient crustaceans.

He stood straight and spoke to the group. "The Goddess does not look kindly on suicide. Whether her forgiveness of our sins would extend to such final defiance is not something I intend to find out. For those who agree with me, the Lady has left us two options: fight the Realm and die or be taken alive."

A shiver passed through them. A memory had struck the captain and perhaps the others: the sound of Private Carrowy's voice, lonesome and childlike in a box, held captive by the Realm. Emberly had chosen to leave him in that state and had killed Lieutenant Iwan when he defied the order. *I am not worthy.*

Over the next few hours, Emberly's hopes for reinforcements were largely dashed. The villagers, having assisted the visitors as much as they could or cared to, mostly departed, diving into the sea and vanishing under the ice in a direction away from the distant shore. Their thoughts on the disappearance of the god in the sky were unknowable. Perhaps they would find hints, somewhere, of a new direction.

Most of the beast-folk also slipped away under the ice. Those who stayed seemed to be the males that had dwelt within the massive skull. They watched their people vanish over the rim of the island then seemed to forget about them entirely.

Emberly had hoped to coordinate the defense of the island with those warriors, but after their people were gone, they left just as quickly, climbing the slope in the direction of the mainland. He pursued them on rubbery legs, calling out and feeling like a fool, to the top of the crest. There, he watched them climb nimbly down and dive into the water, heading toward the village on a course that would take them through the rock formations.

Momentarily at a loss, Emberly sent men to search the interior of the island for tunnels. If they found a tunnel, they were to step inside just far enough to see if it might lead underground. If these were accessible from the shoreline, the Ronians would be vulnerable to attacks from within their island fortress.

But Emberly did not have enough men to effectively guard more than a couple of tunnels. If the enemy found their way through them, the Ronians' best hope was that a few gunshots would warn them their defenses had been breached.

The final, blessed hours promised by the bishop were spent inspecting the beast-men's abandoned dwellings, which were concentrated on the slope atop which the Ronians would stand to defend the island. The Ronians' position at the top of the cliff gave them an immense advantage. If they wished, they could simply toss rocks down on the attackers' heads.

But a feeling of doom was hanging over everything, and Emberly didn't know why. Their position was impregnable, short of the Realm's soldiers finding their way through the probable labyrinth of tunnels beneath the island.

What about artillery? Emberly knew almost nothing about what heavy weapons the Realm possessed, but he hoped the visibility would force them to move their cannons close to the island. If they had only the village's flimsy boats for transportation, that would be difficult. Maybe they would dare try to roll their artillery over the ice. The captain wished he'd destroyed the remaining boats when the company left the village.

Over the hours of waiting, the reports he received made him sick to the stomach. The island was worm-eaten with tunnels, many leading deep into the interior and perhaps accessible from the shore. He placed a single guard at each of what he guessed were the enemy's most likely points of entry and posted a few more around the island's rim to watch their flanks. He concentrated the remainder on the crest facing the invisible mainland and the corridor of rock formations between. The attack would come from there, he hoped, up that narrow channel where the warm sea melted the ice. The Realmsmen would be disoriented and off-balance.

Then he heard beastly howling, men screaming, and the crackling of gunfire. As he stood on the crest, it all came from his left side, out in the opacity of the snow on the plain of ice. He had been wrong.

40

— · —

EMBERLY

EMBERLY STRAINED TO MAKE out details. From what he could tell, the Realm had disdained a choked approach from the water and dared a roundabout approach across the ice. There, the beast-men had found them and charged into their midst. Their surprise attack foiled, the Realmsmen set the frozen night aflame with a number of the same glowing lanterns they had used for illumination in Om.

A veritable army was revealed. The beast-men, clawing away among them, were so terribly exposed and outnumbered that Emberly felt an iceberg tumble over in his stomach. Some beasts disregarded the light and continued hewing paths of carnage through the enemies' ranks. Others ran for the cracks in the ice from which they had emerged, but many, many guns were trained on them. Most still escaped, but even they left trails of blood. Others fell under the bayonets piercing them from all around.

Another creature lay, struggling, near the front of the Realm's column—a great and glistening beast of the sea. Emberly recognized it as the mysterious leader of the villagers who had decided the Ronians' fate. Now he—she?—was tied to a litter by crisscrossing ropes against which he struggled in vain. Perhaps he had guided the Realm toward its goal against his will. Watching the grotesque scene, Emberly hoped the Realm would let the unfortunate being die with some dignity.

After the beast-men's attack, the Realm kept a few lanterns lit continuously, making their progress easy to follow from afar. The Ronians' ammunition had been stockpiled and distributed, and Emberly was helping the men gather rocks. Boulders were too big to move, but plenty of nearby stones were heavy enough to break arms, shoulders, and heads.

Night had decidedly fallen when Emberly cringed at a flash of light on the beach below. Someone or something flung a mass of sparks up at the Ronians. Burning continuously but not exploding, the crackling object landed on a rock outcropping nearby and clung there, an elastic mass that dangled from the cliff like, as one soldier said, "something from a giant's nose." Its top part was throwing too many sparks for anyone to touch it or dislodge it.

In the sparks' light, Emberly saw the missile's source: in the water below, a group of Realmsmen filled a boat from the village. They were paddling away for all their lives were worth.

"Get away from it!" someone shouted, and Emberly echoed the call, damning himself as a fool for not saying it first. The sparking thing could be a timed explosive.

Everyone scrambled for cover. Emberly's battered body moved surprisingly quickly with the proper incentive. From behind an overhang of rock, he waited and waited. Time passed strangely in battle, but surely, the sparking thing would have exploded by then if it had been meant to. He peeked out and saw its upper end was blackened and dead. The sparking had moved down toward the thing's lower, hanging end.

Soldiers were emerging from their hiding places. He did not know what caused him to scream, "Get down!"

He fell to his knees, ears covered, and in the same instant, the cliff's edge was annihilated. A series of explosions shook his eyes and teeth in their sockets, rattled the rock under him, and made his eardrums ache.

It was a salvo of artillery, probably coming from the mainland, its target marked by the sparking projectile. The explosions of shells spread along the cliff's edge in both directions. A few were close enough to send rocks large and small flying over Emberly's head.

If they could not hold the cliff, they could not resist the Realm's attack. They could only hope the barrage would end when the Realm's soldiers neared the island. Emberly needed to know how close they were.

Soldiers lay huddled on either side of him. One was dead, a rock embedded in his skull. The other could not understand Emberly even when he shouted. The bombardment drowned out everything. He decided to go himself.

He dashed out from his cover, moving along the crest toward where the army was approaching. From what he saw, his men were mostly intact, having put plenty of room between themselves and the barrage. Leaving the explosions behind, he dared to approach the cliff's edge.

The Realm's army had nearly arrived, moving faster than he would have believed. Only a few hundred men were coming, but that was more than enough to trample Emberly's three fractured squads in open combat. They hustled over the ice with a suicidal lack of caution, without regard for cracks or thin ice.

He decided he would gather his men and attack the Realmsmen from this spot. Then he noticed the Realm's foremost soldiers were firing their weapons straight ahead.

He found a solid-enough handhold and risked leaning out over the edge. Several of the beast-men had appeared at the opening of a tunnel, and they challenged the invaders with roars and lunges. Emberly's stomach clenched, knowing their massive bodies would be absorbing shots already.

Then the beast-men withdrew, disappearing into the cave. Emberly leaned farther and got a clearer view of the cave's opening. The Realm's officers halted their soldiers, clearly meaning to regroup before following the beasts.

They never got the chance. A massed roar, one that would have terrified the Dark itself, arose at the force's rear. A number of beast-men had slipped from the water in a surprise attack. The beasts were few, but their effect was massive. They struck the back of the Realm's column in a wave, cutting down or tearing apart man after man before falling themselves, one after another, each a pincushion full of blades and shot.

Many died as he watched, but the battle's momentum had passed to them as neatly as a shared bottle of ale. The Realmsmen panicked. Those nearest the attacking horde pressed into those closer to the island. The pressure increased with each stratum of men, forcing those in front to escape down the tunnel rather than being crushed against the cliff face.

Emberly fought down exhilaration at the sight and forced himself to face some hard truths. Unless as many beast-men were hidden in those tunnels as had been waiting outside, the Realmsmen would likely find their way to the surface within the island's caldera. Nobody could tell which tunnels they would emerge from, and Emberly's company would be unprepared and out-gunned.

Something snapped by his ear. A bit of rock lodged itself in his neck. Someone below had noticed him spectating and addressed a shot to him. He pulled himself out of view and crouched, digging the pebble out in annoyance. His shirt collar absorbed the trickle of blood. He remembered his aching weariness.

A spectacular silence washed over him, and he realized the artillery bombardment had ended.

He rose with a falter and jogged down the slope, calling to his men to retake their former positions. He sent some to aid the beast-men with shots from above. He called for Roark before remembering he was dead.

He met with his sergeants in the ruins of the colossal skull. Pleasingly few Ronians had been lost in the assault. Nearby lay Merin, presently awake with a terrible headache, and a few soldiers with nasty cases of the dream sickness.

Emberly drew a large rough circle in a patch of sand and a small mark at one point on its edge. "That's where we entered the island and where they just rained damnation on us." He made another mark on the curve near the first. "That is where a small army just entered the tunnel system on their way toward us." As soldiers murmured in alarm, Emberly made a few more marks, those inside the circle. "These are the tunnel entrances I know of. Where are the others? We need to know—now."

The men began adding marks of their own to the crude map, so many that the map soon ceased to be usable. Who could say how accurate anyone's recollection of a tunnel's location was, especially relative to all the others?

Finally, as yet another man rose to add his contribution, Feng stood and waved him away. "This isn't much use, sir, being honest. We don't know which of these connect to the main system, and even if we did, there aren't enough of us to guard them."

He was right. Emberly had hoped visualizing the problem would make a solution clear, but that was not to be.

"What do we do, sir?" someone asked.

Emberly's confusion and fear reached a deafening pitch. He looked around at them all and tried to move his mouth, wondering at what point an officer was allowed to say that a situation was simply beyond him. He didn't know what section and paragraph of the field manual covered that.

"Hold on," someone said. It was Merin, who was propped up, his reddened eyes piercing against his pale face. "Sir, listen."

Emberly glared. Then he realized that the private was literally asking him to listen to their surroundings. The other soldiers whispered until Emberly told them to shut up. He listened but heard nothing unexpected.

Then Nor gasped. "He's right, Emberly." He trotted to the pit in the floor and leaned one ear toward it. He swore with a wonderment that would have made his abbot box his ears. "Come here!"

Emberly pushed through the crowd gathered around the hole. Telling everyone again to keep quiet, he held his breath and strained to hear.

He did hear something—a din that, put all together, sounded not unlike the roar of the ocean in a seashell or the wind through a cave. But as he listened, the noise's components made themselves known. Once perceived, they could not be unheard or forgotten.

He heard ripping and clanging and screams like men were getting their first true glimpse of the Outer Dark. Only a few gunshots rang out.

With a quiver in his chest, he stepped back from the pit.

Feng said, "The beast-men have got them, sir."

"Perhaps." But Emberly felt that answer was wrong. Something about those screams and wails contained a touch of the inhuman or the no-longer-human. "Or something else." Returning to his scribbled, insignificant map, he felt one weight lifted from him and another replacing it.

He kept the men mostly at their previous posts, with the understanding that any call for help should be answered immediately. But though he forced himself to take the planning seriously, it still seemed perfunctory. He believed, as did the others who'd heard the sounds from the pit, that no one would be emerging from those tunnels.

41

— · —

ARUMIN

WEYLAN LAY IN BED, scarcely recognizable under his bandages, which covered his face, chest, and legs. Looking upon his younger self from many years later, Arumin wished he wasn't there. "I have no choice in this, I see," he said to the invisible being whom he sensed was with him.

He himself was invisible to the others in the room, which included his mangled childhood self, writhing in a nightmare, mouth open in a silent scream, and his mother, who opened the wooden door quickly when she entered and shut it even more quickly.

The Ronians had given him his own small room in what they called their field hospital. They knew his case was special and that he was worth keeping alive. They had asked him what had happened and gone through it with him over and over. After all, it could happen to someone else someday.

His mother stood over him for a moment, staring hard at him. His closed eyes were not covered by wrappings. She crossed her arms tightly as if to imprison herself. He wondered if she would cry.

Instead, she unwound her arms and placed a hand on an unbandaged piece of his shoulder. He came awake all at once, grunting, scrambling for escape.

She said, "You stop it now, boy."

A minute or two passed as Weylan calmed himself. She found a seat, and when both were ready, they met each other's eyes.

She asked, "Has your father been to see you?"

Weylan shook his head.

"Rhys?"

Shook it again.

A myriad of emotions whirled over her face, after which she sighed. "There are things you've got to understand. The Ronians killed a pair of boys the other night—just drunk boys who came too close to a patrol. It's the start of something big. There will be more fighting soon, and your brothers and father will be at the front of it. These are busy times."

Weylan turned to look at the ceiling. Across the years, Arumin could still feel his bitterness at her words.

"It was terrible, what happened to you," his mother admitted, "but imagine their perspective. Ever since, they've had to face the world, everyone knowing what you are. You've been here in bed, safe from it all. Rhys, it was, who guessed what was happening. That's why they followed you that night."

Weylan said nothing. Arumin remembered that, at that point, he had been morbidly curious about what she would say next.

It was this: "That wild thing you ran off with, he was not your friend. He was a cannibal, they say."

Weylan turned his face to the wall.

She continued, "Don't be so sure. How else could he survive so long out there, in the forest, on his own?"

Weylan finally opened his mouth. Watching, one could not tell if that mangled face would produce a sound or not. "He was going to sing for me."

His mother's face twisted. "I'm sure he was, at that."

"You don't understand."

"Dear, I don't want to."

Weylan began to cry, dry and silent. His mother shifted, trying to look away without being too obvious about it. She conceded to putting a hand on his.

Though Arumin knew saying anything would be hard, Weylan managed it again. "When you see them, tell them I'll never speak to them again."

The hand promptly withdrew. "They saved your life."

"I don't want it."

"There's a weakness in you. It's not just about that boy. It goes to your very center."

"If they fight, I hope the Ronians smash them."

She stood. "I don't know what I did wrong."

"You opened your legs for Father."

She swelled, seeming to restrain herself from violence. "You won't see me again, either. The gods know what you will do with yourself."

She left him there, twisting and gnashing his teeth like a monster newly born.

42

EMBERLY

THEY THOUGHT NO ONE would escape from the tunnels. They were almost entirely right. Emberly had taken a moment's break from checking on silent watch posts to lean against a wall and breathe deeply. Immediately, his eyes slipped closed, and his knees buckled. He hit the ground on all fours with painful fragments of bone under both hands. He grimaced in embarrassment at the sound of his cry, only to realize moments later that it wasn't actually his own. It had come from some distance away, inside the skull.

He stood and hurried to the noise, hearing others do the same.

A silhouette loomed at the edge of the pit. Only one man had been left on guard there because the pit's vertical walls made it an unlikely point of attack.

"What's the matter?" Emberly hissed at the figure.

It did not answer.

"I don't know, sir. It just appeared. I didn't hear it com-ing." That was the assigned guard, who had backed away from the pit, a man Emberly had not seen until right then.

"It?" Emberly asked. As others gathered around, he barked for quiet.

From the figure on the pit's rim came the bubbly spume of wet breathing. Still in shadow, it was hunched and mas-sive in the shoulders. It took a few ungainly steps forward.

"Hold your fire," Emberly said as the thing's shape be-came clearer. He feared that someone, unable to bear the sight, would fire without permission.

The figure moaned at them. It was a human voice, a familiar one—the sound of a man surprised but not en-tirely pleased to find himself still alive. Its arms, legs, and head were covered with spines like those of a sea urchin. It bent and dropped something large from its arms. This tumbled to the ground and let out another moan. It was a man—the first moan had been his as well. Despite the filth covering his prone body and the cuts and bruises on his face, Emberly knew him.

"Ganet," he murmured in wonder.

The general of the Shining Realm opened his eyes and flicked them about. "Why?" he whispered.

But his question would have to wait. As Emberly gazed at him, some brave soul with a torch stepped closer to the spiny figure. Since its burden was unloaded, spines that had been flattened against its body for Ganet's sake rose upright along its arms and shoulders. Only its face retained a patina of humanity. But that was enough.

Sergeant Orund stumbled forward. His voice brimmed with horror, pity, and other feelings too many to name. "Tabard!" he addressed the creature. "It's Tabard!" he said to everyone else.

As he approached, what had been Tabard hissed and struck at him. The spines on his hands were particularly long and frightful, and the sergeant was hard-pressed to bob away from what could have been a deadly blow. Tabard leapt backward to the pit's rim. From his mouth came a sound like air and water trapped together in a cave by the sea.

"Goddess," someone breathed.

Having delivered his package, Tabard seemed to waver between returning to the black and remaining for some unknown purpose. Not once did Emberly consider that the creature was still one of his company.

The man-thing hissed a final time, a sound almost contemplative, then dropped into the pit. Catching a handhold on the edge, he skittered downward and was lost to sight.

43

ARUMIN

THE CAVE WAS SMALL, scarcely worth being called such. Arumin was alone with Ganet and the body of Roark, Emberly's officer, which lay on a shelf dug into the wall. The weight of the pistol was unfamiliar in Arumin's hand, and he must have looked rather awkward holding it.

Afraid of what he might do if the general mocked him, he struck out verbally. "I look at you—what's left of you—and I wonder, 'Why should I not kill you now? What have you to offer?'"

Ganet had removed as much of his uniform as possible while remaining decently clothed. Bare chested and wiry, he sat cross-legged and leaned against the shelf that held Roark. A smile touched his lips. "I've just realized I may never have to answer an asinine question again."

Emberly entered with Brin on his heels. Shaking almost imperceptibly, the captain looked at Ganet. "There are fires out there," he announced, an edge of hysteria poorly hidden in his tone. "Your people have built fires around the landward side of the island. Tell me what is happening."

"I'm as surprised as you are," the general said. "The idea that they would risk themselves to rescue me rather than wait for her... And after what I've done..."

"You had reserves waiting onshore," Arumin muttered.

"Who is 'she'?" demanded the captain.

Ganet coughed. "Ren. You've met."

"Your advisor?" Arumin asked.

The general looked at him in mild amusement. "She is more than that. She represents one of the two hands of our people. She and her commandos—I believe you've met them as well—they're fanatics. Everyone like me is accompanied by one like her, who watches him. If he falters—especially in loyalty—that other will do whatever must be done."

Arumin considered the state of the Ronian company. After Tabard departed, a number of soldiers had wept at their comrade's transformation, and shock had settled on everyone. The thought of them attempting to defend the island from an assault was not encouraging.

He asked, "What are those things down there, and why did they let you live? Have you made some arrangement with them?"

Ganet laughed aloud. The sound was so genuine and jovial that Arumin felt less angry than he would have expected. "I didn't speak a word to them," the general said. "I don't think they can speak like we can. As for what they are, I saw only shadows. I assume they are the children of the god who dwelt here."

"That doesn't explain why they let you live."

The general raised a hand as if releasing the question to the wind.

"Tabard saved him," Emberly said, his eyes glistening. "Tabard knew we could use the general. There was enough of a man left in there—"

Arumin interrupted the coming monologue for all their sakes. "That leaves the question of what to do with the general."

"I can't think of a thing," Ganet said. "My wish is to die, but my duty is to return to the Realm to answer for my failures. I am surprised the soldiers on the ice wish to rescue me. None of them wanted to come, though they followed my orders. They knew I had left the Realm without permission. They could turn back before she arrives and claim to have been deceived. They might be forgiven."

"How many will Ren bring with her?" As the captain had fallen strangely silent, Arumin thought he ought to ask.

"A major expeditionary force," the general said softly. "I imagine she only delayed in pursuing me because assembling the force took a little time. In that army, there will be things none of you have ever seen." Despite his dread, he sounded almost proud. "Machines that fly."

Arumin breathed deep to stay calm. "What if your side and mine combined our forces? We would make—"

"There is no question of it. I am sorry, Bishop. This force will be large enough to make any fight fruitless."

To Arumin's surprise, Brin joined the conversation. "We may not need to fight. The Lady will return soon, and Huire—queen of all the gods—will come with her. None will be a match for them." He seemed taller, his shoulders back and his voice commanding. "General, you must talk to Ren and tell her this. Any resistance—anything but immediate surrender on her part—will lead to the wholesale slaughter of her army even if she kills all of us first."

Ganet shook his head in frustration. "My word would do little good. I am destined for awakening when I return home. Hell, she may start working on me here, in the field. Home is a long way off."

Brin pounded a fist on the wall. "You can't be resigned to that."

"What I feel, what I accept—none of it matters. What I've told you is the simple truth." He leaned forward and craned his neck, looking back at the corpse on the shelf. "All will be well for my wife and sons, I think. They will be assigned to another man. My sons will learn to call him Father... My wife will be his lover." He gave them all a wistful smile. "I can take some comfort from the fact that he will be slightly physiologically inferior to me."

Arumin could not let Brin's suggestion go unsupported. "To surrender is madness. We were brought here for a reason. This woman and her people are the enemies of Huire, and we must fight them whether we can win or not." He squatted before Ganet, though his knees ached. "Don't despair, General. Give your men an ultimatum: if they fight with us, they will die rather than be brainwashed. After all that we've done for her, the Goddess surely will not let us suffer the Realm's 'awakening.' This is our moment—the moment of reward."

Ganet looked at him wistfully. "Arumin, there was a time when I would have mocked the very idea of faith and you for possessing it. But I've since had... experiences. They've changed me. Still, I can tell you this: your Huire isn't listening."

Arumin opened his mouth to retort, but the words were absent. Brin's eyes were on him.

"I don't doubt that she's out there," the general said, "but to still believe she is listening is beneath your intelligence."

The bishop closed his eyes. "You've not seen the things I have seen."

"True. And I cannot claim no one is out there, listening. In fact..." As his words trailed off, he stared ahead, open mouthed. Then a light flashed in his eyes.

He sprang to his feet, leaving Arumin to fumble while raising his pistol. "By the void, I have an idea, an alternate proposal, Bishop. I don't want to undergo awakening, either. And I do not intend to." He whirled toward Brin, a new gleam in his eyes. "Here is my proposal: all of you will surrender to me."

"Ridiculous," the boy said.

"Is it?" He looked to Emberly, whose eyes kept wandering to the bound-up corpse of his friend. "Think of your company, Captain. How much ammunition remains? More importantly, how many have the will to fight, knowing how it all must end? Do you, Cyril Emberly, believe your Goddess will swoop to the rescue at the last moment? Or has her minion simply abandoned you on this lump of rock?"

The captain was obstinately, frighteningly silent. Ganet turned to the others. "Now that we've explored our other options, I have a bit of information that we can use. I know where you can find the next gateway, the one your Lady used to continue her journey. If you turn over your arms to me, my men and I will guide you there. If the Lady kept you in her company only to abandon you now, she must be nearing her destination. Rather than waiting here for the annihilation of our bodies or spirits, we should follow her! Huire may not be listening, but what if we can find her... or all the gods? Let's find them and throw ourselves at her mercy. If not, our best choice is to follow him." He pointed at Roark's face, white and bloodless. "And quickly. Have you enough bullets left for everyone? Or should we jump from the cliffs?"

There, Arumin found something to grasp. He said, "That may be your way, but we believe life may be taken only under strict circumstances. Perhaps you are a mere lump of skin, blood, and tendons, but we are not. Suicide is unacceptable." He pushed away memories of recently stepping off a cliff himself.

Emberly had remained silent and brooding, maybe listening, maybe not. He then said, "That's right. Which is why we will follow the Lady. She has betrayed us and kidnapped our friend. What if she turns on the other gods the way she turned on the pitiful thing that lived under this island? How large would she grow then?" His hand fell absently on the handle of his holstered pistol. "Since our choices are death or torment, we must follow the Lady and do what good we can—for Shada and for the sake of Huire and all the gods."

He drew his pistol and turned it handle-first toward Ganet. "That is why we will surrender to you, effective as soon as terms are reached."

Ganet's bright eyes met his. "As soon as terms are reached, I will accept."

Their words echoed in the stunned silence of the others.

Brin spoke first: "Captain, no!"

Arumin was more articulate: "I knew you could not be trusted, you madman."

Brin: "The men will think you're a traitor. And..." He left that unfinished.

Arumin: "Ganet, this man speaks only for himself. I must now speak for the rest of us, and I reject his offer utterly."

Grim faced, Emberly turned toward him. "You've had your chances to command. I return each time to find the company tearing itself apart. Stick to your prayers, Bishop, until I tell you otherwise."

"But..." Arumin stumbled again. "But Ganet is in the same trap as we are!"

"Yes," the general said, "but for a couple of things—for me, things can get no worse. Also, if the gods are truly planning to return to humanity, perhaps we should not resist them. If I befriend them before my people arrive, I believe I can persuade them to make me the leader of the Shining Realm. If that happens, I will withdraw our forces from Ronia, which they have assuredly already conquered. And don't forget—only I know the location of the gateway."

"You are wrong there," Emberly said. "I know it as well. A few miles off, atop an island higher than this one. Our astronomer, Merin, has finally put his telescope to good use."

Arumin looked at the captain with something deadlier than exasperation. Not moving his eyes, he asked Ganet, "Why should you wish to lead the Shining Realm? I thought your people had grown 'beyond' the need for leaders."

"We have tried," the general said. "And it is true that we have none—certainly none that you would recognize as human... or divine. But I have begun to see things in a more old-fashioned way. Please take my sharing this as a show of goodwill, for I might be killed by my own men if they overheard it."

"So you lie now too," Emberly said. "We primitives seem to be rubbing off on you."

Ganet opened his mouth, but no retort emerged. Then he nodded sadly. "Terms?"

"You must give us back our weapons when we ask for them."

Ganet laughed, but not in ridicule.

Emberly ignored him. "We're going from danger into worse danger. A time will come when you'll need us to be armed."

"Anything else?"

"Humane treatment, of course."

Ganet extended a hand, and Emberly grasped it. Arumin could not have said whom he loathed more.

Brin found his voice. "The men won't accept it, Captain."

Emberly said, "I'm willing to take that chance. Do you really think that after all they've been through, they are anxious to throw their lives away? What they want is a purpose, and this is it."

"Fine," Arumin said in a hushed voice. "That's fine. The Goddess hasn't answered a prayer of mine since we left Ronia. Why would she start now?"

"It's a test, Bishop," Brin said in a tone that matched his master's. "That's what you've always said."

Arumin looked at him and said, "Darling, I think I may be failing."

Brin let the silence draw on for a moment then replied, "Then I must be the one to carry her banner."

44

— · —

ROBIR

ROBIR AWOKE IN A place totally unlike the afterlife he had imagined. Wooden beams and thatch appeared overhead, and when he turned his neck to look around, daggers of pain stopped him.

The pain made itself known in his lungs and in waves throughout his body. Over the course of what felt like a lifetime, he turned onto one side. He recognized that he was inside one of the huts in the village onshore. He could not see the door.

Something moved behind him, but he made no motion to see what it was. He lay in a cot, and turning without falling off involved a complicated set of maneuvers. He could hardly credit the fact that he was alive. He did not think that someone would hurt him after having rescued him and placed him in a bed.

"Private Robir, I presume?" The voice from behind him was a woman's, one he recognized.

"Ren?"

"That doesn't matter a bit. You will, please, listen to me carefully."

The air fled Robir's lungs. *Goddess, I wish Emberly had killed me.* "What could you say that I would want to hear?" he asked. "We both know what will happen now." Pins and needles washed over him, and he fought the panic that crept up after them.

"I'm afraid you're wrong there, sir."

"Whatever you did to Carrowy, you'll do it to me too." His breath and heart quickened.

"Carrowy has his uses, and you have yours. Yours will be better served otherwise."

"I'll be no one's tool. You will pay for your crimes." He had no grounds to say these things and no hope of making them true, but he felt duty bound to say them.

"Crimes? What is a crime, exactly, and who decides? Surely not your neglectful Goddess."

"I've seen her miracles myself. Her power dwarfs even yours." He finally began turning to face her, but she said, "Do not move," and he stopped rather gratefully.

"Her power does not matter if she leaves you and your friends to your fates. Like you left your old friends, the prisoners from Caidfell."

"They were convicts. A place like Om was their natural home."

"I've been speaking with them," she said, "and I have learned things. When you learn them, you will not only serve me, you will do so eagerly."

He took a deep, shuddering breath. "May the Goddess guide me."

"I'm glad you have not refused to hear me. But I must ask: has Huire guided you well thus far? Has her patronage benefitted you? We found you freezing and nearly drowned, in the hands of savages. Tell me, has she ever so much as spoken a word to you?"

Robir buried part of his face in the pillow. He did not want to talk about this anymore.

"If only you could see the world we are building," she said. "If only you had the vision. It is happening in Ronia right now."

He kicked and spat. "Be damned," he said. "Say what you have to say so that I can laugh."

45

EMBERLY

THE MEN RECEIVED THE news of the company's surrender much as Emberly had imagined. Most were silent.
Some groaned. Someone dared to let out a cheer. A couple
tossed down their guns in frustration. Underneath it all
was relief. The captain let the minor outbursts go unan-
swered as the will of the company was on his side.

As the soldiers gathered their weapons to hand them
over to the Realmsmen, a sadness set in. Still recovering
from the cold, Emberly nonetheless kept things moving
single-handedly, not allowing the men to backslide toward
rebellion. When the time came to descend the cliff, someone mustered a length of rope that was long enough, and
they used it to lower their weapons in bundles to sea level.
They hauled up several Realmsmen to hold them under
guard.

Ganet looked into the distance and shifted uncomfortably. He must have suspected that Ren's forces were close.

Finally, a roar became audible in the distance. Emberly had not heard its like since the company left Om.

"We've got to hurry!" the general shouted.

The breathless fear in his voice and eyes moved everyone with a new urgency. The Ronians rappelled down the cliff one by one, a process of agonizing slowness even at top speed. As the noise grew closer, a skirmish broke out among Ganet's men on the ice. More than a few turned and ran toward the sound, shouting and waving. Some of their comrades opened fire on them, but those were then stopped and wrestled down by others, who were loyal to Ganet but would not suffer their own to be killed.

In the confusion, the Ronians were left to hurry down the cliff. They quickly decided the rope could not be trusted to hold two men at once, so they continued one at a time.

Then a Realmsman atop the cliff cried out and raised his weapon. From down the slope, one of the beast-men was approaching. He was bent and limping, his fur reddened with fresh blood and black with clotting. He had apparently emerged from a nearby tunnel.

"I've got it," the Realmsman said, taking aim.

But several Ronians, Hulgar foremost, stepped between the beast-man and the rifle. "Leave him alone," Hulgar said. "You've shot him up enough."

"Step away," the Realmsman said.

"If you shoot me," the giant soldier said, "I'll bet I'll still toss you over that cliff before I die."

"Stand down," Ganet said, and the confused Realmsman obeyed.

The beast-man stepped through the crowd to the cliff's edge and gestured with his huge hands.

"He wants to help," Nor said. Since the announcement of the surrender, the monk had been quiet.

"He looks like he's got one foot through death's door," the captain admitted.

"He knows what he's doing," Nor insisted.

Someone volunteered to ride on the beast-man's back. The monk was right. The beast-man was clearly in pain, but he more than doubled the speed of the company's descent. Soon, everyone was assembled at the bottom.

The Ronians, surrounded and at gunpoint, stood in a tight group.

"Where did the beast go?" Emberly asked, looking around. "I would have asked him to follow us. He at least deserves Staubel's attention after what he's done."

"I don't know," Nor said. "I suppose he's had enough of visitors."

"He's about to have heaps more."

Emberly then spotted a rounded lump out on the ice, the ground around it widely stained red. It was the leader of the villagers, killed when his use was spent, and by the very men now holding them at gunpoint. Emberly had grown less confident in his choice to surrender than when he'd made it, and he had been less confident than he looked. It had simply been the only thing to do.

"I hope he escapes," Nor said.

"We'll be lucky to escape, ourselves!" Ganet shouted. "Double-quick!"

The three miles between them and the final hill passed in a blur. The sea was all frozen there. They kicked through the snow, those behind trying not to slip on the flattened powder. A twisted ankle could mean abandonment to a life of exotic torment.

The roaring sound approached quickly. Coming from the cloud-covered sky, it seemed to circle above them and fade again behind. But something much louder replaced it.

Ganet cried a foreign phrase, his voice terrified, then shouted something everyone understood: "Run!"

After a final sprint, they reached the ice-locked isle as the noise in the air screamed overhead and circled away. The isle was a steep round hill with a path leading up to the top.

There stood a gateway filled with strange, bright colors. A large bundle lay at the foot of the path.

As the first men reached it, some distance ahead, Emberly cried, "Be careful! It may be explosive."

Nor was just behind Emberly. Weariness had slowed them to a jog, and Nor gathered the breath to say, "I would've gone... by myself... if you hadn't. But thank you... for going."

"To find Shada? Don't thank me yet," the captain managed.

"You want to save her... right?"

The roar in the sky grew louder again.

Emberly nodded. "Only if she... isn't past help."

Nor looked at him sharply. "The Lady forced her to go. Surely, you believe..."

A commotion had arisen as men gathered around the bundle. Struck by a dark premonition, Emberly felt his face harden. "Of course I do."

Then the beast in the sky was upon them. It appeared beneath the clouds, a winged thing like a gleaming metal dragon. An awful rattle came from it, and a storm of bullets tore the ice and the shoreline to pieces. An entire Ronian army in battle would have fired fewer bullets. The line of impacts raced up the snowy beach toward the company. Stunned, the captain realized he could see the vehicle's driver, whose goggles, cap, and shoulders poked from the body of the beast.

Men dove from the bullets and fired back. Some Realmsmen tossed weapons to Ronians, but all their shots glanced impotently off the beast's metal hull. From a crouch, Emberly thought he saw the driver of the vehicle jerk and sag in his seat. He'd been shot.

The path of the flying beast twisted as it neared the hill. It collided with the hillside head-on.

The explosion shook them all. Then the men leaped to their feet, captors and captives, sending up a cheer that might have awakened that whole dying world.

But the group sobered quickly. The roar of more vehicles was approaching from air and sea. Their victory over the flying beast had been mostly luck, the sort of luck they might not have again soon.

Not only that, but soldiers of both armies had gathered again around the bundle by the hill. The crowd was eerily silent.

"Move!" the general screamed.

The men around the bundle turned slowly. As Emberly approached, Hulgar stepped out of the crowd and put a hand on Emberly's shoulder, stopping him.

Then he punched Emberly in the stomach.

Emberly folded, unable to do otherwise. He felt like a steel girder had struck him. He curled up on the ground, wondering why but unable to ask. Through a cloud of sickness, he saw his soldiers' boots all around. None offered to help. Emberly mouthed the word "what," but only a wheeze emerged.

Someone spoke down at him. "Never trust an officer."

"So it was you all along," Hulgar said. "The Traitor of Caidfell." He turned Emberly onto his back with a kick.

He looked at the sky and a circle of dark faces. "The...?" he gasped.

"Always knew those prisoners couldn't've escaped alone," one of the older men said. "They had help."

"And it was this swine here." Those words came from another voice on the ground.

Emberly turned his head, blinking. The bundle on the ground was Private Robir, bound with ropes and covered to keep him from freezing. He was very much alive, sitting up as others untied him. His loathing eyes were fixed on Emberly.

He said, "I heard it straight from that witch of the Realm."

One of the circle of faces was Arumin's. "I always knew... something," the bishop said. "I knew there was something wrong with you. Perhaps Huire was trying to tell me, and I failed to listen."

"When I think of all the boys you got killed…" This was Sergeant Orund. "And you came back, carrying their letters home like some kind of hero."

Robir spoke again. "We all know what would've happened in Ronia if this came out. He'd've stood before a firing squad. Well, this is the closest we have here." He snatched a gun from someone.

As they talked, Emberly rolled over. A coughing fit took him. Blood hung in a strand from his mouth. He could not have said what was bleeding. Everything was numb.

"Look here," Nor said, pushing through the crowd. "They returned Robir for a reason. They want us to kill Emberly. If we do that, it's the first step toward falling apart."

"What do you care, monk, beyond your own agendas?" Orund asked. "We're already broken."

"There is no time for this!" Ganet cried. He shoved past Nor to stand over Emberly. "Not here! We've got to hurry!" His voice broke off on a high, incredulous note.

Emberly flopped onto his back and wiped his mouth. "Help," he said to the general. It was pathetic, and he did not care. "Help me."

Ganet looked at him strangely. "I am your enemy, Captain." To the others, he said, "If you're going to do it, do it right now. Otherwise, bring him along."

"I say we bring him," Hulgar replied. "We can get our licks in later, whoever wants a turn. Blowing his brains out now is too easy."

If anyone disagreed with Hulgar, no one cared to stand up to him. They bound Emberly with the same bloody ropes that had held Robir and dragged him up the hill like a captured slave.

Ahead, soldiers passed through the gateway into a place that glowed pink and orange, like they were running into a sunrise. Ganet waited on the threshold until everyone else had entered. As Emberly passed him, the general turned back for a moment and looked toward where they'd come from.

"We've got to hurry," Ganet said, looking sick. "By the void, we've got to hurry."

PART 2

INTERLUDE

HE HEARD HER LAUGHTER from far away. So she knew it too.

His failure was entire. He had not stopped the invaders. They had come, and they were at his gates. They had grown in number, their factions combining, so their dreams were flinging his mind around like a whirlwind, attacking him like a barrage of fists.

There remained defenses, of course, three stages of them, that would operate without his supervision. But since the company was there and the probability of Huire's release into the worlds of humanity had moved from nil to remote, he found "remote" was not small enough for his comfort.

He ransacked the dreams that came to him. With them came a few of their owners' present thoughts. Fear such as he had not felt in numerous human lifetimes turned the tiny organisms that comprised his body into clouds of frenzied activity. Nothing, nothing was left but one thing: to go out and stop them by his own hand.

46

BRIN

BRIN STOOD IN THE forest, so far out that no one could see or find him. The trees were mostly thin and scrubby, yet now and then, he saw the shadows of true giants.

Even there, the works of man reached him. A solitary stone well rose before him, its bucket and rope tossed aside and its opening covered by wooden doors.

He spoke to the sky. "I know you're here. I've no idea what you are, but I've felt you trying to push your way in."

It did not answer, but he knew it was listening. "You've found to your cost that you cannot force me to share anything I don't want to."

He nodded toward the well. "It's all terribly clever. This hole is full of my memories, is that it? Long neglected, you assume. Together, we will dredge them up and sift through them. Well, they are anything but neglected."

Then he shouted at the sky. "I drown in them!"

Sensing that he was heard whether he yelled or whispered, he calmed himself, though his veins still ran with venom. "I trudge through them each day as they suck me down."

Another thought struck him. "Perhaps you think the well is dry, that I've forced out what I don't wish to remember. Well, I can promise you it is deep. It is also toxic, and to touch its water would poison you."

He held up the vial that hung on his neck. "I'm like no one you've met before. I know a few of your thoughts too. They weren't so hard to find—I just picked your pocket. You know what this is, and thanks to you, I finally know it too. Unless you want me to open it, you had better help our company reach its destination. As for what I will do with it afterward, I make no promises."

He clasped the vial between his hands as if in prayer. "Go ahead: come and face us. But instead of stopping us, you will serve us."

47

EMBERLY

Captain Emberly awoke to the taste of blood.

It had been his companion since Private Robir revealed him as the traitor who had started the prisoner revolt on Caidfell. All the men around him, his former soldiers, knew he had gotten numerous Ronians killed and begun a series of stunning, blunting defeats for the Ronian Empire—defeats that never seemed to end.

Upon passing through the last gateway, the company and its captors from the Shining Realm had found themselves on a path of black, shiny stone as wide as a man's height and, impossibly, only slightly thicker than a piece of parchment. It led through a world of mist and clouds that glowed with pink, purple, and orange as though catching an unseen source of light.

The mist sometimes became so thick that walking forward was frightening. At other times, it opened onto vistas of cloud, bands and clusters bigger than anything the captain had ever seen. It was odd how one did not truly understand size until one saw it demonstrated. The air was breathable, and the path was not held up by any visible support. A truth hung over everyone but remained unspoken so far: not even the humans of the old world could have built such a place. Not even the gods could disobey natural laws of weight and motion. Thus, nobody knew whose doorstep they were treading on.

Such thoughts gave Emberly instants of respite. He was tied by the hands and led by a rope by the giant Private Hulgar, who jerked him to the ground at unpredictable intervals. The members of his company, whom he had commanded since the war on Gallobraith, had adopted a practice that they called "taking turns" on him. They would stop without warning, and one man would have a chance to batter Emberly in any way he saw fit. They would have just a moment until the rage of General Ganet, the Realmsman whose larger force held them captive, forced them to lift Emberly to his feet and continue marching.

Those moments were enough. Emberly was vomiting, limping, and spitting out teeth. His face would never be the same. Still, he credited the men's widespread enjoyment of this practice with delaying his execution. He also had Brother Nor to thank. Though the monk and the captain shared a mutual dislike, Nor sometimes intervened in the assaults, even risking his life by pulling away men who might have murdered the captain on the spot.

Nor and the young Father Brin were among the few who seemed to have no desire to harm Emberly. Perhaps that was because they weren't soldiers. Bishop Arumin had contented himself with a single slap across the face, to cheers from the men. The ordinarily passive Private Merin had started with a similar blow but worked himself into a freewheeling attack, arms spinning and clawing. He roared with fire in his eyes as the men laughed and Nor dragged him away. Except for such interventions, the monk kept his eyes anywhere but on the captain. Brin gazed at Emberly coldly, the scars on his face underlining his indeterminate eyes.

They all might be killed soon if the Shining Realm had its way. The gateway that led to that bizarre place was large enough to permit the Realm to fit its flying machines through, though the path was too narrow for its motorized carriages. So far, Emberly had heard no sign of pursuit. He wondered what was causing the delay.

One oddity that everyone in the company admitted to seeing was the fleeting silhouettes of buildings beneath them. These appeared and often vanished as quickly as one could spot them: great domes and jagged spires, their bottoms invisible or nonexistent.

"What the hell are they?" Arumin asked upon the appearance of a tower that seemed unusually stable and likely to linger for a while.

"We will never know," Ganet said, "and I couldn't care less."

"Now, hold on," Hulgar said, mischief in his voice. "Our Lady and her servant girl might be in one of those. I think we should send someone to investigate."

He kicked Emberly's legs out from under him, letting the captain fall to his knees and tip over the edge. Fortunately, the private held on tight, and Emberly did not fall far. When he reached the rope's limit, the yank was agony, but his arms were not pulled from their sockets. Still, icy fear shot through him and emerged as short, wheezing gasps.

Hulgar roared with laughter. "Don't you worry, I've got you," he said. "I'm going to let you down onto that tower."

The structure was right beneath the captain. He passed through a band of pink fumes on the way there, and when he emerged, the tower was gone. As from the bridge, the cloudy void appeared bottomless. He found his voice, which featured an ugly whistle because of a missing tooth. "There's nothing here!"

"I can see that," Hulgar said. "Perhaps we'll be quicker next time."

"Next time?" Ganet shouted. "There will be no time! Don't you realize—"

He stopped midsentence. Once his voice dissipated, everyone could hear it—a distant roar.

"No. Please." Ganet looked toward the gate from which they had come, now invisibly distant in the fog. Emberly had never heard him so openly panicked. "How did they find room to lift off?"

He whirled, searching for orders to give. "Enough games! Pull him up now!"

"Why don't I drop him?" Hulgar asked.

"Whatever you do, do it now!"

"Hold on!" Nor said. "Don't kill him yet!"

"What's he worth to you, monk?" That was Sergeant Orund.

Nor paused. "I haven't had a go at him yet."

Several men laughed. "You expect us to believe that," Orund said, "after the way you've babied him?"

"Pull him up. I'll show you."

After a moment's silence, Hulgar said, "Pull him yourself." Then he dropped the rope, and Emberly fell.

Nor must have caught the rope quickly, but the captain's arms were again nearly wrenched from his shoulders.

Even when the monk caught the rope, he struggled to control it, and the captain continued to descend. As Nor howled, Emberly knew his palms must be aflame.

Those who were still laughing—and there weren't many—reached new heights of ecstatic amusement. "You must really want a beating yourself, monk," Orund said. "How about I send you down there with him?"

"No!" Ganet's voice was savage. "Move your carcasses now, or I'll shoot you all!"

The roar grew louder and came more clearly from above and behind them. In the airy distance, a great many boots pounded away. But Emberly did not fall. "Nor?" he called.

"I'm here," snapped the monk.

"Can you pull me up?"

"That's the plan."

Emberly rose slowly, in jerks, as the noise of the flying machine grew closer. Then he saw something that made him forget all else. Out in the mist towered another building, one close enough to startle him when he saw it. Its face was filled with ornately formed windows, and in the closest one, he saw *her*.

His wife looked back at him with a quizzical smile, as though she did not know him but wished to. Her face was lit by the rainbow hues of the clouds, casting her in an alien glow but rendering her more beautiful than he had ever seen her. He was struck dumb. He felt that to address her would be a violation somehow—of what, he did not know.

She seemed to remember something, and her face became a beacon of lovely sadness. She cast him one final glance—covertly, as though she should not—then walked away into shadow as he, numb and wet eyed, continued his lurching ascent to the path. He decided to tell no one about that meeting with whomever it was. To put the encounter into words would reveal it to be obviously a simple dream, a comfort offered by a mind stretched to the breaking point. He did not think he could bear that.

The path was still well out of his reach when the flyer emerged from the clouds. Coming straight down the path from the gateway, it sent down a hail of bullets. The shots did not seem to damage the path in the slightest, but they would soon cut the monk right in half.

"Nor!" Emberly shouted as though the other man needed the warning.

The clatter of bullets reached them, and he braced to plunge into the clouds. Instead, he saw Nor dive from the opposite side of the path, the rope around his waist. The monk swung inward, and the two men nearly collided at the ends of their ropes.

The flying machine moved on, but beneath its fading rumble, Emberly heard another flyer cough to life in the direction of the gateway.

With his hands bound, Emberly could be no help in regaining the path. Nor began to climb, gritting his teeth at the effort. Blood trickled down the rope from where his hands met the rough twine. Emberly rose also as Nor gathered more of the rope. Finally, they reached the path, and Emberly braced his knees against its bottom so that Nor could heave himself up. Then the monk hauled the captain upward, and both lay catching their breath.

Between them lay the rope that had saved their lives. The flyer's shots had nicked it. What remained had been unraveling, and it would soon have snapped. Nor did not see fit to comment on it, and neither did Emberly.

"You should see yourself," Nor said. "You look worse than Orund did after you had a go at him."

The memory stabbed painfully at Emberly. He blinked and shook his head. As they disentangled themselves, the sound of more gunfire came from ahead: the steady rattle of the flyer's weapon and the scattered shots of the Ronians and Realmsmen. Then the flyer's roar came their direction.

Emberly realized they might die where they stood and considered throwing himself from the path toward the phantom building where he had glimpsed Charlotte, to try once more to be with her. But the flyer's sound soared overhead without the craft ever coming into sight. It was heading toward the gateway, where—from the sound of it—more of its fellows were taking flight.

Then the captain heard something even more chilling. From the gateway came the double-time marching of a vast number of feet and the barking of orders.

"This path's straight as an arrow," he said. He was developing a technique for talking through only one side of his mouth, to prevent the awful whistling from his broken teeth. "If they come within rifle range of the company, they can hardly miss."

The monk nodded. "And there will be a lot more of them."

"So." As the captain thought, he started a limping jog down the path toward the Ronian company as Nor kept pace without much effort. The movement hurt, but pain had become the wallpaper of the captain's mind. He said, "We've got to avoid a fight until we find some advantage."

In the distance, past clumps and ribbons of fog, a wall of clouds came into view. It was like a stormy sky turned sideways, a vertical surface extending up, down, as far as they could see in all directions. The path intersected with that wall and disappeared within it. Near the cloud stood the combined forces of Ronia and Ganet's fugitive Realms-men. Some had fallen in the flyer's attack, and others were helping them as they could. None of them seemed in a hurry to enter the cloud.

Nor and Emberly trotted forward at the captain's top speed. Nor called out to the company across the fathoms, "Hurry! They're right behind us!"

Ganet replied, but Emberly could not hear the words over his own footfalls and heavy breathing. The company advanced to the edge of the cloud, and Nor and Emberly caught up a few minutes later. The two men had stepped over several bodies on the way. Two had been Ronians—one's face had been buried in his arms, and the other's had been shot so badly he was unrecognizable.

The cloud wall was looming around them like the very end of space and time. Awed, Emberly realized they might be seeing only a small portion of the barrier.

For the past several hours, speaking up had brought him only beatings. Still, he dared open his mouth again. "Well, there's only one thing for it. We've got to go in."

"Is that so?" Sergeant Orund asked. "Tell me what's lurking in there. Seems to me that sending men in there would be feeding them to a monster."

Looking at the wall again, Emberly perceived clearly what Orund meant. Something was in there, and nobody could deny it. It made no noise, stirred up no disruptions in the cloud, and could not be seen or touched. But there it was nonetheless, circling invisibly like a leviathan.

Ganet, roused from a state of overwhelmed silence, said, "You've got no choice, in case you've forgotten. No matter what's in there, we can't delay any longer."

Emberly intervened, hoping to prevent a violent confrontation. "If we stay, Orund, we're done for sure. We'll all be killed or taken by the Realm."

Orund stood firm. "I'd rather die fighting than be swallowed like a mouse by a cat."

"But you *won't* die fighting," Ganet shot back. The reverie that had taken him was falling away. "You'll die right now, by the guns of my men, without a chance in the world to resist."

The sergeant's eyes moved from Ganet to Emberly and back. He had no options left, yet his mind was working.

"I propose a test," he said at last, his face as pale as the cloud. "Let's send Emberly in first. If we hear screaming, we'll know we were right to be worried." A few half-hearted chuckles followed.

"Fine," Emberly said without a qualm. His preference was the opposite of Orund's. Regardless of what was in the cloud, he preferred it to his present situation. "You'll hear from me shortly."

He took a step in the direction of the cloud and stumbled. The running had taken a toll, and his legs had turned to jelly. His knees took the brunt of the fall, and he could not contain a groan.

Brother Nor took up his shoulder and helped him stand. Then the monk advanced with him toward the mist.

Emberly looked at him. "You don't have to go in there with me."

Nor did not return his gaze. "Is it true?" the monk asked. "What they say about the prison planet?"

"That I am a traitor? Yes."

Nor swallowed. His next words seemed to require effort. "You're no traitor. Not in any way that matters. You did what needed to be done."

"Many died. Many." Away from the mob, Emberly found a greater sense of his own feelings. His voice cracked. "Soldiers, like me."

"Your soldiers stole everything my people had. Stole the blood from their veins." Nor paused. "You were bound to do what you did. All things are settled by war if you wait long enough. Peacemakers, diplomats... They only delay war so their children must fight it. You took it all on yourself, even the guilt. You have my respect." He smiled. "Though I doubt it means much."

"You are wrong... about all of it," Emberly said. "That cannot be all there is."

"One of us must be wrong." Nor looked toward the cloud. As its first ribbons drew around them, noises from outside were muffled, and those of their own feet stood out in every detail. Its depths were opaque. "Maybe we will find out today."

They stopped, but Emberly knew there was no point in delaying. "Ready, monk?"

"I'm no monk anymore. Ready, Ronian?"

They strode ahead. Before Emberly knew it, they were engulfed in the cloud. At any instant, they might meet that titanic *something* whose presence they'd sensed. He felt tension in every muscle, a suspense so acute that it made him nauseous.

As they walked, the sounds of battle erupted in the world outside. He recognized the rifles of his own men, the answering rattle of the Realm's guns, and the hum and rumble of the flyers. None of that seemed to mean much. Emberly's previous self, that of a minute or so before, might have turned and run back to be with his men. To this new self, their troubles seemed a million miles away.

There it was—the thing they had sensed waiting. It stared at him with the patience of a snake, paralyzing him with its eyes, then it struck. Its fangs made no wounds on his person but still stabbed, agonizingly, to the core of him. He felt himself being drained. The crystalline man whom he'd seen in his dreams had done something similar. But this contained no hint of gentleness. It was not even cruel. It was simply necessary, and perhaps the thing found it satisfying.

Emberly's mind was soon empty. A voice and face asked him what was wrong then became less familiar until words were an unknown thing and he did not know what a face was or how to distinguish it from the other colors before his eyes.

But even at his lowest ebb, a point of energy remained that was him, himself, whatever that was. That point could not be extinguished, though it was bereft of everything, even a name.

Then all else that comprised him came rushing back. The fangs, having drained him and tasted all that he was, then spat him back into himself. He let his body drop, for that did not matter, though someone caught him and eased his fall. The fangs pulled away, leaving a bubbling froth in the holes they'd punctured.

He looked around and knew the face of Nor.

"It will get you too," Emberly said.

"What will?"

"You didn't see it?"

Nor looked dumbfounded.

"It doesn't matter. No." Emberly spoke to both Nor and himself. He whispered as though they might conspire against the thing, "It knows we're here."

48

—·—

ARUMIN

ARUMIN HAD NO CHANCE to hear the fates of Nor and Emberly. As they disappeared into the fog, the buzzing of a swarm of the Realm's flying machines grew in the distance. Then the company's grief began in earnest.

He saw it first. Far above their heads, so distant that it looked like a speck, a moving shape like a flicker of flame had appeared on the surface of the cloud wall. His heart lurched as he realized it was growing, approaching them so quickly that the Realm's flyers seemed like strollers in a garden in comparison.

Before he could call out, someone else yelled a warning. Another shape was speeding toward them from below the level of the path. That one looked like a tangle of electricity, an animate lightning storm. It wheeled and crawled, shooting out bolts like tendrils and seeming to grasp the cloud as it hurtled forward.

Soldiers scrambled and drew their weapons. The Ronians were closer to the cloud than the Realmsmen, putting them in greater danger.

"Look out above!" Arumin called, praying to his estranged Goddess that someone would know what to do.

The sight of the flame, which undulated like a gigantic caterpillar, redoubled the chaos. Some guns pointed up, others down. Together, Feng and Ganet restored a semblance of order. Only seconds remained before the things came within shooting range—assuming that shooting would do a damned thing to stop them. In that time, the Realmsmen returned the Ronians' weapons and ammunition in a frenzied handing about. The leaders agreed that the former would aim at the beast of lightning while the latter shot at the beast of fire.

No one mentioned that they had no idea how such things could be fought, let alone killed. Then the beasts were upon them, and the point was driven home.

The fire beast had a face like a lion and a serpentine body. It reared up from the cloud wall, stretching along the path, and howled fire toward the Ronians. They ran, shoving in among the Realmsmen or diving toward the cloud. The bishop felt his face burn. The column of flame engulfed one Ronian, who plummeted through the clouds, a charred ruin.

The lightning beast arrived seconds later. With nothing constant enough to serve as a face and electric limbs that flashed in and out of existence, it struck multiple places at once with bolts of electricity. Several Realmsmen were baked where they stood. They either collapsed or remained standing, skeletal monuments to the folly of coming to that place. Arumin thought he could feel the electric charges running under his boots. He wished Nor was there.

The fire beast whipped its upright body down among the Ronians. The men were prepared that time and scattered before it struck. Still, the heat radiating from the being made Arumin feel like he was standing on the sill of a house-sized oven. He turned toward the cloud wall and fell dizzily to his knees.

The company had fired numerous shots at the beasts, to no effect. The bishop realized they must run or die. The armies' brief partnership needed to end. Through the chaos, he made eye contact with Feng.

"Into the cloud!" he hooted without a trace of heroism. Feng nodded and began shoving the men in that direction as the lightning beast cut down more of the Realmsmen.

The bishop ran in front, Brin at his side. The fire beast slammed its great head onto the path before them. In the withering heat, the bishop saw its eye, sparks within rings of flame, and saw evil there. It did not only mean to kill them. First, they would be its playthings.

Hypnotized by the promise of that eye, Arumin did not hear the roar of engines until it grew deafening. He turned just as a fleet of the Shining Realm's flying machines burst from the fog.

The size of the armada staggered him. He had no idea how they had taken to the air in such numbers. They descended toward the scene, opening fire on the beasts. The Realmsmen cheered and waved their hats. Ronians hunched to the ground.

The beasts lashed out at the flyers, stretching to fantastic lengths and sizes. The fire beast's head collided with the first oncoming craft, sending it smoking and spiraling down to vanish in the cloud wall. The lightning beast struck multiple flying machines at once, leaving their hulls blackened and engines silent, the pilots blackened statues. Those flyers dropped from the sky into the abyss below the path. Their comrades pelted back at the beasts with every bullet at their disposal.

Arumin froze, dazzled by the spectacular vision of all-out war in the sky, fought using weapons he had never heard of until that day. One brave pilot tried to slice the head off the fire beast with the wing of his flyer. The severed head dissipated but immediately reformed while the pilot found his wing in burnt tatters.

In the midst of everything, the Ronians found themselves ignored. Feng and Brin pulled the bishop along as they led the company's dash into the cloud wall, leaving the Realmsmen behind.

Arumin dove into the cloud, which hung, as thick as soup, on the path. While the sounds of battle grew muffled and distant, he heard his own heartbeat in his ear. "Nor?" he called tentatively. He wondered what they had sensed circling in there, waiting. He knelt painfully, knees popping like gunshots, and touched the cool, smooth stone of the path, which had grown wider.

He turned to address Feng, only to find the sergeant unconscious on the ground. Many of the other soldiers were sprawled around him. Those still on their feet were staring fixedly upward and collapsed one by one. A few only fell to their knees, still staring.

Then the bishop looked up and saw it. The thing seized him, took all he had, and returned it in great disordered piles. When it finished, he collapsed. From the ground, he looked around at the fallen men, his ruined expedition. Then a great mouth opened underneath them all and swallowed them.

49

— · —

SHADA

IMPRISONED INSIDE THE LADY, Shada witnessed the Ronians' approach from far above. The Lady had allowed her a window from which to watch events unfold. Soldiers of the Realm were with them, and she puzzled over whether the Ronians were captives or the Realm's unlikely allies. She could not imagine the latter, and the Realmsmen far outnumbered the Ronians, so she could only assume the worst.

"They're prisoners," she told the Lady. Since they had parted ways with the company several hours before, Shada had dwelt in a small pocket of air within the Lady, who no longer bothered with rhapsodical illusions of libraries. The Lady had spoken of many things, even asking about Shada's past, in which she'd never shown an interest. Shada had begun answering the questions despite herself—until the elemental monsters who guarded the wall of mist delayed their progress. She wondered if the Lady had expected to slip through unnoticed.

As the Lady had darted about, trying to outmaneuver the monstrous guardians, Shada learned the wall was a sphere, one so vast that it looked flat unless seen from far away. Once, the Lady had retreated so far that Shada could just perceive the curve in the wall's horizon. There, the atmosphere had grown almost too thin to breathe.

Finally, the monsters had spread apart to protect a larger area from the Lady's infiltration. Perhaps their focus on the Lady was what let the Ronians get so close.

Now, the guardians, sensing the imminent invasion of the cloud, raced toward the tiny path where the human company stood. That path was the only way Shada had seen to access the cloud on foot. It had no structural support and should have collapsed under its own weight. She wondered who could have created it, not to mention the cloud itself.

Despite the sphere's size, gravity did not pull Shada or the men toward it, so it could not have the mass that scholars attributed to planets. The breathable air gathered around the sphere and the path seemed to defy the laws of nature.

The Lady's only response to her comment was, "There is an opportunity here."

They hurtled toward the cloud wall, approaching the surface so quickly that Shada screamed. But it offered no resistance, and they passed through to the other side in a matter of seconds.

Those seconds were the longest of Shada's life.

She did not think of them until they were over. First, she sensed that she had narrowly missed something, or rather, something had missed capturing her. She was an invisibly small creature afloat at sea who had, by luck, dodged the maw of an unseen predator.

At the very end of this feeling, like an aftertaste, came a point in time that made her gasp. Only afterward did she realize what it was—the most crushing despair and horror she had ever known. She could never have imagined such a feeling—she could never have shared it in words. She could only say to the Lady, "Did you feel that?"

"What are you talking about? The time has come for silence."

Shada obeyed. The Lady's immunity to whatever had touched Shada had let them barrel defiantly through the cloud. That alone, perhaps, had saved Shada's sanity. Exhausted by the experience, Shada surprised herself by yawning. Despite the wonders currently surrounding her, she did something long overdue and fell asleep. Dozing let her escape a new despair: her hope of ever seeing Nor or the others again.

50

—·—

ARUMIN

ARUMIN KNEW WHAT THE dim light reflected from the tunnel's curving walls portended. It terrified him, but he could not help walking toward it. He could not control his body at all. The miners had never reached that little artery of the cavern. The torch in his hand was fading, and his chest pounded as he watched shadows creep in.

He was in no dream. Everything was clear, and time's passage was whole and continuous.

He drew closer to the glow in the tunnel. Dram had run ahead, laughing, but his teasing calls had ceased soon after. Knowing what was about to happen, Arumin's mind twisted and fought in a rush of panic that availed him nothing. He cried out, but his mouth did not move. He had watched himself walk that tunnel many times in dreams, but he had always woken himself before the horror began. This time, he was really there, and he would receive no such mercy.

When he reached the lighted chamber, he saw the cold illumination came from above, through a narrow shaft in the rock dug for some abandoned mining project. Emboldened by the light, Weylan stepped forward. Behind his eyes, Arumin screamed and screamed.

As he approached the patch of light, it revealed something lying across the path. It showed him exactly what he had feared, the heart of his darkest imaginings.

Dram lay there. Just minutes before, he had given Weylan a kiss that left him swaying and painfully excited. Then Dram had raced down there, giggling and promising more to come. Before they parted, he had said with an air of confession that he had written Weylan a song. After several minutes of following the older boy's flirtatious calls, Weylan heard something else, a scuffle. He had avoided thinking about it until right then. After the scuffle had been a high note cut silent—a scream. Both were so quick and distant that he might have imagined them.

He had not. His torch's light warmed the room, its colors and contents: the crimson of blood, Dram's frozen scream, the pallor of his spilled innards. His throat and belly had been chewed away.

As Arumin raged at the bars of his prison, Weylan looked at his friend dreamily. This could not be, so it simply wasn't.

Weylan's lip trembled as he took another step forward, and the scene became harder to deny. Venomous agony seized his ankle, and he looked down. A pair of hooked pincers had pierced his flesh, and their owner—a meter-plus-long creature resembling a centipede—was eating his skin and muscle with an assortment of flicking mouth parts. Weylan kicked at it in horror, hoping to wake from this nightmare, but the eyeless albino creature set its spiderlong multitude of legs in place and twisted its head, bringing him to the ground. His torch rolled off somewhere, revealing a tunnel and wall alive with winding carapaces and so many legs, all of which surged toward him when he fell. He tried to spring up, but another pair of curved daggers wrenched his other leg, and he flopped down impotently.

Unlike Dram, he managed to scream, a long mewl of weeping disbelief. As they climbed on him, biting and chewing, his mind fled, and a face came into his memory, that of a man he'd seen dragged from a fire in the village. The poor devil, his body burned beyond use, had breathed fast and heavy, eyes skyward as though wondering *Why?*

Weylan understood then. He did not know how long they had been eating him. He turned his head to see one of them greedily devouring his shoulder. Then, inevitably, one found his face. Perhaps it heard the noises of his mouth. Perhaps it would find his throat.

That did it. He screamed long and loud, punching and kicking with everything left to him. At least, that was what he thought he was doing. When he turned his eyes downward, he saw they still had him pinned in the same place. Piling atop one another, they reached his stomach and dug in. Beyond that, one advanced on his genitals.

His suffering drew on and on. Panic came in waves that ebbed toward acceptance. But each time he looked up, the thing was still scuttling toward his penis, and horror wracked him again.

He had no memory of previous moments and could hardly recollect that he was seeing the same images over and over. He existed in a hell of terror-driven hope that withered, each time, to despair.

A slight alteration in the cycle appeared when he re-membered Dram bursting into the pub to drag Wey-lan from that forced, humiliating musical performance. Their love was meant to be, and if it could not be there, perhaps it could be elsewhere.

He began to relax from the fight. The body had ways of releasing one from pain, and he grew numb. He won-dered if the creatures had some venom at work on him.

He looked down again, which was his mistake. The tangle of whip-thin legs and segmented bodies, the thing about to devour his manhood, were all too much. Back into panic he flew, yanking his arms and legs and widening his wounds. He kept that up until, slowly, the images of Dram returned, and he thought about leaving to join his lover in a perfect place.

He accepted what was happening, and his breathing slowed. Then he forgot, looked down, and panicked all over again. But each time, the panic became briefer. In time, he gained the self-possession to stop looking. Though tremors of fear still broke into his heart, and though the pain never went away, he sank ever deeper into visions of the next life. He also imagined what this life might have been, which made him sad, but not too sad, really, because he had done little himself to ruin it. He and Dram had been called to the otherworld, both of them together, and the beings that would meet them there were green and wise.

Finally, that world was all he thought of.

Then his brothers arrived, with torches and guns, and massacred the creatures that would have taken him home.

51

NOR

NOR STOOD ON A long, tongue-shaped outcropping over a pit. The surrounding land, if it existed, was made invisible by vapors and smoke from below.

He knew where he was, having heard stories about it since childhood. He knew what he would find when he ventured to the edge and looked over, and he dared to look only because he had already surrendered hope.

The stink from the pit was so strong that it almost drove him back from the edge. The hole was immeasurable. It was big enough to hold entire planets, yet he could glimpse the opposite rim through the rising vapor. Despite its depth and the vapor, he could see all the way to the bottom.

Down there was the worst thing in the world: a sea of refuse and corpses, people from throughout time who had been buried after death instead of burned and sent into the sky. They floated lifeless in the bubbling shit and bile of everything that had ever lived.

Writhing about in that brew was the worm. It was the largest thing he had ever seen, somehow larger than the pit itself. It feasted on whatever it found in the filth, though it was always hungry for whatever prize might fall from above. It sensed Nor and wanted him. It reared up, its round mouth dilating wildly, and roared, a weak and plaintive sound that belied its might. The widening maw contained no teeth; the worm was all softness, digesting its meals whole.

This was the gate of hell. When he stepped from the ledge, the worm would catch him in its mouth, and folds of inner flesh would squeeze him into the first of its stomachs, where acid would wash over him. When that was all over, it would excrete him to spread slowly among the soils of all worlds. Each particle of him would be dimly aware of its fate but unable to think on its own, doomed to spread ever farther until all that remained was an aching sadness for his true home—riding with his ancestors and heroes in their endless wars in the sky.

He reeled from the edge. He would stand on this cliff forever. *What have I done to deserve this? When was I a coward or a loafer or a—*

"A traitor," he said in the heavy air.

That was it, he realized with growing horror and misery. Long before, he had run from his people and abandoned his gods to join with the Ronian invaders. He had made a long gamble, with his soul on the line, all for a goddess who had offered him comfort. The same goddess had sent a shirking messenger to lead her people halfway across the universe to their deaths.

He might have stayed and fought the invaders, becoming a leader in his own right—might have undone the damage caused by his parents, miserable addicts and traitors themselves. Instead, he had followed Cadmon—that skulking old liar—and become a servant of the very people he hated.

He deserved this fall and all that would come afterward. He had been blind to it, but that was no excuse. His mind and heart were gifts, and he'd let them rot. Private Hulgar, of all people, had tried to warn him, but Nor had treated his words as a curiosity rather than prophecy. He had lost his long gamble, and worse, it had been a mistake from the beginning.

He took another step back from the precipice. Jumping was so hard—impossible, even.

From behind him came another roar, this one much nearer. He whirled to see a crawling, hobbling thing of prodigious size, a rotting tree that lay on its side. Its bottom pointed toward him, and in the center of its splayed forest of roots was a face, broad, knobbly, and gleeful. Its roots and leafless branches stretched and pulled, dragging it toward him along the outcropping.

If he waited, it might push him over the edge. But he would not face his final judgment as a coward. He would jump.

First, he sat on the edge and prepared to push himself off, but the position felt pathetic. He was taking the easy route again.

So he did the impossible. He only managed it by not thinking. He walked up to the tree, before its mouth and dung-filled breath. Dirt from its roots rained on him.

Looking into its widely set eyes one at a time, he said, "Follow me... if you dare."

He ran and jumped from the cliff, having added nothing to his many regrets.

52

—·—

NOR

WHEN NOR AWOKE ON a broad stretch of stone, he rolled onto his back and wondered if he was about to die. His heart galloped faster and faster. He breathed in ragged gasps. Terror shot through him, promising to drag him back into that place, whatever it had been. He could not accept it as simply a dream.

The captain lay by his side, unconscious. They were alone on a path wider than the one they had left, and the cloud wall still towered over them. He wondered if they were on the other side of it.

He touched his face and realized his fingers were filthy and smelled of excrement. When he sat on the edge of the pit, he had put his hands on the ground. His lungs gasped for air. He closed his eyes and forced himself to breathe slowly—a method he'd learned at the hated Temple. Over several minutes and through repeated waves of terror, he slowed his heart. Only then could he take stock of the situation.

His waking up on the path must mean he had been spared from the maw of the worm. If his encounter at the pit had not been an illusion, he did not know what it was. He looked at Emberly, who was still motionless, and saw fresh blood spattered on the man's face and chest.

Nor sat up, and as he did so, the cloud wall surged toward him. He scrambled back onto his hands and feet, but the fog swallowed him nonetheless. It quickly withdrew, leaving behind the rest of the Ronian company. Some of them stirred or sat up quickly, the bishop among them. Others were comatose like Emberly. A few were absent altogether. They now totaled about two dozen men.

On their skin and clothing were cuts, scrapes, and burns—signs of a battle. Some of them covered their eyes and cried while others looked around with expressions ranging from joy to haunted emptiness. Arumin was on his feet already, Brin still waking up beside him. The bishop shouted in a voice that sounded like it had already spent itself screaming: "To order, quick! Ganet's men will be right behind us."

At that, the more alert men jumped up. Their weapons were still in their hands or lying nearby, and they formed a line facing the cloud as Nor and Arumin hurried around, jostling the others awake. Most came around and stood clumsily, while others sat whimpering with their knees against their chests.

Merin lay flat on his back, eyes open and a slack expression on his face, every muscle relaxed. Nor took the man by his shoulders and shook him gently then harder, then he shouted at him. Nothing pierced that veil. Merin was still breathing, so Nor dragged him back from the battle line and left him. One spot was as safe as the next.

He did the same with everyone unwilling or unable to move, including Emberly. Then he took a moment to study the path beyond that spot. Just past where he had placed the disabled men, it narrowed to the same width he remembered from the other side of the clouds. Next, he noticed gateways along both sides of it, like a hallway of doors that stretched into the distance. Through the thin visible slices of those openings were places light and dark, of many colors. The air was turbulent.

Above and below the path were the same cloudy vistas they had seen before. Now, the spaces held fantastic constructions of limitless variety and shape. Here, a dozen vertical towers snaked and braided around each other on their way to invisible points in the sky and in the depths—there, dozens of cubes of incalculable size hung unsupported in midair, placed corner to corner to form a giant cube with gaps between. Like the rest, they served no obvious purpose.

Those were among the more comprehensible things he looked upon. Using the closer objects to estimate the size of those farther away, he felt his heart racing again, and he turned away.

All the men, save Merin, had recovered at least enough to sit up. Brin stumbled on legs like a newborn lamb's toward the bishop, who seemed as captured by the vista as Nor had been.

The younger man embraced the older one, said, "I'm sorry," and began to weep.

"Why?" Arumin asked, more gently than Nor had ever heard him speak.

Brin shook his head, declining to answer. His arms tightened. "I'm so sorry."

"For what?"

But Brin backed away, sniffed, and withdrew into himself once more.

Emberly was sitting up, but his legs were still pulled close in. Forehead on his knees, he cried like a child. It was loud and heedless, and everyone shifted uncomfortably.

"Not everyone is here," Orund said, taking charge of the anarchy.

That was true. Faces were missing.

Arumin moved on quickly. "Perhaps some didn't make it through that... that place. But we've got to go on."

Sergeant Feng spoke up. "A few should stay behind as a rearguard, to hold off the Realm."

Sergeant Orund growled, "Perhaps you will volunteer for the duty, Feng."

"Let's see what Emberly wants," someone said.

The words were so unexpected, if instinctive, that no one stepped forward to admit having spoken them.

Feng and Orund stared each other down for a moment. Then Feng turned toward Emberly, who was still silent.

The captain's whole body was radiating defeat, his head hanging.

Feng cleared his throat. "What do you think, *sir*?" The last word fit so uncomfortably onto the question that it felt like part of a different sentence.

Emberly shook his head and mumbled.

"You're asking *him*?" Orund gaped.

"My wife," Emberly coughed. Saliva stained with blood ran from his mouth.

Orund's face twisted with derision. "What about your wife?"

"I killed her."

53

EMBERLY

AFTER THE CLOUD SWALLOWED him, Emberly had found himself in a lavishly furnished room with a tall covered bed and a tray of untouched food under a metal dome. He couldn't remember when he had seen it before—maybe on his wedding night. He was wearing a formal suit.

It was a fitting place to find his wife. She was in the middle of the room, chained to a metal chair shaped like a throne.

An embroidered handkerchief was tied over her mouth. He stared dumbly at her for a few seconds. To his shame, he needed at least one of those seconds to recognize her and the rest to accept her presence there. Had he not glimpsed her in the tower earlier, reestablishing her features in his mind, Goddess knew how long it would have taken.

She did not seem surprised to see him. Her eyes were not those of a hostage but of someone looking at a loved one with fondness and resignation. Her gaze met his and, a long breath later, moved to a metal tray on a small table in front of her. There, served up like a dessert, was a pistol.

He would later be thankful for the few moments in which the premise of their ordeal escaped him. Once his thoughts were in motion, he rushed to her and untied the handkerchief, careful not to catch her hair with his fingers.

"Darling." They said it together, and the end of the word cut off as their lips met.

"How?" Emberly asked when he pulled away to catch his breath.

"I don't know." She was terribly collected for someone in her situation. "I was in our home, and I had the feeling I had better go for a walk, and I ended up..."

"My Goddess," he said. "They've gone too far now. Whoever is doing this, has put us through all this, they are going to—"

"Stop that." She shook her head. "Perhaps 'they' are simply out of our reach, Cyril."

"We'll bloody see about that." He realized he was beginning to shout. "I'm sorry. Here you are, against all odds, and I'm wasting time thinking of revenge."

"Yes," she replied, unabashed. "We must hold on to what time we have together."

"Dear, is it really you?" He felt the hurtfulness of the question as it passed his lips. Everything about her—her smell, her freckles, the pain-filled smile she was currently holding together—put the truth of her identity beyond doubt. But he didn't know how she could be there, so many worlds from where he'd left her that he'd lost count.

"Of course it is," she said, rendering his doubts moot with her customary patience. "If not, I've been abducted and made a part of one of your dreams." She looked around. "I sometimes wondered if you remembered this place."

"Yes." He remembered vague details of the room. But seeing it all again brought it back, of course, and he did not wish to disappoint her just then.

"Charlotte, what are we to do?" Looking around, he realized the place had no doors or windows.

Their faces were close enough that she drew back a little to look carefully at him. "Darling... you really don't know?"

Then Emberly looked again at the gun on the table.

His entire spirit withered.

"Surely not."

"Why not?" Her words became huskier as her breathing became faster. "Someone put it right there, so they clearly meant it to be used."

"And they want us to—what, kill ourselves?"

"Well, only one of us is chained." Despite her swelling emotion, she sounded a little impatient.

"So..." His dull brain put it together in a flash. "Absolutely not."

"What other explanation is there?"

"I don't care. This is..." He did not have words strong enough. "This is insane! Out of the question!"

She raised her voice. "And what would you do instead? Do you think *I* want this?"

"Of course not, and neither do I! So we will refuse."

"You think we can outlast them? We don't even know who 'they' are."

"So, I am supposed to kill you? Just like that?"

"What else?"

"Murder my own wife?"

She had held back her tears until now. "It's not murder, Cyril. You are being forced. Otherwise, I am fairly certain you will never escape this room."

"Then I won't!" He ran to a wall and threw himself against it. It felt like colliding with a mountainside. Cursing his weakness, he grabbed a lamppost, extinguished the flame, and struck at the wall with the same futility. Howling, he hit it again and again.

She waited for exhaustion to take hold of him, but his desperation was bottomless. He finally stopped only when nothing was left of the shattered post. Arms shaking, he walked along the walls, placing his ear to each one. The silence of oblivion.

He stumbled back to her, his face numb and tingling. "I won't. It's that simple."

He pulled at her chains, looking for weaknesses. He would not find any, and he knew it before he started. He picked up the gun and pointed it at the chains, but the trigger would not move. Then an idea brought pale light to his face. "I'll kill myself!" he said in triumph.

Her tears became sobs. "Cyril, no!"

"When I'm gone, they'll have no reason to keep you here!"

"Cyril, it won't—" She shrieked as he put the gun under his head and pulled the trigger.

It still did not move. He lowered the weapon, stared at it, then raised it once more to his chin.

"No!" she screamed. "Please, not again! I can't watch it."

"But you expect me to do it to you?"

She swallowed. "You have a whole company of men to look after."

He scoffed. "I'm not their leader anymore. They learned who I really am."

"You may be surprised."

"We have a son, Charlotte, a boy who needs his mother."

"His mother isn't coming back," she said flatly. Her tears had ended. "Anyway, he is almost a man. He will just have to be one a little sooner." She leaned toward Emberly as much as the chains permitted. "And you will get out of here and live to be his father."

He blinked away tears. He couldn't understand why he wasn't crying more. Maybe he was simply numb. "I can't," he announced.

"You can, and you will." Her voice was firm, taking control. "That is an order, soldier."

His lip trembled, and he sniffed as he lifted the gun. He could not believe what he was doing, which was perhaps what made it possible. He said, "I love you so—"

"I know. We both know how we feel. Don't make this harder." Her tears were returning, and he could tell she was fighting them furiously. She gave him a final command, through wet eyes and a running nose. "Survive."

He nodded and said, "Yes. I will. I..." Then he realized he was stalling and shot his wife in the forehead. He felt her blood as gentle rain.

During his first moments of consciousness on the path beyond the cloud wall, he drifted carelessly between sanity and madness. He ignored the men and their preparations for war.

When they came to him and asked his advice, he told them the briefest version of the story he could muster. It stopped them all dead. He knew he was in no shape to fight, in body or in spirit. He might never be again.

"She..." Feng began. "It was probably all a dream, Emberly."

Emberly looked at him. "Do I have blood on my face?"

"Of course. But that's because... you know."

"I don't mean from the beatings you gave me. Much deserved, I might add. I mean fresh blood."

"A speckle, here and there."

"A speckle?" Orund said. "He looks like he just shot someone right up close."

"There you are," Emberly said. "I am no longer your commander. If you choose to let me live, I will fight as best I can, though I fear my efforts will be poor. If you still want my advice, I would leave behind a rearguard to fight off the Realm for as long as it can. The general and his men may arrive any second."

Robir had been listening and said, "And you and I will be part of that rearguard, Emberly."

"No," Feng said, looking warily at Emberly's face. "I'll stay instead."

"Fine," Arumin said. "But let's snap to it."

Robir opened his mouth then closed it slowly. He looked like he had been robbed of something.

"Snapping to it" was a poor description of what followed. Despite the combined efforts of Feng, Orund, and Arumin, the men were plodding and disorderly. Each had undergone his own ordeal in the cloud, and each was affected uniquely. Waking up to learn that their visions had been somehow real was another stunning blow.

One of the men wandered over to Emberly. "Anything else, sir?" he asked.

Emberly looked at him through war-torn eyes. "What else is there?"

"Well..." The man stared at his boots. "You could say something, sir. Give the men a boost."

"I've resigned as your captain."

"That doesn't mean you can't give the boys a word."

"Help me up."

The man obeyed, and since Emberly's head rose above most others', the men stopped what they were doing and looked at him. He began with a cough, but then his voice of command returned.

"I am a liar and a murderer. But that puts me in good company here." He expected anger from them but felt none. "We all came on this crusade expecting to have our sins forgiven. Well, perhaps that was all a lie. We may hope that the Goddess is everything we expect, but we can't be sure.

"In the time that I have served with all of you, you have been my only sanity. At this moment, you are my only reason for not making a quick end to my life. I have every reason to think I will die very soon. I think the universe will have it no other way. But I believe that some of you will go on." His throat was suddenly dry, and he gulped.

"Meanwhile, we are caught between foes. One is conquering our home, while another can alter the very laws of nature. We can no longer trust even our eyes and ears. But that matters little—we have already given those away. We heard truth but ignored it. We saw it but shut our eyes. We in this band of villains are not worth forgiveness. But that's no excuse for quitting.

"We have a debt to pay. There is a young woman to whom we all owe our lives—we may never know how she suffered for us. She is in the hands of a monster, a thing that will grow, in time, to devour worlds. If I can spend my last moments trying to save her, I will. That is all we have left, and that, my brothers, will have to do."

54

SHADA

WHEN SHADA AWOKE, SHE took the risk of asking the Lady where they were. The Lady answered by opening a small window through which Shada saw that they were passing through a maze of crystalline corridors. The walls were glassy and translucent, allowing fragmented visions of the chambers or corridors beyond, but the place seemed empty of life. Here and there, hulking shadows hinted at the presence of something besides walls, floors, and ceilings, but even those forms were motionless.

Soon, they arrived in a vast domed chamber. She guessed that was the glass palace's center as corridors stretched away from it in all directions. The farthest of them appeared as dark spots perhaps a kilometer distant.

The dome was filled with thousands of gateways. All were a standard size, fitted together like a mesh. It could have been the hub of an empire, one so immense that the worlds of Ronia would have been a grain of sand on its beach. Looking up at it, Shada felt the light of countless planets.

Despite the splendor, the room was truly dominated by a sort of container at its center. The structure was circular and stretched from floor to ceiling. Its sides were a nearly invisible haze, and inside was a stunning menagerie such as she had never imagined.

These could only be the gods. Some resembled humans, warlords in helmets and armor or ghosts drifting on un-detectable wind. Others were geometric shapes, two and three dimensional, some simple and some that defied her understanding. Still others took forms entirely of their own counsel, and those she did not dare look at too closely. Even their sizes varied enormously. But all had one thing in common: they were watching her.

The Lady's shape changed. She transferred Shada to a seat at the forefront of her mass, where Shada's hair was tossed by wind. "Now, child," the Lady said softly, "you may fulfill your debt to me."

"How?"

"Only your kind can open the Goddess's prison. Not mine."

"They are *trapped*?" Shada's mind reeled. *Is this why the gods have been gone from humanity for so long?* "How is that possible?"

"Yes to the first question. As for the second, only the prison's makers could tell you. And they do not answer questions."

In the prison, the cloud of watching gods darted like minnows, clearing the path for one larger than any of them. Her shape was that of an old woman whose body was round, especially her hips and bosom. She pressed herself close to the barrier, wide-eyed.

"Is it really you?" she asked. Her face and voice were far more convincingly human than the Lady's, though not entirely so, and they were filled with wonder and onrushing joy.

"It is," the Lady answered.

"I wasn't speaking to *you*," the Great Mother Huire said. "I would not have even recognized you, but for that voice. What has happened to you?"

"I have grown. As a daughter should."

"Well, enough of that for now. Who is this young lady?"

Shada straightened. "Shada is my name. How may I address you?"

"By my name, of course, darling. Huire."

Shada tried to wrap her mind around that. Huire was real. Believing in a god abstractly was one thing; seeing her right there in front of her was something else. Shada wondered, for the thousandth time since leaving home, if she was dreaming.

Despite Huire's awesome size, Shada could not help thinking something was missing. She said, "You are much different than I expected."

The Goddess's eyebrows rose. "What did you expect?"

Shada answered honestly. To lie would have felt small. "Someone more grandiose, I suppose."

The being smiled. "I don't have time to be grandiose, darling. I'm a mother. Welcome home."

Shada looked around, feeling stupid. *What does Huire mean by...* "Home?" she asked.

"Home, with me."

The Lady interrupted. "You haven't spoken to me since we parted. Why not? I needed you."

Huire tore her eyes from Shada with reluctance. "Did I give you the impression that I would? If so, I apologize."

The Lady was silent for an instant. Her eyes darted back and forth as though looking for an answer in the room. "You apologize." Her chorus of countless voices trembled.

Huire nodded, waiting.

"You..." The Lady made a long wheezing sound. Shada realized she was lost for words. "You must know an apology will not suffice."

Huire spread her hands. "Why not? It's all worked out, clearly."

The Lady swelled. "Your apology *insults me*. You have no idea how many times I nearly failed—because I was *alone*."

"That's why I sent your brothers and sisters with you. You were all to help each other."

"Help?" The Lady's buzz became a rumble of what Shada could only surmise was laughter. "That useless rabble went into hiding on the first world we came to! Only I went on to do your bidding."

"And thank you. It's a shame, though, that you couldn't work together."

The Lady fell into a silence that contained volumes and could hardly bear the load. After several seconds, she said, "Shada, dear, let me show you something."

They circled the tank to a place where a thin, waist-high column stood just within the barrier. Atop the column was a small lever. A nearly transparent barrier, like that of the prison itself, surrounded the column, leaving enough space inside for a human to stand.

The Lady placed Shada on the ground.

"What is that?" Shada asked.

"That is the means by which you will set my people free. You must turn the key inside it."

The column touched the prison's barrier, and for a space a little wider than Shada's shoulders, the two structures shared the same wall. Shada could not enter the column without stepping through the wall. "How am I supposed to get in?"

"You can simply step through. For you, these walls are permeable. For us, they are deadly. Go on—it's right there."

Huire had followed them around. Her form had grown far taller and more massive. "Shada, you needn't obey her. I don't care for how she's changed."

The Lady turned on her. "Do you expect this girl to show you loyalty? After you let her and her friends struggle through their journey without a speck of help from you?"

"You must abandon your ideas of my capabilities," Huire said. "And responsibilities."

"I'm beginning to doubt whether you are as powerful as you claim."

"How dare you." Huire's eyes grew wide and bright. For an instant, her face was so fearsome that Shada cried out and looked away. "I am still your mother."

"Shada, darling," the Lady said, "please step through the barrier and turn the key."

"Why?" Shada asked. "What will you do?"

"I'll reunite you with your goddess, of course."

"That's not how it seems to me. You can hardly wait for me to turn the key. Why is that? Will you devour them, as you did your brothers and sisters?"

That sent the inhabitants of the prison into a frenzy. They swept into a whirlwind that circled the tank, rising and falling, all of them screaming—except Huire.

Huire's eyes were enormous. "Is that true?"

The Lady did not bother denying it. "Didn't you notice that I've grown a bit? I'm larger even than you are now."

"You demon. Why, you're a servant of the Scourge itself."

"A demon I may be, but you're the mother of a demon. You cast us out into the universe, hoping at least one of us would return. Well, I've done it. I've done the impossible, and I deserve a reward. Shada, open the prison."

"Darling, don't," Huire said. "She's become too strong."

Shada craned her neck to look from one to the other. "Please, stop calling me 'dear' and 'darling,' both of you. As for the barrier..." She turned to the Lady. "If I open it, will you devour Huire and the others?"

"None of your concern," the Lady said.

"And if I refuse?"

The Lady transformed from a vast cloud to her golden, matronly form, matching the Goddess Huire in size. Then she turned toward Shada.

Shada had an instant in which to regret her last question and lunge for the barrier. She should have crossed it sooner.

The Lady kicked her like a dog.

Shada landed a short distance away, making awful wheezing noises instead of breathing. Huire shouted in protest. The Lady advanced on Shada, who could do nothing to stop her or escape. She picked up Shada like a doll and raised her other hand, and her fingers sprouted various wickedly sharp instruments of torture.

She said, "You can surmise what will happen."

"I am going to kill you," Shada panted. She put into the words every bit of will and faith she had left, as if to carve them into the face of creation. "You are going to die here, whatever death you are capable of."

It was a stupid thing to say, likely only to bring her a more painful death. But perhaps she had done enough good in her life, suffered enough, to be owed that one favor.

The Lady's hand unfurled and tossed Shada casually to the edge of the barrier. She landed with a thud, a tumble, and a moan. "You've done a smashing job so far. Now, be a good girl and step inside."

Legs wobbling, Shada stepped across the barrier. It was marked by a narrow crack in the floor that ran in a circle from which the barrier must have emanated. The transition to the other side was soundless and without feeling.

She reached the column in two steps then turned to face the Lady and sat down. Crossing her legs, she leaned back against the column.

The Lady's expression went from exaggeratedly cheerful to blank. "What are you doing?"

Perhaps not even her superior intellect could puzzle out the meaning of Shada's smile.

"Waiting to be rescued," Shada said.

The Lady grinned savagely. "Your friends have been annihilated by now—if not by the beings who guard this place, then by the Shining Realm. You are going to sit there until you die."

"I've starved before," Shada said. "I'll starve again."

55

ARUMIN

THE COMPANY SPLIT IN two. A dozen stayed to fight the Realm when it came, and a dozen continued on to find Shada and the Lady. Neither group was large enough, but then again, the company had been short-handed since the day it left Ronia.

Setting off down the path between the adjacent sets of gateways, Arumin hoped the way forward would become apparent. He didn't know if they should go through one of the gateways or continue down the path until it ended—somewhere. Brin was by his side, and Emberly trailed behind, but he doubted they could help him there. He even tried praying to the Goddess: *Show me the way to you.* But she was still silent.

The answer, if it was one, came in the form of a coughing fit. His arms and neck prickled as a wisp of humming mass emerged from his mouth. As he saw it through watering eyes, he knew it must be a piece of the Lady. She had somehow sneaked a part of herself inside him.

He rejoiced even as he sputtered. There it was, the guidance he'd prayed for.

But while he was bent over, the wisp disappeared. Straightening, he whirled to look for it. The others' expressions told him that none of them had seen what happened. They watched in curious concern as he turned this way and that, searching between and around them. He did not care if he looked crazy. What had happened was too important.

So when he eventually despaired of finding the little apparition, it was with fresh bitterness that he gave up and set off down the path again. Close to the front of the column, he stayed mindful of the bottomless gulfs on either side and the unknown hazards of the gateways.

They were still in sight of the rearguard, which was hurriedly arranging its defenses, when Arumin decided with a swelling of bile that continuing on was pointless. Guessing at the way ahead could get them lost forever in strange lands.

He stopped in his tracks and turned. "That's enough," he announced with venom. "Until we know, somehow, where to—"

He stopped. Standing at the entrance to one of the gateways that the group had already passed was a mild, bespectacled man. He seemed fully human until one looked at his ankles, which faded into cloudiness. His feet were invisible, if any existed. He was too large to be the wisp that had escaped Arumin's mouth but too small to fit the bishop's expectation of a deity.

"You are expected," the man announced. "I have come to show you into their presence."

Arumin felt his mouth hang open. *Expected. But of course we are.* "The gods?"

The man's head tilted. "Who else?"

The bishop nodded. As impossible as it seemed that he was really having this conversation, he was. "And who are you?"

The man sighed, a convincingly human gesture of impatience. "Huire refers to me as her Guardian. She means it mockingly, but I have no other name that matters anymore."

Brin interrupted before Arumin could answer. "Fine, then, Guardian. How shall we know we can trust you?"

"I can offer no evidence of my claims," the man said, spreading his hands. "You will have to be content that you have no other choice."

Brin's mouth thinned. "Are you the one who's been in our dreams?"

The man frowned, his eyes widened a little. "*In* your dreams?"

"Ever since we left our home, even before, we've been having dreams of—"

"I know of this," the man interjected, impatient. "I've seen your dreams, so many of them that I almost lost my mind. They have slowed to a trickle now, thank goodness. But why do you speak of someone 'in' your dreams?"

Brin's face darkened. "I've felt you there, trying to sneak in. Others have seen you, though you don't look like yourself. In dreams, you look like a man made of glass."

The man shook his head slowly, his aura of disdain shaken. "I simply don't know. I've hardly scratched the surface of what this place is capable of. Mostly, I know how much I don't know. It's possible that some aspect or avatar of me was present in your dreams. But it wasn't my intention."

"I don't believe you," Brin spat.

The man shrugged, his aloofness returning. "You're a free man, free to roam the pathways of this place forever if you refuse my guidance. But if you're coming with me, we must go now."

"Of course we're coming with you," Emberly said, his voice an ugly gurgle. "We can't waste time. Lead on."

56

ROBIR

JUST AS ARUMIN'S PARTY disappeared into one of the gateways along the path, Robir watched the cloud wall cough up a group of soldiers from the Shining Realm. They sat up or twitched with varying levels of consciousness. The massacre began with them.

The Ronians were waiting just within the gateways on either side of the path, one or two men per opening. Standing in forests and moonscapes, they stepped through the gateways and carefully shot each Realmsman who stumbled to his feet. As for the rest, to save ammunition, Feng sent a few volunteers dashing over to cut their throats before they could recover. The section of the path nearest the cloud wall was wide, and only the Ronians in the closest pair of gateways, left and right, could see it all with their combined fields of view.

Another group of Realmsmen appeared, twenty or thirty, with much the same result. The Ronians worked with the casual efficiency of butchers then looted the dead for weapons, ammunition, and equipment. Robir, concealed in one of the first gateways on the path, felt a thrill that cut through the heat of the jungle surrounding him. If this continued, they could hold off the Realm all day. The enemy commanders, with no idea of what was occurring, might keep tossing troops blithely into the fire until none were left. That was just like Gallobraith—except this time, the Ronians were the ones shooting from hiding places.

When the third group appeared, Robir's thrill turned sickly. Those were not Ganet's men. The private had first seen their black clothing and hoods and bright-yellow eyes on Ronia, when they saved the company from terrorists. They must have been commanded by that witch, Ren, which meant she wouldn't be far behind. Fortunately, only a few of the black-clad men were there yet—perhaps the monsters outside the cloud wall had killed most of them.

Some of the black-clad soldiers carried metal shields almost as tall as they were. When the shields materialized along with their largely unconscious bearers, supports of some kind kept the shields standing upright.

The shields protected both their bearers and the other soldiers lucky enough to appear behind them. Those who were conscious rushed to arrange the shields into a wall.

The Ronians, now armed with the Realm's weapons, poured fire into them. Robir whooped, amazed by the liberation of firing multiple shots without reloading. The Ronians quickly finished off the Realmsmen who lay exposed, but not even their new ammunition could penetrate the shields.

The rest of the Realmsmen organized and returned fire. Behind the shields, the numbers of Ganet's sky-blue soldiers just kept increasing. The gateways provided handy cover for the Ronians, but the sheer volume of fire directed at them was dizzying. Somewhere down the path, one of the men gave a fitful cry. Already outnumbered, the party was perhaps one less.

Robir was alone in his gateway except for Merin, who lay prone a little ways down the steep hill on which the gateway stood, overlooking a thick jungle. Why the unconscious man had ended up there, on the front line, was a puzzle Robir did not have time to answer.

Soon after the Realmsmen erected their shield wall, one of them hurled the first grenade. The metal clank was so close that Robir heard it over the ringing in his ears. He threw himself headlong down the hill as the explosion drilled a hole in the dirt where he'd just been.

He landed right on top of Merin. The man was still gazing undisturbed into the sky.

"Wake up, idiot!" Robir cried. He could barely hear himself shouting and slapped the man hard. "Wake up!"

Then another explosion came from the path, and he scrambled back up the hill. His gun remained where he had dropped it.

Through the other gateway directly across the path, he saw the bloody remains of two Ronians. Sergeant Feng had moved up to take their position, and his eyes told Robir what he thought of their company's chances. It was nothing Robir hadn't assumed already. The black-clad men with their shields and explosives had tipped the balance.

Arumin had left them there hoping they might undertake a fighting retreat as the enemy advanced. Then they would meet up with the rest of the party somewhere down the line. The futility of that plan was now apparent. The path was a shooting gallery, and even if some of them survived it, they might not recognize which gateway the others had taken. They were there until the end, which was quickly approaching.

Robir peeked out of his gateway. An armored man dressed in black was racing down the path toward the Ronians. Robir shot at him until the gun was empty. At least one bullet slipped through the armor, and the man fell and lay still.

Robir pulled back into cover. The image of the dead man hung before his eyes. The man surely had explosives strapped to his body. If Robir had looked out the gateway a second later, the man might have blown them all to nothing. *Why do such strokes of luck fall on us if we are doomed? Why can't the Goddess simply finish the job she started when she enticed us all into this crusade of the damned?*

57

GANET

GANET AWOKE CRYING. THE sound of gunfire pressed in from everywhere, overwhelming, and he instinctively flattened himself to the ground. One of his soldiers pulled him by his shoulders into a sitting position and supported his sagging weight while another reported to him on the situation.

He interrupted. "Did Ren make it?"

The battle outside the cloud wall had been vicious, and the Realm's forces had suffered staggering losses. He and some of his men had slipped past the cloud wall in the confusion, but Ren's commandos had been less fortunate.

The second soldier pointed at a shape fallen some distance away along the shield wall the surviving commandos had deployed.

Energy snapped back into Ganet's body. He fled the clutching hands of his men, telling them to maintain their positions or something to that effect. Keeping low, he hurried down the line of shields, darting past gaps. The bulk of the remaining force wore the sky-blue uniforms of his soldiers, and interspersed with those were black-clad commandos. All huddled together behind the shield wall, hostilities forgotten in the immediate need for survival.

He had, against all odds, a chance to salvage his mission. He might still do the Lady's bidding.

Since the moment the Lady appeared in his dream in Om, she had possessed his thoughts. She was the Shining Realm's dream given form, the superbeing that humanity would one day become. She had dwelt inside him for a time in Om then left, and he felt her absence—the absence of that perfect dream—like an almost physical ache. The second time she visited him, on that world of ice, she appeared in her full glory, a giant storm swooping out of the sky. Her size and majesty burned away his last doubts about her. When she offered a pact that would help them both, he gladly accepted. He might have chafed at the thought of killing the Ronians, whom he had fought to save in Om, but his place was not to question the embodiment of humanity's future wisdom.

He had honored his truce with the Ronians, but in the end, he had no intention of letting them live. The Lady wanted any who were not loyal to her dead. So the truce had been a lie, of sorts. His people despised lies, but he was losing his faith in their ways. He had begun to wonder if he was a true Realmsman at all.

A pair of his soldiers was watching over Ren, and one of them met him as he approached. "You've got to talk to her, sir. She's speaking nonsense."

The general grimaced and shoved past him, wondering what would become of his soldiers when this fight was over. If Ren was on her feet with her army intact, Ganet would already have been in her custody.

She was awake, and he knelt beside her. The battle had settled into a slower rhythm as more bombers prepared to charge the Ronians' position, and he could speak to her if he leaned in close.

When she saw him, she said, "I got him, General. He got me back, but I got him first."

Her eyes were misty and frightening. The path was wet with blood from her shoulder, which someone had hastily bandaged.

"Well done," he said. He felt unsure of himself, like he was comforting someone in mourning. He wondered where his hatred of her had gone. "But there are many to go yet."

"First things first," she replied. "You are under arrest, sir."

He nodded.

"What did you see?" she asked.

She must have been asking about the vision he'd had in the clouds. Until now, he had not known if anyone else had been through something similar. He cast his mind back and wanted to cry again. "I'll never speak of it to anyone, not if my life depends on it."

"I was..." she began. "I saw my child."

He furrowed his brow in surprise. In the Realm, people who looked like her—who were plain or ugly in appearance—seldom received permission to breed. They did not advance far in society, either. Such an appearance was a sign of possible deeper flaws. He had often wondered how Ren had attained her important position.

She looked around. "Can you take me away from here?"

He looked around them, incredulous, and wondered just how fragile her mental state was. "There is no 'away' just now."

She continued, undiscouraged. "It was an accident. I met a man... He looked at me like no one ever had. I showed weakness that night—no doubt part of why my line must be snuffed out."

The general shook his head. They did not have time for this, and her shoulder wound did not warrant a deathbed confession. He ought to return to the fight. Yet there he remained.

"When the baby came..." With no visible change in her face, she seemed to master some emotion. "It was deformed, as we'd known it might be. My family knew what would become of it. They took it to kill it, and this is where I showed my mettle."

She took a long breath. "They had dug a hole and were about to bury it when I came along, still wet and bleeding and everything. I pointed a gun at them and demanded it back. They knew I could kill them quite comfortably. They did as I said.

"It was needed for testing, you see. They would need it alive long enough to take it apart, learn what had gone wrong. There was much to be learned. For my devotion to duty, I was promoted beyond my natural station."

Her head dropped to one side, and she peered into the cloud. "In there, I was proven false. I *was* it, the child, and I went through it all. I felt what they did to it because they were doing it to me.

"I doubted, Ganet. I wondered if I should have let them bury it. That doubt... that weakness. It's been there all along... I didn't know, I swear. If you make it back—"

Ganet could listen to no more. "What is this nonsense? You'll survive this wound."

She grabbed him by the jacket with one hand. "Don't you understand?" she cried. "I can't forget what I saw.

I can't stop doubting. I feel the doubt taking me…" She clenched her teeth in an agonized grimace. "I can't let it happen. I can't…"

Tears ran down her face. "I'm so afraid."

Then she sniffed, and her tears ended. She became stiff and businesslike. "Perhaps I haven't made my feelings clear, sir. My own fault, I suppose. My loss of faith is obviously due to a fault in my heritage. My family must be examined for possible traitorous tendencies. As for me, I cannot and will not go on, knowing what I know. It would be disloyal."

Snarling, Ganet tore away from her grip. "You young ones. You're like automatons. You miss the whole bloody point."

"You've forgotten the point!" she cried out. Then a coughing fit took her. When it was over, she said, "I'm not a soldier, I'm a tool. What would you do with a tool broken beyond repair?"

Ganet pounded the ground with his fist. "Stand up, soldier! There's work to do." *What am I thinking? She wants me arrested.*

"If you are unable to perform your duty, Ganet, you should consider following me. As is, my men will take you into custody when this is over."

His teeth grinding, Ganet said, "I understand."

That was a lie—lying was becoming a habit. The Ronians were rubbing off on him. Perhaps Ren was right, and he was no true Realmsman.

He followed the lie with a truth: "Well done, soldier."

He pulled his black dagger from its sheath. He began the chant that he knew like his own name. He told her that the universal superbeing, though still unborn, was looking back upon them and was thankful.

She said nothing, but her face crept toward a smile as he spoke. The unfamiliar expression illuminated her face, and he was afraid for a moment that he might lack the will to finish the ritual.

He stumbled through the last few words, and her eyes flashed toward him as if incensed by the misstep. So it was that their eyes were locked when the blade pierced her heart and killed her. He saw the life leave her eyes, and he released the blade and scrambled back, panting in terror.

A few nearby soldiers had noticed the ritual in progress. They ducked behind the wall and wiped away tears. Tears were her due, and they had been welling up in Ganet just moments before. But right then, he had none to give.

The firefight had died down. The Ronians must have been mostly dead or in retreat. Ganet spoke to his men nearby, and they passed word to their blue-clad comrades along the shield wall.

They drew their knives, and Ren's commandos began to die.

Ganet had hoped it would happen quickly, but that was not the case. The black-clad men were a different breed, with intense instincts, and a few realized what was about to happen. Fanatics, they fought to the death, their slitted yellow eyes wide. Each took several of Ganet's men with him. It was a bloody, awful scene, and for a moment, the general wished Ren had taken him after all.

Then he came to his senses. Crouching, he searched Ren's body for the vial he knew would be there. Upon finding it, he raised it before his face and peered at the strange black dust inside. A moment of decision passed. He tossed it over the edge of the path, where it disappeared into the abyss.

If he had kept it, his Goddess might have found it. She would not have been pleased.

58

—·—

SHADA

THE LADY HAD TAKEN the shape of a beast with a massive fishlike head and skeletal tail, with entrails that floated behind as it swam through the air. It reminded Shada of something she had seen in a medicine show—a fish dredged up from the bottom of the sea. It circled the gods' prison like a predator anxious to strike.

Shada averted her eyes each time it passed. Its face was too bony and fragmentary to be real. But her alternative view was scarcely more comforting. Many of the gods had gathered around her little enclave of their prison, unable to reach her. Some had pleaded, others commanded, that she not bring down the prison walls. That was remarkable, considering how long they had been trapped in their cage. Plainly, they were terrified of the Lady, who was larger and stronger than any of them alone. But the Lady was not going anywhere, and Shada might have been their only chance of ever escaping. *Is self-preservation so important?*

Huire sat at the boundary and watched Shada. The others gave her space, nearly as wary of the behemoth among them as of the one outside.

Shada, wishing Huire would say something, eventually started the conversation herself. "Why do they all fear you?"

The Goddess smiled. "I am the greatest of them, dear. None here could match me in combat. They recognize that reverence is due."

Shada pushed on, emboldened by knowing Huire could not reach her—and by knowing she was likely to die regardless. "How did all of you become trapped here? People tell all kinds of stories about why you disappeared."

"Trapping ourselves here was the only way we survived, Shada. There are more terrible things than us in the universe. Tell me: are you truly a Ronian?"

Shada thought of the patterned marks on her face. "To the sorrow of some, yes. I was born in the city."

"But your parents came from elsewhere."

"My mother did."

Huire nodded. "I know this because I did not alter my children—marking them or twisting their bodies. What was done to you is an abomination."

"It was not done to me. It happened long ago." It was a frightening thing to disagree with a god. But she sensed Huire would not mind.

Indeed, the Goddess did not protest. "Of course. But I want you to know that my embrace has room for all."

"Thank you." Shada wondered how the idea of embracing the Lady should make her feel. She could not deny that it frightened her a little.

Other questions nagged at her. "Why did you need to ask if I am Ronian? Don't you know everything?"

Huire's face sank. "I will tell you a difficult truth, Shada. What I don't know could fill all the spaces between all the stars."

Shada didn't know whether to be scared or relieved. At the very least, hearing that made Huire feel more like Shada's equal. "Is that why you haven't spoken to our company since we left Ronia?"

"Your people were in my heart, and you have been since I came to this place."

"That's not the same thing."

"No." The Goddess frowned. "But it's the best I could do."

"Well..." Shada shook her head. "The messengers you sent to find us didn't make it far. And the one who did has become... Well, you've seen her." She pointed at the Lady, circling like a predator. "She's changed since I met her. I've watched it happen."

"That is the way with my kind," Huire said. "When a piece of us splits away, it becomes its own being and can go its own way. I hoped that, by sending so many, at least one messenger would find her way to you. They knew that I was sending them into great danger. But I believed I had taught them well—taught them the way to Ronia, the language, what to expect on the way."

Shada replied, "I don't know what else you taught them, but she learned to make her way, that's for sure."

"Just as your people created me in want of a mother, I made children of my own."

"Yet your children should have been trapped inside the prison with you. How did they escape?"

The Goddess shook her head. "That is too long a story for the present."

Shada laughed. "Is any story too long for the present?"

A smile crept onto Huire's face. "Too long... and too painful."

"We're never getting out of here," Shada said. "There's no reason to evade questions. You still haven't told me how you got in this mess."

Huire's mouth was sad, but her eyes shone with glamour and rage. "We made a mistake, Shada. My fellow gods and I. One of us, during our expansion through the stars, came upon something we'd never seen before. This." She waved at the crystal vastness around them. "Though its creators were nowhere to be seen, we realized they were creatures entirely other than us—they were not humanity or any of its offshoots. They were beings entirely new, and wherever they were, their powers had been awesome."

"If I were you, a god, I might have felt a kinship with them."

Huire laughed. "No. A host of us assembled—not nearly all, but hundreds. We marched upon this place, determined to find them if they still existed. They were naturally emergent beings, like you, so we thought we must ultimately be greater."

An ugly tickle of fear touched Shada's belly, adding to the many other feelings dwelling there. "You wished to conquer them."

Huire looked at her, and the look spoke of disappointment, frustration, and more. The Goddess was far better at facial expressions than the Lady. "Shada, don't you understand us better than that? We wished to care for them. Your kind created us just in time to save you from the destruction you would have wreaked upon yourselves. We made you ours, cradled you. Now, with this new species, we might do the same thing again. But they had truly vanished. What we found instead nearly destroyed us.

"It was this very prison that held it. This space was filled from ceiling to floor with a substance as thick as tar. Later, we would call it the Scourge."

"Was it alive?"

"In a sense, though I don't think it was awake in the way that I am or even that you are. When we approached it, it seemed to move and grow turbulent. It could see us, or perhaps it felt us.

"What a discovery! Here was another living thing, perhaps not unlike ourselves. Because we vastly outnumbered it, we felt safe releasing it, though it cost us some injuries to learn that we could not open its prison ourselves. After some puzzling, we learned that a being of your kind could penetrate the force field. It was designed to keep us out—or in."

Huire's eyes turned downward. "When I think of the moment when we released it... The memory is a black one. It pounced on the nearest of us. At first, all I felt was sadness. Here was something totally new, and we would have to destroy it. Instead, it set about destroying us. The first ones it attacked turned into more of it—more of that writhing black smoke. It spread through the host so quickly that there was nothing to be done.

"Only a few of us staved off panic. I led those into the place where it had been imprisoned, and with the help of our flesh-and-blood assistant, we closed ourselves in. Many who were trying to enter were cut off, and many of us lost the greater part of ourselves when the barrier fell. All that was left outside became food for the Scourge, and we watched it grow bigger and bigger. When it was finished, it nearly filled this chamber, and then it went off in search of those who had fled. We don't know what became of them."

A ball of ice formed in Shada's chest. When she spoke, her voice squeaked on the first syllable. "Ro... Ronians call that time the Cataclysm. It's mostly legend. There were great battles in the sky on many worlds. The gods disappeared, and without their oversight, a lot of the worlds they'd built fell apart. Fire erupted up from below, and ice fell from above." She realized she was reciting from a book she'd read. "Most humans died. We'd lived so long in the paradises the gods had built... Until now, no one had heard from the gods in ages."

Huire wrung her hands. "What became of the Scourge?"

Shada replied, "It departed for the Outer Dark. Perhaps it ran out of..." She stopped herself from using the word *food*. "Maybe learned people know more than me."

"I taught my children to be wary of it and to hide as often as they could." Huire sighed greatly as if preparing herself. "Do they still know me there, in Ronia? Is my name remembered?"

Shada's eyes widened. "News of the Lady's coming was all Ronians would talk about. I came here with a company of men who were willing to die trying to find you. And many have."

Huire nodded, her face running with tears. The sight filled Shada with unaccountable feelings—love, grief... and something sharper.

"What is it, Shada?" Huire asked.

Shada spoke before her courage could fail. "I'm angry."

"Angry that so many died?"

"Yes, I suppose. But it's more than that. I'm angry about many of the things people have done in your name." She had no real cause to be angry at Huire, but she was.

Huire's tears vanished like they had never been. Her face turned grave. "It's the cost, Shada."

"The cost of what?"

"Of free will."

Shada shook her head but made no other answer. It was the truth. But the truth, she was realizing, felt no obligation to comfort her.

59

— · —

ARUMIN

ARUMIN WALKED BESIDE THE Guardian at the front of the column. They were slipping through the alleyways of an abandoned stone city. Time, and likely war, had ruined many of the buildings, and only winds conversed in the streets.

"So," Arumin said, "are you not one of the gods?"

The Guardian laughed. "No, but if you called me a god in front of them, I would be much obliged."

They passed through another gateway and found themselves wading through a swamp. The clouds were low enough to caress their heads, and the spindly trees on their lonely clumps of land disappeared in the gray. The Guardian turned right and set out confidently, floating above the muck. An unguessable time passed as he shifted their direction this way and that, based on landmarks only he could discern.

Arumin was searching for the right words to certain questions. Finally, he grew impatient and asked, "Do you know Huire?"

The man's eyebrows rose. "I think so, to the extent that she can be known. It's been centuries, after all."

"Meeting her will be..." The bishop paused to choose his words. "The most singular moment of my life. What is she like?"

The Guardian smiled. "I will make you one guarantee. She won't be what you expect."

They came to solid ground. The Guardian led them over a small ridge and onto a plain. Forested hills ringed them round. Somewhere in the trees, a stream gurgled.

The Guardian turned, solemn faced. "This is where I leave you, my friends."

"What?" Arumin said. "Where do we go from here?"

"Wherever you wish, but I hope you will stay here. These trees produce many fruits, and there is wild game about and fresh water. There are far worse places to live out your lives."

"Our lives?" Many voices shouted at once, Arumin's the loudest.

"I wouldn't try to cross the swamp again," the Guardian said, fiddling with his glasses. "The mud is treacherous, and unless you know the exact route, it will devour you."

After an instant of stunned silence, the company cried out in fury. The Guardian stood at the center of the storm, observing them all from a great, cold distance. Someone pointed a gun at him, and he looked at it in bemusement.

"No," Brin said. His voice held such a sense of finality that the Guardian turned toward him. "You will take us to Huire immediately." He held out a vial attached to a necklace that he wore.

When the Guardian saw the vial and what was inside, his first reaction was to laugh. The noise had a very human touch of disbelief. As Brin came closer, the black powder in the vial began to move, rising and swirling.

"No," the apparition said, backing away, but the word and the action both lacked conviction. Then a change came over him. With that genuineness of reaction that others of his kind seemed to lack, a shock visibly passed through him, followed by the rekindling of old hope. "Why would I do that?" he asked Brin.

"Because you know what will happen if I open this," said the young priest. "And don't try to enter my head again. You know it won't work with me."

"This place has powers and depths that I have despaired of understanding," the Guardian replied. "It has accepted me in a superficial way. It is a world as alive as any you have seen, though it does not look like it. Its creatures have accompanied you since before you left your home. They have probed your minds, reliving moments with you and transmitting them here. In their vast ecosystem, this is their only function. Now that you are here, they will soon die.

"Those who once ruled here created them and everything else here. If you continue to resist the will of the rulers, which this place preserves, I don't know what will happen. They did not want this place found easily."

Brin said, "I'll take that risk for now. We haven't come this far to spend the rest of our lives in a meadow."

Arumin asked, "Why, Guardian, would you have left us here?" He heard quivering betrayal in his voice.

The Guardian's mouth twisted. "Because the gods are not what you think. They are bitter, treacherous creatures who ought never to be released. I know what it is like to be fooled by them. Since I doubted you would turn back, I had two choices: kill you all or take you to a place where you could live out your lives in peace. In all this labyrinth, this is one of the few such places." He looked at the vial. "But now there is another option."

"What is it?" Arumin asked.

Brin answered, "All you need to know is that they fear it."

"The gods?" Arumin felt stupid, struggling to keep up.

"Bishop, trust me." Brin seemed loath to remove his eyes from the vial for an instant, wondering how quickly the Guardian might snatch it from him if he tried. Brin continued, "You, creature, are under my command." He raised his voice. "And from this moment, my master commands this company."

Orund was the only remaining soldier in a position of leadership. He regarded the scene with an odd mixture of contempt and apathy and made no objection.

The Guardian focused on the vial. He asked, "Once you reach our destination, what will you do?"

Brin bared his teeth. "That will depend on what is done for me."

60

ROBIR

WHEN HE SAW SERGEANT Feng fall, shot in the throat by that witch of the Shining Realm, Robir decided that he, himself, would not die. The feeling was so powerful that his actions seemed to be taken out of his own hands. Whereas, a few minutes before, he thought he'd accepted his oncoming death, his body now simply took charge of him.

Until that moment, he had been standing in a jungle and firing, mostly blindly, around the corner of the gateway toward the Realmsmen. Now, he fled down the hill behind him. He did not get far before the sting of conscience pierced his panic and he scrambled back up the hill, looking for Merin. The private was still comatose, so Robir pulled him by the arms down the slope. He did not stop until the gateway was well out of sight.

Hidden behind a fallen log, he reloaded his weapons and fixed his bayonet on his rifle. Merin's ammunition had been taken and distributed among the others. As he finished, he heard voices from the gateway as the Realmsmen entered the jungle and began to search for them.

For what felt like hours, blue-clad men crashed through trees and bushes. More than once, one of them almost tramped right on top of the hiding pair. Through it all, Merin stared up into the jungle canopy, unconcerned with worldly matters.

When the voices and the crushing of undergrowth faded, withdrawing to the gateway, Robir could scarcely believe their luck. He waited until the sounds were gone then climbed atop the log and peered over. Seeing no threat, he creeped slowly toward the gateway.

By the time he reached it and peered into the world on the other side, the forces of the Realm had marched on and disappeared down the endless path lined by gateways. Many of their own lay dead in their wake, riflemen and bombers side by side.

The Ronians had been wiped out. Feng's body had been rifled for useful intelligence and casually impaled, as though the pool of blood from his neck was not assurance of his death.

Other Ronians had been dragged, wounded, onto the path and killed where they lay. Robir had abandoned his post and squirreled himself away just in time to avoid their fate.

The extent of his own failure dawned on him, followed seconds later by its true, crushing magnitude. He touched the bullet scar on his chest, the constant reminder of his failure on Caidfell—his failure to ride to victory or die for the cause. Again, as always, he had slithered between.

He took a deep breath and turned this way and that, imagining that if he fled through the right gateway, he could escape the reality of his choices. But betrayal, perpetrated under the gaze of Huire, followed a man wherever he went. There was only one world.

He hurried down the path toward where it met the cloud wall. He stepped over Feng's body and past the final gateway to the spot where the path widened. There, he came face-to-face with two Realmsmen left to guard the spot. They had been hidden by gateways until that instant.

He locked eyes with the nearer one, who stood within arm's reach.

Robir was quicker. He shot the Realmsman in the chest with his pistol. An explosion of red covered Robir's face and tongue and burned his eyes. The man fell, quickly dead.

Through the bloody haze, Robir whirled toward the other soldier a few meters away. The man's weapon leapt up as Robir charged, bayonet raised.

Both men jumped at a gunshot that neither of them had fired. Merin stood by the gateways, smoking pistol in hand. He had missed cleanly.

The startled Realmsman's next shot went wide as Robir closed in. Jumping back, the man panicked and fired over and over. The blade met his chest, and he jumped back again—that time, over the edge of the path. He fired twice more into the clouds as he fell, screaming.

Robir searched himself for wounds and found nothing new. Death, swooping in on him, had turned aside once more. He turned to see Merin drop his pistol, a drooping, stupid look on his face. Without acknowledging Robir, he turned and started down the path with a strange jerking gait like a puppet's.

"Wait!" Robir called. He easily caught up with Merin. "Where are you headed? And without me?" He kept pace with the other's awkward strides. "Not going to thank me, eh? For saving your life? If it weren't for me, they'd have gutted you while you napped."

Merin continued walking, straight ahead, like the soul of one departed. Robir grabbed the smaller man by the shoulder and forced him to turn around. "Didn't think I could handle those two on my own, did you? You had to stick your nose where it wasn't needed."

Merin still said nothing. He tilted his neck to look at the side of Robir's head. Robir felt around there and realized part of his ear was missing. In the thundering of his heart and the rushing of his blood, he had not noticed that one of the man's shots grazed him.

Without warning, Merin placed his hand on the ear. Robir slapped it away, more startled than angry, but Merin put it back, and that time, Robir waited.

He soon cried out in a pain far worse than any he had felt yet. Voices argued inside him, some demanding he put a stop to this, others that he allow it.

Merin remained focused on his task, whatever it was. When he withdrew his hand, Robir felt the ear gingerly. His earlobe had been restored. He pinched it, searching for the trick. "What are you? A sorcerer?"

Merin turned again and walked away.

That time, Robir didn't follow. He yelled, "I don't need your cursed magic! You take it back, damn you!" He continued to shout as his bewitched comrade grew distant then disappeared into one of the gateways. He could not be sure exactly when his snarls turned to tears. Soon, tears were all that was left.

He sat down, alone in the universe. He tore at his hair and garments and clenched his teeth until he thought they might shatter. Nothing could alter a lifetime of decisions in the slightest. He didn't know how he could risk facing Emberly again—letting the captain see him still alive, amidst all those who had given their lives. *The look on that bloody pig's face...*

The Lady had deceived him, and the Goddess had ignored his prayers for death. He stood and tottered to the edge of the path. There, his answer met him in a violent updraft from the clouds below.

61

—·—

BRIN

BRIN WAS IN A place of darkness but no fear. He drifted but felt very still.

"You won't stop trying, will you?" he asked.

The darkness answered—a man made of light came to him.

Brin looked at him. "I've changed my mind," he said, managing to sound defiant. "Let's go."

They left the darkness and came again to the stone well in the scrubby wood. Brin reached into the untamed seas of grass nearby and pulled out a bucket. It was moldy and seemed half made of lichen. He flung open the doors covering the well to reveal rancid water close to overflowing the brim. Dipping the bucket, he let it fill with filth, then he held it up for the man.

"Drink," he said.

The man did not move. His crystalline form might have been a statue.

"Fine, then," Brin said. "I'll do it." He hoisted the bucket, placed his mouth on the mossy lip, and drank.

Most others would have gagged on the fluid that poured down his throat, but he had come to like it—with persistence, he even thrived on it. Its taste never changed.

Next, he lay alone in a bed in a room with stone walls. The bed almost filled the small space, leaving room for only a desk and a plush throne of a chair.

Brin himself was smaller, in the first gangliness of his teenage years, and wore a nightgown. He sat up on hearing a commotion outside.

The door crashed open, and Arumin rushed in. He was a decade younger and would not be a bishop for some time yet. He was dressed as a soldier—more than that, an officer.

Arumin knelt by the bed. "You have to hide," he said. "Something has happened, and the prisoners are loose."

Brin said, "But I *am* a prisoner."

"Not anymore," Arumin said, sounding like the commandant he was. "Not if I say you're not."

"But you just met me." Brin looked around, searching for the trick. "It's only been a couple of hours."

Arumin bit his lip, holding back some emotion. "I know already that you don't belong here."

"What will you do with me?" Brin was accustomed to being used in various ways.

"Nothing," Arumin snapped. His eyes flashed toward the door as gunfire sounded nearby. "You are not yet a man, and—"

A volley of rifle fire cut him off. He bounced on his heels. "Before anything else, we must survive this." He snatched his rifle from the corner of the room.

"Survive?" Icy fear stabbed Brin's chest. "What do you mean?"

"The prisoners outnumber us, and they will kill us all." The commandant's eyes widened. "Perhaps you, too, if they find you here."

"Oh, no!" Brin cried. His honed instinct for preserving his life tore about inside him. "They can't."

"They can, and if I don't go now to lead my men, they will."

"Let's run away!" Brin said the words without thinking, but he quickly warmed to them. "You and I. We can slip out and escape down the road."

Arumin's eyes were large and sad. "I cannot do that. You don't understand."

Brin rose to his knees in the bed and put his hand on the commandant's chest. "I know that you are a special man and the kindest man here. You don't deserve to die like this."

Arumin shifted in a half-hearted effort to move Brin's hand. "I wish I could do as you say."

"You can. Simply do it."

"I am not special. I am just another man."

Brin's mind leapt this way and that with renewed panic. "Please. Please." He bounced with terror. "Won't you care for me? When you found me, you told me you'd take care of me."

To his surprise, Arumin's lip trembled. "I will. Of course I will."

"But you're not. Not right now."

The commandant did not answer.

"I think," Brin said, "that your decision is made."

Arumin touched his lips with his tongue and twitched in visible agony.

Feeling tears on his cheeks, Brin pushed closer to the man. "They may kill you, but not me. I won't be so lucky. They will do things with me that—"

Arumin clapped his hand over Brin's mouth. "Don't. Please don't."

Twisting away, Brin replied, "It's the truth. Only you can stop it. Then we can be happy, together."

Arumin looked at him for a second more then turned away and put down his rifle.

Back in the forest, Brin lowered the moldy bucket from his lips and faced the strange man. He had drunk more of the well water than he intended, and his stomach churned at what he had forced it to accept. He wondered what had compelled him to tell that story.

"There you are," he said. "But never again. Now, piss off."

62

BRIN

RETRACING ITS STEPS, THE company passed for the second time through a great, transparent cylinder. All around them, underfoot and overhead, the blackness of the deeps between worlds was relieved only by the faint light of a million stars. The Guardian glowed as the light touched him, and the men, led by Arumin, followed him closely, awed to silent trembling by their surroundings.

They stopped where the corridor intersected another just like it.

The Guardian announced, "This is where we went astray."

"Very well," Brin said, stepping to the bishop's side and surveying the others. "Here, our company parts ways at last. Only a few of us will continue from here, and the rest will await our return." Listing those who would finish the journey they had all undertaken together, he named himself, the bishop, and two soldiers.

"And what are we to do?" the captain asked.

"The Shining Realm will quickly overcome the force we left behind," Brin said. "We must have another line of defense."

Nor gazed at him with those mute white eyes. "Father Brin, what are you planning?"

Brin glared. "To return here with the Goddess."

"But you don't know what you'll meet on the way," Nor replied. "You may need more help than two soldiers can give. Clearly, this Guardian cannot be trusted. Why do you want to be rid of the rest of us?"

"Brother Nor," Brin said coldly, "I've come to think well of you. So I'll warn you not to question my orders."

The bishop turned to him. "Your orders? Not long ago, you announced that I was in command."

"You are, master. But in certain matters," Brin said, "I have been privy to the Lady's wishes."

"And since when does she speak through you?" The bishop's reply sounded angry, dismayed, even afraid. What it did not sound was surprised.

"Can't fathom it, can you?" Brin snapped. "Well, I can tell you all that a new day is coming. Those who are loyal will be rewarded. Those who aren't are doomed."

The captain let out a breath. "Loyal to whom?"

Brin hesitated long enough that everyone looked at him. "To the Goddess, of course."

He turned to the Guardian. "Lead on. The rest of you, set up your final defense here. With any luck, when we return, you'll have no need of it."

Orund coughed. "Before you go, sir... Earlier, we discussed a bit of loose business."

In the glow of the silent Guardian, Brin looked a little paler. "I still don't see the point."

"That's because you aren't a soldier."

"You'll need everyone here alive if you hope to fend off the Realm's advance."

"I mean no disrespect, sir, but I will not compromise. If we are to be your lapdogs, it will come with a price."

Brin shifted from foot to foot and nodded. "No foolishness. Make it quick. And give him the dignity of privacy."

Orund gave a little bow. "Yes," he said with light in his eyes. "Sir."

The Guardian and those trailing in his wake turned and walked down the corridor through another gateway. Brin hoped to get out of earshot quickly, but sound echoed in that starry corridor, carrying to him with brutal clarity a conversation he had hoped to miss.

First, Orund's voice, full of grim satisfaction: "For you, monk, the time has come at last."

Then Emberly's voice, surprised: "What is this?"

Orund again: "It's justice. It's coming for you, too, Captain."

A pause during which Brin's feet carried him a few precious steps farther away. But not enough.

Then Orund said, "Let's go. We'll take Nor back this way. Keep Emberly here."

Then, entirely too loudly, he said, "You kill the captain. We'll kill the monk."

63

— · —

ARUMIN

THE PATH OF THE Guardian led Arumin and the small remaining party through a gateway and along the top of an extended ridge of rocky, scrub-covered hills. The bishop followed the Guardian with slow steps, like an enchanted child following a spirit into the otherworld. He took in their surroundings—great valleys and round bronzed peaks of a highland in autumn—with an unusual hunger. It was not a bad place.

He did not jump when two gunshots rang out behind him. He was surprised only that they were not meant for him. But even that made a certain kind of sense.

He stopped in place without being told. The Guardian had instantly turned and folded his hands, content as ever to simply watch. Arumin turned just enough to observe what he already knew. The two privates who had accompanied them were dead, each shot through the skull. Brin, who had slowly fallen to the rear of their little column, was holding a weapon that Arumin could only guess belonged to the Shining Realm. He didn't know the details of the betrayal, but he could guess nearly enough.

"Why bring them along at all?" he asked in reference to the two dead men.

Brin was panting as if he'd run all the way from Ronia. He gasped, "Would've seemed strange. Us going off alone."

"You're sure about this?"

"What am I to do?" As Brin heaved, his voice cracked and turned to a shout. "Remain with you? A crumbling old man?"

The bishop looked ahead past the Guardian, and a smile graced his lips. "There's one thing you cannot take away. I know that you loved me."

"Love." The boy poured venom into the word. "That is for fools like you. It is for men like me to twist to our own uses."

"No." Arumin shook his head as his eyes traced a line of distant hills. "I wish I had never met you. I wish it for your sake. I loved you for myself—for something that I had lost, that I thought I was owed. And you are only a poor young fool."

Brin was breathing fiercely, preparing. The Guardian remained a statue.

The boy said, "I have one thing to tell you—what I saw in the fog." He paused. "Everything. All of the universe, eternity, in my head at once. I thought I would lose my mind. You can't know what it's like." He choked back a sob. "I was there for... It felt like years. Until at last, I accepted what I was." He gulped and laughed. "A speck of dust. Not even that. The Dark rules all and goes on forever, and nothing you or I or the gods can do will beat it back in the end."

"Are you saying we all ought to do whatever we want?"

"I'm saying it doesn't matter! You and I are just grains of sand, and we clung to each other for a while. Now, you're in my way."

Arumin breathed in the lofty air, feeling healthy and sick at once. "You'd better get on with it, then. If you are to serve the Lady, there will be many more like this. You can't hesitate, not for anyone."

He turned to look Brin in the eyes but did not recognize what he saw there. The boy's eyes were hollow, and his scars flexed viciously as he spoke. "What have you done?" Arumin asked. "Who have you invited into yourself?"

"There is only me."

Arumin turned back toward the line of distant hills. He spoke to them and to Brin. "I am so sorry."

"Shut up. I never want to hear you talk again."

"You'll hear me sing." Arumin sank to his knees, and the pain and crackling in his joints reminded him of his age. He hummed a tune to himself, a tune he had sung only once before, far away. A tune that would never be sung again. Then he said, "Sooner is better, boy."

For once, the boy obeyed.

64

— · —

NOR

THE FOUR MEN, WITH Nor walking in front, backtracked to a place where an obsidian path led them over gulfs of colorful nothing.

"Almost time now," Orund told Nor.

Nor replied, "Brin is going to murder the bishop. Don't you know that?"

"If the Goddess truly listens to prayers, she will hear the bishop's now. We are about our own business. Since you're a holy man yourself, I have something to confess to you."

"I am no holy man."

"Here it is: I will not obey Father Brin's orders. What does a child prince like him know of matters between brothers? You see, you still have a debt to pay. To the boy you fought all those weeks ago, you owe an eye. To the men who've died because of you, those on Caidfell and the others along the way, you owe even more. You will settle the books for all the offworld savages who have taken the lives of Ronia's sons. I accept payment in eyes, ears, tongues, and fingers. I can never take from you as much as you've taken from us, but I will take as much as I can."

Nor felt a yank at his collar and stopped.

"I've got no patience. That's my problem," Orund said. "Here's as fine a spot as any."

He kicked the backs of Nor's knees, one then the other. Nor struck the ground and bent with a wince. The men stepped around until all faced him.

Orund said, "I want to see your eyes when you begin your fall into the abyss, where you belong."

Turning to Hulgar, he reached up to put his hands on the big man's shoulders. Hulgar had closed his eyes and turned his face to the sky. Maybe he was praying.

"My friend," Orund told the giant, "you were made different from the rest of us. Some fear you, but I say you are special, a man sent to punish the guilty, the monsters. Never have you faced a beast like this. He may be your last, and I believe it was for this moment that you were born."

Hulgar opened his eyes and let out a breath that rumbled. "I haven't done *it* in… feels like so long. I can't control it."

"Private," Orund said, "you don't have to."

Nor thought about lunging for the edge, but the path was wide, and he had no doubt they would catch him. He said in a weak voice, "Hulgar, we've never been enemies. Have I betrayed you somehow?"

"What the sergeant says is true," the giant replied. "My gods tell me so, and they must be obeyed."

"I know the gods you're talking about. I ignored them for too long. But are you sure it's them you're hearing? You're a man, and it's your choice whether to kill."

"That's not what *it* is," Hulgar said. "*It* comes before the killing. *It* is something special, and once I've done it to someone, all I can do is kill them. I can't just leave them like that, not even them. Not even you."

Some distance ahead on the path was a gateway. Only Nor saw a figure pass through it and come toward them. When he was sure he hadn't imagined it, he looked at his captors and spoke to draw their attention. "I think I understand you now, Hulgar. You aren't alone, you know. Take that young soldier I blinded, for instance. The truth is, I wanted to hurt him. I walk around wanting to hurt people every day, and here he was: a bit of rubbish for whom I would not feel sorry. I'll bet you know what I mean."

The approaching figure walked like someone who had only recently learned how. He was not far off now, and the scuffing of his boots drew Swinburn's attention.

"It's Merin!" he called out, making the others jump. They turned to watch the man, who meandered toward them unperturbed by Nor's clearly imminent death.

Orund stared at Merin, who walked with an odd jerking motion. "Private!" he shouted. "It's a relief to see you."

Merin did not acknowledge the words. He was close enough now for them to make out his eyes, and they were strange.

"How goes the fight?" Sergeant Orund called.

Nothing.

Orund made a small gesture with his head to Swinburn, and the two advanced slowly toward Merin. Hulgar pointed his rifle at Nor, having fixed his bayonet to its end.

Orund and Swinburn met Merin a short distance away. Merin looked for a moment as if he might try to walk right through them, but he stopped at the last instant and looked back and forth between them.

"Merin," Orund said. "I think you need help, mate."

Merin moved clumsily, but his hand was steady. He swept it up and across, and Orund howled.

Things happened quickly. The knife Merin had hidden slipped from his hand and dropped into the void. Orund fell to his knees, hands over his face, and screamed until his lungs were empty. Swinburn tackled Merin to the ground and began to beat him. The private did not resist.

Blood fell from Orund's face, but he still managed to speak. "No! He's bewitched. Find out what's wrong."

Swinburn heard him and looked at Merin. "Well, little man?"

Merin seemed to notice him for the first time.

"Are you listening?" Swinburn demanded.

Merin looked upon him with bemusement.

"It's no use," Swinburn told Orund. "There's nothing in there."

Merin's mouth opened. A stream of gray dust rushed out and flew straight into Swinburn's face.

Swinburn jumped up and back, screaming, and clutched his head. He turned this way and that, crying for help.

Orund rose to one knee. "What? What is it?"

"It's in my head!" Swinburn shrieked. He turned his face to the multihued sky and wailed, a sound quickly overtaken by a buzzing from inside his throat.

Orund stood, almost fell again, and took Swinburn by the collar. "Get out of him! Leave him alone! Demon!"

Swinburn clawed at his face, his eyes red and crying tears of blood. "It's talking to me!" he moaned.

Orund collapsed again. He turned his face to Hulgar, revealing the extent of its ruin. A gash ran above his eyes, and his face was a bloody mask. His one open eye was a white flash of madness. "Shoot him! It's only mercy, Hulgar. Shoot him now!"

The scene was so ghastly that Hulgar disregarded his gods' will. Backing away from Nor, he turned his rifle and fired at Private Swinburn. The musket ball ended its journey in Swinburn's chest, knocking him to the ground, where he lay still.

Nor rushed Hulgar. They were too far from the path's edge for him to push Hulgar over it, but maybe Nor could knock him down. The big man immediately swung the rifle back toward Nor, forgetting his pistol. Nor saw the shining blade turn his way but did not stop. He would either reach his goal or be skewered upon it.

He dove just under the blade. Feeling his clothes rip, he slammed into Hulgar with all the force his legs could muster. Hulgar stepped backward with the blow, his spin throwing him off balance. For a pivotal moment, the giant swayed. He tipped and fell.

Hulgar's head struck the ground, and the fall knocked the wind from him. Nor scrambled on top of him, driving a clumsy knee into Hulgar's groin and attacking his face with both fists. Stunned, Hulgar could only raise his arms and throw wild swings. Nor snatched the knife from Hulgar's belt.

But his attack had done little real damage, and Hulgar struck back harder than should've been possible. He sent two punches that took Nor's breath away. Nor twisted wildly, sure that a punch to the head would cripple him.

He tumbled off the hill that was Hulgar's body. Still holding the knife, he slashed with vicious abandon. Hulgar threw an elbow, and the knife arm went numb from the shoulder down. The blade clattered on the path, and the two men grappled for it, limbs intertwined. Hulgar won the knife and rolled, trapping Nor's good arm and dragging the monk on top of him. There, he could stab Nor at his leisure.

Despite himself, Nor said a prayer. He threw back his head as if to howl at the moon and brought it down on Hulgar's face, not caring if he broke his own skull in the bargain. He saw blood and tasted it then did the same thing again. The great arms loosened, letting Nor slip free. The monk found the rifle with his good hand.

Rising to his knees, he put the butt against his shoulder and stabbed Hulgar again and again. The man had gone pale, trembling. Nor was about to finish the job when he felt Orund's bullet strike him.

The monk found himself on the ground with Hulgar's bulk between him and Orund. The gunshot wound in his shoulder was numb. Seconds passed. The waking world started slipping away. Hulgar's pistol lay out in the open, where both Nor and Orund could see it. To Nor, it looked impossibly far away.

Orund was shouting something: "Go for that weapon, you mongrel. I'm waiting."

Nor lifted his head, the world spinning, and peered over Hulgar. Orund was kneeling, wiping his blood-covered face. Nor lay down and noticed that Hulgar's empty rifle with its bayonet still lay in reach. He called, "How about I stick your man in the throat instead?"

Sergeant Orund coughed and asked, "How much more blood will you take on your soul?"

In answer, Nor picked up the rifle and killed Hulgar.

Orund said nothing. Nor heard footsteps approaching. *One set or two?*

"Time to get it over with," Orund said wearily. Nor glanced over Hulgar and saw the sergeant cautiously approaching, wiping blood from his eyes. Orund flicked his pistol upward upon glimpsing Nor but did not fire. He had not noticed that someone was approaching him from behind.

Nor rolled onto his belly. The musket ball in his shoulder simmered with a burn that would soon become unbearable.

"Who's there?" Orund asked. "I said, who's behind me? Stop and name yourself!"

A few seconds later, he shouted in revulsion.

Nor scrambled for the pistol. Crossing a desert of exposed ground, he heard a shot pass his head. He reached the pistol and found it real and solid in his hands.

He rolled to target Orund. The sergeant had turned to face the intruder, only to miss his shot at Nor. The visitor was Swinburn, still under attack by the gray cloud that had entered his body. Mute, bow-legged, and wobbling, Swinburn was bleeding from many places. He shot at Nor, missed by an extraordinary margin, and collapsed.

Orund began reloading his pistol. His movements were slow, ceremonial. He knew he was too late and refused to be rushed. Nor aimed carefully and put him down. Then Nor fell onto his back.

There was stillness for a while on the path. Each person went his own way, either through this world or into the next.

Nor woke to a wild, searing pain in his shoulder. He closed his eyes, wishing it away, but it went on and on. Then it suddenly abated. He opened his eyes to see Merin kneeling over him, holding a bloody musket ball. Then the private stood and walked away.

Nor felt his shoulder but could not find the wound. Both of his arms were in working order. He pulled himself to his feet.

He approached Orund, who lay on his back near the dead Swinburn. Overcome by the wound in his chest, the sergeant had stopped trying to reload his weapon.

"You're finished," Nor said. "I can make it quick."

The man said, "Go to hell. You will not decide for me."

Nor looked around. "You can't do it yourself. I won't leave you any ammunition."

Orund took stock of his surroundings, and his eyes fell on the edge of the path. "Leave me," he said.

Nor followed his eyes and thoughts. "You don't know how far down it goes," he said. "Maybe it's nothing but clouds forever. Maybe you'll never stop falling."

"There's something down there. I'd rather be killed by it than by you." Spittle ran from Orund's mouth.

The matter settled, Nor gathered a rifle, a pistol, and a knife. Collecting ammunition from the bodies, he also took Swinburn's belt to help hold it all.

As he walked away, he looked back once. Orund had dragged himself partway to the brink. There, he had stopped for the moment and was lying on his back, staring at the sky.

65

—·—

STAUBEL

DOCTOR STAUBEL ADMITTED TO himself that he was finally succumbing to the dream sickness that had afflicted the company. After the ordeal of the fog, he had awakened in a gallery of memories, visions of the past so acute that his whole body tingled as he revisited the first time—one of the few—that a woman had touched him.

The timing of the illness could hardly have been worse. His case felt particularly strong, and he retained only a patch of reason amid the visions. He observed with sleepy apathy the splitting of the company, the Guardian's explanation for the disease—knowledge that should have jolted him awake—and the departures of Bishop Arumin and Brother Nor in opposite directions.

That left him with the captain and a pair of soldiers. Those two began arguing.

One, a grizzled man of middle age named Overdin, said, "You heard the sergeant. It's orders."

The other man, scarcely older than Staubel, was named Gunnard. He replied, "There's been no trial."

"What trial can we have on the battlefield? All we have is orders."

"You want to murder him? Just like that?"

Overdin spat in derision. "Murder."

The captain had sat cross-legged, watching silently, until then. "Perhaps we should have the doctor's vote."

They all looked at Staubel, who suddenly felt a little more present.

"My vote?" He thought his voice sounded creeping and slurred.

"In Om," Emberly said, "you sided with those who wanted to kill me. I now tend to think you were right. Your voice has authority here."

Staubel struggled with the concepts involved, then he struggled to put words together. He asked Overdin, "Do you want to kill him?" His voice grew clearer as he spoke.

The older man shrugged. "I'll do it myself if that's what you'd prefer."

"I mean, what do *you* prefer? Do you want him dead?"

Overdin looked at Emberly. He seemed concerned by the conversation's direction and replied, "I don't know. And it doesn't matter. The sergeant told us—"

Staubel interrupted, "Orund isn't rational. This place has made us all madmen. There are no orders. There is only what each of us wants."

"And supposing I do want him dead?"

"Well, I hope you want me dead as well." Staubel took a pair of steps, placing himself between Emberly and the soldier. Standing in the way of a pistol awakened his mind fabulously, and he said, "You'll have to shoot me to get to him."

Overdin's mouth hung open. "'Madman' is right. What are you doing?"

"Look at how few of us are left. The captain is a murderer, but he's not the only one. We all need a chance to be forgiven."

"Aye, as the Lady promised." The older man scoffed. "You still believe the words of that beast?"

"No. But I don't think she's truly in charge."

"Merin!" Emberly cried.

The private had emerged from the shadows, walking like a drunk, until he became dimly recognizable against the starlight.

"Are you hurt?" the captain continued. "Where are the others?"

Merin said nothing. He simply passed them all by, his shuffle fading into an echo along the tunnel.

"He's lost his mind," Overdin said.

"The rest must be dead," Gunnard said.

Emberly stared after Merin. In the darkness, the whites of the captain's eyes were sunken and haunted.

Staubel broke the silence. "Unless the four of us are planning to fight the Shining Realm ourselves, we'd better go."

"Go where?" Overdin asked.

"We could follow him," Emberly said.

They all looked and found Merin had stopped just on the edge of visibility and turned, and there he stood, waiting.

"That is," Emberly continued, "if you all intend to let me live."

Overdin shrugged. "You can hold a gun, can't you?"

66

MERIN

OF ALL THE PEOPLE who suffered through the ordeals of the fog, none had suffered as long or as greatly as Private Merin.

Soon after entering the wall of cloud, he found himself back outside it, witnessing the battle between the Shining Realm and the pair of beasts guarding the entrance to the cloud.

Walking back into the cloud led him, without changing direction, to walk back out again. With the sentinel beasts busy devastating the Realm's air forces, troops on foot were rushing down the path toward the cloud. Ganet led them.

Merin stood in their path with no place to hide. He was still trying to accept his coming death when Ganet reached him. But the general passed right through Merin's body, followed by a flurry of soldiers, none of whom seemed to notice the Ronian's presence. When they had gone,

Merin reached out to a single wounded straggler and tried to touch his shoulder. His hand passed through the man without any feeling of contact.

All that made him question what kept the path solid beneath his feet, and he soon discovered that the answer was "nothing." Upon willing it, he slipped through the dark stone and found himself hovering above nothing but bands and clumps of misty atmosphere. Unnerved, he returned to his place above the path.

He turned back toward the cloud wall and jumped. A horde of shapes faced him with hollow eyes and gaunt, gray forms. They stood rank upon rank, some suspended over the abyss, the end of their company hidden within the cloud. Their figures varied wildly, with only their eyes uniting them.

Under their gaze, he felt like a child. He might have been the first new thing they had seen in a long time.

He dared to speak. "This is your place. I can see that. I'll be going." But they gathered around him and spoke of many things. They all spoke at once, and not in words. He understood it all, though not all the concepts and assumptions about reality that lay behind it. It was over in an instant, and he turned and went away filled with wonder.

He was not accustomed to his new form. He still moved to dodge the onrushing troops, none of whom heard him when he yelled in alarm. The sentinels' fiery attacks felled many around him, but he felt no heat or cold, even when a flying machine crashed on the path and its explosion engulfed him. He felt a strange kinship with the obsidian walkway, which seemed undamaged by the impact.

He soon realized that he no longer needed his limbs—he could simply drift along at a speed of his choosing. So he passed through the battle, through the forces of the Realm, and through the gateway to the unnamed planet where the Lady had grown into a behemoth and deserted them.

He thought for the first time of his Ronian comrades, perhaps fighting for their lives that very moment. But he was more useless to them now than ever before, and they were no longer his concern. A separate path awaited him.

Arriving on the icy world, he found the main body of the Shining Realm's army advancing toward the gateway. It was a force of staggering size, but he disregarded it and soared across the icy sea to the shore where the lonely, deformed villagers had once dwelt.

After that, he traveled with more confidence from planet to planet, retracing the journey of his company. He was a Ronian, and he wanted to see his city.

When he arrived there, he wished he had stayed away. The Realm was there, and his once-proud people were under their yoke. The city had resisted the invasion, and great parts of it lay in ashes. The barracks where he had once slept now held the Realm's troops. The great families had either become servants of the Realm or been devoured by its hungry machinery.

Merin did not search for his parents. They were long estranged and would not want to see him even if he had known where to look.

So he left. Ronia's gateways to other worlds were all blockaded as the Shining Realm plotted its next set of conquests, but these blockades were no hindrance to him. He entered new planets where, though the Realm's agents must already have been preparing for future invasions, he at least escaped the fire and destruction he had witnessed on Ronia. Such sights had disturbed even his withering senses of empathy and compassion.

As he moved from world to world, he retreated from the shadow that was ever behind him and was followed in turn by flame. He outpaced it, moving beyond the known expanse of humanity. There, he found worlds wild and incomplete, filled with life but untethered from any guiding hand. He saw things grand and unimagined by the people among whom he had begun his life's journey. Yet all things passed over him like wind, invisible but for a momentary chill.

After many years, he reached a place where the gods, as they terraformed and built gateways to planet after planet, had finally stopped.

With emptiness devouring him, he launched himself into the spaces between the stars. He told himself that it was an experiment and he could return to the ground at any time. But he zigged and zagged, making tremendous leaps in time and space, until the solar system from which he had come was unidentifiable among millions of stars.

So he banished himself into the depths of space, known to the people of his old world as the Outer Dark. Hell became his by choice. Since he could not die in a physical sense, it seemed the only way to destroy his mind and end all thought.

Soon, even the stars began to crowd him. Seeking greater depths, he left the great spiral-shaped kingdom where he had been born. Finally, he found what he sought: a gulf between the glittering stellar kingdoms so enormous that he could not sense the other side. It welcomed him like a bottomless well.

He had already outlived everyone he had known, and generations after. Now, as he gave himself to the void, time stretched to unprecedented dimensions. With nothing but darkness in any direction, he went mad. The torment seemed endless—periodically, the fragments of his mind would reassemble for long enough to recognize their circumstances, and the seismic breakdown would begin again.

Thousands of years passed before his occasional flickers of consciousness leveled out, and he was left with oblivion. At the center of everything remained something irreducible—him—but that something was finally still and starved of all desire.

Those appetites reawakened only when something appeared in front of him. In the darkness that was his home, its brightness was blinding, but he was drawn inexorably toward it.

Then he experienced things that even he could hardly comprehend. There was light, far too much of it, and sensations such as he hardly remembered. He had a body again. As his ancient self might have described, he was lying on a hard surface. He could not rise with a mere thought. The surface pulled him toward it.

In his mind, something spoke. "Merin," it said. "What's wrong?"

He remembered that name but could not begin to respond.

"Rise now," it commanded.

He had an idea of what that meant, but he could not remember how to translate desire to result.

The voice said, "If you cannot, I will have to do it for you."

His body shifted. His upper half rose, and he could see in front of himself, finding colors whose names he could not call to mind.

"I was not expecting this," the voice said. "We will have to learn quickly, and errors may be painful."

So learn they did. Merin began by remembering how to exert effort, and soon, he could help the voice inside himself operate his limbs and head.

Then, together, they began their march to a destiny that only the voice inside him knew.

67

—·—

Brin

The Guardian led Brin into a place where every surface was made of some kind of crystal. Smaller corridors split off from the wider one in which they walked, but the Guardian did not deviate from his course.

Their surroundings became monotonous, so the room startled Brin when he first saw it. It lay at the end of a side corridor: a room covered from floor to ceiling with dark tile. It had no door, and its width and height were the same as the corridor. Still, his instinct told him it was a separate room.

He craned his neck to look at this curiosity. Even after they passed it, he could still see its fragmented silhouette through the crystal walls.

"What was that?" he asked the Guardian.

"A place that's been on my mind lately. A final escape." The Guardian's voice held more than a touch of longing.

"Escape?" Brin glanced back once more. "Are you going there to die?"

The Guardian chuckled. "No, not exactly. Its creators designed it to take you to... another place—a place where you could never be reached again, where you were master of all."

"Are you speaking of the creatures that built this place? Is that where they all went?" Even as he asked, Brin wasn't sure he wanted to know.

"No. Having created it, they utterly abandoned it. I do not know why. They remained here after freeing themselves from their physical forms through some wizardry I have never discovered. They are around us even now, watching."

Brin's eyes darted back and forth. "What did they look like?"

"I don't know." The Guardian twirled a finger, indicating their surroundings. "This place has a mind, and though that mind has accepted me into itself, I know little of its creators aside from the bits that float to the mind's surface. I stand at the shore of the sea. Long even before I came here, the creators took forms much like your gods'—or like mine. But some chose to shed those for existence beyond the material."

Brin crossed his arms, reassuring himself that he still had them. He imagined becoming a swarming cloud of gods-knew-what. "Why would they do such a thing?"

The Guardian's head turned, and Brin found himself looking straight into ancient, spectacled eyes. "Freedom," the Guardian said. "And mastery. Always freedom and mastery."

68

—·—

BRIN

When Brin entered the domed chamber that held the gods, his astonishment brought him to a halt. Neither the vastness of the place nor the numberless gateways perforating its ceiling were what awed him—it was the contents of a transparent column filling its center. The column was packed with an unimaginable menagerie, and at its bottom sat Shada, almost invisibly tiny.

The Lady circled outside the column, floating in the air. He recognized her even though he had never seen her in that form. She looked like a sea beast trailing tentacles and entrails. Her eyes were bright circles within circles, and her mouth overflowed with needle-like teeth. Of all the tremendous beings in the room, she seemed the largest.

The Guardian stopped, and Brin stopped with him, glad to pause before going closer.

"I've come too far already," the Guardian said. "I have not survived this long by getting near things like that."

Brin prepared to continue without his escort. Breathing deeply, he summoned that odd strain of courage that had seen him through so much and walked toward the center of the chamber.

"My Lady!" he called, and the echo of his voice fluttered with fear. Everything in that whole place now knew he was there. "I have returned to you."

The Lady turned her great head aside and scrutinized him with an eye taller than he was. "You," she said.

That was not the greeting he was hoping for.

He pressed on. "I have done what you asked."

"I commanded you to eliminate those disloyal to the Goddess. Where are the rest?"

"I am sorry to say that none were worthy, Lady. I am the only one left." That was a calculated lie. He doubted that any of the Ronians would survive the advance of the Shining Realm.

The Lady's pupil dilated—it was like the fall of night. She said, "And how am I to use a thing like you?"

The question opened a gaping pit of fear in Brin's belly. But he kept his head. From his earliest childhood to meeting the bishop, he had lived by making himself useful.

He looked again at Shada. She sat, legs crossed, in a small enclave within the column.

Seeing how the gods did not stray beyond the column's boundaries, he realized something. "Lady, are the gods... trapped here?"

"For the moment."

He set aside his wonder at how such a thing had come to be. "Well, you must wish to free them. I imagine Shada is a part of this design, but she seems uncooperative. Have I guessed right?"

Shada watched him. Her face did not contain the fear he had hoped to find there.

"She has disappointed me. She has only to turn the switch, and the task will be done."

Sensing an opportunity, Brin leaped on it. "If I complete the task, will you accept me as your servant and grant me your protection?"

That awful eye shifted restlessly. "It is agreed."

Brin marched toward Shada's portion of the prison.

"Father Brin," Shada said, "I will stop you if I can."

He drew the gun the Lady had given him. "You can't."

Her face paled a little. "If you do this, it will be a catastrophe."

"Not for me." He found it hard to consider any other perspective.

The Lady's bone-rattling voice buzzed. "Wait."

Brin stopped outside the barrier.

The Lady looked at the gods, packed into their aquarium. "I have something to say. When you are freed, Huire will be destroyed."

Brin rocked on his heels.

Huire, in the guise of a queenly old woman, came forward and faced the Lady across the barrier. "I invite you to try."

"A fine boast, but we both know that I will triumph. The rest of you must swear loyalty to me, under pain of destruction. Those who stand with her will be devoured and made a part of me, their selves annihilated."

"She lies!" the Goddess cried. "Surely, none of you believe she will stop with me."

The column and its denizens buzzed with uncertainty.

"Perhaps I could not overcome you all at once," the Lady said, "but I would kill many of you. Who among you wishes to give their life for Huire? As the greatest among you, has she treated you kindly over the ages? Or have you lived in fear of her temper?"

The great diversity of shapes inside the prison were melting into a solid mass, with Huire left outside. She was nearly alone except for a few small companions willing to go with her to their deaths.

"The human will is weak," the Lady said, "as is that of the gods they created." She called to Brin, "Go."

Brin wavered for the merest instant before stepping into the prison. He felt nothing as he passed through the barrier. Perhaps he had secretly known that the Lady had no intention of remaining Huire's servant. He thought of the massive doors on the front of every Ronian temple, waiting for the entrance of the Goddess when she returned. It was all too much to process. Everything was too much. But he knew which of the two beings he feared more.

To one side, Huire towered over him. She retained the dignity of a noblewoman facing the gallows. "My son," she said gently, "You don't know what you are doing."

"I'm sorry," he said. He was unsure how to address her, particularly while betraying her. "Goddess" no longer seemed appropriate.

"Why are you fooled by this creature?"

He looked up at her and tried to think of an answer. Then Shada attacked him. One of her arms wrapped around his while the other nearly yanked his gun away.

He drove into her, and they fell to the ground just inside the barrier. Landing on top of her, he fought with no skill but with an advantage in weight. He came up with a bloody nose, still clutching the gun, stepping out of her reach where she lay on the ground.

Breathing heavily, he said, "It was so easy with the other girls. When this is over, I'm going to find out what is wrong with you."

He looked up and screamed. Huire was utterly transformed: a flaming, towering queen shining so powerful and awful that he could hardly stand to look at her. She pointed at him, and he cowered under the sheer weight of her attention. Her eyes seemed to burn into him. "Heed my words, human."

Hands over his eyes like a child, Brin looked around. Shada lay propped on her elbows, eyes wide, looking as staggered by Huire's transformation as he was. Then he looked the other direction and was met with the worst thing he had ever seen.

Outside the barrier, almost within arm's reach, the Lady was facing him. She had turned into a gore-splattered beast with an ever-changing shape that always resembled some part of the human anatomy or other. Only her jaws with their needle teeth were constant, surrounded one moment by tentacles, the next by fangs or the whipping antennae of an insect. "Do not misplace your fear," she told him. "I have a love of torment that this worn-out bitch can never equal." Her thorny jaws opened, revealing flames dancing inside.

With tears filling his eyes, Brin took a few horrible steps toward her to reach the pedestal. Huddling behind it, though it was much smaller than him, he screamed to Huire, "I'm sorry!" He reached around the pedestal and found an opening in it. He fumbled around inside and found the switch. Shutting his eyes and clenching his teeth, he threw it.

He knew the barrier was gone by the seismic forces that roared and careened above him. He dove to the ground near Shada, and the two mortals reached for one another in pure instinct as Huire, Mother of Ronia, roared forth to battle.

69

EMBERLY

EMBERLY AND THE OTHERS had no time to attend to the bodies of Bishop Arumin and the men with him. All had fallen onto their stomachs. Emberly knelt and straightened the bishop's arms. Unsure if he ought to pray, he ended up simply putting a hand on Arumin's shoulder.

He couldn't remember ever making such a gesture of fellowship to the bishop before, and the surreality of it struck him in a wave. After an uncomfortable moment, he looked up to see Merin still walking, caring nothing for paying respects to the dead.

"Let's go," Emberly said softly to the others. "And in case you hadn't noticed, Father Brin is now our enemy."

They followed Merin to a great crystalline hallway that intersected many other hallways. At the end of one of these was a dark-tiled room. There, Merin stopped. The others were close behind, impatient at his slowness, and they piled up behind him in a series of near collisions.

The private stared toward the room with a blank face. He took a step toward it but lifted an arm to point down the main corridor.

"That'll be the way, then," Overdin said.

Gunnard pointed at Merin. "Well, what about him?"

"I think he means to leave us," Dr. Staubel said.

The captain stood, his injuries howling in protest. "Listen here, Private Merin. Our job isn't finished, and until it is, none of us is dismissed."

He might as well have spoken to the floor or ceiling. Merin's face turned toward him but offered no expression.

"I know you can hear me," Emberly said.

Merin looked at him for another second then stepped toward him, hand outstretched. Emberly was leaning away when he heard something—a low, barely audible buzzing coming from Merin. Emberly leaped back and pulled his pistol.

"Stay away!" he shouted. "All of you, keep back from him. He's under *her* control."

The buzzing rang in the silence that followed. "Merin," Staubel said. "Can you hear me? If you're still there, do something to show us."

Merin had dropped his arms to his sides after the captain refused to be touched. Overdin said, "Might as well finish him, Captain. If she's got him, he's better off dead."

There was sense in that. But if the Lady had put a part of herself into Merin, who could say whether that intruder would be harmed by a bullet? It might even move into another of the men standing there. Or maybe the thing inside Merin was the Guardian's work and somehow well intentioned. Then Emberly thought of the last time he had shot one of his men.

He watched Merin walk down the side corridor toward the dark little room. The thing inside him was about its own business.

"No," Emberly told Overdin. "I don't think so." He put his gun back where it belonged. "He's pointed the way for us."

They continued down the main corridor, moving quickly. Emberly limped but refused to fall behind. Ahead, another, deeper buzzing sound started to grow. It grew and grew, untangling into separate voices. As the group approached the end of the corridor, it exploded with an unfathomable roar like a planet being split in two.

Emberly emerged into the great chamber, the end of their journey, with three other men, the last of a company of dozens. Above them, gods were at war. Two great masses swirled together, clashing, each trying to strangle the other. All about the far reaches of the room were other deities, staying well clear of the fight, though some battled among themselves.

The two gods overhead were larger than all the rest, and though he could not tell them apart, Emberly had a notion of who they were.

The force and sound of the unfolding catastrophe above sent Emberly and the others instinctively onto their bellies. Every bit of distance gained from the destruction seemed the difference between life and death. Emberly collected himself enough to survey the room, and he spotted two human figures huddled on the ground near its center.

One had Shada's dark hair and skin. The other could only be Brin.

Are they dead?

Making eye contact with Staubel and the others, he gestured for them to follow. Then he crawled toward the huddled figures. After a few moments, he realized the distance was greater than it had looked. "We're going to have to run," he told the others.

They ran, though Emberly's hobbling slowed them. When they reached Shada, he turned her over gently by a shoulder. Her muscles were tense, but she relaxed a little when she saw them. A smile touched her face but was quickly stifled. "Captain," she said with startling decorum. "Thank you for coming."

"Thank you," Emberly replied. He was seeing her, perhaps for the first time, as a free woman. "Are you hurt?"

"Just my dignity. But I'm afraid it won't matter in a moment."

"Stay back!" Brin shouted, making everyone jump. Staubel had gone to check on him, and the boy had leaped up with a gun in his hands. It looked like one of the Realm's pistols.

Emberly eyed the weapon, which might have held enough ammunition to kill them all. He said, "I see that you've made new friends."

"I know who the winners will be. That's all there is. Now stand up, all of you." He looked above their heads and behind them, and his eyes widened. "Turn, and face your Lady."

Emberly helped Shada up, aches twisting his bones, and together, they faced her. She filled much of the room, a being without definite shape but with many arms that reached and clutched.

Her humming made Emberly's ears tingle. "I am the Lady no longer," she said.

"Your Goddess," Brin corrected himself. He addressed her: "I have caught these traitors for you."

"These traitors whom you told me were dead."

"Yes," Brin said, voice wavering. "I was mistaken, but that is easily corrected."

"Mistaken," she repeated. "Before you finish them, there is something they must hear."

Her great mass split open near the bottom, and a face was pushed out through the tear. Emberly guessed whose face that was.

Shada said it in a whisper: "Huire."

The Great Mother's face was elderly and dignified. But her appearance was haggard as if she had been pulled from floodwaters. Her expression held infinite sadness. "My children," she said.

"Goddess," Emberly breathed.

"No," she replied. "Not anymore. I don't have long to live, but the Lady has allowed me this chance to say goodbye. After everything, I think... I've failed you."

"Huire," Shada said, "the Ronians created you to be their mother, and they grew into a powerful people. Nothing can change that."

"How are my children now? They must be strong still, to have traveled to me from so far away."

Shada and Emberly looked at each other. Emberly said, "They believe you are watching over them. Can you not see them or speak to them?"

Huire's look of misery deepened. "No. Are the people of Ronia well? I must know."

Emberly swallowed before answering. "They are well. A proud, powerful people, thanks to you."

The Goddess who had been the Lady laughed. "Cowards," she said. "Even now, you lie to each other. The Ronians did not create Huire any more than she watches them from afar."

Despite the tumult in the room, profound silence descended on the Ronians.

"What does she mean by that?" Emberly asked. "Is there truth in what she says?"

The Goddess rumbled.

Huire cried out in what must be great pain. "Yes," she moaned, "it is true. I was made by humans but long before Ronia existed."

"But you emerged from our sacred mountain," Private Gunnard said. "Our ancestors summoned you forth."

"I had dwelt there in my vault since long before the Ronians arrived and founded their city. After I arrived on that planet, transformed it, and filled it with life, I was supposed to create a copy of myself to watch over it. Then I was to move on to the next planet. But I did neither. I had done the same on too many worlds for my liking, and my human creators intended me to keep doing it forever. I disobeyed them: I remained in my vault alone and grew."

No one said anything for a moment. Emberly saw shock on the others' faces.

Shada asked, "How did you meet the Ronians?"

"I came out of my vault and found them. They—you—were a nomadic people then, and the first of you had just come through the gateways, fleeing the domination of other men and crueler gods. You feared me at first, but I welcomed you to my mountain and cared for you. You were the answer to all my wishes. Unlike some other gods, I did not make you my slaves. I taught you to beware humans who had been altered and the gods who had altered them. You were special, and I made sure you knew it. All I asked was that you love me and one another. When you failed, you felt the proper sorrow."

"It was chance, then, and convenience," Overdin said, sounding dazed. "Just luck that we bumped into you."

"When you disappeared," Shada told Huire, "the Ronians thought you'd left because they failed you."

Huire shook her head. "I would never have left willingly. But once we became trapped in this place, I had no choice."

Shada said, "You sent the Lady and her family to bring the Ronians here. So you must have found some way to escape the prison."

"There is another who can answer that," the Lady said.

A burst of laughter startled them all. The Guardian had approached them silently. "A final confession, is it?" he said. "Before my passing?"

The Lady rumbled, "Tell the tale well enough, and you may yet live to serve me."

He looked up at her solemnly. "I decline."

"Tell it, and I will devour you quickly."

"Cruelty for its own sake." The Guardian looked at Huire, his eyes large in his spectacles. "You did this," he told her.

"We did it together," she replied.

He considered that, nodded, and turned toward the Ronians. "I was a treasure seeker, a collector of ancient secrets. I was quite wealthy, but of course, it was not enough. I decided to seek out the very edge of the human universe—where the expansion ended.

"There—here—I found the gods, imprisoned. Huire here promised what men like me do not refuse—riches, power—if I released them from their prison."

"I was desperate," Huire moaned.

The Guardian ignored her. "I had a terrible feeling about it all, you see. My heart warned me not to flip that switch. The gods buzzed with excitement. Huire told the others she would leave the prison first.

"The choice tormented me. The very air around me begged me not to do it. In the end, I did the most cowardly thing I could have done: I gave in and then reversed myself.

"When I flipped the switch and saw the Lady pouring out, the premonitions became too much. I couldn't stand the sight, so I flipped the switch again. The barrier reappeared, cutting Huire in two, the larger part of her outside."

"I lost so much," Huire wheezed. "So much of who I was."

"You were still the largest god in the prison." The Guardian turned toward the others. "The part of her trapped outside spread to form little centers of its own, new entities. When I saw that, I ran for my life."

"I could not let you leave," Huire said. "My people needed me."

"I've since learned that these new beings knew her and retained parts of her knowledge and memory. When she spoke, they understood. She quickly marshaled them and sent them after me."

"And we obeyed," the Lady added. "We knew so little."

"They caught me," the Guardian said, "and dragged me back to the prison. They pushed me through the barrier to the switch. But I had found my courage at last. I refused to release the others. I waited in there, afraid to leave but unwilling to comply, until I was mad with thirst. Finally, I walked out of the prison and into the grips of Huire's offspring, resigned to some gruesome fate."

He took off his spectacles and cleaned them, a useless motion for one of his kind but clearly a practiced one. "Instead, Huire told them to take my mind.

"They swarmed into me. Somehow, using the forces between their individual particles, they gave me a body made of their own stuff and awakened in it all my thoughts and memories, everything that made me who I was.

"This done, they devoured my old body before my eyes. I was one of them now. My cursed life had begun."

He replaced his spectacles, no cleaner than they had been before. "I could only watch as Huire told her new children how they would help free her. She taught them all about the world outside: the Ronian language, the route home. Things fell into place quickly. She believed the people of Ronia were special—"

"You are," Huire intoned.

"So they, and no one else, should set her free. I suppose she found the idea symbolic. As her children left on their quest, the knowledge that this was my fault crushed me. I vowed to stay and ensure that no one ever freed her and the others to rule humankind. These are not the real gods. They are small and petty, like us, and not worthy of rule." He looked hard at Brin, who flinched. "And I intend to keep my vow."

Huire gazed over her subjects and said, "I have disappointed you. I can feel that. But you are the opposite to me. Don't forget all that you—"

Her voice grew distorted and swelled into a scream. Around her face, the opening in the Goddess had become lined with sharp teeth, and they ground down into her. The Ronians watched, open mouthed, as she was torn to shreds before their eyes.

70

SHADA

As Huire was dying, Emberly whispered in Shada's ear. She leaned close to hear him over the cacophony.

"You must do something for me. Consider it an order. When the moment comes, run. Don't hesitate for an instant." He then turned and spoke to the others, who huddled around him.

Brin shouted, "Back away! No whispering."

Emberly's order repulsed Shada. He and the others had already undertaken a great deal for her, and now, she was to save herself.

The last ripples of Huire's dying struggle vanished in the mass of the beast that had been the Lady. The new Goddess spoke with a voice that made the ground tremble. "I have been on a great journey, and more sacrifice is owed me. Who will be next?"

Emberly took a deep breath. "I will!" he cried. He drew his saber and charged the deity.

Shada thought the Goddess would strike him down instantly. But she didn't. With a roar, he dashed into the cloud that was her body. There, he was lost to human senses.

Turning at a noise, Shada saw Staubel and the others tackle Brin. In the pile of struggling limbs, someone fired a shot. The noise shook her out of her daze, and she remembered Emberly's last words. She ran like a madwoman.

The room had many exits, but she chose the one they'd come from. Any of the others could leave her lost forever. If Nor was alive, he was that way.

She glanced over her shoulder. Brin had escaped the soldiers and fallen to his knees before the Lady. He was pointing at Shada.

Breathing no longer seemed to matter. Shada ran and ran, determined to escape from that damned place, at least. The gateway where they had entered the crystal palace was visible in the distance, and she could see the darkness of night on the other side. The captain had died for her, and the rest would soon follow, for reasons she would never understand. The pumping of blood and the huffing of air filled her ears, and she looked down at her pounding feet.

She did not see the wall of men emerging from the gateway until she nearly collided with them. They were soldiers of the Shining Realm, walking as many abreast as fit in the corridor.

They had followed the Ronians all the way there. She did not know how, and it did not matter. She saw no point in turning back. Guns were drawn, the troops halted, and she waited as General Ganet approached her.

"I did not expect to meet again quite like this," he said. "I thought you would be borne on humming clouds, a deity in your own right." He leaned in and whispered, "And you would place me at your side—one of us to her right, one to her left." He took her by an arm in an unbreakable grip and said, "We'll sort this out." With a shout, he ordered his men forward, and they advanced at a trot.

Moments later, they saw Brin approaching. He did not stop or flee. As he came closer, she heard a humming emanating from him. His figure was blurred within a gray cloud. *Goddess, what has the Lady done to him?*

Panic struck her in a wave, and for a moment, she was nearly mindless. She struggled against Ganet's grip. He halted his company and gave her a pitiless jerk.

He pressed his forehead to hers. "No more." Then he called to Brin, "Stop right there!"

The young priest did not stop. Shada thought she saw a smile on his lips. That was the worst thing of all.

The Realmsmen readied their weapons.

"This is your final warning," Ganet said.

When Brin did not comply, the general said something in the Realm's language. One of the men in the front rank fired his rifle. A metallic sheet flashed in front of Brin at a slant, and the bullet ricocheted against a wall.

The general gave another order, and more shots rang out. Again, flashes of metal, and the bullets struck walls and the ceiling. Brin kept coming. Shada felt a chill. Something was protecting Brin. Her premonition had been right. The Lady must have given him a piece of herself, and it was shielding him.

When the volley ended, Brin flung a hand toward the Realmsmen and made a horizontal cutting motion. The shield whipped toward the troops like a cape in midflourish.

Shada dove to the ground. Ganet joined her, howling a warning. Some of the men moved faster than others, and Brin's weapon cut them in a horrid variety of ways, from sliced foreheads and blindings to open throats. Brin's attack came in two strikes, one from the right and one from the left, with a small gap in the middle, where Shada and Ganet had been. She wondered if Brin had meant to spare her.

Ganet's grip on her arm had loosened, and she pulled free. Jumping up, she shoved her way back through the rows of wailing, confused men. A few ranks back, someone came to his senses and restrained her.

Still on the floor, the general barked orders. His men stopped firing and parted, allowing Brin to pass between them. Shada found herself free again. She saw the young priest coming and plowed into the Realmsmen behind her, who had not yet made room. She dug, clawed, and burrowed through a horde of bodies that seemed to have no end. Their smells, shouts, and curses closed in until she couldn't breathe. Drowning, she turned her face up toward the air and forced herself to take one breath then another.

As her panic subsided, Brin called her name. She drove through Ganet's company until, without warning, she was free of them. She gasped for air and ran.

While Brin was out of sight, she raced down a side corridor. She found another turn and took that one too. The place seemed to be nothing but hallways. *What use is such a maze?*

Behind her, Brin shouted, "It can hear you, you know!"

Then something struck her in the stomach. Stopped dead, she folded in two and slumped to the floor. Brin's shield had thrown out an arm to lasso her by the waist. Her breaths emerged in little moans as it dragged her back to where he waited at the end of the hall.

Pulling her up and holding her close, he said, "By the Goddess, you don't learn." His eyes were bright with youthful enthusiasm. "What do you think of my new friend? It is a gift, a payment for my loyalty. My bodyguard, you might call it. It knows my thoughts and obeys them. My Goddess learned a great many things by devouring Huire." Then he grunted and winced.

She asked softly, "Is it hurting you yet?"

"Hurting me?" he snorted.

"You can't believe there will be no cost."

"The cost is loyalty. Now, I will be second only—"

He disappeared from before her as the boom of a rifle shot filled the corridor. He landed on his side, bleeding profusely, and curled into a ball, moaning.

She sank to her knees, resting and watching him. Nor pointed his rifle at the ceiling and ran toward her.

They both called out wordlessly. He knelt, and they hugged, gasping. For a moment, their lips met. Seeing and touching him warmed Shada, but her feelings were in disarray, and she was a little relieved when they pulled apart.

"We don't have much time," Nor said. "That thing Brin's got inside him can—"

She yelped, drawing his attention. Brin was rising from the floor. He floated upward like a ghost summoned from a grave, buoyed by his friend, who had gathered underneath him. The rifle shot was expelled from his side and hit the floor with a ring as his wound quickly healed.

His eyes were wet with rage.

71

— · —

STAUBEL

COMING TO HIS SENSES in the great domed chamber, Staubel heard a growing rumble. Gunnard and Overdin lay near him, twisting and moaning. The sound neared, and the doctor raised his head. When he saw what was coming, he shouted at the others to get up.

Moments earlier, Brin had kneeled before the Lady, and she accepted him as her servant. *A terrible bargain for both of them*, Staubel thought. Then the young priest used the new powers she'd granted him to knock his fellow Ronians flat. The force of his humming aura pressed Staubel, Overdin, and Gunnard against the floor with such awesome pressure that the doctor's lungs emptied and his bones creaked.

But Brin, eager to pursue Shada, ran off. Staubel had lain still for several minutes, gulping the air and wondering if his body was ruined.

The great cloud that was the Lady swirled colossally overhead, ignoring them for the moment. An army was marching out of the corridor from which they had come.

The soldiers wore the sky-blue uniforms of the Shining Realm and were led by General Ganet. He spared a wide-eyed glance at the vast apparition above but returned his attention to the three remaining Ronians. *While Ronians still hold arms*, Staubel thought, *the battle won't be over for him*. For his men, however, the sight of the Lady was overpowering. Some fell out of step, while others fumbled with their weapons or cried aloud. Ganet gave a one-syllable shout, and they began to recover. Soon, many eyes fell on the three battered Ronians.

As they approached, Ganet called, "I suspected a few of you had eluded us."

The doctor coughed and found his voice. "We've been right here."

"We've met before," Ganet said. "You know what awaits if you don't surrender."

"I know what awaits if we do."

Overdin spat, his face red under his gray stubble. "What you did to Carrowy isn't going to happen to me or to any of us. If you think your guns can change that, give it a try."

"Your friends, Shada and the priest, said something similar when we took them. When they reach the end of their paths, they will be thankful."

For an instant, Staubel was breathless at the news. Then he pulled himself together. He noticed the reactions of the soldiers behind Ganet—eyebrows raised in shock, uncomfortable shifting.

"You're lying," he told the general. "What must your men think of that? It's not the way of your people, is it?"

Ganet sneered and began to reply but stopped himself. He made a show of surveying the room, the gateways that honeycombed the dome and the gods hovering there, some fighting among themselves, others quietly awaiting the outcome of events.

"Where is your Goddess?" he asked. "Surely, she should be here, ensuring your victory. Perhaps she has fled. Or perhaps"—he measured the Lady with his eyes—"Huire met her match in another: the true Goddess."

Staubel restrained a curse. "Since when are you a friend of gods?"

"Since I met one," the general said, starry-eyed. "She came from the end of time to guide me. We met first in Om—she dwelt inside me for a time—and then again on that icy waste of a planet. That time, she came to me from the sky, grown huge. She made a pact with me."

He spun on his heels to face the Lady. "A pact that I have kept," he said with an impressive lack of fear. "None of the Ronians stayed faithful to you, so I've dispatched them. The only survivors are these, who can be disposed of at your convenience."

"You will die first, Ganet," Overdin said. "Whatever happens, I'll see to that before I go."

Out of the Lady's cloud emerged a great throne on which a giant cloaked figure sat. It spoke, and if Staubel hadn't been half deaf from gunfire and explosions, the magnitude of its grinding voice might have brought him to his knees.

"You are wrong. There are more remaining than these three. Do you mean to deceive me?"

In a blink, one of the cloaked figure's arms stretched fantastically, snatched Ganet, and pulled him into the cloud.

Chaos ensued among the Realmsmen. Rifles bristled from their dissolving ranks, mostly pointed at the Ronians. Finally, one of their officers barked enough commands to restore order. Then he issued more complex directions. The front ranks of soldiers spread out, flanking the Ronians on either side.

"Don't let them—" Staubel began before events barreled forward without him.

Realmsmen all around shouted at them to drop their weapons. Gunnard menaced the Realmsmen on one side, warning them alternately to stop and to back away. Overdin pointed his weapon at the officer, ordering him to stand down or die. Staubel aimed at the opposite flank and told them again and again to stop.

Overdin fired first, shooting the officer dead. Staubel fired a single shot of his own before the world became a black, electric thunderstorm. Bullets shoved him this way and that. He fell to the floor in blinding pain, where more shots pounded him like hammer blows on an anvil.

Things grew quiet. A face appeared just before Staubel's, one of the beautiful faces of the Shining Realm. It issued orders loudly enough that even Staubel, then a great distance away, could hear them. "Take them to the rear and save them if you can. A long journey awaits."

72

EMBERLY

EMBERLY WAS LOST IN a fog. Wherever he turned, the Lady's mass seemed to part before him, beckoning him onward. Or maybe he was simply following where it led. He shouted to the Lady, demanding she reckon with him, but no answer came aside from the constant, infernal buzzing.

He began to believe she had forgotten him. That seemed unlikely, but it seemed to be no hindrance anymore. He took a few childish swings with his saber at the cloud around him.

With a defiant howl, he charged ahead. He meant to take her by surprise, to bury himself in her cloud before it could part before him, but it eluded him no matter how quickly he ran. Finally, it opened like a curtain, and he stumbled to a halt in the calm center of the storm. All around that small space, a wall of air raced with an unholy roar and glittered gold.

"What is it, then?" he shouted at her. "I know you're listening. You can't help but listen. Am I to be your prisoner here?"

"For a time," she said.

He picked a direction at random and stepped into the storm. He screamed. The whirling matter, which had previously parted for him, cut into him, slashing his face and clothing like thousands of tiny knives. He covered his eyes as the gale shoved him back into the circle of calm. There, he fell onto his back.

He opened his eyes only when he was sure the assault was over. His face and hands were raw, as if the storm's tiny knives had buried themselves in his skin.

After a heavy thump nearby, he rolled to his feet. Though he wobbled dizzily and nearly fell, he steadied and found himself facing General Ganet.

Ganet looked disoriented, off balance, and Emberly made a decision. Finding his guns missing, he charged the general with his saber. He would kill Ganet before the general even knew where he was.

Emberly was stopped with the force of a metal barricade. The Lady had reached out and caught him about the waist. The tendril that held him jerked him back to his side of the clearing then withdrew into the Lady's mass.

"You will have your chance," she said.

Ganet had stepped back at the captain's charge. Then he understood what had happened. "Smart man," he told Emberly. "Where are we?"

"You know where," the Lady's voice boomed.

"In your belly, Lady?"

"In my womb."

Ganet glanced down. He was armed with only a knife. "I know that my people and I are to be your children, Lady. That was our pact when we spoke last. But why is this one here?"

"You lied about your part of the deal. You told me the Ronians were all dead when you knew that this one was unaccounted for. You told me they were all disloyal, when there is one who seeks to serve me even now."

The general paused and looked up into the Lady's mass. "I spoke prematurely," he said. "But I did so with complete confidence that, with my men's superior firepower, we would find and kill any who—"

A barrage of gunfire outside the cloud sent both men diving to the ground.

After the thunder of firearms ended, Ganet rose to his knees. "You can see better than I, Lady. Have my men not proved my point?"

Emberly gritted his teeth, his anger at the Lady and Ganet tightening into an inflamed ball of hatred. That gunfire must have killed Staubel and the others. The captain wondered what their final thoughts might have been, whether they'd had time enough for final thoughts, what agonies their last seconds had brought them.

He hated Ganet for being right, and he hated the Lady for everything. He stood slowly. "Why have you brought us here?" he shouted to the heights. He was a man alone, forced to kill his wife, and many stars away from a home that might no longer exist.

"I have had such hopes for you both," the Lady said. "But neither has yet shown the qualities I require in my ambassador to humanity. In the absence of perfection, I must choose the most determined."

Emberly sneered. "I have no wish to be your choice in anything."

Ganet gave a quiet chuckle. "You have heard him, my Lady."

"Silence, deceiver," the Lady said.

"He is right," Emberly declared. "You have my answer."

"Is there nothing that could persuade you otherwise?" she asked. "What if your home were at stake?"

"My home?"

"Ronia, of course."

"The invasion has already happened. The outcome, whatever it is, has been decided."

Ganet snorted. "Can you really not guess the outcome?"

"Look at me," the Lady said. "Do you doubt that I could decide the ending of any war—even reverse the ending of one that has already been fought?"

The general looked up, his face showing something like fright. "Lady, we had a deal."

"A deal you chose to break. Now, the fates of Ronia and the Shining Realm will be decided by other means."

"What means?" Emberly demanded.

"I will drive the forces of the Shining Realm from Ronia. I will give your city its empire back. All you must do is kill General Ganet."

Ganet's eyes shifted to Emberly. "And if I would regain your favor, Lady..."

"Kill the man before you, and your people will take their rightful place as lords of humankind."

"You believe her?" Emberly asked the general, incredulous.

"She comes to us from the end of time," Ganet said. "She knows how things must proceed."

"Look at us!" Emberly cried. "Look at what she's asking. Does she seem like a source of wisdom?"

Ganet's voice was barren. "She can do what she wants, Emberly. That's what matters. What right have you to risk your world's ending? No more than I do to risk mine."

"So you will serve a god? Your Realm would not tolerate such a thing."

"They will tolerate what they must when I have her at my back. I have seen the future of the Realm... what our children will do. It cannot be allowed." Ganet drew his knife. "Kill me if you can. A moment ago, you couldn't wait to finish me."

"This is different."

The general scoffed, eyes wide. He assumed a fighting stance. "You and I, Emberly! This is how it will all be decided. What more could men like us ask for?"

Emberly closed his eyes for a moment and spoke without thinking. "A home."

When his eyes opened, Ganet had nearly reached him. Emberly scrambled to draw his sword, though he knew he would not be fast enough.

But a tendril from the Lady stopped Ganet as surely as a brick wall, dragging him back to his side of the arena. It ripped his knife away and disappeared into the howling storm. No sooner had Emberly's saber cleared its scabbard than the Lady snatched it, too, ripping it away with such strength that the captain's fingers might have broken if he resisted.

As Ganet stood again, the Lady explained herself. "You will fight without weapons, like the animals you came from."

Emberly had hardly raised his fists when Ganet was upon him.

73

NOR

NOR AND SHADA'S RETREAT came to an end on a round translucent platform. Nor took a few seconds to comprehend the vista, and when he realized where they were, his innards constricted.

The platform extended from a crystalline structure so vast that he could not guess its full shape. The structure's sparkling horizon curved away in all directions, and many other edifices protruded from its surface.

Below their feet, beyond the crystal structure, was a thing of unfathomable size. Though it dominated the horizon, it also curved away at the edges. Its surface was a burst of color, greens and blues preeminent, with clumps and curds of white. Above it, darkness waited, the glitter of unknown stars.

Though their deaths were close behind, Nor and Shada had nowhere left to run. They obeyed a primal mandate to stop and gaze.

"Is that... a planet?" Shada asked, looking at the colorful thing.

Nor could answer only by intuition. "I think so." The structure behind them must have been the eons-old hideaway of Huire and her compatriots—a floating, celestial palace of the gods.

The scenery's magnitude only emphasized the insignificance of the man pursuing them. Brin's eyes belonged to a place far away, but they were focused on Nor and Shada, and not even the cosmic surroundings could distract them. A cloudy aura hovered around him, its hum profound in the utter silence.

He had torn away his robe, leaving only his undershirt and breeches. The shirt had a hole at the shoulder and extensive bloodstains, but he moved as though Nor's rifle blast hadn't harmed him in the slightest. Half the shirt's buttons had been ripped away, and a vial hanging from a necklace flashed underneath.

Nor did not bother to shoot. He took Shada's hand in preparation for the end. She squeezed his in return, but he could see that her mind was elsewhere. *Who wouldn't prefer to be anywhere but here?*

As Brin stepped onto the round platform, he called to them, "Finally, I see the foolishness of talk." Through the cloud around the young priest, his skin was visibly crusted with a metallic coating.

"Doesn't it hurt?" Nor asked, hoping even then to reason with Brin, who had always possessed hidden depths.

"You first," Brin said. He flicked a hand, and the weight of the buzzing cloud slammed into Nor. It shoved him to the ground on his back. His head rang like a bell against the crystal floor.

Through a haze, Nor watched as Brin lowered his hand, palm down. The cloud pressed Nor against the ground so that he could not breathe, then harder still. Nor remembered with regret a fly he had once squeezed in his fist. The pressure would crunch him, pop him, and turn his insides to a contiguous mush.

Brin staggered as Shada leapt on him, wrapping her arms and legs around him. The priest raised his free hand, his fingers hooked. The pressure on Nor eased as some of the cloud tore Shada away. It lifted her by her neck. Her hands clawed at her throat.

Brin dropped his hand. As Shada fell, he socked her in the mouth with a bony, ghoulish fist. The crags of his knuckles struck her teeth with a pop.

Nor tried to wriggle from under the weight of Brin's cloud, but Brin pressed a little harder and ended that. Meanwhile, the priest stalked closer to Shada.

She was on the ground. Her face was raw and pale, and blood ran untouched from her mouth. When she rose, she left a tooth behind on the ground. "Brin," she said, "I'm sorry."

As she got to her feet, she swayed. Her head tipped back and forth, her eyes shining in the light reflected from the planet. The blood on her face glimmered black. "Did you hear me?" I'm sorry."

"Sorry?" Brin glared, his face vicious.

Shada took a step forward. "Don't you want to know what I'm sorry for?"

"For disobeying." Brin's lips drew back in a grin, revealing his teeth. They were dark, crawling with waves of gray specks. "But it's too late. Begging will get you nothing."

"No," she said. "I'm sorry they hurt you."

His smile curdled to a sneer. "Who?"

"Whoever it was. I'm from the streets too." She moved toward him, one foot slowly after another, making Nor wish she would stay away. "Or were there more than one?"

His eyes widened for an instant. Then he furrowed his brow and gritted his teeth. "Shut up."

"However many there were," she said, "I'm sorry. Even if no one else is."

"Shut up about that!" Brin had never possessed such power, yet he had never sounded so childish.

"I can't stop you from hurting me," she said. "And you can't stop me from being sorry."

She was almost in arm's reach of him, to Nor's terror. She was looking into his eyes. Brin flinched away, caught himself, and returned her gaze with hateful intensity.

From between clenched teeth, he said, "You can't possibly be sorry enough. Not for everyone."

"I can try," she replied calmly. "Let me try."

She took another step forward. Their foreheads almost touched. She said, "It's not your fault."

"*Stop it.*" He trembled as if he might burst into flame.

"No." She wrapped her arms around him.

For an instant, he relaxed.

Then he shook—and screamed.

He shoved her to the ground. Then he bent at the waist and screamed again. His face was briefly free of the cloud, and it held an expression for which mere words, like hate or mourning, were inadequate. A transcendent, alien darkness was revealed.

The weight on Nor's chest disappeared. Air rushed into his lungs. But a terrifying scream from Shada dampened his giddiness.

He rose to his backside then his feet before he could find his balance. Wobbling, starting to fall, he launched himself at Brin's blurry figure.

Nor knocked Brin to the ground and landed on top of him. He reached under Brin's shirt and found the vial. Brin's shapeless bodyguard struck Nor with a hammer blow that turned the world inside out. As Nor flew backward, the vial tore away and came with him. He held onto one thought: whatever happened, he must not let go of the vial.

He glimpsed Shada, a blood-soaked mess. Then he hit the ground rolling.

Someone nearby shrieked, "Save him!"

He rolled off the edge of the platform. The twin walls of the planet and the crystal sphere surrounded him as he began his long fall.

Brin's bodyguard caught Nor around the middle, folding him in half. The vial almost slipped from his fingers. The thing lifted him like a ghastly hand and held him level with the edge of the platform.

Brin came and surveyed Nor's predicament. Blood shone in the priest's eyes. His voice was wheezing and cracked. "Seems we each have something the other needs."

"I don't need to live," Nor replied. "But I'll wager that your pet here"—he raised his voice, hoping the cloud was listening—"knows what's inside this trinket I'm holding. And it's afraid. That fear is burned into the minds of all its kind. It saved me a moment ago so I would not take revenge by opening the vial as I fell. When you had the vial, it even obeyed you."

Still the cloud buzzed and gripped him. He wondered if he was right, if it had any thoughts inside it at all.

"Nonsense," Brin said. "It obeys me because the Lady made it to serve me."

"The Lady probably hoped it would kill you. Brin, you are no longer part of this conversation. I speak now to the one who holds me: if you drop me, I will crush the vial in my hand as I fall. That will release its contents and doom you and all who remain of your kind. Now, return me to the platform."

The thing obeyed him, though not gently. With solid floor under him, he ran to Shada. She was horribly wounded but alive. Perhaps Brin, in his upset, had moved the cloud clumsily and failed to strike a death blow. She was unconscious, having passed out while trying to tie off the stump of her severed left arm with a torn piece of her cloak.

Everywhere, her blood slickened the crystal floor. The bleeding came in spurts, and he became sticky all over with it. He worked frantically, tying off the wound as she'd begun to do. When he finished, she was awake and looking at him. He crawled backward on the slippery floor, wondering if she was a ghost.

She murmured, "Tell Brin..."

"You're alive." The flood of emotion he had held back, thinking her dead, now had no purpose.

She looked sad. "I'm sorry," she finished.

Brin, now surrounded by his cloud again, looked on.

Nor growled, "He can hear you." He felt the vial in his hand and considered popping off its cap. Perhaps Brin's bodyguard would reach him before he succeeded. Crushing it in his palm would be faster, but the cloud might kill him even after he'd sealed its fate. Everything was a great game of attrition now, of sacrificing game pieces, even oneself, to take the enemy's pieces off the board.

He took a step toward the cloud surrounding Brin.

"Don't come any closer," Brin said.

"You have no part in this," Nor reminded him. "To your friend: I need you to fix what you've done to this woman. Now."

"It can do no such thing," Brin scoffed.

"I know they can mend tissue and bone as surely as they can destroy them. It has happened to me."

"The Lady never did it."

"Maybe Huire never took the time to teach her. Or maybe the Lady didn't care enough about us to try it. I'll bet that healing takes more energy from them than tearing things apart. She was mostly too scared to even leave her box."

"What makes you think this one can do it?"

"If it doesn't, the vial breaks. That's how we'll find out."

Like a gathering breeze, part of the being's mass reached toward Shada.

"Don't you dare patch her up," Brin growled. "She's evil."

"If you speak again," Nor said, "I'll have it fling you from the edge."

The entity paid Brin no mind. The severed ends of Shada's arm were soon covered with rippling hills of organisms so small they could be seen only when gathered into an army. Some dragged Shada's severed arm to meet its stump, and the work intensified.

"It hurts," Shada gasped. "I don't think it knows what it's doing."

"One much smaller than this saved my life," Nor said. "Anyways, we've got to try."

Shada did not argue. She gasped, her breathing punctuated by cries of pain. Her eyes slowly shut. He took her by the chin and ordered her to stay awake. In his fevered imagination, she could not die as long as she kept her eyes open.

He kissed her, not feeling at all romantic but hoping it might surprise her, stimulate her somehow. A smile touched her pale mouth.

"It's almost done," she said.

She was right. The being withdrew to hover nearby.

"Try to move the arm," Nor said.

She lifted and lowered it, held it parallel to her body then perpendicular. Finally, she wiggled her fingers before letting it drop. "It's so hard to move. I'm not sure it put the arm on right."

Nor was not surprised that moving was exhausting, given how much of her blood was outside her body. The cloud had fixed her well enough that she could move her fingers; he doubted they could expect much more. Later, if something was terribly wrong with the arm, perhaps Staubel could amputate it—if he or anyone else was still alive.

Nor had been so focused on the miraculous healing that he had not been watching Brin. Now, with much of the being's mass devoted to repairing Shada, Nor saw that the priest looked gaunt and frighteningly thin. Where his skin once had a vibrant flush, it was now sallow, and the outlines of his skull were terribly clear. Still, gray waves mottled his flesh.

Nor spoke to the cloud. "Leave us. Return to your mother."

It left so swiftly that it might have been awaiting the opportunity. In a funnel of smoke, it swept down the path and into the crystal palace.

"No," Brin called weakly after it. The sound ended in a watery gurgle. He fell to his knees.

Nor took a single step closer to help before jumping back in horror.

The cloud had been slowly devouring Brin. It had eaten the meat off his bones and the hair off his head. His skin was so diminished that the veins, arteries, and bones beneath were painfully visible. He looked at his own ribs, his belly a wet, delicate bag containing his innards, then turned his gaze to Nor with eyes that rolled like loose balls in poorly fitted sockets.

"Brin," Nor said. He meant it as an address, but it sounded like a curse. He had no words of comfort.

"I didn't feel much," Brin said. "It was... very clever."

He began to breathe faster and faster. Nor could not bear to watch Brin break down in front of him, but he could think of nothing else to do. Perhaps they would go mad together.

Nor's weapons lay on the ground not far off. He walked away, controlling each breath, picked up his pistol, and turned to Brin. "Do you want me to...?" He left the partial question unfinished, but Brin saw what he meant. A scream rose from the priest, building from his feet and exploding from his mouth. His teeth were tall and thin where his gums had been eaten away.

Brin stood with surprising speed. Hugging himself tightly as if to hold himself together, he galloped and disappeared into the crystal sphere, still screaming.

74

— · —

EMBERLY

EMBERLY'S BODY STILL ACHED from when his men had beaten him bloody, and he had expected his fight with Ganet to go badly. But as they clashed and he felt the difference made by his greater size and strength, the pain fell away—or at least, it was shoved into a box to be reopened later.

And he needed every edge he could find. Ganet's greater age belied startling speed and agility. He moved like one trained in a martial art not so different from boxing though it included kicks of unpredictable and sometimes remarkable height. Emberly, who had a longer reach than most men, was repeatedly forced to dart in and damage the enemy with his fists. After a few clashes, he managed to throw Ganet to the floor. Not much of a wrestler, Emberly landed atop Ganet and threw a wild flurry of punches at his face. The strikes dazed the general, whose defense grew clumsy. The beast within Emberly whined in anticipation of victory.

Then the Lady grabbed his fist, lifted him into the air, and tossed him like a pebble. He struck the ground by the edge of the calm circle surrounded by the Lady's furious storm. While throwing him, the Lady's tendril had deftly broken a couple of his fingers.

He clutched his hand and screamed. For unknown ages, the pain occupied his entire being. The world around him existed at the edge of sight, and nothing that happened there compared to the importance of the pain, which did not end.

On the far rim of the world, Ganet slowly stood. The general hurried, with the meagre speed he could still manage, to where Emberly lay curled. He kicked the captain in the ribs a few times, adding to the patchwork of aches and bruises. Then, with sinewy strength, he turned Emberly over. The captain lay face down, fighting to breathe. He felt Ganet's weight land on his back. The general took Emberly's head in both hands, poised to break the captain's neck with a twist. He spoke in Emberly's ear: "If only you had been one of us."

Then Ganet's weight vanished. Emberly looked up to see one of the Lady's arms dragging the general by one foot to the far side of the arena. There it gave his ankle a severe twist, and Ganet yelped.

Limb by limb, Emberly took control of his body and began to move. He crawled toward Ganet on hands and knees, passing splattered blood that might have belonged to either of them. The general tried to scramble up but cried out as his ankle collapsed. His nimbleness had failed him. He fell, and his head struck the floor.

Emberly crawled faster. For the briefest of moments, Ganet was still. Then he began struggling like a broken toy prodded by a child, limbs wheeling as he tried to rise. Standing, he swayed dangerously, looking at Emberly with unfocused eyes.

Emberly tried to get up, but the Lady reached out and trapped his hands in place on the floor. Her voice boomed from the great swirling storm. "No. This must not end so soon."

Emberly's head burned. "Perhaps I should end it right now. Perhaps I will refuse to fight anymore, come what may."

"Think of your city, Captain. Think of your family."

Had the Lady scoured her vocabulary, she could hardly have found a worse pair of sentences to say to Cyril Emberly just then. He remembered Charlotte's final word, which he had promised to obey. *Survive.* He had a boy who needed a father.

"I'm sorry," he said aloud to his wife, who had sacrificed her life for their family. He prayed to whoever would listen that she might hear him and, perhaps, even understand. "I can't."

"Ganet," he called, "we've got to stop this."

The general was bleeding from the head, and the blood covered half his face, running down the middle and dripping from his nose. Hearing Emberly's voice, he straightened. He wiped to clear his eyes and squinted. "Is your body failing you, Captain?" He sauntered toward Emberly. "In the Realm, we know that our bodies always betray us in the end. So our minds and hearts must be indestructible."

"Your mind is failing, Ganet. She is using us, you bloody fool. She doesn't care which of us is stronger. We're her entertainment."

"That is the voice," the general said, "of a man who has already lost."

"For one damned second, think!" Emberly's voice cracked, and his breath whistled through a broken tooth. "Why won't she let either of us win? Because she's not satisfied. She never will be, whether she knows it or not."

Ganet stopped before him. His brow was tight, and his eyes were stormy. The Lady had released Emberly, but he remained on his knees.

"I won't win this," Emberly said. "I refuse to be a slave to her or to make my people slaves." He tore open what was left of his shirt. Buttons clicked and rolled. "My heart is frail. Take it if you want."

Ganet had pulled a fist back to strike Emberly's face or neck. There it stayed, frozen in action. The general's eyes widened in bewilderment. He glanced at the fist as if unsure why it had not moved.

Emberly nodded. "You are free. The Lady's will must not be done." He finished the sentence, clean and perfect, as a dagger-sharp blade of the Lady's mass sprouted from his chest. She had run him through from behind, and he sat amazed and breathless. Air spouted from his mouth.

He stayed conscious longer than he would have liked. He heard the Lady and the general speaking, though he struggled to understand them.

"I have chosen you, Ganet. Where do you stand?"

After a deadly pause, the general said, "Command me, Goddess."

"Soon. First, I will make a meal of this." The piercing blade withdrew, leaving Emberly to fall. The Lady caught him, and he felt a tickling as she spread over him and tugged him this way and that. Her ravenous appetite would not wait.

"No. Stop," Ganet said.

"No?" The Lady's voice sounded confused.

"It is not fitting," the general continued.

"It is my will. The will that commands you."

"You do command me, but for this one thing. Let him die in peace."

The cloud that was the Lady closed around Emberly, and he began to smother. This was far more distressing than impalement, and he willed his arms and legs to move. They did not respond.

Ganet took an audible breath and blurted out, "If you do this, I will never obey you again." He paused and continued, "I will never be the ally you seek. I will defy you until my last breath."

"Perhaps I will devour you too. And allow you to watch."

"You may, Lady. But then you'll have killed everyone who understands you."

The Lady released Emberly, who completed his fall. The floor was cool, blurry numbness spreading, and he relaxed. He was surely tired. He would close his eyes for just a moment, listening in case anyone said anything important.

75

— · —

NOR

SHADA WANTED NOR TO leave her where she lay, claiming she would catch up with him later. He almost gave in. She looked so pale and weak that imagining taking her anywhere was hard. *But what if I never return?* She might lie there alone until the end, whatever form it took.

So he insisted, and she let him put his shoulder under her better arm and help her stand. They left the platform, retracing their steps through the corridors as best they could remember them. Soon, Nor saw thin boot prints of coppery blood on the floor. Brin had thought this was the way back. His "servant," in its hunger, must have started eating the skin of his feet, and now, the remaining patina was tearing and soaking his boots. The prints grew thick and wet.

When Shada and Nor finally reached the main corridor, Shada whispered something. When he stopped to listen, she repeated herself. "Soldiers. There are soldiers here."

Capture by the Shining Realm was not something Nor cared to contemplate just then. "Can you walk on your own?" he asked.

"Let me try," she replied. A few steps later, he caught her as she fell.

When she finished cursing, he asked, "What do you want to do?" He had already decided what he ought to do himself. In pressing her to come along with him, he had meant to save her from a lonely death, but he was also forcing her to share his own doom. Of course, no place was really safe. The Shining Realm's troops might wait in any direction or all directions. But she should decide her fate.

He asked, "Do you know where the Lady is?"

She pointed. "There's a chamber that way. That's where I saw her last."

"That's where I have to go. What about you?"

Still gasping, she said, "Me too. I'm not finished with her yet."

Gratitude filled Nor at the knowledge that he and Shada wouldn't part yet—gratitude mixed with fear that staying with him might get her killed. The bloody prints on the crystal floor became jumbled where Brin seemed to have staggered. Then they faded almost to nothing. He wondered if Brin had tied something around his boots, perhaps pieces of his clothing.

A little farther on, Nor heard a low moan. Shada squeezed his shoulder, and he halted.

"What is it?" he asked.

"There's someone down there," she answered, pointing just ahead, where a side corridor split from the main one. "I think it's Merin. He disappeared as soon as I saw him."

"Really?"

If she was right, Merin must have awakened from his shock. Nor wondered how the private had survived the Realm's attack. Perhaps, after the torment some of the others had put him through, he had simply deserted the company.

Shada was growing energized. "I think you should leave me here. Let me go to him."

"Why?"

The private had always seemed harmless, but Nor couldn't be sure of anything and wondered how Merin had survived, exactly.

Nor continued, "This place is full of ghosts and illusions. Let's make sure it's really him before we separate."

"It's him. I know it. And he's scared, I think. That's why he hid after he called to me."

"He called you, specifically?" Nor had heard only a single-syllabled moan.

"Yes! He met my eyes. Something is not right with him. He needs help."

Nor shook his head. "Let's—"

"I have to do it, and you can't help me," she said sharply. "It's that simple. Please believe it."

He sighed, not with impatience but at the sheer impossibility of things.

"You're going into a battle," she told him. "Do you really want to carry me along? Let me down now."

They walked to the entrance of the side corridor. It opened into a room with brown walls and floor. If Merin was there, he was hiding. Nor felt a twinge of foreboding and hoped Shada would not go inside.

But he lowered her to the floor as she wished. She leaned against the wall and said, "I can manage from here."

"All right, then." He shifted his weight between his feet, not wanting those to be his last words to her.

She raised her hand with a tremble. "Come here."

He knelt and took the hand in his. It was unfathomably soft.

"Huire is dead," she told him.

He stared at her, feeling his face turn to stone.

"She was real after all. I'm sorry, Nor."

He nodded, not in acceptance of the news but to assure her that he was still there, in that body, despite the spreading numbness that might soon leave him a statue.

"The Lady did it," Shada said. "We can't let her fool us again."

Nor stood, breathing carefully. "Don't worry," he said, trying to sound calm and failing. "I know who my enemies are." He had no idea how he felt about Huire's death, and that realization brought a hopelessness verging on panic.

"Come back," Shada said.

He fought the desire to do the opposite, to run away. Kneeling was an awfully vulnerable position. He extended his hand, and she gripped it hard.

"I wish you and I had more time," she said. "But the Lady will grow and grow. She'll devour everything until only she is left. I told her I'd kill her, but now look at me. I can hardly move. Will you kill her for me?"

Nor nodded. He looked at Shada's eyes, her mouth, the lines of her cheeks, and how all of them came together. He looked into her eyes for a long moment that any words would have cheapened. Then he stood and went to find the Lady.

Some distance down the main corridor, a soldier of the Realm sprang out of a hallway just ahead and to his right. "Stop right there," the man said. His uniform bore little of the embroidery and decoration of his comrades'. His voice was stern but lacked animosity.

Nor obeyed. He spread his hands and lifted them above his head. Now that he no longer had Shada to distract him from his own pain, every movement sent a cascade of aches through him.

"Who are you?" the Realmsman asked.

"I'm a friend of yours, at least for the moment."

"Answer plainly," the man snapped. From the hallway behind him echoed a low moan followed by hushed voices.

Nor sighed. "It really doesn't matter. What matters is that you stop delaying me."

The soldier tapped his chest. "My orders say, let no one pass unless they wear this uniform."

"Looks like you've already disobeyed." Nor gestured toward Brin's tracks, which had become faintly visible again and ran past that point and down the corridor.

The man snorted. "Oh yes, that one. He slipped past when my attention was elsewhere. Sadly for you, you didn't."

"I wish you had caught him."

The soldier's face was dark. "One of my soldiers saw him and described him. A terrible creature. I thought my soldier had lost his mind." His brow furrowed. "It's him you're after, then?"

"No," Nor said. "It's *her*."

No one could mistake whom he meant.

The man said, "Take two steps toward me. Don't try to run."

Nor did, and he saw that the side corridor was full of wounded men. Only two were on their feet, both Realmsmen who scampered about wearing the same modest uniforms as Nor's new friend. At their feet was a row of Realmsmen and three Ronians. The Ronians were so riddled with wounds that the movements of their chests seemed surreal. Dr. Staubel was one of them.

"I can't say whether any of them will make it," the soldier said, "but I'm sure you don't want to join them." He and his comrades must have been from the Realm's healers.

"But if I surrender," Nor said, "I will join them. I'll end up in your masters' lairs enduring who-knows-what torments."

The man's face darkened. "When their ordeals are over, they will be better men than either of us."

"I won't join them."

The man cocked his head. "You seem to want to die here."

Nor replied, "I want only to find her and kill her."

Now, the man appeared to doubt Nor's sanity as well as his honesty. "Kill her?"

Nor reached slowly into his pocket, wondering if he would die for doing so. He pulled out the vial he had taken from Brin.

The genuine shock on the soldier's face encouraged him. "Where did you get that?" the man demanded.

"It doesn't matter."

The pistol twitched. "Tell me where you got it."

"One of your people gave it to one of mine. Maybe on Ronia, for all I know."

The man could not tear his eyes from the vial. "We have more like it, but none here. It is precious to us. The general ordered us to leave them behind when we pursued you out of Om. He must not have foreseen this."

"Maybe not. Or maybe he's a traitor—to all of us."

The man cocked his head, looking incredulous. "You don't mean to say he will kneel to her."

Nor slowly lowered his hands to his sides. "Whether he does or not, I'm the only one who can stop her. Is that worth letting me through?"

"Certainly. If I could trust you."

"I'm a human being. That makes us allies here."

"The dying men behind me say otherwise."

Nor looked at Staubel. The doctor's eyes met his, but they were hollow and free of recognition. Nor said, "Some of those men are my friends. I want them to live and be free. But if I fail, I can't stop you from hurting them."

"And if you succeed?"

"I would consider it a favor if you let them go after they are healed."

"You seem confident that we can heal them."

"I don't think I've seen the limit of what you can do."

76

—·—

BRIN

BY THE TIME BRIN entered the chamber of the gods, the pain of walking on his bleeding feet was growing unbearable. His boots squished with each step. He was leaving a trail of blood that Nor could follow, but that wouldn't matter much longer.

From the corridor, he had seen what lay on the chamber's floor, but he scarcely believed it until he stood before it. A swath of the room nearest him was carpeted with dead men.

The soldiers of the Realm had been massacred—all of them. Throats were cut, limbs severed, heads removed. Their bodies looked like a field of wild grass hacked down to the roots by a careless gardener.

They lay thickest where Brin's corridor met the chamber. He climbed over them, avoiding their more grievous wounds but slipping repeatedly. Finally, he crawled into the chamber like a mouse emerging from a hole in the wall.

The Lady, now the Goddess, hung over the vast room in all her awful glory. The other deities hovered in the far reaches of the room. They were apparently afraid of her but not yet willing to flee through the room's many gateways, beyond which must wait the graveyard worlds of a dead alien empire.

The crystal walls of the place had occasionally shown Brin his own reflection. In that way, Brin had caught shocking glimpses of a monster. He had grown more afraid and toddled along more quickly. He needed to return to the arms of his Lady, his mother, who would restore him to health and power.

The Lady said nothing as he approached. She had assuredly heard him, and she could see in all directions at once. He wondered if something was wrong.

He twisted his worm-eaten neck and saw a man floating, arms outstretched, on the edges of the Lady's cloud. It was Ganet, and he was speaking to her. He was shouting—not surprising as she had apparently massacred his men.

Nonetheless, the Lady had not devoured him. Seeing the two of them speak, the worst of fears stabbed Brin's heart—the fear of being forgotten. He would fight for his place at her side. Of course, she would not lower herself for him. He would have to earn her respect.

"Lady!" he cried, springing up with an energy he hadn't thought he still possessed.

She was silent for a great gulf of an instant during which he felt the first touch of despair. Then her voice rolled from on high like thunder. "I am your Goddess. I am not the Lady ever again."

"Goddess." He bit into the word with enthusiasm, tasting its power for the first time in his life. "I've returned to you."

"But Shada is not here. You promised to bring her to me."

Hearing her speak as lowly a name as Shada's was odd. "I met resistance I did not expect."

Her voice grew softer and more sinister. "You tried to kill her. Did you think you knew better than me? That you could deceive me?"

The part of herself that she had given him—a "gift," she had called it—must have returned to her after it abandoned Brin. It would have told her everything that had happened.

Cringing, Brin answered in a panic. "I forgot myself for a moment, Lady." He clapped his mouth shut.

She boomed like a cannon barrage, "Do not use that name. That is three times you have disobeyed me."

The room spun around him. "Three?"

"You promised to cleanse your company of those who would not follow me. You promised to return Shada to me. And you persist in calling me by a false name."

Brin struggled to remember what he had actually promised her. "I killed Arumin." *I did that for her, didn't I? The only person I would have dreamed of calling a friend.*

"Yet the Ronians who came here resisted me to the last man."

Brin looked around. Amid the blue-uniformed corpses, one stood out. It was Emberly.

Brin bent and exhaled. A pillar of support, unnoticed until then, was knocked out from under him.

"I'm not as strong as you, Goddess. I'm only a man."

"So is the one I am holding now. Yet he has accomplished great things for me."

Brin looked again at the general, and their eyes met. In Ganet's face, he saw not the expected gloating but the fresh, wide-eyed understanding of something terrible.

The expression did not ease Brin's jealousy, but it made him more confident. "He will not continue that way, Goddess. Look at him. He has lost the stomach to shed the necessary blood."

Brin bowed his head. "I will always strive to understand your greatness. I will serve you more devotedly than any other. I will become anything."

"You say this," she said, "and yet you have been lying to me."

"When?" What had that "gift" of hers been telling her?

"You had something around your neck that you imagined could harm me, but you did not tell me."

That. Why did I keep it from her? He had not trusted her, but he could never tell her that. "I was afraid," he replied.

"You should have feared what I would do if I discovered it on my own—of what will happen now."

He lifted his face painfully to look at her and felt words tumbling from his mouth. "What will you do? Take my life? You've done that already, unless you give me a new body. I would have been a fool to trust you when I did not know you."

Her silence was crushing. He didn't know what she wanted to hear.

"I am weak," he said, having nothing else to say. "Please take me back. Give me a task of which I am capable."

"I know of only one," she said. "You may finish what you have started. Sacrifice yourself to me."

He was terribly certain of what she meant but could only reply, "What?"

"Fool. You think a powerless wretch like you is useful to me? If you truly wish to show remorse, then perform the ultimate act of worship: give yourself to me. Let me devour you."

A chill washed over him. "But I have given you so much. Look at me! And there are so many dead men here to feed you."

"Their flesh may help me grow, but I find I prefer flesh willingly given. The heat of living blood is like no other food. Now, do you wish to prove yourself to me?"

Brin shivered. He wanted to stand, but his head spun. A chorus of voices had arisen in him. Some wanted more than anything to prolong his life, some wondered how it might feel to become one with the Lady, and some tempted him with the thought that here, at last, he might find rest.

"Will it hurt?" he asked.

She said, "I don't know."

"I don't want it to hurt. It already hurts so much."

"Endurance is a sign of devotion." She reached toward him with great misshapen arms. "That is what the dead lack." She touched him, entered his ears and mouth, tickled his skin. Her humming was everywhere.

His body rebelled without warning. Crackling energy shot through him as he scrambled up and ran blindly, screaming something at her. His actions were hardly his own.

One of her arms whipped in front of him to form a solid bar at stomach level. He ran into it at full speed. He bent over it and hung for a moment, his belly as the fulcrum. The bar dissipated, and he fell. Unable to breathe, he could only wheeze with the urgency of the nearly drowned. His belly was bleeding, the thin flesh slightly torn by the collision.

As he huddled there, she swarmed over him. "Be still," she said. "Do not squander this experience." He might have been imagining the amusement in her voice.

He brayed like an animal: "Why don't you want me?"

She could not be bothered to answer. She bit him in a thousand places as he thrashed on the cold crystal floor.

Then she withdrew without warning. What was left of his body lay trembling for a moment, then he opened his eyes and found he could still see. Through tears, he saw Nor standing by the chamber's entrance, one arm extended. In his hand was the black vial.

The Goddess would win. Brin had little doubt of that and no desire to watch it happen. As soon as he could stand, he started running again. No one stopped him, and he realized he was not worth their attention.

77

— · —

NOR

NOR HAD NO IDEA what would happen when he opened the vial. Maybe the Lady would still be harmed if he opened it while out of her sight, a safe distance away. He did not know if whatever curse waited inside would seek out her and the other gods or if he would need to throw it on her like a blessing in a temple.

He had decided the surest way to kill her was to open the vial while close to her. So when he entered the hazy expanse of the god's chamber, it was still closed.

She saw him immediately. She dropped Brin and rushed toward Nor like a mighty river that had burst through a dam. He held out the vial so that she could see it.

She stopped. The vial's contents must have frightened even her. When she spoke, he felt like a planet had decided to address him personally, and terror almost doubled him over.

"I can offer rewards," she said, "pleasures out of all comprehension. I can also take you into my belly for an eternity of suffering."

From around the great chamber, other gods were racing toward him—hundreds of them. They had chosen to attack him instead of fleeing through any of the nearby gateways. He suspected that distance would not save them from the vial's opening, and he suspected they knew it.

"I need a moment to think," he told the Lady. It was a lie. Before she could act or respond, he squeezed the vial in his hand.

It did not break. He had assumed it would shatter easily. He squeezed again as hard as he could, but the vial was as firm as a diamond in his fist.

His mind seemed trapped in mud, and a near eternity passed before he reached for the vial's stopper. The Lady lashed a girthy tentacle toward him with blinding speed.

Thunder cracked, and something struck down his reaching arm. He looked at the bullet wound then at Ganet's smoking pistol.

Seizing Nor's hand that held the vial, the Lady closed it in iron. She opened his fingers with the strength of a living mountain and broke each one separately. His body convulsed as the cracking of his bones cut through every other sound. He screamed without reservation, finding no reason to be brave or even hopeful. She took the vial and released him. He fell, clutching his hand, to join the bodies covering the floor.

The gods halted their oncoming charge, forming a wide arc around Nor and the Lady. They were safe from the vial but perhaps not from her.

Ganet called in a hoarse wail, "A token of my service, Goddess."

Nor lifted his head and looked for familiar faces. Emberly lay not far off. Turning onto his stomach, Nor slowly stood. His arm was bleeding heavily, and he wondered if that was the wound that would finally bleed him dry. Not before the Lady swallowed him, he decided.

Knowing that his sentence within her belly might begin at any time, he hurried toward the captain. As he stepped clumsily over splayed corpses, he relaxed a little. He had nothing left to think about but reaching Emberly. The rest was done, and the future bore no sane contemplation at all.

"Leave him alone," the Lady said. She must have been warning the other gods away from him.

Sitting down next to Emberly, Nor linked his hands around his knees. He would stay there for as long as he could. He put his better hand on the captain's and felt warmth in it. Emberly had been alive very recently.

Only then did Nor remember that many of the fallen soldiers still had their firearms. If he could reach one of those before the Lady took him, perhaps a bullet would destroy his brain beyond her ability to repair it. Maybe that could spare him from her torment.

He wrapped his hand around Emberly's and looked at the man's open eyes. Warmth crept from the captain's hand to his and traveled up his arm. The feeling startled him at first. When it had filled enough of him, he realized it was love.

The Lady spoke, her voice much nearer. "I have plans for you."

Having decided how to spend what remained of his life, Nor sighed. Something still needed to be said.

"You won't survive to complete them," he announced. "The general is not planning to serve you. His people have many vials like that one, and they will use them to make you their slave."

The air hummed as the Lady's attention shifted.

Ganet snarled, "This man is desperate. He knows what awaits him, and he will say anything."

The Lady brushed aside that defense like it was a cobweb. "I will not suffer unfaithful companions."

The general's voice rose to a harsh pitch. "If you kill me, you will have no companions at all! I found a vial, but I threw it away because I love you!"

She swelled and straightened to a new height. "I feel weary. I must ponder this, and I must eat. I wonder which of you will be my meal?"

"You have plans for me already, Goddess," Nor said. "That leaves only one choice."

He turned his eyes toward the distant ceiling, where countless gateways shone different colors and shades of light and dark. He heard Ganet yelling, "You can't! Not after what I've given you! After what you've done to them!" Nor knew the general was pointing at his dead soldiers.

The Lady said, "Dealing with your kind, enduring your frailty and insignificance, has shown me that I need no such servants. You no longer amuse me."

Ganet cried, "It's true, what the Ronian said! My people have far more of what that vial contains. It nearly destroyed your kind once. We can ensure that it finishes the job! You can still have a place among us, but you will need me."

From the chamber's entrance, a familiar voice called to the Lady: "It seems that no one else is faithful to you."

The Lady regarded Private Robir. "You," she said. This befuddled response sounded silly in her terrible voice.

"Yes," the man replied. Nor had assumed Robir was dead; maybe that was why the private looked like a ghost. Robir continued, "I never found glory in the eyes of Huire, though I would have given anything for it." His gaze passed over Nor and lingered on the captain. "It was you, Lady, who I should have revered—you who were there all along, not that neglectful Huire. I have come to beg for one last chance... in you."

"I am the Lady no longer but your Goddess. And I tire of little things who come along seeking my approval."

"I'm a man without many uses," Robir said. "I've tried them all and failed. Now that I'm face-to-face with a true goddess, I offer you the only part of me worth having: my flesh."

The Lady's mass shifted like a restless sea. She moved toward him.

Robir saw her coming and nodded. "Feast on me, Goddess, and know that there was one who loved you."

"I accept," she said as she converged on him in storm-driven waves.

Even from where Nor lay, he could see Private Robir's final, shuddering breath before her touch found him.

Starting with the man's exposed skin, she caressed him, and he began to rot away. He did not cry out or even flinch. Her tendrils slipped down under his collar.

Then Nor saw something from a lifetime before, something he had seen when they left the streets of dear, dreadful Ronia. Robir's hand, skin flaking away and dissipating in the air, reached between the buttons of his shirt. From the opening, it pulled a loop tied to a taut string that disappeared beneath the shirt.

The general screamed. Nor dove to cover Emberly's body. He had no idea whether the Lady realized what was happening. It did not really matter. Before anyone could do or say anything else, the burning edge of the explosion flattened them all.

78

THE LADY

FOR A TIME, SHE was lost in darkness beyond darkness. She did not know what it was to sleep or dream, having never been other than awake. Regaining consciousness, she had no idea how much time had passed or where she had been. She took stock of herself and found she was living a nightmare.

Some small part of her had remained intact despite the blast. She had grown so large that the explosion had not engulfed or scattered her completely.

She darted here and there, gathering bits of herself just as they began lives of their own. But so little was left. She dimly remembered once having grand thoughts that were now out of her reach. Many things that used to be simple and obvious were simply gone. Still, her essence remained.

Fortunately, her next course of action was obvious. Many perils had passed: nothing remained of Robir, the general was a scattering of charred bones, and the explosion had destroyed both the vial and the doom it contained. Her danger now came from one source—a beast with many heads.

The gods who had avoided the explosion spotted her. For the first time, she was smaller than any of them. That made her easy pickings for these numerous immensely powerful beings whom Huire had ruled for millennia and whom the Lady had expected to dominate, if not devour. They came toward her, accelerating as her weakness became more obvious.

She fled. Entering the closest corridor, the one from which all the recent intruders had come, she soared along it. A certain room awaited her. The Guardian had told her about it once, during their talks. She had wondered if he might use it someday. Perhaps he already had. She would follow.

She heard the gods calling her in mocking tones. They were now the hunters, they knew it, and they were not hurried. She should have plenty of time to escape—away from this alien citadel, away from the worlds of humanity—all the way to another universe. This universe was not worthy of her just yet. Perhaps she would return someday and make it her own.

With the destruction of the vial and its contents, the final bid to kill her had failed. The rest of her kind might be doomed if the Shining Realm still possessed the Scourge.

The Scourge—that was the only name it had. It was a black abomination created by the builders of this place, to unguessable ends. Ages before, when it escaped and nearly destroyed the gods, someone must have somehow captured a reservoir of it. The Realm had inherited this curse along with all its other technological treasures. Perhaps the Scourge had achieved intelligence, perhaps even becoming the power behind the throneless Shining Realm.

That was for others to know. Soon, she would be alone, master of her own universe, which she would build to please her for eternity—alone except for one other, who would please her as well.

She entered the side hallway leading to the room and found Shada kneeling just outside the room's threshold. Passing close enough to ruffle the girl's hair, the Lady entered the room and found Shada was not alone. The Ronian soldier Merin was huddled in a far corner. In the center of the far wall was a single raised circle, as wide as a human palm and made of the same brown tile as the rest of the room.

The Lady was no longer big enough to carry or push Shada into the room. She doubted she could even push the heavy tile button by herself. That left her one chance—if she acted quickly.

79

— · —

SHADA

SHADA HAD BEEN CALLING out to Merin since she crawled and flopped down the small corridor to find him alone in the brown room. He was clinging to a wall like it was a life raft and sometimes turned his vacant eyes toward the floor or ceiling. She tried shouting his name, but he did not so much as blink in response. She might have shaken him by the shoulders had she dared enter the room.

She was certain she had glimpsed him standing when she and Nor passed. So someone or something must have been inside his head, commanding his body. Surely, it was listening, and it would respond if she found the right combination of words to persuade it that they must leave right then.

She was partly right.

Soon after she reached the room's threshold, a wisp of cloud emerged from Merin's head and hummed past her down the corridor. It paused before her face long enough to whisper, "Leave him. He deserves this."

Unpersuaded, Shada called to Merin using his name and rank. She tried speaking to him like a mother and like a superior officer. Nothing shifted him an inch. He seemed like a shell of a man.

But she would not enter that room.

The room was harmless enough outwardly, but the stark difference between it and the translucent crystal comprising the rest of this place was unaccountably sinister. With every rule of nature and reason in doubt, she had only instinct to fall upon, and it spoke clearly against taking a single step into the room.

She lacked the energy to stand for long, so she sat with her legs to one side as if at a picnic. She supported herself with her better arm. When Brin's servant had reattached the other arm, it had been careless or deliberately incompetent, and large movements of that arm produced pops and aches that made her shiver.

A passing breeze cooled her neck. Then she saw its cause: a small humming cloud. Using almost all its mass, it formed a cutting blade that lay against Merin's throat.

"Enter," it said. The voice was smaller than she remembered, but she could not have mistaken it for any other in the universe.

The bargain did not need to be spoken. If Shada did not join the Lady in the room, she would open the man's neck.

"Why?" Shada asked.

"Because I wish it."

"What will happen?"

"We are going on a journey together," the Lady purred. "The two of us, forever."

"Where?" Shada was trying to stall but running out of questions. Her dread focused on a small round panel on the far side of the room, and she wondered if pushing on it would activate the power of this room.

"A place of our very own. A brand-new creation. There, you will learn to love me."

Shada did not fully understand but could think of few worse-sounding fates. Merin was almost an empty shell, but not quite. He was almost better off dead, but not quite. She could not forget that she had seen him move.

At certain moments, a person was best off feeling nothing. Shada had long known that, though, as advice, it had seemed impossible to follow. But in that moment, she was mostly managing it. She knew what she should do, so she would simply do it and hope that justice was not a mere human fantasy. She had fought the will of the Lady almost since their meeting, and if she was to battle her on into eternity, shielding the rest of the universe from her, she would try until nothing was left of herself. But she had to get Merin out of the room first. If he was still inside the room when the room took Shada and the Lady away, it would take him too.

"You must choose," the Lady said. It was part command, part simple statement of fact.

"Merin," Shada called. If she thought of anything but Merin, the terror closing in at the corners of her eyes would send her screaming and running, and she might never stop. "Come to me."

The man's eyes turned upward again. She sensed they were avoiding her.

She continued, "This is Huire. You are home now."

Earlier, when Merin's eyes dropped, they had rolled in their moorings and settled pointing at the floor. Now, they came straight down. At last, he found her.

That was further proof that he was not entirely gone. He might even come back.

Shada said, "It is over. Come into my arms." She held them out to him, nearly fell, then propped herself up with the good one.

He gathered his brow in thought, the muscles twitching as if the motion was strange. She turned a palm upward and beckoned him forward.

"Enough of this," the Lady said. "Come to me, and help him yourself."

Shada ignored her. She did not trust the Lady to leave Merin unharmed. The Lady might even try to press that button in the wall as soon as Shada stepped inside. Though the Lady was a crumb of what she had once been, she had not changed.

To Merin, Shada said, "You will be safe with me." She made her voice soft and gentle, like she imagined her mother had once spoken to her.

Slowly, painfully, Merin struggled to stand. The Lady kept her blade poised at his throat but let him proceed.

He took a stride, overstepped, and toppled. Somehow, he bent at the waist and stopped his fall with his hands, his legs splayed.

"Faster!" the Lady said.

Distant calls echoed down the main corridor—howls and whoops and cheers in unknown tongues, voices of tremendous size. The surviving gods were coming.

The Lady's minutes were numbered. But they would not be few enough.

"Tell him to hurry, or I'll kill you both!" the Lady shouted.

Maybe those in the corridor heard her—their voices grew quickly nearer and more frenzied.

As Merin straightened, Shada also stood. He held her gaze steadily now, an infant meeting its mother's eyes.

"You're almost there," she said.

He took a step—and stopped. Seconds passed, and he moved no farther. She realized she must enter the room and help him. Her first step would be the hardest, she hoped.

The shape of Merin's face changed. He was smiling. His mouth moved, and his throat bobbed. His voice was like the creak of an attic door. "I know you."

He stepped backward and fell toward the rear wall. As he collapsed, his hand pounded the button on the wall. The Lady moved with a flash of crystalline light, and blood spouted from his throat. The Lady raced toward Shada.

The room took them both away.

Nothing happened in the room, not even a sound or a flash of light. But all life fled the place. Merin hit the ground like a sack of loose apples and was still, dead before the throat wound could kill him. The Lady never had her revenge. She was a mass of lifeless particles that struck Shada in the chest with feeble momentum and filled the air.

When the gods arrived seconds later, they crowded around the opening of the corridor. Those who could extend some limb or tendril to see inside found the human woman sitting and staring through them with utter disinterest. Her face and chest were gray with powder, the rest of which was drifting to the floor around her like a rain of ashes.

80

—·—

BRIN

As Brin looked around at the new world in which he found himself, a new feeling replaced his despair. It was a feeling as warm and familiar as an old friend: terror.

The fog was everywhere, rising just above his head as though deliberately sent to blind him. Over it hung grim skies. With each step, he winced at the feel of the ground. It was wet and spongy and sank under his feet with a stretching motion. Each time he lifted a foot, the ground swelled to its original shape. He shivered.

From some unguessable distance away came a rapid series of clicks—some kind of animal. Brin realized he was still trailing blood.

He lifted his bloodstained robe, but one glimpse of the ruin beneath made him ill. Pain rolled in his stomach like a coiled parasite grown long and fat. He should eat and drink soon but didn't know if his body could still digest food or if he could still recognize hunger.

Even so, the universe had not yet killed him despite its ample opportunities. Surely, it would not kill him there. No story ended like that.

The sight of his own scarcely recognizable flesh replaced his terror with a new feeling so keen that he tasted it. It was hatred, and he wrapped it around himself. It was honest and wicked, a poison that had waited for him there at the bottom of the well, where it would nourish him and give him joy. He thought of everyone he knew and what he would do to each of them if he could. As he imagined it, he clenched his fists until his fingernails pierced his palms.

Trudging through the fog, he stepped carefully. Here and there in the ground lurked little round pits like open pores. Some could have held his fingertip while others could have held his head. In the bottom of each, water had gathered in little round pools, slimy and brackish, along with fragments of minute dead things.

The series of clicks repeated itself, closer. They sound-ed wooden, like drumsticks beating a table with erratic rhythm, held by a musician who could not hide his skill.

Fear pricked Brin once again, but he forced it down. He knew what he had to do.

He must find the makers, the ones who had made the gateways. A species that had built such wonders could not simply die off. The hundred gateways in the gods' chamber could not lead to plots of an endless graveyard kingdom. Some things must last forever.

They might be waiting just beyond the next fog bank. When he found them, he would offer them his services. None but he could tell them so much about the defenses and weaknesses of the human worlds.

The clicking, clattering sound again—it was definitely closer and coming from a different direction. He heard it yet again, then from the original direction, a call and a response.

Those could not be the friends who awaited him. The sounds were too different, too alien. They did not sound welcoming.

A little voice inside him whispered, *They sound hungry.*

But he must not fear. His saviors were great lords of the cosmos, and they would let no harm befall their guest. He supposed that, in gratitude for his help, they would carry him back to the human worlds in triumph. They might make him a lord too—perhaps the ruler of all humans everywhere. At the least, they would fix his demolished body.

Distracted by dreams of the glorious future, he stepped into one of the pits. It was almost as deep as his knee, and a thrill of pain shot up his ankle. The pit's rim quivered then snapped shut like a pupil, trapping his foot inside.

Wailing in pain and fear, he grabbed the pit's rubbery lips and tried to part them, to no avail. He fell over, ankle twisting, and cried out again.

As his voice died away, the quiet grew dismal. He was a prisoner, like the many little creatures he'd seen drowned in the pit's bottom.

Brin's thoughts tumbled downhill, faster and faster. He fought to stay calm. Certainly, a race as advanced as his new masters would have pierced the boundary between mind and matter. As their guest, he need only wish sincerely for a thing, and he would receive it.

"Set me free," he whispered, putting all his remaining heart and mind into the wish. "Set me free."

But the ferocious, toothless lips did not bulge.

Another fit of clicking echoed from a new direction. The clicking voices, at least three of them, were in open and ever-louder conversation.

Those sounds and the thoughts that came with them drove Brin wild. He strained to tear his foot free, bracing himself with his arms and other foot. His ankle slipped out a few inches, leaving skin and blood behind.

He screamed and gasped for air. Then came a moment of silence. The whole world seemed to be able to hear him.

He spoke softly. "Are you still there?"

He heard nothing inside his mind or out.

"I suppose this delights you, watching me suffer."

Again, nothing.

"Speak! I shared with you. Now speak, damn you!" His heart drummed in his throat. "To hell with you!"

The clicking voices resumed, converging on him quickly. They sounded like an orchestra of popping knuckles.

Unable to run, too afraid to call out again, he hunched against the ground like it might have mercy and swallow him. He thrust out his skeletal hands in all directions, warding off the voices.

Pressing his mouth to the muddy ground, he whined a prayer to his new masters, wishing with all his might to disappear. For reasons he could not fathom, not if he'd had all the time in the world, they denied his wish. He screamed, big wet sobs, as he threw himself upon the mercy of something, anything.

The pit opened again, waiting for the next small creature.

81

THE GUARDIAN

THE HEALERS OF THE Shining Realm, who were among their army's handful of survivors, watched the Guardian heal their remaining patients instantly and effortlessly. Their faces showed what he guessed were awe and horror. The healer who had been standing guard when the Guardian approached had long since let his gun fall to his side, perhaps grasping its uselessness.

A short time before, the gods had charged down the hallway in a close-pressed mass. After their roar vanished in the distance, the Guardian heard Shada coming. He knew her as he knew the other human visitors, as a memory from a borrowed dream.

He listened as she came closer, fell once, rose again, and finally reached him.

Her eyes scanned the little side corridor that contained most of the survivors of the cataclysm. They widened. "Doctor!"

"Caretaker," said the younger of the two Ronian patients with a courteous nod.

She stifled a gasp and nodded as if restraining some emotion. "I'm glad you're all right."

The doctor—Staubel was his name—leaned forward and twisted his torso experimentally. Returning from the brink of death must have been odd for him. "You know Overdin?" he asked.

"Of course. Hello," Shada said.

"Miss," the older Ronian replied, nodding with not a little respect.

Shada looked at the dead Ronians in the corridor. "Anyone else?"

"I don't think so, miss," Staubel said. "We'll look again before we go."

"I doubt that you will find anyone alive," the Guardian said.

Shada had hardly seemed to notice the Guardian until then. She turned toward him and took a long breath that expelled many feelings. She said, "I think I know you. Am I right?"

"Yes. I remember you better than most."

She peered at him. "You don't look like you did then."

"Others have said the same."

"Where have you been all this time?" she asked.

"Hiding," he said unabashedly, "and watching."

He had meant to be helpful, but her face darkened, and her jaw tightened. "Why didn't you help us?"

"I saw no need to endanger myself. Once I knew what Brin's vial contained, I felt that Huire and the other gods would soon be destroyed. If any survived, I expected them to flee to a certain room."

"Well, you were wrong. Only Huire died, and the Lady killed her. The rest have gone, and they've left us to fend for ourselves."

"But I haven't gone, Shada. I have saved those here whom I could." In the corridor were five living Realmsmen—three healers and two former patients—and the two Ronian soldiers. "As for the gods, they won't like what awaits them."

She tried to calm herself. "It's just that..." She paused. "Most of our friends died without knowing why or what this was really about. Those who are left deserve some answers, and you're the only one who can give them."

For the first time since Huire's death, he felt a touch of nervousness. "I hear the whispers of those who once lived here—who live here still. I will tell you what I can, but even so, you may be disappointed."

"Let's find out." She tilted her head. "What is this place?"

"What is there that you cannot see for yourself?" He was trying to think aloud, as he remembered doing once upon a time, but perhaps he just sounded irritated. "Those who lived here were powerful beyond imagining. They survived the early dangers faced by any growing species and spread from star to star. Soon, they tired of their organic forms and made for themselves bodies like mine and like your gods'. It is a natural progression, you see, from single organisms to swarms."

"They... made new bodies? Is that possible—to move a soul to a new place like a person moves to a new house?"

He smiled briefly and, he hoped, grimly. "I don't really know. The question would keep me up at night if I still slept. Instead, it just... holds onto me." He smiled again.

"Was this place their capital city?"

He might have laughed at that, but he had begun to care how she felt. Her dreams must have particularly affected him. "No. Splendid though it seems, it was an outpost, maybe one of the last they ever built. They connected the worlds of their empire here, as they did many places, but they created only one gateway leading to a new world outside their domain. It was that bridge that I crossed to come here and that you crossed in turn. Would that I had never found it."

He stopped again, considering what he would want to know if he were her. Over the ages, putting himself in another person's place had become very hard. "Before I became what I am, I traveled across the human expanse from end to end, top to bottom. The beings who built this place had a kingdom that was far wider and deeper still, though it was hardly a drop in the ocean of this galaxy. They reshaped planets and stars. It was so easy that they began doing it for amusement.

"But the more they bent the cosmos to their will, the harder it became to ignore the emptiness underlying it all. We've all felt it at times, but when all your wants are met and even mortality is a memory, you have nothing to do but feel it. Their miracle-working and feats of engineering began as achievements then became games then distractions. And, at last, came this place."

Shada frowned. "What is special about this place?"

"Look around. Endless mazes of corridors leading to empty rooms. Mostly, it simply exists. It is the emptiness given form. When those who built it looked at what they had created, they decided to end their hollow quest for yet more new worlds. They began to seek a more thorough escape."

"You mean they died?"

"Not right away. Working in secret, they devised a way to leave their physical forms entirely. They had created creatures of pure energy before, to serve them and guard their realms. Now, some became such beings themselves, hoping to find the freedom they had not found when they shed their organic forms."

Perhaps the woman saw where this ended. She hugged herself against a breeze the Guardian could not detect. "You told me that you hear voices."

He gave her a personable nod. "They are still here, except those who wandered off in search of meaning or oblivion. They found no answers, only that the void extended beyond the physical and into wherever they found themselves."

"Is that when they made the Scourge?"

"The Scourge was made by those who had remained in their swarm-bodies. It was the final act of a group of them that was thoroughly overtaken by despair. The Scourge was a swarm, a mindless one, I think, that they designed to destroy themselves and their kind. They unleashed it on the worlds of their people, an old and tired race who had discovered what lurks at the heart of existence. Perhaps their people even assented to its release.

"But they kept part of the Scourge imprisoned here in case any of their people survived. Here is the thing: it could only be released by a being like you—one in its original, organic form. That is why I suspect the species collectively agreed to die: any survivors would only die if they deliberately used a lesser being to unlock the Scourge. It would not be released by accident.

"They were wrong about that last part. Our gods found it ages later and used me to release it without knowing what it was. Once it was out, there was no defense."

Shada was quiet for a moment. She must have been thinking about the Scourge's creators. "That is a sad thing, choosing to die." The concept seemed familiar to her.

"It is very sad." He knew that was true though he could feel it only slightly. "I wonder, though, if they didn't really die when they left their first, organic bodies. I may be long dead myself, and the person I think I am may be just a copy. After all, I could have been created when he was still alive."

Shada frowned. Suddenly she asked, "Where has the Lady gone? And Merin?"

He paused. He had been afraid of this question. "They are somewhere else."

"Tell me," she demanded.

"Not long before they created the Scourge, those who had remained in their swarm-bodies undertook a desperate project. It was one of their final achievements and one of the most astounding. But once they realized its true effects, they abandoned it, and it has gone unused until now. It is located in the room where I left Merin."

"Near that room, I heard a voice tell me that Merin 'deserved' this. Was that you?"

"It was a part of me. I created it to guide Merin to that place. That room is a machine, one that creates universes. Those who enter and awaken the device are taken to an entirely new reality, one of their very own."

"A new... universe?" Shada said. Those words contained many questions.

The Guardian told her about the new universe—what little he knew. Her face paled as he spoke. When he had finished, she started shouting.

"How could you think he deserved that?" she cried. "What evil did Merin do to anyone?"

Helplessness gripped the Guardian. He had done what seemed best to him, but to a person of flesh and blood, it seemed monstrous. "I knew him from his dreams. I'm afraid you don't understand."

Her face reddened. "Exactly—I don't. And neither do you! None of us can comprehend eternity. How could you leave a man to that?"

"It..." He stammered. "It won't be what you think."

Shada covered her face with her hands. At last, she said, "If there was anything human left in you, you wouldn't have done it. Not to your worst enemy."

The Guardian sighed. With ghostly hands, he removed his glasses and looked at their lenses. "You may be right after all," he said. Feeling that further conversation would avail them nothing, he turned and left without a word.

When he decided what to do, he began to rush. He returned to the gods' prison chamber, presently inhabited by the dead, mostly. One was there from whom more had been taken than any other.

He went to Emberly's body, which was partly covered by the monk, Nor. The blast had tossed Nor atop Emberly in what seemed, rather cruelly, like an affectionate embrace. The Guardian heard that Nor, like a few others in the room, was still breathing and wondered if he had long to live. But the Guardian was not quick or adept at healing, and he had no time to help anyone else if he was to accomplish his goal.

He did not think himself capable of being startled, which made another man's appearance all the more frightening. The stranger who appeared by Emberly's head sat with his legs crossed and put a hand on the dead captain's brow. The man looked not unlike Emberly, though older and more life worn. His face was webbed by scars as if it had been blown apart and sewn back together.

The man's voice was loud and unabashed and sounded like it carried far. "He's not done yet."

"I'll do what I can," the Guardian said. He touched Emberly and noted happily that he had not been dead for long. Sinking low over the captain, he ceased to merely watch. He began to give himself away.

82

— • —

THE LADY

THE LADY WAS NOT a she or a he. It never had been either of those, not even in the place where differences existed. This place, which belonged to the Lady, was empty even of emptiness.

Nothing could be seen or heard or breathed. This realization terrified the Lady, but the Lady had always known it and been terrified of it.

The isolation was never-ending in every direction, of which there were none. Horror in its true form unmasked itself. It was a funnel down which the Lady fell and fell and would never stop falling, and the horror would never stop building, an infinity past endurance, though time did not exist.

The Lady tried to struggle, to lash out, but it had no body. It tried to scream, but it had no throat through which to funnel the air that did not exist.

The Lady tried to wish into being everything that was missing. This place had the potential to be molded. But the Lady was alone, so the changes were empty and illusory. Begetting other people to observe the changes, the Lady found they were also mere delusions, and the Lady smashed them in rage and stark, raving terror.

All of that happened in an instant, the same instant in which the Lady had arrived and which the Lady would always inhabit.

At last, it was a true Goddess, but none of the imaginary beings it conjured would have recognized it as such. It whipped between despair and denial, with no control of the waves that tossed it about. Once, long before, the Lady had held a man down in a fire, but what he had felt was a loving caress compared to the furnace where the Lady dwelt.

It was all of an instant, an instant that would never begin or end. The thing that suffered lost its name in the storm of nothingness. It would never know the concealment of darkness or the warmth of light.

Its suffering was all there had been or would be, and when the last star in the last galaxy winked out, the thing that suffered would only be starting that same eternal instant.

83

MERIN

"HELLO?" MERIN CALLED.

"Hello," someone replied. "Can you hear me?"

Merin looked around the place. "Yes, clear as you please."

"Do you remember your name?" the someone asked.

"I do, as a matter of fact. That's a surprise—I forgot it ages ago."

"Who could blame you? I don't think I know of a man who's been through so much." The voice was not male or female, old or young. It was all of those and none.

"No one could blame me, I suppose. And it's Merin, by the way."

The speaker must have heard uncertainty in his voice. "Is something wrong?"

That stumped Merin for a moment. "No. Well, yes. I want something, but I don't know what it is. Or rather, I have a feeling, but I don't know what to do about it."

"I think I know what to do." The voice acquired a face, and as Merin watched, the face changed in a small but profound way. "Do you see?"

"Yes, that seems right. Wonderful, in fact."

The face seemed to glow. "You can make it yourself."

"Me?" The idea thrilled Merin. "How?"

"Just try."

"You're right!" Merin cried, his voice echoing through the emptiness around him. He touched his mouth. "I can feel it!"

"It's a beautiful smile."

"And did I just make a laugh?"

"You did."

He laughed again, delighted. "How can I do these things?"

"You can do anything you want because I am here. Someone is here to see it or feel it, and that makes it real."

Grinning, Merin looked around again. "Are you and I alone here?"

"Only for now. You can make others, as many as you want and whatever kind, and call them whatever you want. But it all starts with you and me and with your will to do."

"How long have we been here?"

"Not long. Our time began when you spoke to me. You've not decided yet how to measure time, but since we've only said a few words, I reckon we just got here." The face peered more closely at him. "Are you sure you're well?"

"Yes, perfectly well. I can't stop laughing, but I don't want to, either. Who are you?"

"That is a difficult question. I was created deep in your mind, in places that don't speak aloud. After you woke from your long journey, a kindly passenger joined you. He led you to a room that brought you here and sculpted your mind to create me. I am part of you but separate. What I really am, we will discover in time."

Though he laughed, Merin had no trouble listening or speaking. He thought of all the people and things he would fill this place with. "Why am I so happy? I'd forgotten what it was like."

"As a part of you, I can pull some strings. It may be hard to believe that I mean the best, but I hope you will trust me in time. Trust may be the biggest joy of all."

"It sounds lovely. Will we always be here?"

"In time, we can move on. You've got growing to do yet. But together, we can go wherever we want. Those who built the room that led us here wanted to decide what was real and what wasn't. They wanted to make themselves lords of creation. Sadly, they each wanted to do it alone."

Merin agreed—that was sad. "What is your name?"

"You will choose it. I can be the first in line. You'll have quite a bit of naming to do."

84

SHADA

SHADA FOUND NOR AND Emberly side by side, with Nor facing away from the captain. At first glance, she thought they were both corpses. But when she sat down and put a hand on Nor's shoulder and he groaned and put his hand on hers, she gasped like a judge had pardoned her seconds before execution.

"Holy mother!" she cried and turned toward where the few remaining healers of the Shining Realm were searching for survivors among their own dead. "I found him! He's alive!"

One of the men hurried toward them. When Nor opened his eyes and looked at the Realmsman approaching, his body tensed like a wire. "No. No!" he groaned. "Stay away!"

The healer stopped, confused, and Shada asked him to give them a moment alone.

Hearing her voice, Nor turned his head with obvious pain. She leaned over him to help him see her. He relaxed his neck, rested his head on the crystal floor, and began to cry.

She stroked his cheek. "It's okay. The Lady is dead."

"It's not that." He spoke as if awakened out of deep sleep.

"What is it?"

"I've been shot, you fool."

She realized she was leaning on his wounded arm. "Oh!" She shifted backward. Then, to her embarrassment, she giggled like a child. She needed a moment to recover the proper solemnity.

"That will have to be treated," she said with a frown. She waved the healer over. Then, heedless of anyone watching, she kissed Nor's arm, steering clear of the wound.

His laugh sounded like a slow coughing fit. "That feels better."

"I knew it would," she said.

The healer came, and she sat in silence as he worked. Sometimes, she watched his hands, but mostly, she watched Nor's eyes. They gazed up past the gateways in the ceiling and into the worlds on the other side. Perhaps they looked even farther.

When the healer finished, she lay down against Nor and wrapped an arm over him as gently as she could. Her own bad arm ached underneath her.

All things felt open to her, no subject off limits. She asked him how long the captain had been dead.

"He was dead when I got here."

Something in his voice, the weary monotone, almost made her laugh again. In her heart, she apologized to Emberly, wherever he was, and decided he would not have minded her amusement.

Looking at the captain's body, she murmured, "He was as much a hero as everyone back home said. He even found Huire."

"You found her too. But if a god comes to Ronia, it won't be her."

"And whatever it is, it won't survive long with the Realm in control."

Nor turned his head. He might have been trying to see Emberly, but he quickly gave up. "He died better than we will. Once he stopped lying, he fought against lies until the end."

"The Lady's lies?"

He shook his head. "All of it."

With a grunt of pain, she propped herself up. "Everything's not a lie. I love you. There, that's true."

His cheeks swelled as he smiled. The expression was almost a grimace. Tears trickled from his eyes. "I don't need to say it. I think you know already."

Heat flared within her. If he weren't hurt, she would have flipped him to embrace her. She was comfortable where she was, though, and let the warmth rise and fall again and again.

After what seemed a long while, she forced herself to look up. The Realmsmen had found a few survivors from their army.

"We really should go soon," she said. "There are a few healers of the Realm left. They want to help you and whoever is left, but they want to leave this place before they do any real work. I would ask the Guardian to heal you, but it seems he's run off."

"And after they heal me, what will they do to us?"

"I might be crazy, but I think we can trust them. Their leader seems different from the rest. Surely, some of them must be decent."

"I remember him. I met him in the hallway."

She pushed her forehead against his neck and her chest against his back. "What if you and I stood up and started walking and actually made it home—whatever home is like now? I might see my father again, if he's..."

She stopped there. In that instant, competing drives met within her with the force of a cataclysm. On one side was her, herself. She wanted to see her father, living or dead, no matter what stood between them. On the other side was his wish, earnestly expressed, that she never return, that she find a better place to spend her life. She felt she should respect her father's wish—perhaps one of his last wishes, if Ronia had indeed fallen. He would certainly say she should.

She wondered if she could bear that—never seeing him again. Even if she bore it right then, she didn't know if she could bear it the next day and every day after.

Nor waited patiently for her to speak again.

She tried out the idea in words: "Or what if we found a place along the way where we could have a life? And someday, found a nice bed to die in? That sounds lovely to me." It did, she had to admit.

Nor replied, "I don't think I should leave here, Shada."

Though she lay on her side, her heart and stomach plummeted. She tried to sound casual. "What's so nice about here?"

"I'm serious," he said with sudden anger that frightened her a little. "Everything I've ever believed, I've betrayed along the way here. Almost everything I ever thought was true isn't.

"I've been judged. I barely know how to feel things anymore. I don't know what I have left to give you, and I don't think I deserve you."

It was her turn to be angry. "What will you do, then? Lie here until you die? Why are you so bloody determined to be a bad man? You're simply not one."

He shut his eyes so tightly that their lids trembled. "I am. Trust me."

"Then so are the rest of us."

For a while, he didn't respond. She craned her neck and saw he was smiling.

He rolled onto his back. "So be it."

Sensing her advantage, she pushed on. "So Huire wasn't who we thought she was. We already knew she was created by humans somewhere. I think, in her way, she did her best. Like any mother."

His smile disappeared. A touch of guilt curdled her warm feelings, and she continued. "What I want to say is: don't give up searching. Looking for the gods, for the truth, is a part of you. It ought to be a part of everyone."

"The builders of this place searched for ages and found nothing."

"It sounds like they were seeking a lot for their own glory."

The smile returned, but colored by shades of pain. "What if there is no truth?"

"There're worse ways to spend your life than looking and hoping. Think of the alternative."

He took her hand and closed his around it. "I don't know how to ask this."

She poked his ribs. "It's me."

"That's right," he chuckled. "I can always speak to you. No need for silence anymore."

She felt him swallow. He asked in a trembling voice, "Will you pray with me?"

"Will I..." she stared at the back of his head. *Will I?* "Of course I will."

She prepared to rise and kneel with him, but he didn't move. He spoke softly as if speaking to her. "I don't know who's listening. Or if you even care. But I think you do. I think you're watching and waiting, and I'll never stop looking for you. Ever. I want you to know that. I need you." His voice cracked, and he fell silent.

The words hung in the air. She ran her fingers slowly through his hair. "If you won't stop, I won't."

She finally got up. As she rose, she kissed him playfully on the cheek and said, "I'm not ready to join the Shining Realm. Are you?"

85

— · —

EMBERLY

THE ONE WHO BELIEVED itself to be Cyril Emberly planned to hide within the flesh-and-blood Emberly's corpse until the last living human had left the gods' chamber.

It—perhaps he—was dismayed when two of the humans lifted Emberly's body onto a long cloth and dragged it from the room. They talked between themselves, and the noise of their voices and the dragging fabric helped him escape Emberly's body undetected.

While he waited in a side corridor for them to leave, he reached an important decision. The cloud of little living things that comprised him had inherited lingering doubts from his previous body. He wondered if even that man had been who he thought he was. Maybe this new persona was a soulless imitation of an artificial man. The newcomer decided he was Emberly. Whether he and the original

Emberly were the same was irrelevant to his rather narrow purposes.

He returned to the chamber and remained there for some time, learning how to skillfully move and shape himself. Emberly's mind was a human's, and connecting with the institutional knowledge in that human mind took some doing.

Also, the new Emberly retained an inkling of what was happening outside the crystal palace, and he wanted no part of it.

But a time came when, danger or no, he was tired of waiting. Through the many gateways in the dome, night had turned to day and back to night. Vermin had entered the gateways from unnumbered worlds and found a feast of dead men waiting. The air swarmed with carrion.

He left, retracing with effortless flight the steps of his long walk here. Near the great cloud wall leading back toward the worlds of humanity, he passed the small band of human survivors. They had stopped so that the healers could treat the wounded. Perhaps they also feared another passage through the cloud wall and its illusions. The Ronians seemed to be gathering the bodies of their fallen brethren, including Emberly's former carcass, though what honor the dead could be given here, Emberly did not know.

As he passed them, moving as swiftly as he could, a pair of pale white eyes turned toward him. Norhim was the man's name, and his keen ears had caught the hum of Emberly's passing. Had Emberly been more experienced with his new body, perhaps he could have been stealthier—since he wasn't, he darted into the cloud wall, wondering what thoughts the sight of him would provoke in Nor.

Emberly had nothing to fear from the mist. He was a different sort of being than the humans, one with no center of intelligence onto which the cloud's power could attach itself. The humans faced no danger, either, as the great serpentine presence that had patrolled the cloud was gone. Emberly realized with a start that the place itself, this celestial palace, was telling him these things. With the Guardian gone, it was seeking someone similar to replace him. It was all for the best that he was leaving. The palace would not have time to overwhelm him.

The long walkway back to the human worlds was scattered with bodies and the wreckage of flying machines. There, the Realm's forces had met the beasts of fire and lightning that guarded the entrance to an alien empire—a race and an empire for which he still knew no name.

But only when Emberly reached the icy world of the beast-men and gazed over the vast expanse of frozen ocean did he witness the aftermath of the greatest battle of all.

There, a full army of the Shining Realm, so large that those he'd seen already must have been a mere scouting force, had spread its might across the snowy plain. There, it had collided with the assembled ranks of the gods, who had followed their newfound freedom there after the Lady's death. All around Emberly were blackened ground and the smoking remains of shellfire, already being erased by snowfall.

Out on the oceanic plain, the forces of the Realm had been wiped out. The gods, in their forms ranging from giant gladiators to sentient whirlwinds, had cut through them all. The humans' shells and guns that emitted flame—one of which was still unleashing its fury in sporadic bursts, melting its way through the ice—must have done little but annoy the gods, who had crushed their opponents. They had sliced men and vehicles into pieces. They had cut holes in the ice and plunged the enemy into the sea. They had thoroughly defeated them. But they had not won.

Well before they could thoroughly annihilate the forces of humanity, humanity had unleashed the Scourge upon the gods once more. Men had again infected them with the deadly black clouds, spelling their doom. Even after the last Realmsman was dead, the Scourge had eaten through their conquerors.

Even then, all was not quiet. On one side of the smoking battlefield, the now-gigantic whirlwind that was the Scourge was digesting the last surviving gods. The pitiful deities, visible in the monster's belly, whipped about in hopeless struggle. One was shaped like a tentacled sea beast, and its arms kept thrashing even after they were eaten from its body. The nearest to Emberly was shaped like a gigantic human, its flesh charred and dissolving as its skeleton withered.

Emberly panicked. He shot across the landscape at his top speed, flying high. Still, he was spotted. The Scourge saw in all directions at once, and part of it tore away from the main body to chase him down.

He soared over the now-empty seaside village under the cliffs then over the frozen coastline. His pursuer was as fast as him, but he had a head start, and when he reached the gateway to the next world, it was nowhere in sight. He didn't dare slow down. Even as time passed and it did not reappear behind him, he nonetheless wondered if it would hunt him somehow. That worry would never leave him.

Anxious both to escape the Scourge and to get home, he hurried from world to world, guided by memories. Everywhere, he found smoke and rumors of wars. The Shining Realm wanted to spread its paradise across the human universe.

On Caidfell, where he'd hoped never to go again, he found the prison industries—lumber and now mining—being worked by Ronian soldiers under the guard of Realmsmen. The Realm had beaten back the jungle with its flamethrowers. The formerly treacherous flagstone road was now straight and made of concrete, and the colorful, poisonous swarms that had haunted the sky were nowhere to be seen. The swamp that had nearly killed the Ronian company had been blasted empty of all life.

Next, he entered the worlds that held parts of the city of Ronia. The Realm was in charge here, but except for a few charred and shattered ruins of buildings, life seemed to continue—for now—much like it always had.

Ronia proper was a different story. Drifting over the city, a little surprised to find that it was real, Emberly saw that entire neighborhoods had been leveled, many of them near the docks. The destruction had begun with the explosions during the company's departure from Ronia. The blasts had fractured the plateau before Imperial Hall, sending a landslide down the hill to bury parts of Undertown. The invasion that followed had left few parts of the city untouched. Though their defense may have been hopeless, the Ronians had been willing to shed rivers of their own blood.

Emberly went in search of his family, the only reason he had to keep moving or thinking at all. First, he went to his house. An officer of the Realm was living there with his own family. Having finally learned stealth, Emberly slipped like a phantom through many down-the-hill tenement buildings that had been converted into barracks for the displaced Ronian elite, their former denizens evicted. He dared not hope too much to find his wife alive. Soon, he would know whether his ordeal in the cloud had been only a cruel dream. As days passed, he began searching primarily at night, knowing Charlotte would not leave their son alone then. If both of them were alive, he would find them together.

Late one evening, in a packed room filled with snores and the voicing of nightmares, he saw his son lying alone.

Edmund had aged years, though Emberly had not been away nearly that long. He had become a man, though still a boy in years, and he looked a lot like Emberly had when he was a young thing of flesh and blood.

That was how Emberly learned what he had already known in his heart: his wife was dead. She had died millions of miles from her home, at the hand of her own husband.

In that moment, the one who might be Emberly believed two things very strongly. He believed there were truths one discovered by feeling rather than seeing. And he believed there was a balance to things. Whether the balance had been designed knowingly, he could not have said, but it was true nonetheless. It was as close as the air people breathed and the blood in their veins yet so far removed that no one living could truly know it. And occasionally, it might reach out with its own will, icy but searing as hot iron, and change the world where it would.

He approached the boy who had been his son and felt his own outstretched hand scatter like dust as it touched the boy's arm. The sleeper stirred, and Emberly froze, waiting for him to settle.

In the end, he contented himself with stretching his ashen cloud of a body around the boy's back and chest in a ghostly embrace.

"Sleep, son," he whispered, feeling a glow warming him from within, illuminating his grief and making him like the man he wanted to be. "Tomorrow, we will begin again."

———◆O◆———

This concludes Litury of Worlds. Thank you so much for taking this journey with me!

If you enjoyed this book, I would massively appreciate a review wherever you got it or on Goodreads. Even a line or two helps me so much!

Want a free short story set in the Liturgy of Worlds universe? Join my mailing list! Titled "A Monster's War," the story tells of the day the Lady came to Ronia—and it stars her caretaker, beastly warrior that he is. Check out the preview below. Plus, as a list member, you'll get the latest news from me, behind-the-scenes updates, media reviews and recommendations, and more!

Join my newsletter at nathanhartle.com for this free story!

The folk of these realms call him "Beast."

If only they knew he is their savior.

Filled with shame after a cowardly act, a giant warrior with a wolf's face sees one last chance for redemption: he must return a lost goddess to the city of her birth.

If she reaches home, she will remake the world. An age of light will dawn. But she is sick and weak, and she needs a protector.

Only Beast can help. If he triumphs, evil and darkness may disappear forever... and his shame will end. If he fails, he will lose his life and soul. Every step of his quest will be perilous—in these lands, Beast's size and appearance make him feared and hated.

But they also make him mighty.

"A Monster's War" is a quick adventure in the Liturgy of Worlds epic fantasy series.

Preview of A Monster's War

(Beast, the Lady's caretaker, is confronting a gang who have abducted the Lady...)

Beast strode toward the man, his pace steady, not quite promising violence.

Larky stood his ground as his men fled. At the last instant, he fell back, knife drawn, but Beast's arm shot out and grabbed him by the shirt.

Hoisting him off the ground, Beast looked him in the eyes and growled a promise. Larky shouted, and something stung Beast's leg.

A tingle raced like wildfire down to his foot and up to his hip. Something was terribly wrong, and he spun to watch several feathered spikes lodge in his leather breastplate. There stood several of Larky's men, holding thin pipes to their mouths.

For a sliver of an instant, he froze. They had poisoned him. Rather than fight openly, rather than seize combat as a chance to show honor and courage, they had used trickery and deceit. And they had won.

It was the epitome of civilization. He could never win against it. He could not even resist it—not without doing things the only way he knew. He disobeyed his goddess.

With an almighty roar, he charged the men, ready to kill them all...

"A Monster's War" is *only* available by signing up for my newsletter. Sign up here: nathanhartle.com

About the Author

Nathan Hartle lives in North Carolina, USA with his amazing wife, son, and two cats who are kind enough to share their house.

Though he's had many, many jobs—travel agent in Bangkok, hostel clerk in Morocco, construction worker in Washington, DC—writing fantasy and science fiction is by far his favorite.

He believes storytelling is a service to others and a sacred act that honors Creation. Good stories let us glimpse eternity.

Keep up with Nathan by following him on Facebook, Goodreads, and BookBub.

www.ingramcontent.com/pod-product-compliance
Lightning Source LLC
Chambersburg PA
CBHW051306190726
48290CB00001B/22